W9-AGZ-880

Uncommon Type

Uncommon Type

SOME STORIES

Tom Hanks

PHOTOGRAPHS BY
KEVIN TWOMEY

ALFRED A. KNOPF

NEW YORK

2017

THIS IS A BORZOI BOOK PUBLISHED BY ALFRED A. KNOPF

www.aaknopf.com

"Alan Bean Plus Four" first appeared in *The New Yorker* on October 24, 2014.

LIBRARY OF CONGRESS CATALOGING-IN-PUBLICATION DATA
Names: Hanks, Tom, author.
Title: Uncommon type : some stories / by Tom Hanks.
Description: First edition. | New York : Alfred A. Knopf, 2017.
Identifiers: LCCN 2017006246 | ISBN 9781101946152 (hardcover)
ISBN 9781101946169 (ebook) | ISBN 9781524711313 (open market)
Classification: LCC PS3608.A71522 A6 2017 |
DDC 813/.6—DC23 LC record available
at https://lccn.loc.gov/2017006246

LIBRARY AND ARCHIVES CANADA CATALOGING IN PUBLICATION
Hanks, Tom, author
Uncommon type : some stories / Tom Hanks.
Issued in print and electronic formats.
ISBN 978-0-7352-7383-2 | eBook ISBN 978-0-7352-7385-6
I. Title.
PS3608.A5575U53 2017   813'.6   C2017-901561-3

Jacket images by FlamingPumpkin/iStock/Getty Images
Jacket design by Oliver Munday
Emoji art on page 16 supplied by EmojiOne

Manufactured in the United States of America
3 5 7 9 10 8 6 4 2

For Rita and all the kids.

Because of Nora.

Contents

———

CONTENTS

Uncommon Type

Three Exhausting Weeks

DAY 1

Anna said there was only one place to find a meaningful gift for MDash—the Antique Warehouse, not so much a place for old treasures as a permanent swap meet in what used to be the Lux Theater. Before HBO, Netflix, and the 107 other entertainment outlets bankrupted the Lux, I sat for many hours in that once-splendid cinema palace and watched movies. Now it's stall after stall of what passes for antiques. Anna and I looked into every one of them.

MDash was about to become a naturalized U.S. citizen, which was as big a deal for us as it was for him. Steve Wong's grandparents were naturalized in the forties. My dad had escaped the low-grade thugs that were East European Communists in the 1970s, and, way back when, Anna's ancestors rowed boats across the North Atlantic, seeking to pillage whatever was pillageable in the New World. The Anna family legend is that they found Martha's Vineyard.

Mohammed Dayax-Abdo was soon to be as American as

Abdo Pie, so we wanted to get him something vintage, an *objet d'patriotic* that would carry the heritage and humor of his new country. I thought the old Radio Flyer wagon in the second warehouse stall was perfect. "When he has American kids, he'll pass that wagon on to them," I said.

But Anna was not about to purchase the first antique we came across. So we kept on hunting. I bought a forty-eight-star American flag, from the 1940s. The flag would remind MDash that his adoptive nation is never finished building itself—that good citizens have a place somewhere in her fruited plain just as more stars can fit in the blue field above those red and white stripes. Anna approved, but kept searching, seeking a present that would be far more special. She wanted unique, nothing less than one of a kind. After three hours, she decided the Radio Flyer was a good idea after all.

Rain started falling just as we were pulling out of the parking lot in my VW Bus. We had to drive slowly back to my house because my wiper blades are so old they left streaks on the windshield. The storm went on well into the evening, so rather than drive home, Anna hung around, played my mother's old mixtapes (which I'd converted to CDs), cracking up over Mom's eclectic taste, in the segues from the Pretenders to the O'Jays to Taj Mahal.

When Iggy Pop's "Real Wild Child" came on, she asked, "Do you have any music from the last twenty years?"

I made pulled-pork burritos. She drank wine. I drank beer. She started a fire in my Franklin stove, saying she felt like a pioneer woman on the prairie. We sat on my couch as night fell, the only lights being the fire and the audio levels on my sound system bounding from green to orange and, occasionally, red. Distant sheet lightning flashed in the storm miles and miles away.

"You know what?" she said to me. "It's Sunday."

"I do know that," I told her. "I live in the moment."

"I admire that about you. Smart. Caring. Easygoing to the point of sloth."

"You've gone from compliments to insults."

"Change *sloth* to *languorousness*," she said, sipping wine. "Point is I like you."

"I like you, too." I wondered if this conversation was going someplace. "Are you flirting with me?"

"No," Anna said. "I'm propositioning you. Totally different thing. Flirting is fishing. Maybe you hook up, maybe you don't. Propositioning is the first step in closing a deal."

Understand that Anna and I have known each other since high school (St. Anthony Country Day! Go, Crusaders!). We didn't date, but hung out in the same crowd, and liked each other. After a few years of college, and a few more of taking care of my mom, I got my license and pretended to make a living in real estate for a while. One day she walked into my office because she needed to rent a space for her graphics business and I was the only agent she could trust because I once dated a friend of hers and was not a jerk when we broke up.

Anna was still very pretty. She never lost her lean, rope-taut body of a triathlete, which, in fact, she had been. For a day, I showed her some available spaces, none of which she wanted for reasons that made little sense to me. I could tell she was still just as driven, focused, and tightly wound as she had been at SACD. She had too keen an eye for the smallest of details and left no stones unturned, uninspected, unrecorded, or unreplaced if they needed replacing. Adult Anna was exhausting. Adult Anna was no more my type than Teen Anna had been.

Funny, then, that she and I became such solid friends, much closer than when we were kids. I am one of those lazy-butt loners who can poke my way through a day and never feel a second has been wasted. In fact, as soon as I sold my mom's house and parked the money in investments, I walked away from my fake business and settled into the Best Life Imaginable. Give me a few loads of laundry to do and a hockey game on the NHL channel and I'm good for an entire afternoon. In the time I spend lollygagging over my whites and colors, Anna will drywall her attic, prepare her taxes, make her own fresh pasta, and start up a clothing exchange on the Internet. She sleeps in fits and starts from midnight to dawn and has the energy to go full throttle all day. I sleep dead to the world as long as possible and take a nap every day at 2:30 p.m.

"I am going to kiss you now." Anna did just as she said.

We had never done that, other than those pecks on cheeks that go with brief hugs. That night, she was offering a whole new version of herself, and I tensed up, confused.

"Hey, relax," she whispered. Her arms were around my neck. She smelled damn good and tasted of wine. "It's the Sabbath. A day of rest. This is not going to be *work*."

We kissed again, this time with me a collected and invested participant. My arms went around her and pulled her close.

We leaned into each other and loosened up. We found each other's necks and worked our way back to our mouths. I had not kissed a woman like that in close to a year, not since the Evil Girlfriend Mona not only dumped me but stole cash from my billfold (Mona had problems, but kissing? She was fabulous).

"Atta baby," Anna sighed.

"Shabbat shalom," I sighed back. "We should have done that years ago."

"I think we could use some time spent skin on skin," Anna whispered. "Take off your clothes."

I did. When she took off hers, I was a goner.

DAY 2

My Monday morning breakfast was buckwheat pancakes, chorizo sausage, a huge bowl of berries, and *percolated* coffee. Anna opted for some herbal tea I had long ago tucked away in the pantry and a tiny bowl of nuts she chopped up with a cleaver. She counted out eight blueberries to round out her nutritious breakfast. I shouldn't say that neither of us wore clothes as we ate, as it will make us sound like nudists, but the fact is we tumbled out of bed without the slightest inhibitions.

As she was getting dressed for work she told me we were signing up for scuba diving lessons.

"We are?" I asked her.

"Yep. We are going to get certified," she said. "And you need to get some workout clothes. Running shoes and sweats.

Go to the Foot Locker in the Arden Mall. Meet me for lunch at my office right after. Bring the wagon and the flag for MDash and we'll wrap them."

"Okay," I said.

"I'll make dinner at my place tonight, we'll watch a documentary, then we are going to do in my bed what we spent last night doing in yours."

"Okay," I repeated.

DAY 3

Anna ended up taking me to Foot Locker, making me try on five different pairs of shoes (we settled on cross-trainers) and four versions of sweatpants and tops (Nike). Then we bought food and drinks for the party Anna wanted to throw for MDash. She said my house was the only place for such a bash.

Around noon, MDash was one of sixteen hundred soon-to-be Americans standing on the floor of the Sports Arena, right hands raised as they swore allegiance to America—new citizens who would preserve, protect, and defend what was now their Constitution as much as it was for the President of the United States. Steve Wong, Anna, and I were in the bleachers, witnessing the naturalization of a sea of immigrants, their skins all the different colors of human nature. The sight was glorious and made the three of us emotional—Anna the most. She wept, her face pressed into my chest.

"It's . . . so . . . beautiful," she kept sobbing. "God . . . I love . . . this country."

MDash's Home Depot co-workers who could get the time off showed up at my place with a lot of cheap American flags, purchased with their employee discounts. Steve Wong set up a karaoke machine and we made MDash sing songs with "America" in the lyrics. "American Woman." "American Girl." "Spirit of America" by the Beach Boys is actually about a car, but we made him sing it anyway. We used the Radio Flyer wagon as an ice chest and six of us planted the forty-eight-star flag like we were the Marines on Iwo Jima, MDash being the guy in the very front.

The party went long, until only the four of us were left watching the moonrise, listening to Old Glory flitter and flap on its pole. I had just opened another beer from the slosh of ice in the wagon when Anna took the can out of my hands.

"Easy, baby," she said. "You're going to need all your capabilities, just as soon as those two go home."

An hour later, Steve Wong and MDash headed out, the new American citizen singing "A Horse with No Name" (by the band America). As soon as Steve's car was out of the driveway, Anna took my hand, leading me to the backyard. She put cushions down on the soft grass and we lay there, kissing, then, well, you know, putting my capabilities to the test.

DAY 4

Anna runs whenever she can jam a few miles into forty minutes, a habit she was going to force upon me. She took me to one of her routes, an uphill path that loops around Vista

Point and back, and told me to get going. She would zip along ahead of me and meet me coming back down, knowing I'd never keep up with her.

My exercise is an option-only affair. Occasionally, I'll ride my old three-speed to Starbucks or play a few rounds of Frisbee golf (I used to belong to a league). This morning I was chuffing up the dirt road, Anna so far ahead I didn't see her, my feet breaking in my new cross-trainers (note to self: move up a half size). My blood was surging up and down my body in unfamiliar fury, so my shoulders and neck tensed up and my head pounded. When Anna came charging down from Vista Point, she was clapping her hands.

"Atta baby!" she called out, passing me. "Good first effort!"

I spun around to follow her. "My thighs are on fire!"

"They are rebelling," she called back over her shoulder. "In time they will submit!"

Anna reorganized my kitchen when I was in the shower. She thought I kept my pans and lids in the wrong cupboards, and why was my flatware drawer so far from the dishwasher? I had no answer. "Let's get going. Can't be late for our first scuba lesson."

The Scuba School smelled of rubber wet suits and the chlorinated pool. We filled out papers and were given workbooks to study, along with the schedule for our classroom sessions, as well as options for the date of our open water certification. Anna pointed to a Sunday four weeks away and reserved our berths on the boat on the spot.

We went to the Viva Verde Salad Cafe for a lunch of salads

made of salads with salad on the side, after which I wanted to go home for a nap. But Anna said she needed my help moving some stuff around her house, a chore she had been putting off. This was barely true, almost a lie. She actually wanted me to help her rewallpaper her hallway and home office, which meant I had to move her computer, printer, scanners, and graphic equipment, then do her bidding all afternoon.

I never made it home that evening. We had dinner in—vegetarian lasagna with vegetables on the side—and watched a movie on Netflix about smart women with idiot boyfriends.

"Look, baby," Anna said. "This is about us!" Then she cackled and reached into my pants without so much as kissing me. I either was the luckiest man in the world or was being played for a sucker. After Anna let me reach into her pants as well I still wasn't sure which.

DAY 5

Anna had to work at her office. She employs four no-nonsense women and an intern who is an at-risk girl from high school. Last year she landed a contract for doing the graphics for a textbook publisher, steady work but as boring as wallpapering for a living. I told her I was going home.

"Why?" she asked. "You've got nothing to do today."

"I'm going to get a run in," I said, making that up on the spur of the moment.

"Atta baby," she told me.

I went home and did put on the cross-trainers, then jogged

around the neighborhood. Mr. Moore, a retired cop whose house shares my back fence, saw me running by and hollered out, "What the fuck got into you?"

"A woman!" I yelled back, and not only was that true, but I felt good saying it. When a man thinks of a lady and looks forward to telling her that he ran forty minutes, well, partner, he's living in Girlfriend Territory.

Yes. I had a girlfriend. A girlfriend changes a man from the shoes he exercises in right up to how he cuts his hair (which Anna did the very next day, in front of my barber)—alterations I was due. Fooled by the adrenaline of romance, I ran farther than my body could stand.

Anna called just as I had given up on a nap because my calves were as tight as beer cans. She told me to get over to her acupuncturist; she'd call to arrange an immediate treatment.

The East Valley Wellness Oasis is in a minimall/professional building with underground parking. Driving my VW Bus, which has no power steering, around and around those descending circular ramps took physical effort. Figuring out the multiple elevators of the facility taxed my brain. When I finally found office 606-W, I filled in five pages of a Wellness questionnaire, sitting beside a fountain that made more noise from its electric pump than from its cascading water element.

Do you accept the practice of Visualization? Sure, why not? *Are you open to Guided Meditation?* I don't see how it could hurt. *Explain your reasons for seeking treatment. Please be specific.* My girlfriend told me to bring you my tired, my poor, my balled-up leg muscles yearning to be freed.

I handed in my answers and waited. Eventually, a white lab coat called my name and took me into a room. As I stripped down to my skivvies he read paperwork.

"Anna says your legs are bothering you?" he asked. He'd been working on Anna for the last three years.

"Yep," I said. "My calves, among other muscles in revolt."

"According to this," he said, tapping my paperwork, "Anna's your girlfriend."

"A new development," I told him.

"Good luck with that. Lay on your stomach." When he put the needles in me, my whole body tingled and my calves twitched uncontrollably. Before leaving the room, he hit play on an old CD boom box for my guided meditation. I heard a woman's voice tell me to clear my mind and think of a river. I sort of did that for half an hour, wanting to fall asleep, but couldn't because I had needles sticking in me.

Anna was waiting for me at my house, having made us a dinner of leafy plants with seeds and rice the color of dirt. Afterward, she rubbed my legs so hard I winced. Later, she said she had not made love five nights in a row since college, but was going to give it a whirl.

DAY 6

She had set the alarm on her phone for 5:45 a.m. because she had to get a lot done. She made me get up, too, allowed me a single cup of coffee, then made me put on my running clothes.

"My calves still hurt," I told her.

"Only because you are telling yourself they hurt," she said.

"I don't want to run this morning," I complained.

"Tough titties, baby." She threw my sweatpants at me.

The morning was cold and misty. "Perfect for roadwork," she said. She forced me to imitate her twelve-minute stretching routine right there in my driveway, setting a timer on her phone with a tone that *bing*-ed every thirty seconds. There were twenty-four body positions I had to hold, each one stretching some sinew or muscle inside me, each one making me wince, cuss out loud, and get light-headed.

"Atta baby," she said. Then she explained the route we would take around my neighborhood, twice for her, once for me. Mr. Moore was getting his morning paper from his front lawn just as I was running by.

"Was that your woman? Who ran by a minute ago?" he called to me. I was panting so hard I could only nod. "What the fuck she see in you?"

A few minutes later, Anna lapped me, spanking my buttocks as she passed. "Atta baby!"

I was home and in the shower when she joined me. We kissed a lot and touched each other in our wonderful places. She instructed me on how to scrub her back and told me to come to her office at lunch so we could study our scuba workbook. I had yet to read the first few pages, but she had already completed half of it. When she had the time is beyond me.

I spent the afternoon hanging around her office, answering multiple-choice questions about scuba equipment and its uses, scrolling through some real estate listings (I still dabble), and trying to amuse the women who were bent over their graphic work. No dice. All this while Anna took a long conference call with a client in Fort Worth, Texas, designed new title pages for a series of textbooks, proofread three projects, helped her at-risk intern with her geometry homework, reorganized a supply closet, and completed the second half of the scuba assignments. We had yet to take our first classroom session.

Not that it mattered. We were the only students. We watched videos about the glorious underwater world, then got into the pool. We stood in the shallow end while Vin, our instructor, explained to us every piece of the self-contained underwater breathing apparatus. That took a long time, mostly because Anna had at least five questions for every bit of gear. Finally, Vin had us put the regulators in our mouths, drop to our knees so our heads were submerged, suck in the metallic-tasting pressurized air, and blow out bubbles. The class ended with us taking a water fitness test by swimming ten laps. Anna went to the task like an Olympian and was out of the pool and drying off in a few minutes. I swam a languid breaststroke, finishing a distant second in a race of two.

Afterward, we drove to the East Village Market Mall to meet Steve Wong and MDash at Ye Olde Sweet Shoppe for milkshakes. Anna had a small cup of sugar-free nondairy yogurt with a dusting of real cinnamon. Sitting there, enjoying our treats, Anna tucked her hand in mine, a gesture of affection that did not go unnoticed.

In her bed that night, Anna was going through her pre-sleep iPad scroll when I got a text from Steve Wong.

SWong: U boffing A???

I pinched out my reply.

Moonwalker7: Your bizniz?
SWong: Yes/no?
Moonwalker7: 😄
SWong: U Nsane??????
Moonwalker7: 🏆 🎣 🚀 ◎ 🪁 ‼ 🏁 😌

Then MDash joined the chain—

FACEOFAMERICA: 😮
Moonwalker7: I was seduced
FACEOFAMERICA: "when cooks fuck the stew burns"
Moonwalker7: who says that? The village shaman?
FACEOFAMERICA: "when coaches fuck the team loses"
    Vince Lombardi

And so it went. Steve Wong and MDash saw no good
coming out of the pairing of Anna and me. Too bad! That
very night Anna and I went at it like stew cooks in Green
Bay, Wisconsin, hell-bent on pleasure.
😌

DAY 7

"Should we have a chat about our relationship?"

That was *me* asking. I was standing in Anna's kitchenette,

wrapped in only a towel after a shower, plunging her Swiss press coffee apparatus for my morning elixir. She had been up for an hour and a half and was already in her running togs. Luckily, my cross-trainers were back at my place, so no marathon training for me.

"Do you *want* to have a chat about our relationship?" she asked, cleaning up the few outstanding coffee grounds that had fallen onto her surgically spotless countertop.

"Are we an *item*?" I asked.

"What do *you* think?" she asked back.

"Do you think of me as your *boyfriend*?"

"Do you think of me as your *girlfriend*?"

"Is either one of us going to make a declarative statement?"

"How should *I* know?"

I sat down and took a sip of coffee that was too strong. "Can I have some milk for this?" I asked.

"Do you think that gunk is good for you?" She handed me a small bottle of nonpreservative almond milk, the kind that has to be used up in only a few days, the kind that is sold as "milk" but is actually liquefied nuts.

"Could you buy real milk so I can have it in my coffee?"

"Why are you so demanding?"

"Is asking for milk a demand?"

She smiled and took my face in her hands. "Do you think you're the man for me?"

She kissed me. I was about to make a declarative statement, but she sat on my lap and undid the towel I was wearing. She didn't get in her morning run.

DAYS 8—14

Being Anna's boyfriend was like training to be a Navy SEAL while working full-time in an Amazon fulfillment center in the Oklahoma Panhandle in tornado season. Something was going on every moment of every day. My 2:30 naps were a thing of the past.

I was exercising regularly, not just the morning jogs but also swimming in scuba class, doing yoga stretches for what grew into a half hour, and joining Anna in a hot-room spinning class that was so taxing I upchucked. The number of errands we went on was maddening, and they never came from a to-do list or shopping helper app, but were all spur of the moment, ad hoc. Incessant. If unoccupied with work, working out, or working me over in the sack, Anna was making something, looking for something, asking to see what the store had in the back, driving to an estate sale across town, or going to Home Depot to ask Steve Wong about a belt sander for me, as the top of the redwood picnic table in my backyard needed smoothing. Every day—all day—I spent following her orders, which included precise driving instructions.

"Make the next left. Don't get off here. Take Webster Avenue. Why are you turning right *now?* Don't go past the school! It's almost three o'clock! The kids are just getting out!"

She organized a rock-climbing demonstration for Steve Wong, MDash, and me at a newly opened adventure superstore that had a climbing wall as well as an indoor rushing river to demonstrate white-water canoeing and a skydiving chamber—a huge fan that blew straight up a silo with so much force it simulated free fall for helmeted customers. Need I say that in one evening the four of us did all of them? We were there until closing. Steve Wong and MDash felt like he-men after a full day's work wearing those unisex aprons at Home Depot. I was exhausted, having been on Anna's overloaded schedule too long. I *needed* a nap.

We had time for protein snacks at the Energy Stand at the front of the store when Anna left for the restroom.

"What's it like?" MDash asked.

"What's what like?" I said.

"You and Anna. Sitting in a tree. K-I-S-S-I-N-G."

"You holding up?" Steve Wong asked. "You look exhausted."

"Well, I did just go faux skydiving."

MDash threw his uneaten half of a protein bar in the trash. "I used to look at you and think, That guy has figured it all out. He has his sweet little house with a nice backyard, he doesn't work for anyone but his own self. He could throw away his watch because he never *has* to be anywhere. To me, you were the America I hope to live in. Now, you kowtow to a boss lady. Alas."

"Really?" I said. *"Alas?"*

"Tell him that proverb you told me," Steve said.

"Something else the village shaman taught you?" I wondered.

"Actually, the village English teacher," MDash said. "To circle the globe, a ship needs only a sail, a wheel, a compass, and a clock."

"Wise words in a landlocked nation," I said. MDash grew up in the sub-Sahara.

"Anna is the compass," MDash explained. "You are the clock, but you keeping time with her means you've become unwound. Your hands are right only twice a day. We'll never know our longitude."

"Are you sure Anna isn't the sail?" I said. "Why can't I be the wheel and Steve be the compass? I don't follow this analogy."

"Let me put this into a language you can understand," Steve said. "We are like a TV show with diversity casting. African guy, him. Asian guy, me. Mongrel Caucasoid, you. Strong, determined woman, Anna, who would never let a man define her. You and her pairing off is like a story line from season eleven when the network is trying to keep us on the air."

I looked at MDash. "Are you getting this pop culture metaphor?"

"The gist of it. I have cable."

"The four of us," Steve explained, "are a perfect square. You taking to the sheets with Anna is going to misalign our geometry."

"How?"

"She makes things happen in our lives. Look at us. It's nearly midnight and we've been dangling and rowing and parachuting indoors. Stuff I'd never do on a school night. She's our catalyst."

"You've used sailboats, TV shows, geometry, and chemistry to point out why I shouldn't see Anna. And I still don't buy it."

"I predict tears," MDash said. "For you, for Anna, for all of us. Tears shooting out of our eyes."

"Look," I said, pushing away a protein brownie that actually tasted like a brownie. "One of these things is going to happen between me and my girlfriend. Yes, *girlfriend*." I stole a look at Anna. She was far away chatting with an employee at a counter with a sign over it saying, INVEST IN ADVENTURE! "One. We get married, have kids, and you are their godfathers. Two. We break up in a public display of hurt feelings and recriminations. Both of you will have to choose sides: remain pals with me or go against the established rules of gender and stay friends with the woman. Three. She meets some other guy and dumps me. I become a melancholy loser, and *do not* say that's already what I am. Four. She and I part ways, amicably deciding to be *friends*, as seen on TV. What memories remain are those of pseudo–rock climbing et al. and the finest sex I've had in a lifetime. We can handle any of those fates because we are all big boy grown-ups. And admit it—if Anna wanted to make out with you like she does with me you'd be all for it."

"And *you'd* be the one predicting tears," Steve Wong said.

Just then Anna returned, waving a thick and glossy color brochure, a smile on her face. "Hey, guys!" she said. "We are to go to *Antarctica!*"

DAY 15

"We'll need the correct gear." Anna was dipping a fresh Rainbow Tea Company tea bag into a mug of hot water. She was in her running clothes as I was putting on my cross-trainers. "Long johns. Parkas and shells. Fleece pullovers. Waterproof boots. Walking sticks."

"Gloves," I added. "Hats." The trip to Antarctica was three months, many time zones, and thousands of miles away and Anna was already in Full Planning Mode. "Won't it be summer at the South Pole?" I asked.

"We won't make it to the pole. To the Antarctic Circle maybe, but only if the weather and sea cooperate. Still gonna be a lot of ice and wind."

We went outside to do forty-five minutes of stretches on my front lawn, getting our downward dogs and cobras wet from the morning dew. *Bing.* The timer went off and I bent over, trying to touch my forehead to my kneecaps. Fat chance.

Anna was able to fold herself up like a card table. "You do realize," she said, "the Apollo astronauts went to Antarctica, to study the volcanoes." Anna knew of my *jones* for all things spaceman related. But she didn't know just how well I knew that stuff.

"They trained in Iceland, young lady. If any astronauts went to the South Pole, it was long after they retired from altering the course of human destiny by cheating death in NASA rocket ships." *Bing.* I tried to reach out and grab my ankles, setting my poor calves afire.

"Going to see penguins and whales and science stations," Anna said. "And B15K."

"What is B15K?"

"An iceberg the size of Manhattan, so large it's tracked via satellite. Broke off from the Ross Ice Shelf in 2003 and is independently moving counterclockwise around Antarctica. If the weather holds, we can book a chopper and land on it!"

Bing. That was the final exercise. She took off running. I tried to keep up with her but no way that was going to happen, not with her all pumped up about B15K.

As I trotted by Mr. Moore's house, he was just getting into his car, a travel mug of coffee in his hand. "That girlfriend of yours ran by a second ago. She was hauling ass."

After showers and a breakfast of avocado on toasted spelt bread, Anna took that belt sander she bought from Steve Wong and started grinding down my picnic table. I joined her with some sandpaper of my own.

"After you take it down to the grain, you'll need to repaint this. Do you have paint?" I did. "You should have this done by tonight. Then come to my place. We'll have dinner and sex." Fine by me, is how I felt. "I have to go to work now." Before leaving she pointed out other wooden objects that needed sanding and paint as well—a bench, the back door to my kitchen, and the old shed where I keep my lawn toys and sports equipment. I spent the rest of the day on the work detail.

I was sweaty, dusty, and splattered with paint when Anna texted me.

AnnaGraphicControl: dinner in 15

I got over to her place in half an hour, but needed a shower before dinner. We ate in the living room—huge bowls of Vietnamese *pho*—watching two episodes of *Our Frozen Earth* on Blu-ray. For over three hours we learned all about the chinstrap penguins and crabeater seals that live only in *guess which part of our planet.*

I fell asleep before we got around to any sex.

DAY 16

Anna had scheduled an early morning scuba class without telling me.

Vin had us in full wet suits—the tanks, the weight belts, everything—sitting on our knees at the bottom of the deep end of the pool. We had to remove every piece of the scuba apparatus, including our masks, hold our breath, then put it all back on again. Afterward, Vin said I was behind in my workbook and had better get cracking.

"Why haven't you finished the workbook?" Anna wanted to know.

"A date with a belt sander took up my time."

Driving home, I felt a chalky tickle in the back of my throat, like I was getting a cold.

"Don't say you are getting a cold," Anna said. "If you tell yourself you are sick, you *allow* yourself to be sick."

Her phone went off and she took the call hands-free; it was one of her clients in Fort Worth. A fellow named Ricardo told jokes about color templates, making Anna laugh as she pulled into my driveway. She stayed in the car to finish that call. I went inside.

"We have to go to Fort Worth," she announced when she finally came into my kitchen. I was making chicken noodle soup from a packet.

"Why?" I asked.

"I have to hand-hold Ricardo through a presentation. That is not soup, by the way, that's a sack full of sodium."

"I'm allowing myself to be sick. Soup will help."

"That shit will kill you."

"I have to go to Fort Worth with you?"

"Why not? You aren't doing anything. We'll stay overnight and see the sights."

"Of Fort Worth?"

"It will be an adventure."

"My nose is running and I feel like a hive of bees are swarming in my head."

"You can make it stop if you stop saying such things," she said.

In response I sneezed, coughed, and blew my nose into a tissue. Anna just shook her head.

DAY 17

Here are the sights I saw in Fort Worth:

The huge airport. Jammed with so many travelers it seemed like the Texan economy had collapsed and the population was fleeing.

Baggage Claim. Under renovation and therefore a place of chaos and borderline fistfights. Anna had checked three suitcases, which were among the last to come shooting down the chute.

A bus. Painted all around in huge letters that said PONY-CAR PONYCAR PONYCAR. PonyCar was a new travel option in competition with Uber and the rental companies. Anna had a voucher for a free weekend—why, I don't know. The bus took us to a lot filled with tiny cars also painted with the PonyCar logo. I have no idea where PonyCars are manufactured, but they are clearly designed for small people. The two of us and our luggage had to be squeezed into a vehicle sized to fit the two of us and one-third of our luggage.

The DFW Sun Garden Hotel. Not so much a hotel as a collection of efficiency suites and vending machines meant for business travelers with limited expense accounts. Once we were in our little room, I lay down. Anna changed into professional clothes while she was on her cell phone with Ricardo. She waved goodbye to me and was out the door, trailing her professional rolling bag behind her.

In a fog due to my lousy health, I could not get the TV to work. The cable system had a menu unfamiliar to me. All I could get on screen was the Sun Garden Hotel Channel, which showed the glories and wonders of all the Sun Garden Hotels in the world. New branches were opening soon in Evansville, Indiana; Urbana, Illinois; and Frankfurt, Germany. I could make no sense of the phone system, either. I kept getting the same main voice menu. I was hungry, so I dragged myself down to the "lobby" to shop in the vending machines.

The machines were in a separate little room shared with a small buffet table that held bowls of apples and dispensers of breakfast cereals. I took some of each. One of the vending machines sold pizza by the slice, another offered toiletries, including a few cold remedies. After four tries at getting the machine to accept my crinkled twenty-dollar bill, I bought some capsules, some pills, a few single-dose liquids and something in a small bottle called Boost-Blaster! that bragged of its megadose of antioxidants, enzymes, and whatever good stuff is in Swiss chard and certain fish.

Back up in the room, I made a cocktail of two of every purchase, tearing off the safety foil, figuring out the childproof caps, and chugging down the Boost-Blaster! in one pull.

DAY 18

I woke up with no idea where I was. I heard a shower running. I saw a crack of light from under a door and a stack of textbooks on the nightstand. The bathroom door flew open in a flash of illuminated steam.

"He's alive!" Anna was naked, drying herself off. She had already been out for a run.

"Am I?" My cold was no better. Not at all. The only new feeling I had was wooziness.

"You took all this stuff?" She waved at the small desk littered with the debris left over from my self-medication.

"Still sick," I said in feeble self-defense.

"Saying you are still sick makes you still sick."

"I feel so rotten your logic actually makes sense."

"You missed it, baby. Last night we went out for organic Mexican food. It was Ricardo's birthday. There were about forty of us and a piñata. After, we went to a racetrack and drove miniature hot rods. I called you, texted you, but nothing."

I grabbed my phone. Between 6:00 p.m. and 1:30 in the morning AnnaGraphicControl had called and texted me thirty-three times.

Anna started getting dressed. "You better pack. Gotta check out of here, and then go to Ricardo's office for a meeting. To the airport from there."

Anna piloted the PonyCar to an industrial park somewhere in Fort Worth. I sat in the reception area, feeling horrible, blowing my nose again and again, trying to focus on a book about astronaut Walt Cunningham on my Kobo digital reader, but I was just too foggy. I played a game on my phone called 101, answering true/false and multiple-choice questions. True or false: President Woodrow Wilson used a typewriter in the White House. True! He hunted and pecked a speech on a Hammond Type-o-Matic, hoping to drum up support for World War I.

After a long sit I needed some air, so I took a slow walk around the industrial park. Every building looked the same and I got lost. I found my way back when, luckily, I spotted a parked PonyCar that turned out to be ours.

Anna was there, cooling her heels with her clients, waiting for me. "Where were you?"

"Seeing the sights," I said. She introduced me to Ricardo and thirteen other textbook executives. I shook hands with none of them. I had a cold, you see.

Returning the PonyCar was as effortless as promised, but the courtesy bus to the airline terminal took forever to show up. To make our plane, Anna and I had to run through the DFW airport like two characters from a movie that was

about either wacky lovers on vacation or federal agents trying to stop a terrorist attack. We did make the plane, but not
in time to get seats together. Anna sat up front, I was way in
the back. My clogged ears were killing me on departure and
hurt even more hours later on descent.

On the way to my house, she stopped at a liquor store for
a small bottle of brandy. She had me drink a large shot of the
booze, then put me into bed with a pillow tuck and a kiss on
my forehead.

DAYS 19 AND 20

I was ill, pure and simple, with bedrest and liquids being the
only remedies, as has been the case with colds since the first
Neanderthal came down with the sniffles.

Anna, though, had her own ideas. For two days she was on
a mission to cure me sooner rather than gradually. She had
me sit naked in a chair with my feet in a tub of cold water. She
wired up my limbs to something akin to an EKG machine,
made me take off any metal I was wearing, which was none,
then flipped a switch. I felt nothing.

But in time, the water around my feet turned first murky,
then brown, and then began to congeal until the tub looked
like the most unappetizing Jell-O mold imaginable. The goop
was so thick that pulling my bare feet out was like extracting
myself from swamp mud. And the stuff stank!

"That's the bad juju coming out of you," Anna said as she
flushed the slop down the toilet.

"Out of my feet?" I asked.

"Yes. It's proven. The bad food you eat, the body poisons and fats. They leach out of your feet."

"Can I go back to bed now?"

"Just until your steam shower."

"I don't have a steam shower."

"You will."

Anna installed a series of plastic curtains in my shower with a portable steam maker set on high. I sat in it on a footstool, sweating, until I was able to polish off three big bottles of weak tea of some kind. This took some time, as the tea tasted like gutter water and a man's bladder can only hold so much gutter water.

An exercise bicycle was delivered. Anna had me ride it every hour and a half for exactly twelve minutes, until I had worked up a sweat to prove I had raised my body temperature.

"This is to cook out the mucus and such," she said.

For three meals in a row she fed me bowls of watery stew with chunks of beets and celery.

She had me do one-hour, slow-stretch sessions from her iPad, but I had to move *exactly* as did the instructor on the video.

She plugged in this thing the size of an electric bar of soap that made a *humming* sound and vibration, a bit of homemade medicine with Russian lettering on the box. She had me lie naked on the floor and rubbed my entire body, both sides, with whatever that thing was. The Commie machine made different sounds over different parts of my body.

"Atta baby!" Anna said. "We're getting to it now!"

Without telling her, I chugged some NyQuil and chewed up a few Sudafeds just before I crawled back into my bed to disappear into the Land of Nod.

DAY 21

I felt better in the morning. My sheets were so damp with my night sweats I could have wrung them out like a chamois.

Anna had left a note taped to my percolator.

Left you sleeping deep and silent. I like you like that. You will no longer be ill if you finish the soup in the refrigerator. Drink it cold in the morning, hot at lunch. Do the exer-bike twice before noon and take an hour for the stretch routine on the link I emailed you. And RE-STEAM, until you've downed three bottles of distilled water! Leach that sodium! A.

I was alone in my house on my own terms, so I immediately ignored Anna's instructions. I had coffee with hot milk. I read an actual print copy of the *Times*—not the online version, which Anna preferred because newsprint paper was a sin against the earth, regardless of my recycling. I treated myself to a nutritious breakfast of eggs with fried slices of *linguica* (a Portuguese sausage), a banana, a strawberry Pop-Tart, papaya juice from a carton, and a large bowl of Cocoa Puffs.

I did not do any stretching. I did not get on the stationary bike nor did I go into the plastic steam stall. I did not open her email link, thus stretched not a whit. Instead, I spent the morning doing laundry—four loads, including the bedsheets. I played my mixtape CDs and sang along. I reveled in obeying not a single one of Anna's commands. I lived the best life imaginable.

Which meant I had answered the question Anna had put to me two weeks earlier: No. I did not think I was the man for her.

When she called to ask how I was, I confessed to ignoring her instructions. I also said that I felt healthy, rested, and like myself and despite how wonderful I thought she was and what a dope I am and *blahditty blah-blah dittity-blah.*

Before I could muster the vocabulary to actually break up with her, Anna did it for me.

"You are not the man for me, baby."

There was not a smidgen of rancor in her voice, neither judgment nor disappointment. She said it straight out of her face in a way I couldn't. "I've known for a while," Anna said, chuckling. "I was wearing you down. Would have destroyed you over time."

"When were you going to let me off your hook?" I asked.

"If you hadn't backed out by Friday morning, we'd have had the Talk then."

"Why Friday morning?"

"Because Friday night I'm going back to Fort Worth. Ricardo is taking me hot-air ballooning."

A bit of my man-pride had me instantly hoping that this Ricardo fellow would not be the man for Anna, either.

———

He wasn't. Anna never told me why.

For the record, I did get my scuba certificate. Anna and I

joined Vin and a dozen other divers, offshore in the kelp beds. We breathed underwater, swimming through what looked like a tall forest of sea trees. There's a great picture of Anna and me, on board afterward, our wet-suited arms around each other and big smiles on our cold, wet faces.

We leave for Antarctica next week. Anna arranged a big shopping spree, seeing to it that we have all the necessary gear. She spent extra time with MDash, making sure he was going to have enough layers to stay warm. He's never been to a place cold enough for chinstraps and crabeaters.

"Antarctic Circle, make way," I hollered, modeling my green parka and shell. Anna laughed.

We'll fly to Lima, Peru, then change planes for Punta Arenas, Chile, where we'll board a boat to make the crossing from South America to the old science station at Port Lockroy, our first stop. The seas in the Drake Passage can get pretty rough and tumble, they say. But with a strong sail, a firm wheel, a true compass, and a reliable clock, our ship will journey south, bound for the Antarctic Circle and adventure galore.

Oh, yeah. For B15K, as well.

Christmas Eve 1953

Virgil Beuell didn't close the shop until nearly dinnertime, when a light snow began falling. The road
back home was slick and getting slicker so he drove slowly,
wonderfully easy to do in the Plymouth with the PowerFlite
automatic transmission. No clutch, no shifting, an engineering marvel. Skidding off the icy road and getting stuck in the
snow would be a disaster tonight; in the Plymouth's trunk
were all the treasures due in the morning from Santa, kept
hidden and undiscovered there since the kids had declared
their wishes weeks ago. Those presents had to be under the
tree in a few hours, and transferring them from the trunk of
a snowbound car to the cab of a tow truck would alter Christmas Eve horribly.

The drive home took longer than usual, sure, but the
length of the trip did not bother Virgil. The cold was what he
hated. PowerFlite or not, he often cursed the folks at Plymouth, who were unable to build a car with a heater worth a
damn. By the time he slowly pulled up to the house and the

yellow spread of the headlamps played on the screen of the back porch and there was the *hush* of tires coming to a stop on the gravel drive, he was aching slightly from the cold. Virgil had to be extra careful not to slip on the front walkway, as he had done too many times before, but he still got inside the house as fast as a working man could.

As he stamped the snow off his overshoes and hung up his layers of warm clothing, Virgil's body softened in the warmth pumping up from the cellar through the grates. After buying the house, he self-installed a furnace that was far oversized for the modest home. He put in, too, a beast of a hot-water heater, a commercial unit that never, ever ran out of the liquid heaven that allowed for the kids' baths and his own long showers. The winter fuel bills were worth the comfort, as was the price of two cords of firewood every winter.

A fire was going in the family room. He had taught Davey how to build one by stacking the wood the way he did his toy Lincoln Logs, like a square house around the kindling, never a pyramid. The kid now viewed making the fire as his sacred duty. Come the first frosts of November, the Beuell home was the warmest place for miles and miles.

"Dad!" Davey came running from the kitchen. "Our plan is working *great*. Jill is completely *fooled*."

"Good news, Big Man," Virgil said, giving his boy the secret handshake known in the entire world only by the two of them.

"I told her we'd write the Santa letters after dinner, then lay out some snacks, just like you did with me when I was little." Davey was turning eleven in January.

Jill was setting the kitchen table, her specialty being the straightening of napkins and silverware. "My daddy is home, hooray hooray," the six-year-old said, lining up the last of the spoons.

"He is?" Delores Gomez Beuell asked, standing as she cooked at the stove, baby Connie straddling the nooks of her elbow and hip. Virgil gave each of the women in his life a kiss.

"So he is," Del said, pecking him back, then dishing fried potatoes with onions onto a platter and getting it to the table. Davey brought his father a can of beer from the new, huge Kelvinator and ceremonially levered the two opposing openings in the top with a church key, another sacred duty.

Dinnertime with the Family Beuell was a show. Davey was in and out of his chair—the kid never sat through a meal. Connie squirmed in her mother's lap, content with a spoon she worked around in her mouth or banged on the table. Del cut food for the kids, wiped up spills, placed bits of mashed-up potato into Connie's mouth, and, occasionally, had a bite herself. Virgil ate slowly, never repeating a bite of any one food, but working his fork around his plate in a circle as he enjoyed the theater that was his family.

"I'm telling ya, Santa needs only three cookies." Davey was explaining, for Jill's sake, the facts surrounding the evening's expected visitor. "And he never finishes a whole glass of milk. He's got so much to do. Right, Dad?"

"So I hear." Virgil gave his son a wink that Davey tried to return, but he could only scrunch up the one side of his face to force one eye closed.

"Anyways, everyone leaves him the same snack."

"Everyone?" Jill asked.

"Everyone."

"I can't figure out when he comes. When does he show up?" Jill needed to know.

"Not at all if you don't touch your dinner." Del tapped Jill's plate with her fork and separated some of her potato from her meat. "Bites get Santa here sooner."

"Right when we all go to bed?" Jill asked. "We have to be sleeping, right?"

"Could be anytime between bedtime and when we wake up." Davey had answers for every one of his sister's queries. Since he had figured out the deal with Santa over the summer, Davey had assigned himself the task of keeping his little sister a believer.

"That could be hours. If his milk sits out too long, it'll go bad."

"He can make it cold with just a touch! He just sticks his finger in a glass of warm milk and does a *whooshy* thing and boom. Cold milk."

Jill found that fact amazing. "He must drink a lot of milk."

After dinner Virgil and the kids did KP, Jill standing on a chair over the sink drying the forks and spoons one by one while Del was upstairs putting the baby down and grabbing a short, much-needed nap. Davey opened his father's final can of beer for the night and set it on the telephone table right beside what was called Daddy's Chair in the front room, by the fire. Once Virgil was sitting and sipping, Davey and Jill lay in front of the phonograph and played Christmas records. With the room lights off, the tree threw colored magic onto the walls. Jill found Virgil's lap while her brother played the Rudolph record over and over until they knew all the words and started adding their own.

Had a very shiny nose.

"Like a lightbulb!"

Used to laugh and call him names.

"Hey, Knothead!"

When it came to the line about going down in history, they yelled out, "And arithmetic!"

Del came downstairs, laughing. "What would you goofballs make of 'Joy to the World'?" She took a sip from Virgil's beer before sitting in her corner of the sofa, tapping a cigarette from her leather case with the snap clasp, and lighting it with matches from the ashtray set beside the phone.

"Davey, poke that log a bit, would you?" Virgil said.

Jill perked up. "Lemme poke the fire!"

"After me. And don't worry. Santa's boots are fireproof."

"I know. I know."

After Jill took her turn stabbing the fire, Del sent the kids upstairs to change into their pj's.

Virgil finished his beer, then went to the hall closet to pull out the portable Remington typewriter. Delores had bought the machine brand new for Virgil when he was in the Army hospital on Long Island, New York. He had typed letters to her with his one good hand until the therapists taught him to use what he called five-and-a-half-finger touch typing.

He took the writing machine out of its case on the low coffee table and rolled in two sheets of paper, one on top of the other—always two sheets so as not to damage the platen.

"Leave your messages for St. Nick or Father Christmas or whatever his name is," he told the kids when they came back downstairs smelling of toothpaste and fresh, clean flannel.

Jill wrote hers first, one *clack* at a time, letter by letter, key by key.

dear santaa clas thank you for coiming again and thank
you for the nurse kit and my Honey Walker I hpoe
you give me bothh merry chirstmas I love you JILL
BEUELL

For his letter Davey insisted on his own separate piece of paper. He told Jill that he didn't want to confuse Santa. Getting the two pages into the typewriter and lined up straight took him a few tries.

12/24/53

Dear Santa Clause. My sister Jill believes in you and so. Do I. still. You know what I want for this chrismas and believe me you have NEVER DISAPPOINTMED ME..!"Hear is some cold milk of course and 'snack cakes' thar tar also called cookies. Next year you have to bring presents for baby Connie beecause she will be old enuogh by then Okay????? if the milek is warm make it cold with yuor finger.

David Amos Beuell

Davey left his letter hanging out of the typewriter carriage, posing the machine to face the fireplace, where Santa was sure to see it.

"You guys should arrange your presents in piles under the tree. To make things simple come morning," Virgil said. Santa always left the wished-for presents that were his responsibility unwrapped on Christmas morning, ready for immediate play, so Virgil and Del would have time for their morning coffee. The family gifts—from Uncle Gus and Aunt Ethel, from Uncle Andrew and Aunt Marie, from Goggy and Pop, from Nana and Leo, from as far away as Urbana, Illinois, and as close as Holt's Bend—had been collecting under the tree, wrapped in colorful paper, for days, growing with almost every stop at the village post office.

Once twin stacks of gifts labeled DAVEY and JILL had been built up, the kids put the records back in their sleeves and the albums back up on the shelf. Del asked Jill to tune the big cabinet radio to the Christmas Eve Programs, for seasonal music that was not about a deer with a red nose.

Cookies had been baked on December 23. Jill pulled them out of the Kelvinator and arranged them on a plate while Davey poured milk into a tall glass, then they carried the snacks to the coffee table, setting them beside the Remington. From then on it was a waiting game. Davey added another log to the fire as Jill reacquainted herself with her father's lap while the radio played Christmas carols celebrating wise men and holy nights and the birth of Jesus.

Not long after, Virgil carried his sleeping daughter up to

her bed, sliding her between the covers, marveling at the softness of his little girl's closed eyes and the lips that were Del's in perfect miniature. In the front room, Davey was on the sofa, leaning close against his mother as she played her fingers in his hair. "She swallowed it hook, line, and sinker," he said.

"You're a good big brother," Del told him.

"Ah, heck. Anyone would do it." Davey was looking into the fire. "When Jill first asked me if Santa was really real, like she was afraid to ask you and wanted it to be a secret between just us, I didn't know what to say."

"How'd you handle it, honey?"

"That's when I came up with the plan. To have an answer for every question she had. How does he make it to every house? He goes superfast and there aren't all that many houses anyway. What about a house with no chimney? He can use the oven or the furnace."

"Touching the milk to make it cold," Del whispered to her son as she brushed hair off the soft skin of his forehead. "So smart. So quick."

"That was cinchy. He's a magic man."

"You'll have to do the same for Connie soon."

"Of course. It's my job now."

Virgil came back downstairs to Daddy's Chair as a carol, in Latin, was crooning out of the mouth of Bing Crosby.

"Dad, how does radio work?" Davey wanted to know.

———

At quarter past ten, Davey went off to bed, announcing this might have been the best Christmas Eve ever.

"Should I put on some coffee?" Delores asked.

"You'd better," Virgil said, following her into the kitchen, where he stopped her from reaching for the coffee can, wrapped his arms around her, and kissed her. She kissed back, both of them feeling that such a kiss was one of the reasons they were still married. The kiss lasted longer than either of them expected, then they smiled at each other. Del prepared the coffee as Virgil stood next to her at the stove.

"Next year, let's try to get to the Midnight Mass," Delores said. "We are raising godless kids."

"Just Davey." Virgil chuckled. Davey had been born seven months after their wedding day.

"The Midnight Mass is so beautiful."

"Three kids up all hours on Christmas Eve? The drive all the way to St. Mary's? If we'd tried that tonight with the snow?"

"The McElhenys manage."

"Ruth McElheny is as nutty as a can of Planters. Ed doesn't dare cross her."

"Still. The candles. The music. So pretty." Del knew that in years to come they'd make the drive to Midnight Mass. Not because he didn't dare cross her but because he loved to give her what she wanted. But for this Yuletide, there was just his hand over hers in the quiet, warm kitchen of the snowbound house as they sat with their coffee.

Virgil put his overshoes back on and pulled on his heavy coat, cracking open the front door just wide enough for him to slip through. Nearly three inches of snow had collected. Hatless, he went to the Plymouth's trunk to retrieve Santa's bounty. Not wanting to risk a fall on the frozen walk, Virgil made two trips carrying small loads. Closing the trunk, he paused a moment to ponder the final hour of Christmas Eve 1953. A cold night, yes, but Virgil had been colder.

Stepping carefully, he felt the pull of a ghost pain where his lower left leg used to be. He took the five steps to the front door one at a time.

Del laid out the nurse's kit by Jill's stack of treasures. Honey Walker, the walking doll "just like a real little girl," needed batteries. Santa had batteries. Before too long Davey would find his Space Rocket Launch Base, with towers and soldiers and spring launchers that, once Virgil assembled the components, actually flung spaceships into the void. Connie would delight in a new play blanket and a set of blocks direct from the North Pole. When all was laid out and Honey Walker had taken a test stroll, Virgil and Del sat close together on the sofa and kissed some more.

After they'd sat, arms entwined, quiet and still for a while, Del eyed the fire, then rose up. "I'm done in," she confessed. "Try to answer on the first ring, honey. And give him my love."

"I will." Virgil checked his watch. It was almost 11:30. Seven minutes after midnight, the shrill peal of the phone broke the silent night. As instructed, Virgil picked up before the first ring gave way to the second.

"Merry Christmas," he said.

An operator was on the line. "This is a long-distance call for Virginia Beuell from Amos Boling."

"Speaking. Thank you, Operator." As always, the operator had gotten the name wrong.

"Sir, your party is on the line," the operator said, clicking off.

"Thanks, honey," said the caller. "Merry Christmas, Virgin."

Virgil smiled at his nickname. Because of Amos Boling, the whole outfit had come to call him Virgin. "Where the heck are you, Bud?"

"San Diego. I was over across the border yesterday."

"You don't say."

"Lemme tell you something about Mexico, Virgin. The place is loaded with cantinas and cathouses. Nice and hot, too. How deep is the snow up there in Dogpatch?"

"Seen worse. But I'm sitting by a nice fire, so no complaints."

"Delores still burdened with you?"

"Gives her love."

"You are one lucky son of a bitch and that gal could have done better."

"I know that but haven't told her."

Both men chuckled. Amos "Bud" Boling forever joked that when Delores Gomez was taken off the market by Virgil "the Virgin" Beuell, there was no longer any point in getting married. There had been a time, more than thirteen years before, when someone else in the outfit might have come along to snag Delores. Ernie, Clyde, or Bob Clay, or either of the two Johnny Boys would have all taken a run at her had Virgil not met her first. A dance at the Red Cross Center was so chockablock with soldiers, sailors, and airmen that Virgil needed some air and a few moments away from the crowd. He stepped outside for a smoke and found himself lighting a cigarette for a brown-eyed girl named Delores Gomez. By the end of the next morning she and Virgil had danced, laughed, had griddle cakes with lots of coffee, and kissed. Two lives changed forever.

———

In the years since, Bud had not married and Virgil knew he never would. Not landing Delores had nothing to do with it. Virgil had, years before, figured Bud was one of those men, like his father's youngest brother, Uncle Russell. Virgil had been around his uncle rarely, the last time during the long day that was his grandmother's funeral. Uncle Russell had driven from New York City with a friend, a man named Carl, who called Russell "Rusty." After the service, the burial, and a reunion dinner at the house that ended with coffee and pie, Carl and Rusty drove off into the night, headed all the way back to New York City, still wearing their funeral suits. Virgil remembered his father later saying, under his breath, that "women were neither the weakness nor the passion" of his kid brother. Bud Boling had plenty of weaknesses and a few passions, but just as for Uncle Russell, none of them involved women. "So," Virgil said. "How you been, Bud?"

"The same, the same," Bud answered. "Came down here three months ago from a town up north near Sacramento.

That's the state capital, you know. Bought a Buick second-hand and drove it down. Nice town. Navy town. Every cab-driver will tell you he was at Pearl Harbor."

"You working at all?"

"Not until someone makes me."

"I know I say this every year, but here it is: I've got room for you at the shop. In fact, I could use you with the way things have been going."

"Doing well, are you?"

"Bud, I've got so many orders I'm working six-day weeks."

"Hell on earth."

"I'm serious, Bud. You come work with me and you'd be set for years."

"I'm already set for years."

"I'll pay you more than you're worth."

"I ain't worth a flat plug nickel, Virgin. You know that."

Virgil laughed. "Then just come by for a visit. In the summer. Hop in that Buick and we'll go fishing."

"You country boys always make a big deal about fishing."

"I'd just like to see you, Bud. Del, too. Little Davey would be over the moon to meet you."

"Maybe next year."

"You say that every Christmas." Virgil kept going. "Come see us, Bud. We'll go to Midnight Mass. We'll say prayers for all the fellows."

"I've already said all the prayers for all the fellows I'm ever going to pray for."

"Aw, come on. Next year will be ten years."

"Ten years?" Bud let the static crackle on the long-distance line. "Ten years for *who*? Ten years for *what*?"

Virgil felt like a fool.

———

Bob Clay had been killed in Normandy on the same day that Ernie, wounded in his right thigh, had bled out. No one realized his artery had been severed because the pool of blood under Ernie never spread, but was absorbed by the damp ground. Nobody saw it. Attention was not paid as closely as it should have been since there were Germans trying to kill them from somewhere on the other side of a thick hedgerow in the French *bocage*. Mortar rounds coming at them from the unseen enemy kept the outfit pinned down for nearly an hour. Bud and Virgil were in two squads sent to hack through the roots and trees—impossible but for the use of grenades. They flanked the enemy position and killed all of them, but at a cost. Bud's squad leader, Corporal Emery, was cut in two, literally, by a German machine gun. Virgil was unsuccessful giving first aid to Sergeant Castle, who took three rounds in the chest that severed his spine. Burke's head wound was beyond aid, and a fellow named Corcoran lost an arm that was cut clean from his shoulder and he was moved back to an aid station. No one knew if he lived or not.

A week later Johnny Boy disappeared and the other Johnny Boy cracked, and one by one, others in the outfit were lost in ways soldiers are lost. For fifty-eight days, from the seventh of June to early August, the outfit was either fighting or moving toward the fighting. Bud was promoted to corporal and Virgil's teeth began to go rotten from eating nothing but K rations.

On Day 59, the outfit rested at a camp in France—there were cots with blankets and relatively warm showers, hot food, and all the coffee a GI could stomach. Later, a big tent served as a theater where movies where played. Clyde was transferred to Intelligence because he spoke decent French. Every airplane in the sky was either the RAF or the USAAF, and the word was the Germans were on the run, that the worst of the fighting had happened and they'd all be home by Christmas. New guys came in from the replacement depots and had to be drilled and trained. Bud was tough on all of them, and Virgil didn't want to learn any of their names.

In the middle of September the outfit was given new uniforms, rearmed, and loaded into transports for an offensive in Holland. Four of the trucks slammed into each other in the dark of night. Five soldiers were killed, three were so injured they were no good for the war anymore. The trucks were repaired and moving by daylight. Three days later the outfit was surprised by a German attack just before dawn. The command post was blown up, leading to a confused, chaotic battle that had Virgil and Bud fighting the enemy hand to hand. By chance, three tanks, British Cromwells, were close enough to roar in and overpower the German advance. Many of the new guys were killed in what was their first time in combat, and plenty happened that made no sense, no sense at all.

Virgil lost count of the days before he found himself back in France, where he and Bud slept and slept and slept. They walked around huge, ancient cathedrals and played football. Movie stars came to put on shows. There was a cathouse not far from the barracks, a place called Madame Sophia's. While many of the officers had three-day passes in Paris, Bud and Virgil and the other enlisted men drilled and trained more replacements, even in the rain. There was a different movie every night. Then came the coldest December on record, and the Germans roared into Belgium. The outfit was loaded onto trucks, driven hell-bent into the night, and dropped off on a road somewhere between Paris and Berlin. Virgil appreciated the spirit of one driver—a colored fellow—who gave him a pack of Lucky Strikes and a wish for God to look out for him.

The outfit marched on roads and across ice-solid fields, along trails dragged out in the gathered snow, hauling ammo and supplies for themselves as well as for others who were already up ahead in the fighting, which Virgil could see in the distance like Fourth of July fireworks. They fought along with the paratroopers who had taken heavy casualties, moving forward in a show of arms meant to convince the Germans that an entire division was at the ready to take them on. The ruse worked. But lives were lost.

The outfit came under artillery fire in the Belgian woods and some guys were blown apart, vaporized. Then Virgil, Bud, and the outfit were sent marching the other way, through Bastogne proper. They passed a neatly arranged stack of dead soldiers just outside the church, burned-out, useless tanks with their treads thrown off, and a pair of cows eating hay a farmer had stocked. The farmer and the cows seemed oblivious to the Germans, who were trying to retake the port at Antwerp, and to the general hullaballoo. The cold cut them all to the bone. It was inescapable. The cold killed some men in the outfit. Sleep was so rare, some guys went nuts and had to be sent back into Bastogne. The hope was that they could gather themselves so they could return to the cold and the fighting.

———

A new kid—Something Something, Jr.—had the watch. Virgil was in the hole, under the roof of branches, on top of the pine needles that lined the floor, wrapped in a single GI blanket. Sleep was a joke. He had a few Charms fruit candies left in a roll, so popped two into his mouth. One remained, so he rose up from the frozen-ground floor of the hole and palmed the final square of hard candy into the hand of the new kid.

"Merry fucking Christmas," Virgil whispered.

"Thanks, Virgin."

"Junior, call me Virgin again and I'll crack you one."

"Isn't your name Virgin?"

"Not to fucking new guys."

The hole was at the far left of these woods, two trees in from the edge of the rise, overlooking, in daylight, a Belgian farmer's barren field and, just beyond it, a collection of houses built along a narrow road leading northeast. At night, there was only the void. Somewhere down there were supposed to be the German soldiers. The rest of the outfit was in holes and shelters of their own, spaced off to the right. This was the main line of defense, theoretically. In reality, the idea of an MLD was as laughable as that of a cozy nap. The line was so thin there was no listening post forward of the trees. There was little heavy armor in the rear. The big guns had only a few shells left. There was no kitchen and thus no hot food for miles.

This hole was the seventh Virgil had chipped out of the frozen ground and covered with tree limbs since they had walked through Bastogne. Virgil didn't want to dig any more of them. Moving to another position meant shouldering weapons and gear, carrying it who knew how far or for how long, digging another hole, and building another shelter, working up the sweat that, in the subzero winter, caused a man's uniform to freeze to his back. Frostbite had taken more men off the line than wounds from enemy fire. Some of the freezing guys had been able to get out before the encirclement. Those that hadn't had already lost toes and fingers, some even their feet and hands.

Virgil didn't want to be one of those guys. He kept his one extra pair of socks tied together and draped across the back of his neck under his uniform to hang in his armpits. His body temperature, what was left of it, would dry the socks out some. He hoped he could always have that reserve of semidry socks to avoid frostbite. He also hoped Hitler was going to come walking across the field waving a white hankie to surrender personally to PFC Virgil Beuell. Right after Rita Hayworth dropped by to offer a blow job.

"I sure could use some coffee," Junior whispered.

"Tell you what," Virgil whispered back. "I'll start a warm and toasty fire to percolate us up a couple of pots. I got some cake mixings, too, and we'll make a batch for the whole squad and shut the fuck up, you fucking fucker."

"Butterfly. Butterfly!" A sharp whisper came from the dark to the left of the hole, the password for the day.

"McQueen!" Virgil hissed in response.

A second later, Sergeant Bud Boling tumbled into the shelter, weaponless. He had been trying to sleep during daylight hours, covered up in a hole of his own. Once it got dark he roamed the front in silence, alone, returning at daylight to report whatever he had seen to the CP before tucking away in his dark hole again.

"Krauts. Twenty-five of them. Who the fuck are you?" Bud meant the new guy, Junior. Before a name could be offered Bud said "never mind" and gave an order. "Gimme your rifle and get to the CP and tell them a Kraut probe is coming on the left."

Junior's eyes went wide. He had yet to be in any combat. As he kicked his way up and out of the hole, Bud repeated "Kraut probe on our left." And the kid was gone. Bud readied the M1 rifle, tucking spare ammo clips into his jacket.

Virgil lifted the machine gun in one piece, tripod and all, and faced it at the foxholes nine o'clock. "I was right ahead of them, Virgin."

"They see you?"

"No fucking Luger-head ever sees me." The men whispered with the confidence of experienced soldiers, which they were, not like twenty-two-year-old boys, which they also were.

A footfall from the darkness cracked hardened ice.

"Light 'em up," Bud hissed.

PFC Vigil Beuell pulled the trigger of his machine gun, spitting fire into a column of enemy soldiers not three yards in front of him. Bright muzzle flashes and red tracer rounds illuminated the shapes of bodies and the trunks of trees as other American boys took to their weapons. A fury of fighting lit up the woods, and the thin line of defense took on the look of an impenetrable wall. In a flash as well defined as that from a Speed Graphic camera ringside at a prizefight, Virgil saw the helmet of a German soldier explode in a cloud of fine, blood-red mist and soggy clumps of what had been the man's head. The German soldiers spread out quickly and spewed death themselves. Bud raised up just high enough to aim his rifle and squeeze out a full clip into the invading force—eight continuous *BLAM*s—spreading his rounds with a geometric precision until the *pi-cling* of his empty clip flying out of its breach meant his ammo was spent. Instinctively, Bud reloaded and was raised up again when a body came crashing into the shelter through the pine branch roof.

The German was firing as he fell, hitting Virgil in his left knee without Virgil feeling a thing. Another shot made the fingers on Virgil's left hand sting like a hornet's bite.

"Fuck you!" Bud yelled, driving the butt of his M1 across the German's jaw. "Fucker!" he yelled, smashing the German's face twice more. Someone began firing parachute flares that lit up the woods in a harsh limelight, and Bud saw he had broken the nose and smashed the jaw of the German, who lay glassy-eyed and motionless. He spun his rifle around, pointed the muzzle at the middle button on the soldier's uniform, fired two rounds point-blank, and ended the man's life. "One less of you fuckers," he said to the dead enemy soldier.

The small reserve force of American boys was coming forward now; what had started as a probe by the enemy had become a severe and deadly mistake for them. A pursuit was under way as the Germans retreated. Virgil ceased fire and was breaking down his weapon to join the move forward when he realized something was wrong. His hand was sticky and his leg was numb.

"My leg fell asleep!" he yelled. Trying to stand, Virgil fell back, on top of the faceless, lifeless German. He tried to stand again, but his left leg bent the wrong way at the knee and Virgil could not figure out what had happened. Luckily Bud Boling was there to help him up. But rather than getting him on his feet, Bud squatted, pulled Virgil over his shoulders, and lifted him clean off the ground.

That much, Virgil remembered of Christmas Eve 1944. Somewhere between the foxhole and the aid station to the rear, he slipped into the slumber of the unconscious.

―――――

Virgil felt like a *god damn* fool.

Next year was an anniversary for him because the war ended for PFC Beuell on Christmas Eve 1944. He awoke at an aid station in Bastogne proper, after the American tanks had come and the German advance had collapsed. A few days later, he woke up again at a field hospital in France. Weeks later he became one of thousands of wounded men in hospitals in England. When Germany surrendered and the war was over in Europe, Virgil began to think of himself as one lucky bastard. His left leg was gone, severed above the knee, and three fingers of his left hand were now stumps, wrapped in so many bandages he looked like he was wearing a gauze catcher's mitt. But he still had two thumbs, one good leg, his sight, and his manhood. Compared to many other guys in those hospitals and on the ship home, Virgin felt like he had won the 1945 Irish Sweepstake. All he really wanted back was his wedding band, which had been lost somewhere in those woods in Belgium.

Amos "Bud" Boling stayed in Germany for his full enlistment, which meant the duration of the war plus six months. While Virgil was being treated for his wounds and the deadly infections that came with them, Bud was attacking the Siegfried Line and killing his way into Nazi Germany. Then he breached the Rhine River and later the Elbe, swept south into pockets of enemy country that had seen no signs of the war in the four and a half years it had raged around him.

Bud had never been wounded but he'd seen too many who had been, and too many killed. He had also killed a great many German men and boys. He had ended the lives of German soldiers who had been looking to surrender and survive but instead found Sergeant Bud Boling's merciless eyes. Eighteen German officers were shot dead by his hand, alone or two or three at a time, off the roads and under the cover of trees, behind farmhouse walls or out in open fields. Bud used his .45 sidearm to wring a justice out of the war that made sense only to him. Bud killed one last German in August

1945. He had heard stories about a particular local, a former Nazi Party official who was using the false name of Wolfe. He found the man standing in a line of refugees who were hoping to return to their home cities in different parts of what had been the Third Reich. When Wolfe produced his papers, Bud ordered him out of the line. Behind a low brick wall Bud drew his sidearm and shot Wolfe square through his neck and calmly stood over the former Nazi bigwig as he thrashed about for the last few moments of his life. Bud Boling never talked of any of this. He never talked of the camps he'd seen, either. Virgil never knew any of the specifics. But he suspected. He saw the emptiness, the difference in his friend.

———

"How long you thinking of staying in San Diego, Bud?"

"Maybe a week, maybe a year. May head up to Los Angeles for the New Year and catch that big parade."

"The Rose Parade?"

"Yeah. Supposed to be gorgeous. I'd ask you where're you headed but I already know. The shop for six days a week."

"I like my work, Bud. Don't know that I could just amble about like you do."

"Virgin, I'd rather punch a cop than a clock."

The men laughed.

"Merry Christmas to you. And you'll be mighty welcome should you amble our way sometime."

"Always good to talk to you, Virgin. Glad you're a happy man. You deserve such blessings."

"Thanks to you, Bud."

"Almost 1954. Can you believe it? There you are with Del and Davey and Jill and, uh, Connie? I get the new one's name right?"

"Connie it is."

"Virgil the Virgin has three kids. I understand the biology but the reality's a fucking mystery . . ."

The men gave each other a round of holiday wishes, repeated goodbyes, and hung up. They would talk again in a year.

Virgil sat in the quiet, watching the fire until one in the morning. Then he pulled up out of Daddy's Chair to bank the flames so that Davey would have embers to start up the Yule logs. He found the plug for the Christmas tree lights and yanked it from the wall socket, using the thumb, forefinger, and knuckle stumps of his left hand. After almost forgetting, he stopped in front of the plate that held Santa's cookies and ate three of them. He hesitated, then took a bite out of a fourth cookie, put it back on the plate, and drank a few sips of the milk that had gone warm.

In darkness, he found his way to the stairs, climbing one riser at a time, his left shoe matching his right foot. He checked on both of the sleeping kids and Connie in her crib beside Del's side of the bed. Del always laid his pajamas out for him, so once he was out of his trousers and had undone the straps and buckles of his prosthetic leg, he set the thing to rest beside the chair and wriggled into his sleeping clothes.

A short stutter of a hop got him into bed. As he did every night, he found Del's lips and kissed them softly, causing her to purr through her sleep. Virgil pulled the covers over him—the sheet, the two heavy blankets, and the thick quilt. He rested his head on his pillow after the long day and, at last, closed his eyes.

As he did almost every night, he saw the lightning-like image of a soldier's helmet exploding in a cloud of blood-red mist. He saw the soggy clumps of what had been the man's head. Virgil forced himself to think of something else, anything else. He searched his mind for an image and settled on a vision of Bud Boling as a young man, twenty-two years old, standing in the warm sunshine on a California street, part of a great throng of people, all with smiling faces, cheering on a parade of floats covered with roses.

A Junket in the City of Light

What brown fox jumped quickly over dogs that are lazy?

Hey, this writing machine actually works!

What the <u>hell</u> has happened? Who am I <u>today</u>? Still Rory Thorpe, I guess, but who is <u>he</u>?

Last night—just hours ago—I was the guy in a huge movie that everyone was talking about, the guy who made out with a glamorous beauty, a guy with a fine ass. In the capitals of Europe—and America—I was hustled around like a politician, into cars and into ballrooms filled with camera-totin', question-hollerin' reporters. I waved to seas of people, many of whom waved back, even though no one knew who I am, even though I am, in fact, a no one. Although, I have in my possession...certain documents...that reveal Willa Sax's TOP-SECRET CODE NAME (it's Eleanor Flintstone!).

I was 2 Days into taking the City of Paris by storm, with a 3rd to go, and Day 3 was going to have FIREWORKS! I had all my expenses paid. I was wearing free clothes. I could ask for a sandwich whenever I wanted, even though I was kept so busy I didn't have time for much more than a few bites.

But this morning all that is <u>over</u>. I have to be out of my room at checkout time. Too bad. This is a nice hotel. The Nazis stayed here.

A good rule of thumb when traveling in Europe—stay in places with a Nazi past. The place in Rome had been Gestapo headquarters during the war. Big rooms. High ceilings. A beautiful garden. In Berlin, the hotel had been leveled when the Russians clobbered the Nazis who were hiding in it. To rub in their victory, the Commies never bothered to rebuild it or much of anything else in that part of East Berlin. When the wall came down, the hotel went back up and now the joint has a special room just for smoking cigars. In London, the old lady of a grand hotel had been bombed by the Luftwaffe sometime between the Nazi glories of Rome and the ass kicking they took from the Reds a few years later. The Queen has had dinner there twice since 1973.

Finally, this Parisian hotel had been the headquarters of the German Occupation Staff. They say Hitler had a cup of coffee on one of the balconies before he drove around to take in the sights of his conquered City of Light.

All this has been free of cost for me, including the hotels in L.A. and Chicago and New York, on the studio's dime, because I play Caleb Jackson in *Cassandra Rampart 3: Destiny at Hand.* (Cassandra Rampart a.k.a. Willa Sax a.k.a. Eleanor Flintstone!)

Day 3 of my junket—sorry, my Press Tour—would have been another wild ride of a day. Instead, I have to pack my bags and check out by 1:00 p.m.—I'm sorry, by 13:00 ...

TO: RORY THORPE
CC: IRENE BURTON, etc.
FROM: ANNETTE LABOUD
RE: PARIS PRESS SCHEDULE

Welcome to Paris!

We know you must be exhausted, but want you to know how thrilled we all are to be working on the French release of CASSANDRA RAMPART 3: DESTINY AT HAND! Our colleagues in Rome, Berlin, and London tell us the movie has been welcomed with wild enthusiasm . . . thanks to you! Our tracking numbers are strong, just 3 points off CASSANDRA RAMPART 2: AGENT OF CHANGE and only 10 points off CASSANDRA RAMPART: THE BEGINNING. For a sequel, these are fantastic numbers! It seems audiences are responding to the sexual tension between Cassandra and Caleb.

We all feel France is a good territory for the film, as the Cassandra Rampart universe has a megafollowing on all social media platforms.

As Irene Burton and the Marketing Dept. may have already explained to you, France does not allow the promotion of films via paid spots on television—which is why you may notice a few more on-camera interviews during your stay with us. These interviews are crucial in the French market. You have done so well on the U.S. tour and in Rome/Berlin/London there is no question you are warmed up!

So have fun!

Below is the schedule for the next three days. (Separate schedule for Eleanor Flintstone.)

DAY 1

*1:10 (approx)—Arrive Charles de Gaulle Airport from London—
Transport to Hotel.*

7:10—Grooming in Room 4114.

*7:40–8:00—Live appearance on "¡Nosotros Cacauates!" This is the
most popular Young Adult morning show in Spain with a strong
On-Line presence (4.1 million views). They have come to Paris
especially for CR3:DAH.*

8:05—Transfer to Media Center on 3rd Floor.

*8:15–8:45—Print Media Round Table #1 (approx 16 outlets. List
available)*

*8:50–9:20—Print Media Round Table #2 (approx 16 outlets. List
available)*

*9:25–9:55—Print Media Round Table #3 (approx 16 outlets. List
available)*

*10:00–10:30—Print Media Round Table #4 (approx 16 outlets. List
available)*

*10:35–11:05—Print Media Round Table #5 (approx 16 outlets. List
available)*

*11:10–11:40—Print Media Round Table #6 (approx 16 outlets. List
available)*

11:45–11:50—Reddit A.M. Session (for U.S.)

BREAK

*12:00–13:00—Social Influencers Mini-Interviews (3 to 5 minutes
each). The Social Influencers have at least 1.5 million followers.
Each will have a specific request for their postings. Some will be
very quick; others will be limited to 5 minutes.*

13:05–14:00—Photo Shoot on Hotel Roof (Note: Eleanor Flintstone will join you for last 10 minutes.)

14:05–14:45—Lunch/Interview with PARIS MATCH. (Note: A photographer will be present.)

14:50–15:00—Radio interview with TSR-1

15:05–15:15—Radio interview with RTF-3

15:20–15:30—Radio interview with FRT-2

15:40–16:00—Informal Coffee with approved Social Media Outlets (approx 20) with minimum of 3.5 million followers. (List on request)

16:05–16:10—Touch-Ups

16:15–16:45—Live TV remote from Balcony for Belgian TV "PM TODAY." (Note: Eleanor Flintstone will be joining you at 16:30.)

17:00—Proceed by car to Studio du Roi for Air France promotional shoot. This will play on all Air France International flights to support CR3:DAH opening. Shoot will take approx 3 hours.

20:00 (approx)—Proceed by car to Restaurant Le Chat. Dinner hosted by UPIC. (Note: A photographer will be present.) After dinner you are free to stay or return to hotel.

Rory Thorpe thanked his lucky stars for Irene Burton; those stars had been mighty benevolent over the last two years. He'd been in a movie with none other than Willa Sax—Cassandra Rampart herself! He had money in the bank for the first time in his life! And he was getting a free trip to Europe out of the deal! All he had to do was give some interviews over there! His enthusiasm had Irene Burton mutely laughing her ass off.

Irene was sixty-six years old, had worked in marketing for every one of the six major film studios, and now lived in semiretirement in a beach house in Oxnard—far enough away from Hollywood to avoid the daily stresses of showbiz yet close enough to pop in when she was needed to clean up the occasional PR flameout. Eleven years ago, she escorted a young, talented, and beautiful actress through the press tour for a horrible movie called *Dementia 40*, which did lousy business but is now legendary for introducing audiences to the young, talented, and beautiful Willa Sax. The press called her Willa Sex for a few years—a fitting moniker—but now Willa was Cassandra Rampart, a one-woman industry who had her own line of exercise clothes, a home for orphaned pets, and a foundation that promoted literacy in third world nations. The first two Cassandra Rampart movies had grossed $1.75 billion worldwide. Willa Sax didn't just command $21 million a movie plus profits, she commanded respect.

"Irene," Willa told her on the phone. "You gotta help me."

"S'up, punkin'?" Irene called all her young actors punkin'.

"Rory Thorpe is as dumb as a box of hair."

"Who is Rory Thorpe?"

"The guy in my latest thing. I just saw his EPK." The electronic press kit is a house-controlled interview given to the press as background for a movie. "Most of his answers start with 'Well, um. It's like, you know . . .' We have the junket coming up and I can't go around the world with Doofus McGillicuddy as my costar. He needs to be told what the fuck not to do."

"I can do that."

So Irene did. She took Rory shopping at Fred Segal and Tom Ford for the clothes he'd need—casual-look outfits for interviews and black-tie tuxes for premiere galas. No charge. She took him luggage shopping at T. Anthony for the right trunks and suitcases—at a steep discount the studio covered—so those outfits would be ready to don at a moment's notice. He'd be photographed in two-shots with one of the most beautiful women in the world and needed to look like he rated the position. He'd be answering the same questions a thousand times over, so she drilled into him the talking point memos the studio had provided: *CR3—DAH brings the C. Rampart universe its most compelling & sophisticated film, for she is not just a heroine for our times but a **woman for the ages**. Please use "**woman for the ages**" whenever describing Cassandra.*

Irene had perfected her ability to keep her laughter to herself when one of her clients said something really stupid or naïve—in Rory's case, his thinking his first ever trip to Europe was going to be free.

"Oh, punkin'," she told him. "You'll be working your ass off."

The junket began in Los Angeles: three days jammed with interviews, photo shoots, video conferences, Q and A sessions, forums with fan bases, and as many talk show appearances as possible, each needing an hour of preinterviews with the segment producers. Irene saw to it that Rory was well dressed, well groomed, and well versed in what the fuck not to do. And there was the trip to the Comic-Con convention in San Diego. Willa Sax needed a team of bodyguards to keep the fans at bay; many of them were costumed as Cassandra, the former Secret Service agent with computer chips implanted in her brain, formula-enhanced, superstrong sinews, able to communicate subconsciously with the Seven, the extraterrestrials who live among us, aliens who may be good guys, may be bad guys, and who et cetera et cetera et cetera you get the idea. Many Comic-Coners were costumed as the Seven. No one was dressed as Caleb Jackson, pro surfer/software whiz, because no one had seen the movie yet. The fans seemed thrilled at the screening of a twenty-minute teaser of the movie, making it a trending topic for most of the day on both Twitter and Poppit!

Two days later in Chicago, the teaser was screened on the campus of Northwestern University, the alma mater of Willa Sax herself. Her old dorm was renamed in her honor. Irene steered Rory through two days of interviews, a parade, a charity volleyball match, the dropping of the puck at a Blackhawks hockey game, and a screening of the movie to benefit literacy in Africa that was held at the same theater where the gangster John Dillinger had been gunned down.

Four days of junket were held in New York City, starting with a press conference staged in the ballroom of the Waldorf Astoria, attended by 152 media outlets. Rory did not get a question until Willa had talked for thirty minutes, mostly of the challenges of shooting with the new FLIT-cam digital process and the new SPFX system called DIGI-MAX. She was a producer on the film, after all, having optioned the rights to the Cassandra Rampart graphic novel in 2007 for a mere ten thousand dollars.

She laughed off questions about her husband's investment genius and his supposed bedroom prowess. "Guys!" Willa protested. "Bobby is a banker!" Bobby was her husband, and he was worth $1.2 billion. Willa told the press that he really was a regular dude who had to be told to take out the trash.

That led to Rory being asked, "How does it feel for a guy like you to kiss the most beautiful woman in the world?"

"It's a kiss for the ages," he said. Irene smiled, knowing she'd done her work well. The crammed room remained silent, save the clicking of camera shutters. When the press conference ended, Willa was whisked away as more questions were shouted at her. Irene escorted Rory into a smaller ballroom set up with multiple round tables, each crowded with journalists and their microphones. Rory spent twenty minutes at each table, one after another, with no break, answering versions of the same three questions.

What is it like working with Willa Sax?
What is it like kissing Willa Sax?
Is that really your ass in the hurricane scene?

Irene took him to the Media Center on the eighth floor, to sit through a total of fifty-seven television interviews, lasting no more than six minutes each, all held in the same room, Rory seated in the same chair with a one-sheet of the movie behind him. In the poster, Willa was staring off into space, a look of ferocious concentration on her beautiful face, her torso clad in a tight sweater, a rip exposing her shoulder and the top sphere of her left breast. Behind her was a mosaic of images from the movie—an explosion, dark figures running in a tunnel, a massive, cresting wave, and Rory wearing a headset and looking at a computer, serious as all hell. WILLA SAX IS BACK AS CASSANDRA RAMPART was printed in big letters. Rory's name was in the cluttered billing block at the bottom of the poster, in typeface the same size as that of the film's editor. Irene kept him plied with green tea, protein bars, and small bowls of blueberries.

The movie was promoted on *CBS This Morning* the entire week. Every morning at 7:40 and 8:10, Rory reported the national weather in front of a green-screen map. Willa Sax was a guest host with Kelly Ripa on *Live with Kelly*. The two women did Pilates on the air.

The premiere of the film was supposed to take place on one of the piers on the Hudson—special facilities had been constructed with seating for five thousand people, but a predicted thunderstorm put the kibosh on that. Instead, cinema screens all over the city were booked for simultaneous digital projections of the movie. Rory and Irene were delivered to every one of them by SUV—a total of twenty-nine personal appearances. Willa Sax attended only the special screening held at the Museum of Natural History to raise money for its Programs for Young Scientists.

At the end of the nine days of the domestic press junket, Rory was exhausted, talked out, dizzy; he had seen little more than cars and rooms and cameras. Worst of all, the questions had been the same for four-hundred-plus interviews.

What is it like working with Willa Sax?

What is it like kissing Willa Sax?

Is that really your butt in the hurricane scene?

Rory now felt that working with Willa Sax was like eating a peanut butter sandwich on a motorcycle, kissing Willa Sax was like Christmas in July, and the butt in the hurricane was that of a talking horse named Britches.

"Welcome to the big leagues, punkin'," Irene told him. "Tomorrow, Rome."

Willa Sax flew to Italy on a chartered plane, along with her team, her posse, and her handlers. The studio plane took the other five producers, all the executives, and the marketing heads. With no seats available for either Rory or Irene, they flew business class on TraxJet Airways, changing planes in Frankfurt.

Three days of press were held in Rome, each as busy as those in the U.S. On the last night the teaser was shown outside at the Circo Máximo—where the chariot races were held in ancient times. To Rory it looked like just a big field. Scenes from the movie were projected onto a huge temporary screen, but not until after a local soccer team was presented with the trophy they had won in some championship. The crowd was estimated at 21,000. When Rory appeared onstage to wave to the Romans, nothing happened. When Willa appeared to do the same, fistfights broke out as a tide of fans in soccer jerseys rushed the barricades to get to her. The Italian carabinieri got into a melee with the thugs as Willa was hustled into an armored car and whisked away to the airport. The next morning, Rory and Irene took a commercial flight—Air Flugplatz—to Berlin, where another three days of press were on tap.

In Berlin, Rory's body clock was so jet-lagged that he found himself flush with energy at 3:00 a.m., so he went out for a run. Leaving the hotel, he was ignored by the dozens of fervent German Cassandra Rampart fans who'd lingered all night and would continue to do so all morning, hoping for a glimpse of her. He jogged along the dark paths of the Tiergarten, stopping to do push-ups on the steps of a monument to the Russian Army, complete with actual tanks, that crushed Berlin in 1945. At noon the next day he was so tired he felt like a sleepwalker. He talked like one, too, telling the entire staff of *Bild*, the national newspaper, that as both a fan of the movies and the latest costar of Willa Sex (he actually said "Sex" instead of "Sax"), he felt that "Sandra Caspart was the most complimental and sophisticationed of any and all films, for Willa Sex is heroin for our times, and a *woman of the four ages.*" Then came the questions.

What is it like working with Willa Sex?
What is it like kissing Willa Sex?
Is that really your butt in the hurricane scene?

"Try not to call her Willa Sex," Irene told him in the car back to the hotel.

"When did I do that?" Rory asked.

"Just now. To Germany's largest daily newspaper."

"Sorry," he said. "I'm no longer sure what the words are that come out of my mouth."

The German screening of the teaser took place later that night, projected onto the Brandenburg Gate to six thousand fans. When she appeared at the balcony of the hotel to wave to them, Willa Sax was disappointed there were no fistfights.

"I guess I'm no Willa *Sex* tonight," she said at the gala dinner afterward, held in the same museum that displays Nefertiti's bust.

By the time Rory and Irene had flown to London (CompuAir into Gatwick), the international press junket had turned Rory into blabbering toast.

DAY 2

7:30—Grooming in room

8:00—Transfer by Car to Gare de l'Est

8:10–9:00—Red Carpet Interviews prior to Boarding CASSANDRA EXPRESS

9:05–13:00—Train ride to Aix-en-Provence. En route 15-minute interviews in special Media Car. (Outlet list available on request)

13:00–14:00—Red Carpet interviews upon arrival at Ancient Roman Theater

14:30–16:00—Ancient Roman Theater. Re-creation of Hurricane Scene for Press. (Note: This is broadcast live on RAI-Due TV.)

16:30—Reboard CASSANDRA EXPRESS. Live appearance on "Midi & Madi" TV broadcast from Observation Car.

17:15–21:45—Return to Paris via CASSANDRA EXPRESS. En route

15-minute interviews for non-French media in special Media Car.
(Outlet list available on request)
22:00 Transfer by car to Cocktail Reception/Dinner at Hotel
Meurice, hosted by Facebook France.
After dinner you are free to stay or return to hotel.
Irene will be provided the ADVANCE SCHEDULE FOR ASIA before
arrival in Singapore/Tokyo.

Getting the job was a fluke, a scratch-off lottery win. Rory had given up on Los Angeles after a six-month stint as a model-actor-bartender with all of two credits on his SAG-AFTRA card. He'd booked a yogurt commercial, playing touch football on a beach. For three cloudy days in San Diego he ran around shirtless—Rory looked damn fine without a shirt—with a group of racially mixed "pals," then they all snacked on yogurt. They were coached on how to dip the spoons into the minipacks and place the yogurt in their mouths. There was a trick to it.

Nine weeks later he was cast in a one-episode role on the rebranded *Kojak* series for CBS. Rory played a tattooed-shaved-head meth dealer who was *pretending* to be a handicapped Iraq War veteran, so *obviously* he had to die. Rory met his end in high style—shirtless (of course), dragged off the roof of an office building by his fraudulently gained motorized wheelchair, New Kojak jumping to safety just in time.

With little else going on but car payments and gym work-outs, Rory grew bored with Southern California, and took his yogurt-*Kojak* money to Utah for the ski season. When New *Kojak* finally aired, one of the several other producers on Cassandra happened to be watching and texted Willa Sax: *Think I saw CR's next bit o' honey.* A few days later, Rory got a call from his agency to get back to town because something *huge* was on deck, in the brew, cooking in the hopper.

The first time Rory met Willa Sax—who was crazy beautiful, beyond-real-life beautiful—was over cups of green tea in her offices in the Capitol Records Building on Vine Street in Hollywood. The home she shared with her venture capitalist husband was somewhere in the hills nearby. She could not have been a nicer person, chatting with Rory about art and raising horses. Rory knew very little about either. Willa changed the subject to Fiji. She had been to the islands to do research for the movie. She told Rory about the beauty of the night sky and the clarity of the water and the happy faces of the locals, especially during the traditional kava ceremonies that were held to welcome visitors. She had learned to surf there. The movie would shoot in Fiji for at least two weeks.

The meeting lasted a little over an hour, but before Rory was in his car and at a standstill in the afternoon traffic of the Hollywood freeway, his phone exploded with texts: *WSaX Loved you!$$$$.* Two weeks later he was officially cast as Caleb with a crazy payday of nearly half a million dollars, to be spread over three films, which could or could not be part of the Cassandra Rampart universe. The next time he saw Willa was at the studio for camera tests. A production assistant took Rory to her trailer. When he climbed up the steps wearing his torso-clinging Caleb Jackson surfing outfit, she sized up her no-name yet gorgeous costar and said, "Well, ain't you hot shit!"

The start date of the movie was delayed for a few months as the script was rewritten, then pushed to after the new year so Willa could enjoy the holidays with her husband; they spent Christmas in a castle in Scotland. Rory's first day playing Caleb Jackson was in late March on a soundstage in Budapest. Willa had been shooting for three weeks and had her own makeup trailer, so the two did not see each other until they were on the set. The scene called for them to make out in a shower, but the water was not hot enough to hiss out any real steam, so the Hungarian SPFX crew rigged the stall with a smoke machine. When Willa came to the stage in her bathrobe, her three security guards circled her chair. She asked Rory if the hotel was working out for him, then told him that now that she was married she never kissed on screen with an open mouth.

Over seven months, Rory shot only a few days a week—in Budapest, Mallorca, back in Budapest, in a stretch of desert in Morocco, then in Rio de Janeiro for a scene that called for Willa and Rory to run through the crowded streets of Carnival, a scene that took four days to prep and sixteen minutes to shoot. Rory himself shot a week in Shreveport, Louisiana, while Willa took time off with her husband in the Seychelles. They met up again for a day of additional running-through-Carnival scenes, but this time in New Orleans. Because some of the film financing came out of Germany, tax laws forced them to shoot one scene in Düsseldorf. They ran out of a building and jumped into a taxi—the extent of the Düsseldorf filming. After ten days of reshoots in Budapest, they had only the surfing scenes yet to do. They never did go to

Fiji. Instead, Rory and Willa grabbed shots against a green screen at the exterior water tank in Malta, pretending to surf on SPFX gimbals as stagehands doused them with very cold water from dump tanks.

DAY 3

7:30—Grooming in room

8:00–9:00—Hotel Restaurant. Breakfast with contest winners.
(Note: Eleanor Flintstone will join for coffee at 8:50.)

9:05–12:55—Principal TV interviews (12 minutes each)

13:00–13:20—Lunch in room. Room service menu to be provided.

13:20—Touch-Ups

13:25–16:25—Principal TV Interviews continue

BREAK

16:30–16:55—TV Interview "Le Showcase" (hosted by Rene Ladoux,
a French icon of film criticism)

17:00–17:30—TV Interview with Petit Shoopi (Petit Shoopi is a
puppet who will ask you to sing along with her. Song TBD.)

17:35–18:25—Join Eleanor Flintstone in Ballroom for TV Interview
with Claire Brule for FTV 1 (this is France's most widely watched
Women's Show)

18:30–19:00—Photo Shoot with Eleanor Flintstone for Le Figaro

19:05–19:55—Photo Shoot for Orphaned Pets Organization. (Note:
There will be cats, dogs, birds, and reptiles.)

20:00—Transfer to Motorcade

20:30—Arrival at Jardins des Tuileries

20:30–21:00—Work Red Carpet Press Line, Interviews, Photo Call

21:05–22:00—Concert by popular French rapper (TBD)

22:05–22:30—Live Remarks to crowd (Note: you will introduce
  Eleanor Flintstone. See Irene for suggested remarks.)

22:35–22:45—Fireworks

22:50–23:00—French Paratroopers re-create Cassandra-Caleb
  drop into volcano caldera

23:05—French Air Force Flyby

23:10–23:30—Unveiling of CR3: DAH Holographic Billboard (Note:
  Crowd will be provided with holographic glasses upon arrival.)

23:35–24:15—Performance by popular French Pop Star (TBD).
  Eleanor Flintstone to proceed to Airport. Stage is cleared.

24:20 (Approx)—Screening begins.

  You are free to stay for screening or return to hotel.

NOTE: TOMORROW WILL BE TRAVEL DAY TO SINGAPORE

French telephones do not ring. They go *bleat-bleat, bleat-bleat, bleat-bleat.* At 6:22 a.m., the sound is like having a barn animal in your hotel room. Rory had to stop that sound.

"Yeah?" The receiver felt like a toy up to his ear.

"Change of plans, punkin'." Irene was on the phone. "You get to stay in bed."

"Say what?" Rory was still a bit woozy, having taken advantage of the Hotel Meurice's bar until just four hours ago.

"The schedule for today is in flux," Irene said. "Go back to sleep."

"Watch this." Rory put the phone back in its cradle, rolled over, and was out like a glass-jawed boxer.

He woke up three hours later and stumbled into the sitting area of his hotel suite—good enough for Nazi officers in the day and just fine and dandy for Mrs. Thorpe's only boy. The schedule for his Day 3 in Paris was on the desk beside the room service menu and a media packet on CASSANDRA RAMPART 3: DESTINY AT HAND. At 9:46, Rory was supposed to be giving TV interviews of twelve minutes each, but neither Irene nor anyone else had come to fetch him. Tomorrow he'd be flying business class on IndoAirWays to Singapore, so he ordered up a few café au laits and a bakery basket from room service.

He had spent very little time in any of the hotel rooms save for exhausted sleep and grooming, always by two women, one for makeup and one for hair, both ushered into the suite by Irene while Rory showered. Alone, in his underwear and sipping coffee and hot milk, Rory checked out the place.

The hotel had been recently renovated in Hipster-Millennial, which would have been a blow to those Nazi occupiers of long ago. A black screen was the TV. The remote for it was long, thin, heavy, and incomprehensible to any American. The lamps were all touch-controlled, but only if you knew where to touch them. Four bottles of Orangina drink were arranged neatly on the square coffee table, ironically next to four porcelain replicas of oranges. The sound system was a retro turntable with a collection of LPs by the Elvis of France, Johnny Hallyday, one record going all the way back to the 1950s. There were no books on the shelves, but there were three old typewriters—one keyboard was Russian, one French, and one English.

Bleat-bleat. Bleat-bleat. Bleat-bleat.

"I'm awake!"

"You sitting down, punkin'?"

"Gimme a second." Rory poured himself the last of the hot milk and a final cup of coffee, balancing his cup and saucer as he rolled back on a leather recliner. "I am actually reclining now."

"The press tour is canceled." Irene was old school. *Press junkets* were what corporations organized to sell product. *Press tours* were what movie stars did to promote their films.

Rory spit café au lait all over his bare legs and the leather recliner. "Huh? Wha'?" he said.

"Go online and you'll see why."

"I never got the wi-fi password."

"Willa is divorcing that venture capital vulture of hers."

"Why?"

"He's going to jail."

"He do something crooked and piss off the feds?"

"Not the feds. Hookers. In his car on Santa Monica Boulevard. Seems he was in possession of something other than his medical marijuana, too."

"Wow. Poor Willa."

"Willa will be fine. Weep for the studio. *Cassandra Rampart 3: Destiny at Hand Job* will take a hit at the box office."

"Should I call Willa and tell her how sorry I am?"

"You can try, but she and her team are on a plane somewhere over Greenland. She'll hide out at her horse ranch in Kansas for a few weeks."

"She has a ranch in Kansas?"

"She grew up in Salina."

"What about the big events on the docket for today? Fireworks and the French Air Force and all those orphaned pets?"

"Canceled."

"When do we go on to Singapore and Seoul and Tokyo and Beijing?"

"We don't," Irene said, without an ounce of regret in her voice. "The outlets want only one thing, Willa Sax. No offense, but you're just the guy in her movie. Rory No One. Remember that poster I had in my office that said 'What if they gave a press conference and nobody came?' Oh, wait. You've never been to my office."

"What happens now?"

"I leave on the studio plane in an hour. Not looking forward to that twelve-hour bitchathon. The movie opens domestically in four days, and the first paragraph of every review will be about hookers, OxyContin, and the man who paid for sex while wed to Willa Sax. Sounds like the plot of *Cassandra Rampart 4: The Parole Hearing.*"

"How do I get home?"

"That'll be handled by Annette in the local office."

"Who is Annette?" Rory had met so many people throughout the junket the names and faces might as well have been of Martians.

Irene called him punkin' a few more times, told him he was just aces all around, a real mensch, and that she thought he was going to have a fantastic career should *CR3: DAH* make its money back. And, she liked the movie, actually. Thought it was cute.

I don't speak Russian. The French language has too many letters and punctuation marks to make sense to me. Good thing this other type-writer is in English.

I think Willa Sax—a.k.a. Eleanor Flintstone—is a great gal who doesn't deserve this. She deserves a better guy than one who likes streetwalkers and hillbilly heroin. (A guy like me! Not once in one thousand interviews did I ever confess my deep and constant crush on that lady. Irene told me not to be that honest with the press. "Tell just enough of the truth, but never lie.")

I have a pocket full of money. Per diem. In every city Irene handed me an envelope of cash! Not that I had a chance to spend any of it. Not in Rome. Nor Berlin. In London I had no free time. Maybe I should see what pleasures a few euros will buy me here in Paris...

LATER!

I went outside of a hotel on my own for the first time since Berlin.

Hey, Paris ain't bad! I was expecting the usual hordes outside the hotel, the fans hoping for a glimpse of Willa. Hundreds of them, mostly men, duh, have been waiting outside, photographers, auto-graph hounds, et cetera. Willa called them the Paper Boys. They are gone now, the word probably having gone out that Willa Sax has left the City of Light.

Annette LeBoogieDoogie says just because the junket is can-celed I don't have to fly home immediately. I am free to linger in Paris, in all of Europe if I want, but on my own money.

I just did some wandering around, in fact. I crossed the river via a famous bridge, then walked right by Notre Dame. I dodged the scooters and the bikes and the tourists. I saw the glass pyramid of the Louvre Museum, but did not go in. No one recognized me. Not that they should. Not that they would. Rory No One, that's me.

I walked into the gardens—the place where we were going to have a huge event with rock bands and jets flying by and fireworks and thousands of people wearing free 3-D glasses. Instead, crews were breaking down the stage and the screen. The barricades were still up but were made moot. There was no one to keep back.

Beyond the gardens was a big traffic circle called Place de la Concorde—millions of cars and Vespa scooters, lanes and lanes of them going both ways and around and around a monument needle in the center. A huge Ferris wheel has been there since 1999. Bigger than the one in Budapest—when was that? When did I make the movie there? In junior high? The one in Paris is not nearly the size of that one in London, the one that goes around only once, very slowly. When did we have that huge press conference in front of that thing, the event that had the children's choir and the Scottish Mounted Light Cavalry and one of the lesser members of the royal family? When was that? Oh, right. Last Tuesday.

I bought a ticket but did not have to wait long for the Ferris wheel to let me on. Hardly anyone was in the line so I had the car all to myself.

I went around a bunch of times. Up high I saw the city stretch to the horizon, the river wind its way to the south and to the north, with many fancy, long boats sliding beneath all the famous bridges. I saw what is called the Left Bank. And the Eiffel Tower. And the churches up on the hills. And all the museums along the broad avenues. And all the rest of Paris.

Before me was the whole of the City of Light and I saw it for free.

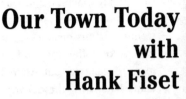

Our Town Today
with
Hank Fiset

AN ELEPHANT IN THE PRESSROOM

SO MANY RUMORS here at da Paper! The Bull Elephant in the room says the *Tri-Cities Daily News/Herald* is giving up the economic ghost of a printed version of our Great Triple-Metropolitan Newspaper. If/when such a business move is made, the *only* way you'll be reading my column and everything else you now hold in your hands is on one of your many digital devices—your phone, maybe, or a watch that needs recharging every night.

* * *

SUCH IS PROGRESS, but it makes me think of Al Sim-monds, a rewrite man at the old Associated Press. My career at the AP lasted close to four years, but I would have been quickly pink-slipped were it not for Al Simmonds, who took the choppy prose and schoolkid syntax from my reporter's notebook and turned those scribbles into bona fide news copy. Al is long gone, bless his heart, so he never saw the advent of reading a newspaper on a laptop or pad. He passed away before the idea was any more real than the Starship *Enterprise*. Not sure the man even had a TV, as he complained that nothing good was on the radio since Fred Allen went off the air (this story is now carbon-dating me!) . . .

* * *

AL'S TYPEWRITER WAS a Continental—a beast nearly the size of an easy chair—bolted to his desk, not because anyone would try to steal the thing. You'd have been foolish to have tried to *lift* it. Al's desk was a small, narrow altar of editing. He would bang out his version of my copy—leaner, crisper, better, dang it—then flip up the typewriter on hinges, and on the cleared space go at his own stuff with a blue pencil. The man made quite a racket doing his job a few hundred times a shift—the *chonk-chonkka* of his typing with the *ba-ding* of the bell, the *krannk* of the carriage return, the *shripp* of the copy ripped from the machine, then the *ka-bump* of his tossing back of the massive tool of his trade to scribble away with an even more primitive mode of writing. Al was at one with

that typing machine and was never more than a yard away from it and his desk. He sent me out for coffee and food on many occasions, but when I came back with the delivery he'd be hacking away at some copy and I'd have to set the food on a nearby stool until he flipped up the Continental and made room for his lunch. If Al Simmonds sounds like a stereotype, a cartoon version of a newsroom denizen, he was in every way but one: he didn't smoke and hated all the dopes at the AP who did.

* * *

QUIET! REPORTERS WORKING would be a superfluous sign here at the *Daily News/Herald* these days. We've been on computers since the eighties, though the first generations of them were called word processors—that was what we called *ourselves*. The point being, Al Simmonds would not be able to fathom how we have been reading our newspapers in ever greater numbers over the past five years—bent over our hand-held miracle machines. Too, he'd not recognize how we've put out the newspaper for the last three decades. "Where's the roar and fury of a newspaper going to press?" he'd holler. At me.

* * *

IN AL'S HONOR here's an experiment: if you are reading this on your phone, I'll write some of it on mine. My edited, proofread, stream of consciousness . . .

* * *

"I'M GOING TO miss reading a physical copy of the paper, on newsprint, delivered to my front lawn seven days a week by a fellow named Brad who scoots by in a car, chucking my copy out the window with but the smallest of deceleration, or from the copy I read at the Pearl Avenue Café (on Pearl Avenue) a few days a week. I'll miss the sensation of a story placed above the fold

on page one, and the shame of a story being relegated to page B6. I admit I get a kick out of seeing my face and my byline—my column—on the back page—so easy to find, and did you know a reading of the column and the timing of a soft-boiled egg are a perfect match? If/when the *Tri-Cities Daily News/Herald* goes all-digital/no print, this reporter will be sad/resigned at the advent of this thing we call Reality. And Al Simmonds, in Rewrite Heaven, will scratch his head in confusion, his typewriter flipped up forever." . . . Now, an auto-corrected version, pinched out on my phone . . .

* * *

I'M GOING TO miss reading a physical copy of the paper, on newsprint, delivered to my front lawn seven days a week be a fellow named bark who scours be uv a cat, chi hubs my cope it the window Eugene the shanked the dr fjsrstik, or FYI. The color I eat at the peak avebure cadge on Zoesrka-vfnud a few days a week. I'll miss the sensation of a dying place Abu d to gold page one and the shame oif a duties relegate to osfs h6. I admit I gat a kick out is seeinmy fx e and my belie—my Viking—on gage back page—so esu to find, and did you know a reading of the volume and the timing of a foot hooked egg is a perfect match? If/when the tri-

cities Zfaiky need/heard hies all-digital thus rouoter will be sad/resigned at the advent of hugs gjjng called result And All Simmonds in Rewrire Heaben, will scratch his head in confusion, hostyoeetotoer flipped up forever . . .

* * *

GOTTA RUN NOW and get my copy down to the pressroom . . .

Welcome to Mars

Kirk Ullen was still asleep, in bed, under a quilt and an old Army blanket. As it had been since 2003, when he was five years old, his bedroom was also the back room of the family home, one he shared with the Maytag washer and dryer, an old, chipped, out-of-tune spinet piano, the idle sewing machine his mother had not used since the second Bush administration, and an Olivetti-Underwood electric typewriter that had been rendered inoperable when Kirk spilled a root-beer float into its innards. The room had no heat and was always chilly, even on this early morning in late June. His eyes were rolled up into the back of his head as he dreamed he was still in high school, unable to dial the correct combination for his gym locker. He was on his seventh attempt, turning right, then twice around to the left, then once back to the right, when a flash of lightning made the locker room blindingly white. Then, equally suddenly, came a darkness that encompassed his whole world.

There were more flashes, like sheet lightning, then blackness again—everything white again, then an impenetrable black, over and over. But there was no rumbling thunder, no claps of Thor echoing off the distant canyons.

"Kirk? Kirkwood?" It was his father. Frank Ullen had been snapping the overhead light on and off—his idea of an amusing wake-up signal. "Were you serious last night, kid?" Frank began singing. *"Kirkwood, Kirkwood. Give me your answer, do."*

"Wha'?" Kirk croaked.

"About going to Mars? Say no and I'm gone. Say yes and we start your birthday like true Ullen men, brave and free."

Mars? Kirk's brain flickered into consciousness and he remembered now. Today was his nineteenth birthday. Last night after dinner he had asked his father if they could surf in the morning like they had the day he turned ten and, again, the morning he turned thirteen. "You bet!" his father said. Conditions at Mars Beach would be good. There was a swell coming from the southwest.

Frank Ullen had been surprised at the request. His son had not joined him in the water for some time. Mr. College-Kirk was not as willing to brave the elements as he'd been in high school. Frank tried to remember the last time he and his son had surfed together. Two years? Three?

Kirk had to ponder his schedule for the upcoming day, which was hard to do right out of his dreamland fog. Birthday or not, he had to be at his regular summer job, manager of the Magic-Putt PeeWee Golf Course, at 10:00 a.m. What time was it now? 6:15? Okay, this could work. His dad, he knew, had only one job site going, the new minimall on Bluff Boulevard. Yeah, this was doable. The two of them could pound the waves for a good two hours. Or until their shoulders dislocated.

It would be good for the two of them to be back in the water, once again the Submersible Ullen Boys, *Princes de la Mer*. Kirk's dad was a carefree man in the water, on his paddleboard in the morning. The hassles of the job and those flare-ups at home were left onshore—all those complicated family moments that came and went, as unpredictable as brushfires. Kirk loved his mom and his sisters as dearly as life itself; the fact that they were such squeaky wheels on such bumpy roads was something he had accepted long, long ago. His dad, the father of the pride, had to work two full-time jobs—provider and peacemaker—with never a day off. It was no wonder the man took to surfing as both his physical tonic and his mental astral-plane therapy. For Kirk to head out with his dad would be a bracing vote of confidence, a manly huddle, a backslapping "we are in this together, you and I" birthday embrace. Name a father and son who didn't need that.

"Okay," Kirk said, stretching with a yawn. "I'm comin'."

"No law against staying under the covers."

"Let's do it."

"You sure?"

"You trying to avoid getting wet yourself?"

"No way, knothead."

"Then I'll be your huckleberry."

"Excellent. Breakfast fit for a long-haul trucker. Twelve minutes." Frank disappeared, leaving the light on, making his son squint, protectively.

Breakfast was savory perfection, as always. Frank was a master in the morning kitchen; his forte was timing. The kielbasa got to the table hot off the stove top, skillet biscuits were soft and butterable, the coffeepot was eight cups deep (an old Mr. Coffee), and the eggs were never dry, so the yolks were fluid gold. Cooking a dinner was beyond his capabilities, something about having to wait around for a shank to roast or potatoes to boil. No way. Frank Ullen preferred the bang-bang immediacy of a breakfast—cook, serve, eat—and he had made the morning meals fun when the kids were young and the family lived on a schedule, the breakfast conversations as heated (sometimes too heated) and thick as the coffee-laced hot cocoa Frank gave them, starting in third grade. But these days Mom slept so late, she was never seen at breakfast; Kris had escaped to San Diego, where she lived with her boyfriend; and Dora had declared long ago that she would come and go as she pleased, on her own clock. So it was just the men at breakfast, dressed in baggy surf sweats, unshowered, since what was the point if they'd be in the water?

"I'm going to have to make some calls about eight thirty. Business shit," Frank said, flipping some biscuits onto a plate. "Won't take too long. I'll leave the water to you for an hour or so."

"If you gotta do it, you gotta do it," Kirk said. As always, he'd brought a book to the table and was already absorbed in it. His father reached over and slid it away from him.

"Architecture in the nineteen twenties?" Frank asked. "Why are you reading this?"

"For the racy parts," Kirk said, soaking up Polish sausage grease and egg yolk with a biscuit. "The Jazz Age was a building boom until the Depression. Postwar engineering and materials changed every skyline in the world. I find it fascinating."

"Those exterior-supporting structures made for wedding cake buildings. Everything got smaller the higher you went. You ever been to the upper floors of the Chrysler Building?"

"In New York City?"

"No, Dime Box, Texas."

"Dad, you raised me, remember? When did you ever take me to New York City to see the upper floors of the Chrysler Building?"

Frank took two travel mugs down from the shelf. "The top of the Chrysler Building is a *fekkin* rabbit warren."

The last of the coffee went into the mugs, which Frank placed on the dash of the truck while Kirk pulled his board—all six feet six of it—out of the storage shed. He tossed it into the camper, where Frank's eleven-and-a-half-foot paddleboard—the *Buick*—took up most of the room.

Six summers before, the camper was brand-new, purchased for a momentous vacation—a two-thousand-mile loop up the coast to Canada, across the two-lanes of British Columbia, Alberta, and Saskatchewan, all the way to Regina. The trek was a long-planned Ullen Family Retreat and came off as promised, for the first few hundred miles, anyway. Then Mom started sharing her opinions and insisting on behaviors. She wanted to establish her rules of the road and began giving orders. Thus rang the opening bell, beginning the first of what became many punishing rounds. The verbal jousts became serious disagreements, escalating into full-throated, mean-spirited arguments that *had* to be won by the mother of the family. Kris, as was her wont, turned her rebelliousness up a few notches. Dora's righteousness devolved into deep-crevassed silence, punctuated with outbursts so fast, loud, and vitriolic as to be near-Shakespearean. Frank, at the wheel, sipping on his cold coffee or warming Coca-Cola, acted as referee, therapist, fact-checker, and cop, depending on the point made or offense taken. Kirk, as his defensive stance, pulled out book after book, reading like he was a chain-smoker with a carton of menthols. For him, the psychodrama faded into a background din not much different from the wheels of the camper humming across thousands of miles of asphalt.

They argued their way across Canada, continued as they came south through the vast American Prairie, the space so open, so endless it was said to have driven some of the original settlers insane. The Ullen family went certifiably daffy in Nebraska when Kris bought pot from some guy living out of his car at a KOA campground. Mom wanted to call a cop and turn in both the dealer and her own daughter. She went DEF CON ballistic when Dad allowed no such thing by simply packing them all up and driving away, fleeing the scene of the crime. The camper went frosty, like a bitter family Christmas in July; no one talking to anyone while Kirk finished all of William Manchester's books on Winston Churchill. By the time they turned due west in Tucumcari, New Mexico, everyone wanted off the road, out of that truck, and away from each other. Kris threatened to hop a Greyhound bus the rest of the way home. But Dad insisted they do some camping in the desert, which they did under protest. Kris got high under the stars, Dora went on solo hikes until after dark, and Dad bedded down outside in the tent. Mom slept in the camper, guaranteeing she'd be alone, in peace *at last*, by locking the door. That was a problem, as it cut off access to the bathroom. Thus ended the last family vacation for the Ullens. The last family *anything* for the Ullens. The camper stayed bolted onto the King Cab pickup, serving as Frank's mobile office–surf buggy, one that had not been cleaned or vacuumed in 21,000 miles.

In his youth, Frank Ullen had been a real, shaggy-haired surf bum. Then he grew up, got married, had kids, and started an electrical wiring business that took off. It was only in the past year that he had once again begun to leave the house before anyone else was awake, to make the point break at Mars Beach, a tight right-hander best in a rising three-to-four-foot tide. When Kirk was a kid and a part-time beach rat, father and son would park on the highway shoulder and carry their boards down the well-beaten path to Mars. To young Kirk, hefting his original sponge board, the beach seemed as rocky and far away as the bottom of Valles Marineris on the Red Planet. The Economic Boom Years had drastically altered the place—there were inland luxury apartment complexes built on what had been marshes; and five years ago the state had paved over a square of weeds and dirt, creating a real parking lot for three dollars a car. Mars was no longer free, but it was conveniently accessible; surfers headed left at the sand, regular beachgoers veered to the right, and county lifeguards kept the two apart.

"You haven't seen this." Frank was exiting the highway at Deukmejian State Recreation Area. Kirk glanced up from his book. What had been a field was now flattened and surveyed; the little flagged posts were already planted, with a sign advertising the site of a future Big-Box Mart. "Remember when the nearest business was a taco stand back at Canyon Avenue? It's now a Chisholm Steakhouse."

"I remember taking a shit in the bushes," Kirk said.

"Don't swear around your old man."

Frank pulled into the lot, parking in an empty slot one row away from the path gate. "Well, whad'ya know," he said, as always. "Welcome to Mars!"

A collection of shops had evolved on the other side of the highway under low-slung roofs made to look like Mexican adobes. There was a surf gear shop, a recent and ubiquitous Starbucks, a Subway sandwich place, a Circle W convenience store, and the office of a lone insurance agent named Saltonstall, who had set out his shingle there so he could surf when the phone wasn't ringing. An AutoShoppe/FastLube & Tire franchise was under construction at the south end of the shopping center.

"A lube job while you surf," Kirk noted. "That's environmental consumer integration."

"Here's your handbasket. Enjoy hell," Frank said.

The parking lot showed a collection of aged and rugged vehicles—Rancheros and station wagons loaded with tools, owned by construction workers who were grabbing waves before work. There were old vans and self-painted VW Buses owned by surfers sleeping overnight, despite posted ordinances that exclaimed NO CAMPING. When the county sheriffs periodically rousted the surf bums there were always lengthy legal discussions about the difference between "camping overnight" and "waiting for daylight." Lawyers surfed Mars, too, as did orthodontists and airline pilots, their Audis and BMWs strapped with roof racks for the boards. Moms and wives would be in the water, good surfers and kind people. Fistfights had once been frequent, when the high surf attracted kooks from all over, but this was a weekday and not all the schools were out yet so Kirk knew the crowd would be easygoing and manageable. And the Martians, as they called themselves, had all gotten older, mellower. Except for a couple of asshole lawyers.

"Sweet break this morning, Kirky-bird," Frank said, eyeing the water from the parking lot. He counted over a dozen surfers already in the water as large waves—the Swell—were shaping in regular intervals outside the lineup. He unlocked the door to the camper. They pulled both boards out, and Frank's paddle, standing them up against the truck as they yanked on their summer wet suits with the short legs and built-in rash guards.

"Got any wax?" Kirk asked.

"In a drawer in there," Frank told him. His paddleboard had a mat, so he didn't need wax anymore but kept some for those who might need some stick for their *sticks*. Kirk found a cake in a drawer full of junk including short-end rolls of duct tape, old mousetraps, a hot-glue gun but no sticks of glue, boxes of staples, and a set of channel locks that was going to rust in the salt air.

"Hey," his father said. "Put my phone in the refrigerator, would you?" He handed over his mobile.

"Why the refrigerator?" Kirk asked. The thing had not worked in many years.

"If you broke into this camper and wanted to steal anything of value, would you look in the busted icebox?"

"You got me there, Pop." When Kirk opened the door, not only was there the dank smell of years of nonuse but there was also the sight of a small, gift-wrapped box.

"Happy birthday, son," Frank said. "How old are you again?"

"Nineteen, but you make me feel thirty." The gift was a waterproof sports watch, a newer model than the watch Frank was wearing, all black and metal, a heavy-duty military chronometer already set to the correct time. Strapping it around his wrist made Kirk feel like he was about to board a military helicopter to go kill bin Laden. "Thanks, Dad. This makes me look cooler than I am. Didn't think that was possible."

"Hoopy boofy, Junior."

As they carried their boards down the path to the beach, Frank said again, "I told you, I'm going to have to make a few calls around eight thirty. I'll holler at you when I get out of the water."

"I will salute my recognition."

Standing in the sands of Mars, they watched a set of waves

play out as they attached their board leashes to their ankles with Velcro straps. About a dozen large, well-shaped curlers came along before the surf lessened, allowing Kirk to run into the tide and hop on his board and paddle out, duckbutting through the smaller waves as they broke over him. He'd be lining up just beyond the break with the younger surfers, those who shredded the faces of as many waves as Poseidon sent their way.

As a paddleboarder, Frank sought the larger waves off of Mars, those well outside, beyond the lineup, where along with the other stand-up surfers he'd wait for the larger sets of heavy water, the waves generated by storms in the South Pacific that grew muscular with mileage. Before too long, he easily caught the shoulder of a wave, rising up six feet or so above its floor, riding gracefully in wide turns. As he was the surfer closest to the curl, the wave was rightfully his own, the other Martians peeling off to leave him to it. When the wave closed out, he hopped off his board and held his position in the shallows until the set died. Then he hopped back up, his feet shoulder width apart, dug his paddle into the ocean, and crested each ridge of incoming water until he was outside again.

The air and water were cold, but Kirk was glad he had gotten out of bed. He recognized old Martians like Bert the Elder, Manny Peck, Schultzie, and a lady he called Mrs. Potts—the veteran long boarders. And there were kids around his age, some of the pals he grew up alongside who were now, like him, in college or the workforce. Hal Stein was in graduate school at Cal, Benjamin Wu worked as an aide to a city councilman, "Stats" Magee was studying for his CPA license, and Buckwheat Bob Robertson was, like Kirk, still an undergrad, still living at home.

"Hey! Spock!" Hal Stein called out. "Thought you'd died!"

The five of them waited in a circle between rides, comparing the notes they'd kept since adolescence. Kirk was reminded of just how good Mars had been to him. Living within driving distance of its waves had allowed Kirk access to a world all his own. At Mars, he grew comfortable in the powerful waves of the place. Mars was where, alone, Kirk tested himself and excelled. Onshore, he was a statistic, a tick mark smack in the middle of a bell curve, neither a dropout nor a scholar, not an ace or a deuce. Other than a couple of English teachers, Mrs. Takimashi the school librarian, and the crazy, gorgeous, honey-haired Aurora Burke (before her new stepfather whisked her off to a new family in Kansas City), no one had ever singled Kirk Ullen out as being *special*. But in the water of Mars, Kirk was master of all he surveyed. He was glad he'd been coming to the place for years and could be there this day as he turned nineteen years old.

After so many rides he had lost count, Kirk was pooped, so he rested in the lineup. When the morning sun came out, he could see the tops of the vans and his dad's camper in the parking lot, the tile roofs of the shops across the highway, and the rocky, scrub-brush hills beyond. With the blue water against the brightening sky, Mars took on the look of a sepia-toned photograph of some legendary surf locale in Hawaii or Fiji, a color image long since faded to an amber tint, turning green mountains into yellow and brown hills.

If Kirk squinted, the Mexican-themed shops became *bures* on a slip of beach, native huts on an atoll in the middle of the Pacific Ocean. Again, Mars became a different world and Kirk was its king.

Sometime later he heard his father calling him from the beach. Frank had laid his board on the sand, planted his paddle like a flag, and was making the hand gesture universally translated as "I am going to make a phone call."

Kirk saluted his father just as Mrs. Potts screamed, "Outside!" Sure enough, a set was shaping up well offshore, the waves as visible as humps on a washboard, breaking at least fifty yards early, making for dozens of long, aggressive rides. Everyone paddled furiously. Kirk was tired, but he was not about to sit out a great set. He stroked hard and steadily until experience told him to wheel around and paddle toward the beach. He caught the third wave that came his way.

As he was rising up on the apex of water, instinct timed his springing to his feet for the drop into the wave's trough. This wave was gorgeous, well shaped and smooth faced. And huge. A monster. Kirk kicked out of the trough and climbed up the face, just in front of the curl of white water, a compressed whisper of wind at his back. He jerked left and shot down perpendicular to the arc, pulled right at the bottom, and again sluiced up the face. He topped the very crest, bounced along the rim, then dug once more into the slot, retarding his speed to allow the break to catch up to him. He knelt as low on his board as his physique allowed until water was bending over his head and he occupied the little green room of the curl. Rushing water was on his left, the smooth glass of the surface on his right. He dragged the fingers of his free hand in the wall of green like the fin of a dolphin, a knife in the water.

As ever, the curl closed on him, the water smacked him on the head, and he wiped out, no big deal. Churning in the white water, he relaxed, as he had learned long ago, letting the wave roll beyond him and allow him time to find the surface and fill his lungs. But the ocean is a fickle mistress, Mars indifferent to human effort. Kirk felt his leash go taut in the Velcro around his ankle. In the foam and chaos his board snapped back, nailing him hard in the meat of his calf. The hit had the same blunt force as the blow from the croquet mallet Kris had once taken to him in the backyard, which sent him to the doctor and her to her bedroom. Kirk knew he was done for the day.

He felt for the sandy bottom, knowing the next monster was about to crush him. He lunged up for a breath, sucking in air, seeing seven feet of white water roaring down on him. He ducked under the wave, blindly felt for the Velcro of his leash, and ripped it off his foot so his board would get tossed toward the beach and away from him.

He floated in, no panic despite the pain in his leg. When he made contact with the sand again, he was farther inland and could hop on one foot to get his head above water. The next incoming wave pushed him closer to shore, another did the same, then a few more. He crawled out of the water and onto the beach.

"Fucker," he said to himself. He sat on the sand, his leg so deeply gashed that white tissue showed along with torn flesh and pulsing blood. He was going to need stitches, sure as shooting. Kirk remembered a day when he was thirteen, when a kid named Blake got hit by his own board and had been pulled unconscious from the water. Blake had been nailed in the jaw and needed months of dental work. This wound was not as serious as that, and Kirk had suffered a few lumps in his time, but this chunk taken out of his leg was worthy of a Purple Heart.

"You okay?" Ben Wu had come out of the water after retrieving Kirk's loose board. "Oh, shit!" he yelled at the sight of the cut. "You need a ride to the hospital?"

"No. My dad is around. He'll take me."

"You sure?"

Kirk stood up. "Yes." There was pain, and blood was trailing down his lower leg, splattering drops of scarlet in the sand of Mars, but he waved Ben away and said, "I got it. Thanks."

He took his board and limped on up the path toward the parking lot.

"You're gonna need, like, forty sutures in that thing," Ben called out before leaping back into the surf atop his board.

Kirk's calf was throbbing in time to his heartbeat. He limped up the path, his leash trailing in the sand-covered walkway. More beachgoers had arrived, so the lot was two-thirds filled, but Frank had parked close. Kirk expected to find his dad inside the camper at the table, talking business on his phone with papers spread in front of him. But when he rounded the back of the truck, the camper door was locked and his father was nowhere to be seen.

Kirk stood his board against the door, then sat on the bumper to inspect his leg, which now looked like a kielbasa had exploded. Had the board hit him a bit higher it might have shattered his kneecap. Kirk felt lucky, but the sooner he got to an emergency room the better.

His dad was probably across the highway, in a store grabbing a drink or a protein bar, the key to the camper in the zippered pocket of his wet suit. Kirk didn't want to hobble across the highway carrying his surfboard, nor did he want to leave it for a thief in the parking lot. He looked around to make sure that no one was observing him, then he stood on the bumper on his nonbleeding leg, shoving the board up onto the camper roof, where it would be out of sight from the ground. The leash hung down, so Kirk knotted it into a messy ball and tossed it up as well. So much for protective measures, he thought, and then headed for the highway.

An overgrown bush provided shade as Kirk waited for an opening in the morning traffic. When a gap showed, he made his move, skip-hopping across the four lanes. He checked the Subway and the Circle W, looking through windows but not seeing his dad. The surf shop would make sense. Maybe he was picking up sunblock. Heavy metal music blared from inside but no one was in the place.

His last and best bet was the Starbucks at the north end of the shops. Coffee drinkers were reading papers and working on laptops at the outside tables and benches. Frank was not one of them, and if anyone bothered to look up at Kirk with his open wound, they didn't say anything. He entered, expecting to find his dad, roust him off the phone, and set off for the appropriate medical attention. But Starbucks held no Frank.

"Holy shit!" The female barista saw Kirk standing there, bleeding. "Sir? Are you okay?"

"It's not that bad," Kirk said. Some customers looked up from their cups and laptops without responding.

"Should I call 911?" the barista asked.

"I've got a ride to the clinic. My dad," Kirk said. "Has a Frank been in, ordering a Venti drip with a shot of mocha?"

"A Frank?" The woman thought a second. "A lady ordered a Venti drip with a shot of mocha a while ago with a decaf soy latte. But not a Frank." Kirk turned to go back outside. "We have a first aid kit."

Kirk scanned the parking lot again and the walkway of the shops but still did not see his father. On the off chance there were tables on the other side of Starbucks, he eased his way to the corner but found no tables, and no Frank, just parking spaces under eucalyptus trees.

A single car, a Mercedes, was parked on the other side of a thick trunk of one of the trees. Kirk could see only the front end and a bit of windshield. Starbucks cups, two of them, were sitting on the dash. From the passenger seat, a man's hand reached out for what Kirk knew to be a Venti drip with a shot of mocha because he recognized the black band of his father's military-style chronometer, a watch just like the one Kirk now wore on his own wrist. The windows of the Mercedes were rolled down, allowing Kirk to hear the lilt of a woman's laughter along with his father's amused cackle.

Kirk didn't feel his leg anymore, no pain at all, as he edged closer to the tree, able to see that much more of the car, as well as the face of a woman with long black hair and a smile aimed at his father. Frank was facing the woman, so Kirk saw only the back of his head. He heard his father say, "I better get back," but his father didn't move. Kirk knew from the relaxed, quiet tone that his dad wasn't going anywhere.

Kirk slowly backed off around the tree to the corner, then around to the door of the Starbucks. He went back inside.

On the wall opposite the entrance, windows spread over three small tables that looked out onto empty parking spaces in the shade of the eucalyptus trees.

Kirk went to the windows and craned his neck. He saw the woman with long black hair, her arm resting across Frank's shoulder, her fingers playing in his sea-salted hair. His father was swirling his drip mocha in its cup. He was sitting on a beach towel that covered the passenger seat as though his wet suit had not already dried. The woman with the long black hair said something and laughed again. His father laughed, too, in a way Kirk rarely saw him laugh, with his teeth showing, his head raised back, and his eyes squinting, a silent movie, the dialogue muted by the window of Starbucks. Kirk heard only the tapping of fingers on laptop keyboards and the commerce of premium coffee drinks.

"Why don't you take a seat?" It was the barista again, named Celia according to her tag. She had a metal first aid kit. "I can put on some kind of bandage, at least."

Kirk did sit. Celia wrapped his leg in gauze, the white staining red immediately. A glance back out to the shade of the eucalyptus tree showed the woman with the long black hair leaning forward, her mouth open, her head tilted in the body language known universally as a prelude to a desired kiss. His father leaned in toward her.

Recrossing the highway was a blur, but Kirk did think to retrieve his board from the roof of the camper. He walked back down the path to Mars. The surf line was still crowded with riders, the high tide about to turn in the hours-long recession to the low-water mark. Beside his father's board and planted paddle, Kirk sat in the sand, his mouth dry, his eyes unfocused, his ears deaf to the roar and rush of the waves. He looked at the bloodied bandage on his calf, remembering that he had been cut deeply by his own surfboard, but it had happened—when? Weeks ago.

He slowly ripped the tape from around his leg, then unwrapped the scarlet-stained gauze, kneading the sticky heap into his fist. He dug a hole in the sand, a deep hole, then put the snarl of trash in the bottom and covered it up again. The wound immediately began to bleed, but Kirk ignored that, as well as the swelling and the pain. He sat, confused, suddenly ill, feeling like he was going to cry. But he didn't. Whenever his father returned he would find his son recovering from a surf accident, waiting for him to finish his business calls so they could go get forty stitches, at least.

No one came by him, neither up out of the water nor down the path from the parking lot. Kirk sat, alone, dragging his fingers in the sand like a small rake for who knows how long. He wished he had a book to read.

"What the fuck?" Frank was striding across the sand, his eyes wide at the sight of his son with such a gash. "What happened to your leg?"

"My own board," Kirk told him.

"Jesus!" Frank knelt in the sand, inspecting the wound. "Must have made you say *ouch*."

"I did say *ouch*," Kirk told him.

"Wounded in the line of battle," Frank said.

"Helluva birthday present," Kirk told him.

Frank laughed, like any father would when his only son takes a hit and shakes it off with a stoic humor. "Let's get you to the clinic, get that cleaned out, you sewn up." Frank gathered his board and paddle. "You're gonna have one sexy scar."

"Sexy as hell," Kirk told him.

Kirk followed his father up the path, away from the surfline, leaving Mars for the last time and forever.

A Month on Greene Street

The first of August is usually only so notable—the start of the eighth month in the middle of summer on what might or might not be the hottest day *ever*. But this year, *yowza*, a lot was going on that day.

Little Sharri Monk was sure to lose another tooth, a partial lunar eclipse was due around 9:15 p.m., and Bette Monk (mother of Sharri; her older sister, Dale; and her younger brother, Eddie) was moving them all into a three-bedroom house on Greene Street. The home so picturesque she knew she would live there the moment she saw the real estate listing. Bette had a vision—*pop*—of herself and the kids in the kitchen for a busy breakfast. She was manning the stove-top griddle, turning pancakes, the kids in school clothes finishing their homework and fighting over the last of the orange juice. Her mental image was so focused, so particular, there was no question the house on Greene Street—oh, that massive sycamore tree in the front yard—would be hers. Theirs.

Bette had visions—was there any other way to put it? Not

every day and never with any spiritual glow, but she would sense a flash, she'd see a *pop*, like a photo of a vacation taken long ago that held complete memories of all that happened before and all that came after. When her husband, Bob Monk, had come home from work one day—*pop*—Bette saw a full-color snapshot of him holding hands with Lorraine Conner-Smythe in the restaurant attached to the Mission Bell Marriott Hotel. Lorraine did consulting work with Bob's company, so the two of them had many chances to sniff each other out. In that nanosecond Bette knew her marriage with Bob had gone from just fine to over. *Pop*.

If Bette were to count all the times she had such visions—from when she was a little girl—and how those visions came to pass, she could have regaled a dinner party for a full evening with examples: the scholarship she would win four years after learning of its existence, the dorm room she would have in Iowa City, the man she would sleep with for the first time (not Bob Monk), the wedding dress she would wear at the altar (opposite Bob Monk), the view of the Chicago River she would enjoy once the job interview with the *Sun-Times* went her way, the phone call she saw coming the night her parents were hit by a drunk driver. She knew the sexes of her children the moment she saw the test results over the sink in her bathroom. The list went on and on and on. Not that she made a big deal out of any of the visions, claiming no special clairvoyance or an all-seeing mentalism. Bette thought most people had the same kind of visions, they just didn't realize it. And not all of her visions came to pass. She once saw herself being a contestant on *Jeopardy!* but that never happened. Still, her accuracy ratio was awfully impressive.

Bob wanted to marry Lorraine as soon as their affair was discovered, so he paid for the privilege, assuring Bette's financial security until the kids were off to college and the child support ceased. Buying the house on Greene Street required hoop jumping with the bank, glowing inspections, and a six-month escrow, but the deed was signed. The lawn, that sycamore, the front porch, all those bedrooms, and the minioffice attached to the garage made for a Promised Land, especially after the narrow, split-level condo in which she had first parked her money and where the four of them lived like kittens in a box, all on top of each other. Now they had a backyard, so deep and wide! With a pomegranate tree! Bette saw her kids—*pop*—in T-shirts covered in purple dribble spots come October!

Greene Street was isolated, with almost no traffic except the residents, making it safe for street play. On August 1 the kids begged the movers to unload their bikes and Eddie's Big Wheel before anything else so they could cruise their new turf. The moving crew was a bunch of young Mexican guys who had kids of their own, so they were happy to oblige and to watch the children play, carefree, as they unpacked and carried a household's worth of stuff.

Bette spent the morning testing her high school Spanish, sending boxes to the right rooms, and having furniture placed according to her intuition—the sofa facing the window, bookshelves bordering the fireplace. Around 11:00 a.m.,

Dale came running in with a pair of chubby boys, maybe ten years old, probably twins, both with the same bashful look and matching dimples.

"Mom! This is Keyshawn and Trennelle. They live four houses over."

"Keyshawn. Trennelle," Bette said. "Howdy do?"

"They said I could have lunch with them."

Bette eyed the boys. "Is that true?"

"Yes, ma'am," said either Keyshawn or Trennelle.

"Did you just call me *ma'am*?"

"Yes, ma'am."

"You, Keyshawn, have good manners. Or are you Trennelle?"

The boys pointed to themselves, saying their names. Since they dressed differently, not like twins in some movie, Bette would always know who was who. Plus, Keyshawn had his hair in perfectly tied cornrows while Trennelle's head was shaved nearly clean.

"What's on the menu?" Bette asked.

"Today we have franks and beans, ma'am."

"Who is making this lunch, exactly?"

"Our Gramma Alice," Trennelle told her. "Our mother works at AmCoFederal Bank. Our father works for Coca-Cola, but we're not allowed to drink Coca-Cola. Only on Sunday. Our Gramma Diane lives in Memphis. We don't have granddads. Our mother will come to your house when she comes home and will bring you flowers from our garden to say 'welcome wagon.' Our father will come by, too, with some Coca-Cola, if it's allowed, or Fanta, if you prefer. We didn't ask Gramma Alice if there is going to be enough food for Eddie and Sharri, so they can't come."

"Mom! Yes? No?" Dale was just about to burst.

"Have something green with the franks and beans and I'm thinking yes."

"Would apples be good with you, ma'am? For something green? We have green apples."

"Apples would do the trick, Trennelle."

The three kids lit out of the house, off the porch, down the steps, under the low-hanging limbs of the sycamore, and across the lawn. Bette followed just far enough to watch them rush through a front door four houses away. Then she hollered for Eddie and Sharri to park their bikes on the front lawn and come in for the sandwiches she would make as soon as she found the fixings.

———

The movers were done and gone by three, leaving Bette to the pleasure of unpacking her kitchen directly from box to drawer or shelf. She no longer had any of Bob's gimmicky appliances, the one-use inventions he collected for his so-called culinary hobby. Bette never loved cooking, but since the split her no-nonsense meals had developed some frills. Her creamed spinach had actually gotten the kids to ask for spinach. Her ground-turkey burritos were stuffed with beans and cheese, but never fell apart when eaten by hand. The kids celebrated when Bette formalized Tuesdays as *Turkeeto* Night and looked forward to them every week. When the boxes were empty and the shelves looked like they made sense,

Bette fired up the one appliance she truly prized, the espresso maker. Made in Germany, the stainless-steel behemoth had cost a thousand predivorce dollars, took up nearly a square yard of counter space, and sported as many gauges and valves as the submarine in *Das Boot*. She so loved the apparatus she often greeted it in the morning with "Hey, big boy."

She sat down, finally, on the living room sofa with a massive mug of espresso and steamed 2 percent milk. The big window looked like a cinema screen showing a movie called *I Live Here Now*. A cavalcade of kids was entering and exiting the frame, a group that either lived on Greene Street or made the block their Our Gangish HQ. A towheaded girl was inspecting Sharri's mouth like an advance agent for the tooth fairy giving an estimate of what to expect. A pack of boys set up a T-ball stand, each taking whacks with a plastic bat while others shagged the hits. Dale and another girl were dangling from the low limbs of the sycamore. Keyshawn and Trennelle must have had a sibling, a dimpled girl in braids, who was helping Ed ride her pink two-wheeler, running alongside of him as he coasted up onto the front lawn of the house across the street.

That lawn belonged to the Patel family—was that what the real estate agent said? Patel? An Indian name for sure. The Patels must have had a kid every eleven months, judging from the black hair and brown skin of five kids out there, each a perfect match of the brother or sister, just a head shorter. The older Patel girls had iPhones or Samsungs, which they checked every forty-five seconds. They took a lot of pictures of Eddie on the pink bike.

Bette tried to count all the kids, but like with a school of fish in an oversize aquarium, the roiling action made it impossible. Call it a dozen children out there, teeming, laughing, *bolting* to and fro in varying shades of flesh.

"I've moved into the UN," she said to no one. That struck her as something to tell Maggie, her oldest friend and the woman who had coached her through every step of the shattering of her marriage—from that first *pop* to the reality of her desperate unhappiness, the separation-of-no-return, the search for a lawyer, and the three-plus years of Marriage Dissolution mumbo jumbo and nights of red, red wine. Her phone was in her purse, sitting in the middle of the living room floor. She was reaching for it when she saw Paul Legaris coming up her driveway.

He was an older fellow wearing baggy cargo shorts and a faded red T-shirt with a crinkled Detroit Red Wings logo. He wore glasses that were a tad too angular and hip for a man his age, which Bette figured was around eight years her senior. He had flip-flops on his feet; it was summer, after all, but since it was a weekday, Bette took the lack of shoes to mean that here was a guy between jobs. Though maybe he worked nights. Maybe he'd won the Powerball. Who knew?

Paul was carrying a bag containing a HoneyBaked ham— this was not one of Bette's *pops;* the brand was advertised on the bag. Though the front door was wide open—it had been all day, what with movers and kids streaming in and out like subway patrons—he rang the doorbell without a follow-up of "Anyone home?"

"Howdy do?" Bette offered, stepping to the threshold.

"Paul Legaris. Your next-door neighbor," he said.

"Bette Monk."

"Though I come in no official capacity," he said, holding out the ham bag, "welcome."

Bette eyed the HoneyBaked. "You know, with a name like Monk . . ." She let that trail off. Paul looked confused, like an actor who had dropped a dialogue cue. "I could be a Jewish mother," Bette said." A bag of pork would then be . . ."

"Treif." Paul knew his lines after all. "Forbidden."

"But I'm not."

"Okay then." Paul offered the sack and Bette took it. "When I moved in, someone on the block left one on my welcome mat and I lived off the thing for weeks."

"Thanks. Can I offer a coffee in kind?" Bette did not really want to spend any more time with her neighbor, a single man (she had clocked his lack of a wedding band), who, by living right next door, was the only unanticipated and undesired reality of her new life on Greene Street. Still, she had to be polite.

"Nice of you," he said, remaining on the porch, on the other side of the plane that was the open door. "But on moving day you must have a million chores on the punch list."

Bette appreciated the decline. She did have a million things to do. She nodded toward the pack of kids out on Greene Street. "Any of those yours?"

"Mine live with their mother. You'll see them come the right weekend."

"Got it. Thanks for this." She nodded at the ham in the bag in her hand. "Maybe some ham-bone soup, come Friday."

"Enjoy," Paul said, beginning his retreat from the porch. "Greene Street will be good to you. Has been for me. Oh . . ." He turned back, stepping once again into the doorway. "Are you doing anything tonight?"

Are you doing anything tonight?

Bette had heard those very words too many times in the last few years. *Are you doing anything tonight?* From men divorced, single, unattached, and lonely—guys who had kids who lived with ex-wives, who lived in apartments, who searched Internet dating sites for any kind of intellectual or romantic or sexual hookup. Guys who took one look at her and thought, I wonder if she is doing anything tonight.

Pop!

The vision: Paul is keeping an eye out his window, looking to see when Bette Monk, divorced, attractive (still) pulls into the driveway right next door. When she does he saunters over with an excuse to take up some of her time—a piece of her mail that accidentally came to his box, word of a lost dog in the neighborhood, concern for Eddie's sprained ankle. He'll linger too long, chat too idly with a look on his face hinting of neediness.

Bette's mind processed the vision, the very first blemish in the fabric of her new life on Greene Street—the guy next door looking for a woman.

"I'm busy with the house," she said. "Lots to do." She drank some of her coffee.

"Nine or so I'm setting my telescope up," Paul said. "There's a partial lunar eclipse tonight that will max around a quarter after. Nice red shadow of the earth will cover about half the moon. It won't last long, but you could have a look."

"Ah," Bette said, leaving it at that.

Paul flip-flopped off the porch and across the lawn, just as Sharri came bounding up with something small in her hand, a little pebble of pure white.

"Mom! Look!" Sharri squealed. There was some blood on her fingers. "My tooth!"

———

In the dying light of that first afternoon, the street quieted down as everyone broke for various family suppertimes. Bette fed the kids ham slices and a salad of lettuce and tomatoes that had made the move from the condo. Earlier, Darlene Pitts, the mother of Keyshawn and Trennelle, had brought a basket of flowers picked from her own garden along with a card asking *Won't you be my neighbor?* As they were chatting on the porch, her husband, Harlan, showed up with two big bottles of Sprite and Diet Sprite. Together they gave Bette the rundown on some of the neighbors.

"The Patels have first names that hurt my tongue," Harlan joked. "I call them Mr. and Mrs. Patel."

"Irrfan and Priyanka." Darlene shot a look at her husband. "And would it hurt you to learn their kids' names?"

"Actually, yes it would."

These were Bette's kind of folks.

Darlene rattled off the names. "Ananya, Pranav, Prisha, Anushka, and the youngest boy is Om."

"Om, I got," Harlan said.

The Smiths *over there* gave away apricots from their tree by the bushel. The Ornonas *over there* had the ski boat that never left their driveway. The Bakas family in the big blue and white house had huge parties every Greek Easter and if you didn't show up the family would bring up your absence for the rest of the year. Vincent Crowell operated a ham radio at all hours. His was the house with a huge antenna on the roof.

"And Paul Legaris teaches science at Burham. The college. Has two older kids." Harlan reported. "Heard his son is joining the Navy."

"A teacher," said Bette. "Thus the footware."

"Come again?" Darlene asked.

"He gave us a ham in flip-flops. On his feet, not on the ham. I thought a man wearing flip-flops in the middle of a weekday was, you know . . ."

"Comfortable?" said Harlan.

"Unemployed."

"No classes in session in August." Harlan sighed. "I envy a man in flip-flops on a day like today."

Pop! Bette saw Paul on campus, between classes, sitting on a bench on the quad, surrounded by coeds, pretty girls who had Legaris for Introduction to Biology, and he was always so free with his time. One of those coeds was sure to have a thing for older men in positions of authority, or so Paul Legaris hoped.

The warm summer evening beckoned the kids back out onto Greene Street as Bette cleaned the dishes, then headed upstairs to find linens and make the beds. From the window of the bedroom shared by Dale and Sharri, Bette saw Paul wheeling a large tube out of his garage—his aforementioned telescope—on a hand-made dolly, aided by some kids. By the time darkness fell completely, Bette had plugged in her Bluetooth speaker and paired it with her phone so Adele could provide a mournful score for the evening's chore of lining closet shelves and untangling hangers. Bette was still organizing dresser drawers when she heard one of the kids slam the front door and stomp up the stairs.

"Mom?" Eddie yelled, coming into what was going to be his room. "Can I make a telescope?"

"I admire your spunk."

"Professor Legaris made his own telescope and it's *amazing* to look through."

"*Professor* Legaris, huh?"

"Yeah. The man who lives right next door. His garage is full of *amazing* stuff. He keeps a bunch of wires and tools in a big wooden thing called a chifforobe. He has three old TVs with knobs on the side of them and a sewing machine you have to pedal." Eddie jumped onto his bed. "He let me look into the Cosmos, whatever that is, through his telescope. I saw the moon and, like, a shadow of the sun was covering part of it."

"I'm no professor, but I think it's the shadow of the Earth."

"It was funny. With just my eye, the moon looked like it was being sliced out of the sky, but through the telescope, you could still see the cut-up part, but it was red. Craters and everything. He made the telescope himself by hand."

"How do you make a telescope?"

"You get a round piece of glass and grind on it for a long time, then make that part shiny, then put it on one end of a tube, like for carpets. Then you buy eyehole things."

"Lenses?"

"Opticons, I think he called them. He teaches a class on how to make your own telescope. Can I?"

"If we can find a tube, like for carpets."

The kids went to bed late that first night on Greene Street, but having spent so much energy running around they all conked out, pronto. Before she could forget, Bette put three dollars under Sharri's pillow in exchange for that tooth, the fairy being rather flush with cash.

The day finally over, Bette opened a bottle of red, red wine and called Maggie, telling her about all the neighborhood kids, the Pittses and the Coke connection, and yes, her vision of Paul Legaris.

"What is with your luck with men?" Maggie asked.

"It's not my luck," Bette said. "It's the men. They are all so sad. So obvious. So desperate for a woman to define them."

"Desperate to fuck you," Maggie deemed. "And there you are, right next door. If he comes over next time smelling of some Rat Packesque cologne? Bolt the door. He's after you."

"I hope he's aiming for his students. Teaching assistants. Sorority girls."

"Those could get him fired. The hot divorcée who moved in next door is legal game. He may have binoculars trained on your windows right now."

"If he does he'll see Eddie's Star Wars curtains. My room is on the other side of the house."

As August yawned deeply into its dog days, Bette avoided contact with her next-door neighbor, not wanting to hear *Are you doing anything tonight?* again. She drove home, scanning Greene Street for signs of Paul Legaris. Once he was on his front lawn and he waved as she pulled into the driveway, calling out, "How you doing?"

"Just super, thanks!" she said. She hustled inside like she was very busy with something when, in fact, she had nothing going on. Another time, there he was watching the neighbor kids kicking footballs in a game called Pig on the Fly, so she grabbed her idle phone and pretended to be on a call as she went into the house. Paul waved at her, but she just nodded back. During the evenings she feared the doorbell would ring and there he would be, freshly showered and smelling of Creed, asking if she wasn't doing anything, would she be interested in dinner at the Old Spaghetti Factory? She had once taken her dentist up on that very offer. He turned out to be such a narcissistic bore she changed her dental care provider. Around then she declared an Armistice in the Dating War, and now she was hell-bent on keeping her new life on Greene Street void of attachments and thus disaster free.

As it turned out, the kids saw more of Paul Legaris than she did. He was washing his car on a Friday evening (who washes a car on Friday evening?) when Bob picked them up for his weekend of custody. Bette showed her ex-husband around the lower floor of her new house as the kids packed their weekend bags, then she watched as they all piled into

Bob's car. Paul came over when Eddie wanted to introduce his dad to the guy who taught Cosmos at the college. The two men chatted longer than necessary, Bette decided. When Bob and the kids drove off, Paul went back to washing his car. Though she did not have a vision about the exchange, she wondered if the two men had compared notes on, well, *her*.

The next morning Bette slept in, wonderfully late on a Saturday morning without the kids. She came down the stairs of the quiet house barefoot, in a pair of yoga pants and a light cotton hoodie, carrying her iPad.

"Hey, big boy." In bare feet she steamed up her morning elixir, taking it out to the backyard before the sun broke over the roof and the heat became too much. She took her iPad with her; it seemed like years since she had used the thing anyplace other than in bed. She sat in a plastic Adirondack chair under the backyard tree, scrolling through back issues of the Chicago *Sun-Times* Sunday magazine, then lingering too long on the *Daily Mail* website, when she heard *klock klock klock klock klock*.

A woodpecker was doing the woodpecker thing some-where.

Klock klock klock klock klock.

She scanned the branches of the trees for a sign of the bird but found none. *Klock klock klock klock klock.*

"Persistent fives," Bette said, counting the *klock*s.

She looked at the exterior of the house, happy she didn't see the bird damaging the siding by digging for insects, then came again *klock klock klock klock klock*.

The sound was coming from over the fence, from Paul

Legaris's backyard. The tall fence—which even on Greene Street made for good neighbors—blocked any view of next door, save the higher tree branches. There were no signs of Mr. Peckerhead up in them, but the *klock klock klock klock klock* sounds kept coming, which made Bette curious. She wanted to see how big this woody-bird was, so she moved her chair to the fence and stood on it, hoping to see the bird in action.

Klock klock klock klock klock.

Paul Legaris kept his backyard neat and organized, with a vegetable garden with drip irrigation and beanpoles. An antique plow, rusted and in need of a horse, sat in the center of a patch of grass beside, incongruously, an array of solar panels. Toward the back of the yard, distant from the patio, was a massive brick BBQ and one of those freestanding, mail-order-catalog hammocks.

Klock klock klock klock klock.

Paul himself was sitting at a picnic table on a redwood deck under a sloping canopy, already dressed in his uniform of baggy shorts, polo shirt, and those flip-flops. His too-cool eyeglasses were set on the top of his head, and he was bent in concentration over a hunk of machinery that looked like it had been made in the 1800s.

Klock klock klock klock klock.

The machine was a typewriter, though it looked like no typewriter Bette had ever seen. The thing was ancient, something out of the Victorian era, a mechanical printing apparatus with hammers arcing onto paper rolled into the carriage. Paul hit a key five times—*klock klock klock klock*

klock—added a touch of oil to the inner levers of the type-writer, and repeated.

Klock klock klock klock klock.

This was how Paul Legaris could ruin a peaceful morning on Greene Street, servicing a writing gimcrack straight out of Jules Verne.

Klock klock klock klock klock.

"Yowza," Bette mumbled. She went back inside for another jolt of caffeine and stayed there, reading her iPad in the relative quiet at her kitchen table, still hearing the muffled *klock*-ing of her neighbor's ironclad word processor.

That afternoon, when the sun was turning Greene Street into both the frying pan and the fire, Bette was on the phone with Maggie.

"So he's got telescopes and typewriters laying around his house. I wonder what else," Maggie wondered.

"Old toasters. Dial telephones. Washtubs with wringers. Who knows?"

"I checked some of the dating sites on the Web. Couldn't find him."

"CreepyNeighbor.com? SadSacks4U?" Bette was looking out the front window when an unfamiliar car pulled up across the street—one made in Korea the color of red nail polish. A young man, the driver, got out along with a girl a few years younger, no doubt his sister. As they walked across the street, angling toward Paul Legaris's front door, Bette recognized the Legaris gait in the boy.

"Kid alert," Bette told Maggie. "Guess who just showed up."

"Who?" Maggie asked.

"Pretty sure it's the offspring of Professor Lonesome next door. Son and daughter."

"They showing tattoos or Birkenstocks?"

"Nah." Bette eyed the kids for signs of youthful rebellion or oddity. "They look normal."

"Normal is a setting on a washing machine."

The girl let out a squeal and ran toward the front door of the house. Paul Legaris was heading for her when they intersected on the lawn. She took him in a headlock and bull-dogged him into the turf, laughing. The son joined the fracas, two kids dog-piling on the father they had clearly not seen in a while.

"I may have to call 911 soon. I think a separated shoulder is due," Bette opined.

That night Bette, Maggie, and the Ordinand sisters met for dinner at a Mexican cafe made of cinder block and with paper shades over the lights, a place so authentic they were afraid to drink the water, but not the margaritas. The night filled with laughter and stories about former husbands, lousy ex-boyfriends, and men who lacked both common sense and sanity. The talk was fun and saucy, much of it about Paul Legaris, none of it flattering.

When her Lyft driver dropped her off at Greene Street, the sky had been dark for two hours and once again the tele-scope had been wheeled out onto Paul's front yard. His car was not in the driveway; his kids were manning the search of the heavens. Bette was making straight for her door when the son's voice reached across the driveway.

"Good evening" was all he said.

Bette gave a nod and made a sound like *g'deve* but didn't slow.

"Wanna see the moons of Jupiter?" This was the girl asking. "Smack in the middle of the sky and cool as hell?"

"No, thank you," Bette said.

"You're missing one gorgeous show!" The girl had a voice like Dale's, open and friendly, prone to enthusiasm over the smallest things.

"No eclipse tonight?" Bette was getting her front door keys from her purse.

"Those are infrequent. Jupiter is out all summer long," the girl said. "I'm Nora Legaris."

"Hi. Bette Monk."

"Mother of Dale and Sharri and Eddie? Dad said your kids are a hoot." The girl headed Bette's way, stepping onto the driveway. "You bought the Schneiders' house. They moved to Austin, the lucky punks. That's my brother." Nora pointed to the telescope. "Tell Ms. Monk your name!"

"Lawrence Altwell-Chance Delagordo Legaris the Seventh," he said. "You can call me Chick."

Bette looked confused, like a woman with three margaritas in her, which she was. *"Chick?"*

"Or Larry. Long story. You want to see what Galileo saw centuries ago? Changed the course of human history."

To wave off such an invitation, to flee into her house, would have been rude, very un–Greene Street. Nora and Chick were charming kids. So Bette said, "Put that way, guess I better."

Bette crossed the boundary of her house into Legaris territory, her first ever visit. Chick stepped back from the telescope, offering Bette access. "Behold Jupiter," he said.

Bette put her eye up to the lens at the open end of the carpet tube.

"Try not to bump the telescope. It should be lined up right."

Bette blinked. The glass of the lens brushed her eyelash. She couldn't make any sense of what she was looking at. "I don't see a thing."

"Chick," Nora sighed. "You can't say 'behold Jupiter' and fail to have Jupiter beholdable."

"Sorry, Ms. Monk. Let me see." Chick looked through a much smaller telescope mounted on the huge carpet tube and made adjustments up and down and left and right. "Bang solid fat as a goose!"

"I sure hope you behold Jupiter now," said Nora.

With her eye again so close to the lens her mascara could have marred it, Bette saw, at first, nothing, and then a brilliant pinhole of light. Jupiter. Not only Jupiter but four of its moons in a straight line, a single moon to its left, and three to its right, as clear as could be.

"Yowza!" Bette cried. "It's as clear as can be! That's *Jupiter*?"

"King of the planets and the Jovian moons," Chick said. "How many can you see?"

"Four."

"Just like Galileo," Nora said. "He put two bits of glass in a brass pipe, pointed it at the brightest object in the Italian sky, and saw just what you are looking at. Slammed the door on the Ptolemaic theory of the universe. Got him in some hot water."

Bette could not take her eye away. She had never looked deep into the Cosmos and seen another planet with her own eyes. Jupiter was gorgeous.

"Wait till you see Saturn," Chick said. "Rings and moons and the whole shebang."

"Show me!" Bette was suddenly hooked on celestial views.

"Can't," Chick explained. "Saturn doesn't rise until very early morning. If you want to set your alarm for quarter to five, I'll meet you here and line it up for you."

"Four forty-five a.m.? That will not happen." Bette stepped away from the telescope and those Jovian moons. "Now, explain Chick to me."

Nora laughed. "Abbott and Costello. The skinny one was Chick in one of their movies. We watched it about a thousand times and I started calling my brother by it. Chick stuck."

"Better than La-La-La-Larry Le-Le-Legaris."

"I get that," Bette said. "I was Elizabeth, along with seven other girls in fourth grade." She looked at Jupiter again through the telescope and once more marveled at the sight.

"Here comes the old man." Nora saw the headlights of her father's car coming down Greene Street. Bette thought to bolt for her front door, but to do so now would be such an obvious dis that she waved off her flight instinct.

"What are you punks doing on my lawn?" Paul said, getting out of his car. Another fellow, a redhead not much older than Chick, climbed out of the passenger seat. "Not you, Bette. These two scalawags."

Nora turned to Bette. "Dad uses words like *scalawags*. Sorry you witnessed it."

"This is Daniel," Paul said, pointing to the redheaded fellow, who, Bette could not help but notice, was very, very thin, possibly malnourished. He was wearing clothes that were brand new and surely not of his own taste, he wore them so uncomfortably. The kids exchanged greetings and Bette said hello.

"You have the Big Guy in sight?" Paul looked at the gas giant in the sky. "Daniel, you ever see Jupiter before?"

"I have not." With no other comment, Daniel stepped to the big tube and looked into its eyepiece. "Wow," he said with no expression.

"Bette? You have a gander?" Paul asked.

"I did. Made me say *yowza*." Bette looked at Nora. "Sorry you witnessed me saying *yowza*."

"*Yowza* is good," said Nora. "A catchall superlative. Like *big-time* or *super-duper*."

"Like *swingin'*," said Chick.

"Or *bodacious*," said Paul.

"Or *tits*," said Daniel. Again, no expression.

No one knew what to say to that.

———

The Daniel fellow spent a few days at the Legaris place. Bette heard the two men talking in the mornings, their distant voices coming over the fence in the backyard. She saw them leaving together in the evenings around 7:00 p.m., and then one night the skinny redhead was gone. Greene Street became, once again, a place of bikes, balls, and kids playing with a decided headiness since the beginning of school was bearing down. The end of summer was suddenly in the air, palpable.

On the final evening of August, Bette took the kids for pizza at a place that was wall-to-wall arcade games. When they returned home, the block was a quiet heaven after all that noise. The Patel kids were playing with a garden hose on their lawn, so Eddie and Sharri joined them. Dale went into the house. Bette lingered out front in a cooling, lovely breeze that stirred the leaves of her sycamore. Some of the spare pizza made it from the take-home box and into her hand as she leaned against one of the lower limbs, nibbling away.

There was no sign of Paul Legaris. His car was not in his driveway, so she felt relaxed in the calm of Greene Street, though guilty over what was her fourth slice of pepperoni, olive, and onion. As she tossed the thin crescent of uneaten crust into the grass—some bird would soon find it—she thought she saw a very large insect crawling across Paul Legaris's driveway.

She nearly let out an *eek* of terror—that could have been a huge spider—but then realized it was only a set of keys lying on the ground, right where Paul's car would have been parked.

Bette, then, found herself in something of a dilemma— what was a neighbor to do? She *should* pick up the keys, hold on to them until Paul came home, then knock on his front door and return them. If indeed they were his keys, as was most probable, she would save him the angst of a fruitless search. Anyone *would* do that, but—*pop*—Paul would be so happy at getting his keys back he would insist on repaying Bette with a dinner he would cook himself. Say! How's about I BBQ some ribs in the backyard with my own sauce recipe!

Bette did not want to go there. The simple solution would be for her to have Eddie return the keys. When Paul came home her son would scamper over and do the good deed and Bette would be inside her own house and that would be that.

She reached down and picked up the keys. There was a fob with the seal of Burham Community College, a couple of house keys and two industrial types with serial numbers stamped into them, a bike-lock key, and, the largest item on the ring, a plastic poker chip held in place by a hole drilled through its rim.

The chip was worn down, its serrated edges smoothed over. It had once been red but now was only flecked with faded spots. Still visible in the center was a big number 20. Paul must have won twenty bucks at one of the fake riverboat casinos at the state line. Or maybe the chip was all that remained of a two-thousand-dollar stake. She turned the chip over and saw *NA* on the other side. The letters were exotic and stylized, like a tattoo, sitting inside a square set on its corner like a baseball diamond. In the fading evening light, she saw some writing in the open areas of the chip, but it, too, was worn down and illegible save for a few letters—a *g* here, an *oc*, and what looked like *vice* but could have been *riot* or *ribs* or any four-letter word.

Across the street, the kids were playing Punch Ball against the Patel garage door. Bette took the keys inside to hold on to until she could assign Eddie the mission to return them.

Dale was on her laptop in the living room, watching You-Tube videos of horse jumping.

"You busy?" Bette asked her. Dale did not answer. "Hey, kid-o-mine," she said, snapping her fingers.

"What?" Dale did not look up from her computer.

"Can you google something for me?"

"Google what?"

"This poker chip." Bette held up the key chain.

"You want me to google 'poker chips'?"

"This poker chip."

"I don't need Google to tell you. That is a poker chip."

"Where is it from?"

"A poker chip factory."

"I am going to bounce this off your head if you don't google this."

Dale sighed and looked at her mother and the key ring and the poker chip and rolled her eyes. "Okay! But can I just finish this?"

Bette showed Dale the detail of the chip—the faded red, the 20, the *NA* on the other side with the rubbed-out letters—leaving the key chain behind to go wash her hands of pizza crumbs. She was loading the dishwasher when Dale hollered something from the living room.

"What?" Bette called back.

Dale came into the kitchen carrying her laptop. "It's a thing for narcotics."

"What is?" Bette was putting silverware into the top rack of the dishwasher.

"The poker chip," Dale said, showing her mother a collection of images on her computer. "*NA* is for Narcotics Anonymous. Like AA, but for narcotics. I entered *poker chips with NA* and a site came up, then I searched for images and there you go."

Bette was looking at the same design as was on the key ring. *NA* was in a baseball diamond, with the words *Self, God, Society, Service* in the open spaces.

"They give them out to celebrate 'sobriety,'" Dale said. "That means for not doing drugs. For thirty days on up."

"But this one says twenty." What was Paul Legaris doing with a poker chip from Narcotics Anonymous?

"I think that means twenty years," Dale said. "Where did you find these keys?"

Bette hesitated. If Paul Legaris had anything to do with drugs or Narcotics Anonymous, she didn't want Dale to know until she knew more herself.

"Found it someplace," Bette said.

"I need to google anything else? Potato chips or the rules for poker?"

"No." Bette went back to loading the dishwasher. When she was finished she called Maggie.

"Sure, Narcotics Anonymous," Maggie told her. "AA for drunks. CA for cokeheads. They have an Anonymous for everything."

"NA is for junkies?"

"Not narcoleptics." Maggie was curious. "You sure they are *his* keys?"

"No. But they were in his driveway, so let's assume—which will make an ass out of you and me . . ."

"Guys in twelve-step programs always sleep with someone else in the twelve-step program. Sarah Jallis had a niece who married a guy from her AA group, but I think they divorced later."

"If Paul Legaris is in NA, has *been* in NA for twenty years, I wonder what for."

"Well." Maggie paused. "I'd guess narcotics had something to do with it."

Eddie and Sharri came in an hour later, wet from the Patels' garden hose. An hour after that, all three kids were bathed and in front of the PlayStation watching a movie in HD. Bette was in the kitchen on her iPad, looking up Narcotics Anonymous on website after website. She did not hear the knock on the front door.

"Professor Legaris is here." Eddie had come into the kitchen. Bette looked at her son with no reaction. "He's at the front door."

And there he was, on the porch, just on the other side of the doorway, dressed in jeans and a white shirt with leather deck shoes on his feet. Bette closed the door slightly behind her to block the sound from the movie.

"Hi," she said.

"Sorry to bother you. I wonder if I can use your backyard to access my backyard."

"Why?"

"Because I am a knucklehead. Locked myself out of my house. I think my sliding door is unlocked. I'd go over my own fence but I'd land in my garbage cans."

Bette looked at Paul, at the same face that had brought her a HoneyBaked ham a month before, at the same guy who washed his car on Friday and thought her kids were a hoot, the neighbor who made his own telescopes and fixed old typewriters. *Pop!* Paul Legaris is sitting in a circle of men and women, all on folding chairs. He is listening to Daniel, the skinny redhead, talking about his days scoring heroin. Paul nods his head, recognizing his own behavior of twenty years prior.

"Wait right here," Bette says.

She returned seconds later with the key chain in her hand.

"My keys," Paul murmured. "You swiped my keys? That's a joke."

"They were in your driveway. I thought it was a big bug, but nope."

"My car remote must have fallen off without me noticing, one more event to which I am oblivious. I had no clue where I'd lost them, so thanks."

"Credit Greene Street and its good neighbor policy," Bette said. Now would have been the time for her to close the door on any more interaction with the guy who lived next door, the guy who wore flip-flops, the guy whom she had been avoiding since she had moved in. But she surprised herself with a question. "What happened to that Daniel fellow with the red hair and the lofty vocabulary?" she asked.

Paul had turned to go but stopped, facing Bette in the doorway. "Ah, Danny." Paul paused. "He's in Kentucky."

"Kentucky? He from there?" Bette was now leaning in the doorway, casually, comfortably. She found herself relaxed with Paul in her doorway, something she had never felt, not since that first *Are you doing anything tonight?*

"He's from Detroit. A spot opened up at a place in Kentucky, so he took it for ninety days, if all goes well. I hope there was no problem during his stay with me."

"No. I did want to give the guy a sandwich to fatten him up."

"Yeah. Danny needs to eat better." Paul stepped away again, leaving.

"You know," Bette said, "in olden times redheads like him were considered demons. Because of the devil-colored hair."

Paul laughed. "He's got his demons, but no more than any of us."

Bette looked down at the keys in Paul's hand, at the poker chip that celebrated twenty years of sobriety, two decades narcotics-free. She did some math in her head. Chick Legaris was at least twenty-one years old, which would have made him a baby when his father hit his own rock bottom, when Paul began his journey from wherever that was to this night in August.

In that wink of an eye, Bette was even more assured she and the kids belonged here, on Greene Street.

"Thanks for saving me a ton of hassle," Paul said, waving his keys.

"De nada," Bette said, watching him step away toward his house next door.

She was just turning back into her house when—*pop*—she saw herself in her kitchen, early in the morning, with dawn still hours away and kids all still asleep in their beds.

"Hello, big boy," she is saying to her espresso machine, steaming her morning latte and, in another mug, a double cappuccino with just a frothing of foam.

Then she is carrying both wake 'em ups out her front door, down her porch steps, across her lawn, and under the low hanging limbs of her sycamore.

Paul Legaris has set up his telescope on his driveway. The instrument is pointing at the deep, dark blue of the eastern sky over Greene Street.

Saturn is just rising. Through the eyepiece, the ringed planet is a glory, bang solid fat as a goose and cool as hell.

Alan Bean Plus Four

Traveling to the moon was way less complicated this year than it was back in 1969, as the four of us proved, not that anyone gives a whoop. You see, over cold beers in my backyard, with the crescent moon a delicate princess fingernail low in the west, I told Steve Wong that if he threw, say, a hammer with enough muscle, said tool would make a 500,000-mile figure eight, sail around that very moon, and return to Earth like a boomerang, and wasn't that fascinating?

Steve Wong works at Home Depot, so has access to many hammers. He offered to chuck a few. His co-worker MDash, who'd shortened his given name to rap-star length, wondered how one would catch a red-hot hammer falling at a thousand miles an hour. Anna, who runs her own graphic design biz, said that there'd be nothing to catch, as the hammer would burn up like a meteor, and she was right. Plus, she didn't buy the simplicity of my cosmic throw-wait-return. She is ever doubtful of my space program bona fides. She says I'm always "Apollo missions this" and "Lunokhod moon landing that," and have begun to falsify details in order to sound like an expert, and she is right about that, too.

I keep all my nonfiction on a pocket-size Kobo digital reader, so I whipped out a chapter from *No Way, Ivan: Why the CCCP Lost the Race to the Moon*, written by an émigré professor with an ax to grind. According to him, in the mid-sixties the Soviets hoped to trump the Apollo program with just such a figure-eight mission: no orbit, no landing, just photos and crowing rights. The Reds sent off an unmanned Soyuz with, supposedly, a mannequin in a spacesuit, but so many things went south that they didn't dare try again, not even with a dog. *Kaputnik.*

Anna is as thin and smart as a whip, and driven like no one else I have ever dated (for three exhausting weeks). She saw a challenge here. She wanted to succeed where the Russians had failed. It would be fun. We'd all go, she said, and that was that, but when? I suggested that we schedule liftoff in conjunction with the anniversary of *Apollo 11*, the most famous space flight in history, but that was a no-go, as Steve Wong had dental work scheduled for the third week of July. How about November, when *Apollo 12* landed in the Ocean of Storms, an event now forgotten by 99.999 percent of the people on Earth? Anna had to be a bridesmaid at her sister's wedding the week after Halloween, so the best date for the mission turned out to be the last Saturday in September.

Astronauts in the Apollo era had spent thousands of hours piloting jet planes and earning engineering degrees. They had to practice escaping from launchpad disasters by sliding down long cables to the safety of thickly padded bunkers.

They had to know how slide rules worked. We did none of that, though we did test-fly our booster on the Fourth of July, out of Steve Wong's huge driveway in Oxnard, hoping that, with all the fireworks, our unmanned first stage would blow through the night sky unnoticed. Mission accomplished. That rocket cleared Baja and is *right now* zipping around the Earth every ninety minutes and, let me state clearly, for the sake of multiple government agencies, will probably burn up harmlessly on reentry in twelve to fourteen months.

MDash, who was born in a sub-Saharan village, has a super brain. As a transfer student at St. Anthony Country Day High School with minimal English skills, he won a science-fair Award of Merit with an experiment on ablative materials, which caught fire, to the delight of everyone. Since having a working heat shield is implied in the phrase "returning safely to Earth," MDash was in charge of that and all things pyrotechnic, including the explosive bolts for stage separation. Anna did the math, all the load-lift ratios, orbital mechanics, fuel mixtures, and formulas—the stuff I pretend to know, but which actually leaves me in a fog.

My contribution was the Command Module—a cramped, headlight-shaped spheroid that was cobbled together by a very rich pool-supply magnate, who was hell-bent on getting into the private aerospace business to make him some big-time NASA cash. He died in his sleep just before his ninety-fourth birthday, and his (fourth) wife-widow agreed to sell me the capsule for a hundred bucks, though I would have paid twice that. She insisted on typing a receipt on one of her husband's old typewriters, a green Royal Desktop, a behemoth, just one of many that he collected but failed to maintain, as there was a stack of them growing rust in a corner of the garage. MUST TAKE DELIVERY IN 48 HOURS she typed, as well as NO RETURNS/CASH ONLY. I named the capsule the *Alan Bean*, in honor of the lunar-module pilot of *Apollo 12*, the fourth man to walk on the moon and the only one I ever met, in a Houston-area Mexican restaurant in 1986. He was paying the cashier, as anonymous as a balding orthopedist, when I yelled out, "Holy cow! You're Al Bean!" He gave me his autograph and drew a tiny astronaut above his name.

Since four of us would be a-comin' round the moon, I needed to make room inside the *Alan Bean* and eliminate pounds. We'd have no Mission Control to boss us around, so I ripped out all the Comm. I replaced every bolt, screw, hinge, clip, and connector with duct tape (three bucks a roll at Home Depot). Our privy had a shower curtain for privacy. I've heard from an experienced source that a trip to the john in zero gravity requires that you strip naked and give yourself half an hour, so, yeah, privacy was key. I replaced the outer-opening hatch and its bulky lock-EVAC apparatus with a steel-alloy plug that had a big window and self-sealing bib. In the vacuum of space, the air pressure inside the *Alan Bean* would force the hatch closed and airtight. Simple physics.

Announce that you are flying to the moon and everyone assumes you mean to land on it—to plant the flag, kangaroo-hop in one-sixth gravity, and collect rocks to bring home, none of which we were going to do. We were flying *around* the moon. *Landing* is a whole different ball game, and as for stepping out onto the surface? Hell, choosing which of the four of us would get out first and become the thirteenth person to leave bootprints up there would have led to so much bad blood that our crew would have broken up long before T minus ten seconds and counting. And let's face it, that crewman would have been Anna anyway.

Assembling the three stages of the good ship *Alan Bean* took two days. We packed granola bars and water in squeeze-top bottles, then pumped in the liquid oxygen for the two booster stages and the hypergolic chemicals for the one-shot firing of the translunar motor, the minirocket that would fling us to our lunar rendezvous. Most of Oxnard came around to Steve Wong's driveway to ogle the *Alan Bean*, not a one of them knowing who Alan Bean was or why we'd named the rocket ship after him. The kids begged for peeks inside the spacecraft, but we didn't have the insurance. What are you waiting for? You gonna blast off soon? To every knothead who would listen, I explained launch windows and trajectories, showing them on my MoonFaze app (free) how we had to intersect the moon's orbit at exactly the right moment or lunar gravity would ... Ah, hell! There's the moon! Point your rocket at it and put on a show!

———

Twenty-four seconds after clearing the tower, our first stage was burning all stops, and the Max-Q app ($0.99) showed us pulling 11.8 times our weight at sea level, not that we needed iPhones to tell us this. We ... were ... fighting ... for breath ... with Anna ... screaming ... "Get off ... my chest!" But no one was on her chest. She was, in fact, sitting on me, crushing me like a lap dance from an offensive lineman. *Kaboom* went MDash's dynamite bolts, and the second stage fired, as programmed. A minute later, dust, loose change, and a couple of ballpoint pens floated up from behind our seats, signaling, Hey! We'd achieved orbit!

Weightlessness is as much fun as you can imagine, but troublesome for some spacegoers, who for no apparent reason spend their first hours up there upchucking, as if they'd overdone it at the prelaunch reception. It's one of those facts never made public by NASA PR or in astronaut memoirs. After three revolutions of the Earth, as we finished running the checklist for our translunar injection, Steve Wong's tummy finally settled down. Somewhere over Africa, we opened the valves in the translunar motor, the hypergolics worked their chemical magic, and—*voosh*—we were hauling the mail to Moonberry RFD, our escape velocity a crisp seven miles per second, Earth getting smaller and smaller in the window.

The Americans who went to the moon before us had computers so primitive that they couldn't get email or use Google to settle arguments. The iPads we took had something like 70 billion times the capacity of those Apollo-era dial-ups and were mucho handy, especially during all the downtime on our long haul. MDash used his to watch the final season of *Girls*. We took hundreds of selfies with the Earth in the window and, plinking a Ping-Pong ball off the center seat, played a tableless table-tennis tournament, which was won by Anna. I worked the attitude jets in pulse mode, yawing and pitching the *Alan Bean* for views of some of the few stars that were visible in the naked sunlight: Antares, Nunki, the globular cluster NGC 6333—none of which twinkle when you're up there among 'em.

The big event of translunar space is crossing the equigravisphere, a boundary as invisible as the International Date Line but, for the *Alan Bean*, the Rubicon. On this side of the EQS, Earth's gravity was tugging us back, slowing our progress, bidding us to return home to the life-affirming benefits of water, atmosphere, and a magnetic field. Once we crossed, the moon grabbed hold, wrapping us in her ancient silvery embrace, whispering to us to *hurry hurry hurry* to wink in wonder at her magnificent desolation.

At the exact moment that we reached the threshold, Anna awarded us origami cranes, made out of aluminum foil, which we taped onto our shirts like pilots' wings. I put the *Alan Bean* into a Passive Thermal Control BBQ roll, our moonbound ship rotating on an invisible spit so as to distribute the solar heat. Then we dimmed the lights, taped a sweatshirt over the window to keep the sunlight from sweeping across the cabin, and slept, each of us curled up in a comfortable nook of our little rocket ship.

When I tell people that I've seen the far side of the moon, they often say, "You mean the dark side," as though I'd fallen under the spell of Darth Vader or Pink Floyd. In fact, both sides of the moon get the same amount of sunshine, just on different shifts.

Because the moon was waxing gibbous to the folks back home, we had to wait out the shadowed portion on the other side. In that darkness, with no sunlight and the moon blocking the Earth's reflection, I pulsed the *Alan Bean* around so that our window faced outbound for a view of the Infinite Time-Space Continuum that was worthy of IMAX: unblinking stars in subtle hues of red-orange-yellow-green-blue-indigo-violet, our galaxy stretching as far as our eyes were wide, a diamond-blue carpet against a black that would have been terrifying had it not been so mesmerizing.

Then there was light, snapping on as if MDash had flipped a switch. I tweaked the controls, and there below us was the surface of the moon. Wow. Gorgeous in a way that strained any use of the word, a rugged place that produced oohs and awe. The LunaTicket app ($0.99) showed us traversing south to north, but we were mentally lost in space, the surface as chaotic as a windblown, gray-capped bay, until I matched the Poincaré impact basin with the "This Is Our Moon" guide on my Kobo. The *Alan Bean* was soaring 153 kilometers high (95.06 miles *Americanus*), at a speed faster than that of a bullet from a gun, and the moon was slipping by so fast that we were running out of far side. Oresme Crater had white, finger-painted streaks. Heaviside showed rills and depressions, like river washouts. We split Dufay right in half, a flyover from its six to its twelve, the rim a steep, sharp razor. Mare Moscoviense was far to port, a miniversion of the Ocean of Storms, where four and a half decades ago the real Alan Bean spent two days, hiking, collecting rocks, snapping photos. Lucky man.

Our brains could take in only so much, so our iPhones did the recording, and I stopped calling out the sights, though I did recognize Campbell and D'Alembert, large craters linked by the smaller Slipher, just as we were about to head home over the moon's north pole. Steve Wong had cued up a certain musical track for what would be Earthrise but had to reboot the Bluetooth on Anna's Jambox and was nearly late for his cue. MDash yelled, "Hit PLAY, hit PLAY!" just as a blue-and-white patch of life—a slice of all that we have made of ourselves, all that we have ever been—pierced the black cosmos above the sawtooth horizon. I was expecting something classical, Franz Joseph Haydn or George Harrison, but "The Circle of Life," from *The Lion King*, scored our home planet's rise over the plaster-of-Paris moon. Really? A Disney show tune? But, you know, that rhythm and that chorus and the double meaning of the lyrics caught me right in the throat, and I choked up. Tears popped off my face and joined the others' tears, which were floating around the *Alan Bean*. Anna gave me a hug like I was still her boyfriend. We cried. We all cried. You'd have done the same.

Coasting home was one fat anticlimax, despite the (never spoken) possibility of our burning up on reentry like an obsolete spy satellite circa 1962. Of course, we were all chuffed, as the English say, that we'd made the trek and maxed out the memory on our iPhones with iPhotos. But questions arose about what we were going to do upon our return, apart from making some bitchin' posts on Instagram. If I ever run into Al Bean again, I'll ask him what life has been like for him since he twice crossed the equigravisphere. Does he suffer melancholia on a quiet afternoon, as the world spins on automatic? Will I occasionally get the blues, because nothing holds a wonder equal to splitting Dufay down the middle? TBD, I suppose.

"Whoa! Kamchatka!" Anna called out as our heat shield expired into millions of grain-size comets. We were arcing down over the Arctic Circle, gravity once again commanding that we who went up must come down. When the chute pyros shot off, the *Alan Bean* jolted our bones, causing the Jambox to lose its duct-tape purchase and conk MDash in the forehead. By the time we splashed down off Oahu, a trail of blood was running from the ugly gash between his eyebrows. Anna tossed him her bandanna, because guess what no one had thought to take around the moon? To anyone reading this with plans to imitate us: Band-Aids.

At Stable One—that is, bobbing in the ocean, rather than having disintegrated into plasma—MDash tripped the "Rescue us!" flares that he'd rigged under the Parachute Jettison System. I opened the pressure-equalizing valve a tad early, and—oops—noxious fumes from the excess-fuel burnoff were sucked into the capsule, making us even queasier, what with the mal de mer.

Once the cabin pressure was at the same psi as outside, Steve Wong was able to uncork the main hatch, and the Pacific Ocean breeze whooshed in, as soft as a kiss from Mother Earth, but owing to what turned out to be a huge design flaw, that same Pacific Ocean began to join us in our spent little craft. The *Alan Bean*'s second historic voyage was going to be to Davy Jones's locker. Anna, thinking fast, held aloft our Apple products, but Steve Wong lost his Samsung (the Galaxy! Ha!), which disappeared into the lower equipment bay as the rising seawater bade us exit.

The day boat from the Kahala Hilton, filled with curious

snorkelers, pulled us out of the water, the English speakers on board telling us that we smelled horrid, the foreigners giving us a wide berth.

After a shower and a change of clothes, I was ladling fruit salad from a decorative dugout canoe at the hotel buffet table when a lady asked me if I had been in that thing that came down out of the sky. Yes, I told her, I had gone all the way to the moon and returned safely to the surly bonds of Earth. Just like Alan Bean.

"Who's Alan Bean?" she said.

Our Town Today with Hank Fiset

AT LOOSE IN THE BIG APPLE

NEW YORK CITY! On my own for three days as my wife let me tag along as she celebrated her Twenty-fifth College Reunion with her Sorority Sisters of Gotta Getta Guy. I had not been to the isle of Manhattan since *Cats* was on B'way and hotel TVs were not high-def.

* * *

SO, WHAT'S *NOO* in Noo Yawk? Too much, if you have fond memories of the place, but little if the Naked City leaves you feeling, well, *naked.* I think NYC comes off way better on TV and in the movies, when a taxi is just a whistle away and superheroes save the day. In the real world (ours) every day in Gotham is a little like the Macy's Thanksgiving Day Parade and a lot like Baggage Claim after a long, crowded flight.

* * *

HITTING THE STREETS of the Big Town ASAP is a requirement, especially when the Mrs. takes the family credit history off to all those big stores with one name: Bergdorf's, Goodman's, Saks, Bloomie's, not a one of which is any better than our own Henworthy's, which has been open at Seventh and

Sycamore since 1952. For my money (a dwindling supply) those fancy places charge too much for just shopping bags. But give NY, NY, this—walking those streets is a show unto its own. I mean, where is everyone *going*?

* * *

CENTRAL PARK, MAYBE? That big rectangle of greenery has more musicians than the East Valley High School Marching Band, but they're all solo acts. Those sax blowers, horn players, violinists, accordion squeezers, and at least one Japanese samisen musician are all in competition with the fellow starving musical artist who performs a few yards away, making for a funky fugue that mars the relative peace of the park. Add in hundreds of serious joggers, power walkers, cyclists, an equal number of lollygaggers, tourists on rental bikes, tricycles towing passengers, and the horses and buggies that make the park smell of a petting zoo,

and you'll yearn for our own Spitz Riverside Park, with less postcard views, true, but at least our Tri-Cities squirrels look a lot happier. On foot, you cross the park from the East Side streets tall with former tycoon mansions to the West Side avenues jammed with Starbucks, the Gap, and Bed Bath & Beyond. Had I just stumbled into our own Hillcrest Mall in Pearman? Looked like it, but where was the convenient parking?

* * *

NOT WITHOUT MAGIC is Metropolis, a.k.a. New York City, I admit. When the sun drops behind the towers and stops baking the pavement, it's nice to cool one's heels at a curbside table with a cocktail in your fist. That's when Yankee-Town has the charm of our own Country Market Patio Bar and Grill. I sat and sipped and watched as a world of Knickerbocker oddballs strolled by. I saw a man with a cat on his shoulders,

European tourists in the tightest pants imaginable, a team of firemen pull up in an engine, go into a high-rise apartment, only to come out later talking about a bad smoke detector, a man rolling a homemade telescope up the street, the actor Kiefer Sutherland walk by, and a woman with a big white bird on her shoulder. Hope she avoided the guy with the cat.

* * *

A CAESAR SALAD is the true test of any hotel restaurant—write that down! Our own Sun Garden/Red Lion Inn at the airport serves a beauty, but at a Times Square eatery—pretheater dinner with the Wife and still-foxy coeds—my salad was limp and the dressing too tart. *Hell, Caesar!* After I picked up the check, the girls headed off to see the B'way production of *Chicago*—like the movie, but without the close-ups. I don't know much about musical theater, but I bet cash money what the girls saw that night was not any better than the Meadow Hills Community College Drama Department's production of *Roaring-Twenty-Somethings,* which went to the American College Theater Festival last year. Does the Great White Way beat out the best of the Tri-Cities? Not according to this reporter.

* * *

IF YOU'RE HUNGRY and crave a frankfurter, they're for sale all over Manhattan—on street corners, every few yards in the park, in subway stations, with papaya juice. None of them beat a tube steak from Butterworth's Hot Dog Emporium on Grand Lake Drive. A bagel in Manhattan is the stuff of theologians, but Crane's West Side Cafeteria serves up a heavenly leavened bun to all in the Tri-Cities. Much is made of N'york, N'york–style pizza, but I fork my money over for a slice of Lamonica's Neopolitan, and, yes, they deliver within a ten-mile circle of each of their fourteen locations. And speaking of Italian food, Anthony's Italian Cellar in Harbor View has all the authenticity of any joint in Little Italy without the mobster rubouts.

* * *

ANYTHING NEW YORK has that we lack in our own Tri-Cities? Not so much, since TV gives us all the sports and media in the world and the Internet provides all else. I admit the multitude of museums on Manhattan is fine, dandy, impressive, et cetera. Being able to walk into, say, an ancient temple from Dendur or a hall full of assembled dinosaur bones makes for a great excursion, even when you have to share it with schoolkids from all over the state and tourists from all over the world. I had a whole day of museums when the women booked facials, massages, and pedicures—a.k.a. hangover cures. I saw paintings I will never understand,

an "Installation" that was nothing more than a room filled with torn-up carpet samples, and a sculpture that looked like a huge, rusted, dented refrigerator. *Ars Gratia Artis* (Art for Art's Sake), moaned the MGM lion.

* * *

MY FINAL MUSEUM was the place for Modern art, where I saw a movie that was nothing more than time passing— really, a lot of clocks ticking and people looking at their watches. I gave it ten minutes. Upstairs, there was a blank canvas with a knife slice down its middle. Another canvas was colored a light blue at the bottom that became a dark blue at the top. In the stairwell, an actual helicopter was hanging from the ceiling, a whirlybird frozen in flight. Up the steps a pair of Italian typewriters, large and small versions of the same model, were kept behind glass as if they were studded with valuable gems but they weren't!

Nor were the machines more than fifty years old. I couldn't help but think the Tri-Cities could put together a collection of used typewriters and charge admission. The now vacant Baxter's Ham Factory on Wyatt Boulevard is available. Anyone civic-minded enough to get cracking on that?

Who's Who?

O n a Monday morning in early November of 1978, as
she had been every day for the past six weeks, Sue
Gliebe was up and out of the apartment before her roommates were awake. Rebecca was asleep, eight feet off the floor
in the loft bed in the living room, and Shelley, probably, was
still conked out behind the locked door of the apartment's
single bedroom.

Sue had showered quickly and quietly in the half tub with
the rubber hose running up from the faucet, the dribbling
water a weak stream that was alternately tepid and then as
hot as the surface of the planet Mercury. Since she had come
to New York, she had yet to feel truly clean and her scalp had
begun to itch. She dressed in the fog of the tiny bathroom,
slipped on her shoes from under the living room sofa, where
she slept, strapped her big leather purse crossways from
shoulder to opposite hip, then grabbed the umbrella she had
bought on Friday. Another storm was due, the news said, and
Sue was prepared; she had already paid five of her dollars to

one of the many men who appeared with boxes of umbrellas the moment the clouds grew thick with rain. As quietly as possible, Sue exited through the front door, making sure the lock clicked behind her. She had once failed to confirm that click and Shelley had angrily lectured her on the dangers of an unlocked apartment door in New York City in 1978. No click was a major no-no.

Her roommates had come to view her as an unexorcised poltergeist, one that had to be negotiated around. Then again, they were not really her roommates but her hosts, making Sue feel as welcome as an abdominal parasite. Rebecca had been so friendly the last summer when she was working costumes for the Arizona Civic Light Opera, and Sue, a local hire, was playing three featured roles. They were gal pals, then. On days when her duties were slack, Rebecca swam in the pool at the Gliebe family home and partied with the company on the Gliebe patio. She had offered Sue her couch for "a while" whenever—if ever—she came to New York City. When Sue showed up with three suitcases, eight hundred dollars in savings, and a dream, Rebecca's *actual* roommate, Shelley, nodded her assent to the deal with a "yeah, okay." But that was seven weeks ago and Sue was still spending every night on the couch in the small living room. The vibes in the one-bedroom apartment just off Upper Broadway had gone from benign acceptance to Arctic-level iciness. Rebecca wanted Sue out; Shelley wanted her dead. Sue hoped to purchase extra sofa time and goodwill with contributions of fifty dollars to the rent as well as providing milk, Tropicana orange juice, and, once, a thing called blackout cake that Shelley ate for breakfast. Such gestures were not so much appreciated as expected.

What could Sue do? Where could Sue go? She was hunting for her own New York City apartment every single day, but the agencies named Apartment Finders and Westside Spaces had "listings" that were in dark, urine-stained tenements where no one answered the buzzer, or were no longer available, or never existed in the first place. Shelley told her to post a Need a Roommate notice on the board at Actors' Equity, but Sue confessed that she had yet to join the union— she couldn't until she had an acting job. Shelley gave her a half-lidded look of supreme disappointment and another "yeah, okay," then added, "Next time you go to ShopRite, get a big can of Chock Full O'Nuts, please." In this eighth week— the start of her third month on the isle of Manhattan—the bundle of Arizona talent who had played Maria in *West Side Story* (just last season at the ACLO) was prone to weeping at night, silently, in her bedroll on the couch, in the diamond-shaped silhouettes made by the window's security gates (were such things actually burglarproof?). On the subway, which cost her fifty cents a ride, she often fought back tears, worried that someone would see a pretty young girl undone by her struggles and, well, rob her or worse. For Sue, moving to New York was an act of faith, faith in herself, in her talent, and in the promise of the city that never slept. It was supposed to be an adventure, like something out of the movies, where she would come out of a stage door after a performance and kiss a handsome sailor on shore leave, or a TV show like *That Girl*, where she'd have an apartment with a big kitchen and louvered shutters and a boyfriend who worked for *Newsview* magazine. But New York was not cooperating. How could things be going so sadly for Sue Gliebe, who was the very definition of a triple threat; she could sing, dance, and act! Her parents had recognized her raw talent when she was a little girl! She had starred in all the high school plays! She had been selected from the chorus at the Civic Light Opera to become their lead actress for three seasons running! She had done *High Button Shoes* with Monty Hall, the host of TV's *Let's Make a Deal*! She had had a going away party with a big banner reading ON TO BROADWAY!

So why was New York, New York, making her cry? Her first night in the city, when Rebecca took her via the bus to see Lincoln Center, Sue had looked at all the locals along upper Broadway and actually asked, "Where is everyone going?" She now knew that everyone was going everywhere. This morning, she was going to the bank, the Manufacturers Hanover branch where she had opened an account five weeks before. From behind a Plexiglas (bulletproof) wall, a disinterested female teller slid a ten-dollar bill, a fiver, and five ones through a slot, leaving it to Sue to note that her savings were now down to exactly $564. She had spent more than $200 in New York City and had nothing to show for it but a five-buck umbrella, a blue one with a telescoping handle.

From the bank, Sue went to a donut shop for one plain cake—which was the least expensive—and a coffee with sugar and half-and-half. That was breakfast. She ate standing at a counter sticky from bits of sugar glaze and spilled java. Barely fortified, she walked to the office of Apartment

Finders on Columbus Avenue, which was up a wide flight of stairs and above a Hunan Chinese restaurant. The posted listings on the wall had not changed since Saturday, but Sue searched the bulletin board anyway, for a diamond chipped off a ring, for an overlooked gem, for a place with her name on it. Apartment Finders had cost her fifty dollars a month, money she might as well have used to light candles. She would come back later in the day, when, supposedly, new listings were posted, but she already knew her hopes were sure to be dashed again.

Sue decided she was adapting to Gotham, because she turned on her heel and headed back over to Broadway with an agenda for the day. She would not blow time by idly walking in Central Park, with its weedy lawns and cracked benches, dirty sandlots and pathways littered with discarded coffee cups, spent condoms, and other trash. She would not filter through the record stores and bookstores without buying any of the titles. She would not spend money on the trade papers—*Show Biz*, *Back Stage*, or *Daily Variety*—looking for notices of Equity Principal Interviews or auditions for Non-Equity Showcases. Not today. Today, she was going to the Public Library, the famous building at Forty-Second and Fifth, the landmark building with the stone lions in front.

Two blocks from the Eighty-Sixth Street subway station, the rain started. Sue halted, reached for her umbrella, pushed the button on the telescoping handle, but the handle did not telescope. She pulled on the fabric of the thing, forcing it open, but in doing so bent some of the spokes. When she tried to slide the plastic knob up the shaft, the umbrella bent like the leg of a card table. She shook the umbrella and tried forcing the knob, but only half of the cover deployed. With the rain getting heavy, she recocked and again tried to get the umbrella open, but it inverted into a scoop and more of the spokes disconnected like severed ribs.

Giving up, she tried to jam the worthless skeleton into an overflowing trash bin at Broadway and Eighty-Eighth, but the umbrella seemed to fight back, refusing to go in with the other garbage. It took her four tries before it stayed put.

Sue hurried to the subway station. Her hair was dripping from the rain as she stood in line at the kiosk to purchase the two tokens she would need for the day's travels.

The local trains were delayed. A flood on the uptown tracks. The crowd grew on the platform, large enough that Sue was edged ever closer to the yellow safety line. One bump and she could have fallen onto the tracks. Forty minutes later, she was standing in a subway car so crowded the riders were crammed against each other, their body heat making steam rise from their heavy, rain-soaked coats. The car was so stuffy and hot Sue began sweating. At Columbus Circle the car stopped and did not move for ten minutes, the doors jammed shut, preventing escape. Finally, at Times Square, Sue pushed herself out of the car and into the stream of people who had managed to find the stairs. She tramped up and up and through the turnstiles, then up more stairs and out into the chaos of the Crossroads of the World, where everybody was going everywhere.

Times Square was an exterior version of the station below—filthy, flooded, and overcharged with people. Sue had learned a primary lesson since her arrival in the city, to *keep moving*, to walk with purpose even when she had none, especially along Forty-Second Street, dodging the human debris that collected there for the drugs, the porn, and, in the rain, to peddle five-dollar umbrellas.

She'd navigated the area before, seeking appointments at the lesser talent agencies, those with offices close by the big X where Broadway crossed Seventh Avenue. She had been surprised to find normal people at normal desks doing normal business just floors above the hissing concrete of Times Square. She had no luck with any of the agents—she never made it past the outer offices—so was reduced to leaving her résumé with secretaries who would say, "Yeah, okay," in a tone remarkably similar to her temporary cohost Shelley's.

On this Monday, her agenda *was* her résumé.

During her last month in Scottsdale, Sue had done two TV commercials for Valley Home Furniture, sweeping her arms wide, exclaiming, "Every room, every style, every budget!" Then, for four weekends, she had acted at the Autumnal Renaissance Faire, quoting Shakespeare as a Lusty Wench for thirty dollars a day. She had added those credits to her résumé with a ballpoint pen, but she knew it looked, well, *amateurish.* So she was going to retype the whole thing, get an offset printer to make a hundred copies, then staple one each to the backs of her head shots, the photo that made her look like Cheryl Ladd from *Charlie's Angels* but with real cleavage.

The problem was that she had no typewriter, nor did Rebecca. When Sue asked Shelley if she had a machine she could use, she didn't say no but did tell her, "They rent them at the library." That's why Sue Gliebe was umbrellaless, navigating eastward on Forty-Second Street, passing a stoned-looking teenager who had pulled his penis out of his pants and was pissing as he stumbled along. Not a single person made note of the sight.

The exact moment Sue discovered that the Main Library was closed on Mondays, a flash of lightning bleached the scraped sky of Mid-Manhattan. She stood at the side entrance to the landmark building, its door locked, unable to comprehend the meaning of those three simple words: *Closed on Mondays*. Just as a roll of thunder outblared the honking horns of traffic, she lost the battle against tears, the collective disappointments simply too much: New York City roommates were not friendly soul sisters; Central Park was a place of naked trees, unusable benches, and spent rubbers; windows had security gates that locked rapists out and victims in; no cute sailors were waiting to meet a girl and get a kiss. No. In New York City real estate parlors took your money and lied to you, drug addicts relieved themselves in plain sight, and the Public Library was closed on Mondays.

Sue was crying, right there on Forty-Second Street between Fifth Avenue and Sixth or, according to the map, the Avenue of the Americas. Sobbing, gasping, tears, the big show. As many people as had made note of the stoned guy's penis stopped to help or even look at the girl who was having so terrible a day that she was weeping aloud in public. Until . . .

"Sue Gliebe!" a man's voice called out. "You little titmouse!"

Bob Roy was the only man in the world who called her a

titmouse. Bob Roy had been the general business manager of the ACLO but lived in New York City. He was a Theater Professional contracted for the season and a homosexual. He had once been an actor on Broadway and he'd done commercials in the 1960s but went into theater management for steady work. Running the Civic Light Opera out west was a summer camp for him—he did it every year—and took his duties a little less seriously than he did laughing and gossiping. Bob Roy seemed to know everything about the Theater, and if you worked in his company, if he signed your paychecks, he either loved you or loathed you. Your treatment completely depended on which way his judgmental wind blew.

He loved Sue Gliebe from the moment he saw her at a dress rehearsal for *Brigadoon* in the summer of '76. He delighted in her youth, her halo of honey-blond hair, her clear eyes full of good nature, and her conscientious work ethic. He adored her for showing up on time, knowing her lines, and having ideas for her onstage business. He was fascinated by her tanned body and firm boobs and her lack of self-consciousness, ego, and spite. Every straight man—all seven of them—at the ACLO wanted to fuck her, but she wasn't that way. Most actresses craved such adoration and demanded the largest dressing room, but Sue Gliebe wanted nothing more than to be onstage. After three seasons, she had not changed a whit and Bob Roy loved her all the more.

He was in a taxi at the curb, the window rolled down with the rain falling between them. "Get in this cab right now!" he ordered.

He slid over to make room for her and the cab moved

along. "I'd have bet on seeing Eva Gabor on Forty-Second Street before you. Are you *crying*?"

"No. Yes. Oh, *Bobby!*"

Sue explained: She had been in the city for two months, sleeping on Rebecca's couch. Her savings were running out. No agents would give her the time of day. She saw a man pissing in the street. She was crying now, in particular, because the only movies that told the truth about New York City were about needle parks and taxi drivers on killing sprees. Bob Roy laughed out loud! "You've been in *Noo Yawk* for two months and haven't called me? Naughty, Sue. Naughty, naughty."

"I didn't have your number."

"What were you doing in Slime Square?"

"Going to the library."

"To check out the latest Nancy Drew mystery? I'd have guessed you'd read them all by now."

"They have typewriters. I need to create a new résumé."

"Titmouse," Bob said. "Start with a new *you* first. How about a cup of tea or hot Postum? Whatever soothed Baby Sue growing up in Indian Country."

The taxi took them to Bob's apartment downtown—to a terrible neighborhood where all the buildings were six-story tenements and the sidewalks were lined with beaten-up trash cans. He gave the driver six dollars and asked for no change. She followed him out into the rain, up the stoop, through the heavy main door, then four flights up a narrow, zigzagging stairway to apartment 4D. He needed keys for three different locks on the door.

From the dingy, dimly lit hallway, the walls more dirty gray than the original green, the floor a maze of broken and mismatched tiles, Sue stepped into a haven that smelled of candles and lemon-scented dish soap, a cabinet of curiosities, one of which was the bathtub smack dab in the middle of the small kitchen. Bob Roy's railroad flat was four tight, connected rooms, each stuffed with koombies, knickknacks, doodads, furniture pieces of any style, shelves, books, photos in frames, trophies bought from flea markets, old records, small lamps, and calendars from decades before. "I know," he said. "It looks like I sell magic potions in here, like I'm an animated badger from a Disney cartoon." He lit a burner on the stove with a huge kitchen match, then filled a shiny, Olde English–style kettle with water from the tap. As he prepared cups on a tray he said, "Tea in minutes, titmouse. Make a home for yourself."

The room off the kitchen was really a hallway, a narrow passage through treasures and castoffs. The sitting room featured three large chairs of different eras, one a La-Z-Boy, each covered with a colorful throw of some kind. A circular coffee table, nearly too large for the square space, was covered with stacks of books, a cigar box full of sharpened pencils, a vase with an artificial orchid, and two assembled toy bugs from the Cootie game, posed like they were either fighting or mating. The rain was still coming down hard outside, but window curtains that could have come from an antebellum mansion muffled the roar of the storm. The last room in the railroad flat was Bob's bedroom, most of it taken up by a four-poster bed.

"I can never move out of this place, it would take me years to pack," Bob called from the kitchen, only eight feet away. "Turn on the radio, would you?"

"If I can find it," Sue said and heard his laugh in response. She had to focus out so much clutter, like she was in a Lost and Found Forgotten by Time, until she saw it. The radio was a blond-wood-paneled box as big as an ice chest, with circular knobs like thick poker chips and four lines of numbers for different frequencies. She turned the ON/OFF VOLUME until its satisfying *kock* was so loud Bob heard it from the kitchen.

"The tubes have to warm up," he said.

"Does this get shortwave from the Soviet Union?"

"How'd you know?"

"My grandma had a radio like this."

"So did mine! In fact, that's it."

Bob came in with a tray on which were two cups, a pitcher of milk, a sugar bowl with a painted honeybee on the lid, and a plate stacked with Oreo cookies. "Feel free to take off your coat, unless you like being damp." Orchestral music came from the radio just as the teakettle sounded its harmonic *toot*.

Sweet tea with milk, three Oreos, and Bob Roy's snug and cozy flat helped Sue breathe deeply for the first time in months. She let out a sigh as big as a cresting wave and leaned back into a chair so soft it put the *z* in *cozy*.

"Okay," Bob said. "Tell me everything."

She opened up about, well, *everything*, cued by Bob's sympathy. He uttered his support at every story, every anecdote: New York was the only place for Sue to be! Shelley and her "yeah, okay" attitude were to be expected from such a *see-you-next-Tuesday!* The subway was survivable as long as you never made eye contact with anyone. You found an apartment by reading the Rental classifieds in the *Times* and *The Village Voice*, but you had to get them early, at seven in the morning, and then you had to hightail it to the apartments with a bag of donuts because the super would always open up for a pretty girl who shared her donuts. From there, they moved back in time, reminiscing about the summer seasons in Arizona, comparing the backstage gossip to that from the front office, the love affairs gone horrible, and how Sue thought Monty Hall was a solid professional. Bob spilled his tea, laughing.

"Have you had any lunch?"

"No. I was going to treat myself to a slice of pizza pie." At half a dollar per wedge, pizza had become Sue's standby meal at midday.

"Let me go out for deli. You strip out of that uniform of yours and take a hot bath. I'll leave you a robe I stole from a spa in the desert, then we'll eat like middle class Jews."

In the kitchen, he removed a large butcher board that covered the bathtub. Why a tub was in the kitchen had something to do with the original plumbing of the old building. He turned on the water, so hot plumes of steam hazed the security-gated window, and laid the robe across a chair. A delicate wicker basket held scented soap, shampoo, conditioner, an organic sponge, and a pitcher to fill with water and rinse with.

"I'll take my time. You soak." Bob locked two of the front door locks behind him.

After the weak, abbreviated showers uptown, Sue relished the feel of hot water on her skin and the pouring of water over her head. It was funny, taking a bath in a kitchen like this, but she was alone, the bath was like the hot tub on the Gliebe family patio, and Sue scrubbed, rinsed, and soaked her way to being truly, wonderfully *clean*. She was still soaking when the front door locks were opened and Bob returned carrying a large bag of deli.

"Still naked, I see." Bob didn't bother averting his eyes, and Sue didn't mind. If "backstage was no place for modesty," as they said in the Theater, Bob Roy's kitchen was no place for blushing.

Sue's now pale limbs were swimming in the man-size terry-cloth robe as she sat at the coffee table, running a comb through her damp hair. Bob set down some half sandwiches, small cartons of soup, coleslaw, pickle wedges, and cans of what was called seltzer and, over lunch, they talked about movies and plays. Bob said he could get her free tickets to the lousy shows on Broadway and cheap seats for the hits, so there would be no more evenings in New York with nothing to do but be unpopular on Rebecca's couch. He'd call around to his friends for tips on agents who could arrange a meeting or two, no promises beyond that. He knew a few rehearsal pianists who would help with her audition numbers, with sheet music, transposed for her key. "Okay, titmouse," Bob said, clapping rye crumbs from his fingers. "Let me see this résumé of yours."

Sue pulled the old version out of her purse as Bob grabbed

a pencil. After a quick once-over, he drew a big *X* on the paper with a sigh. "Standard. So standard."

"What's wrong with it?" Sue was hurt. She had worked hard on the thing. Her stage career was on that piece of paper. All the plays she had done in high school, including the one-acts, asterisked with *Thespian Society Award*. Every performance she had ever given at the ACLO, from member of the chorus right up to last year's turn as Nellie Forbush in *South Pacific*. Five seasons and eighteen musicals! The productions at the Gaslamp Playhouse Dinner Theater—Emily in *Our Town* and the Ensemble in *Zoo Story*. The Narration she did for the Diabetes Walk-a-thon public service message. Every performance Sue Gliebe had ever given was listed on that résumé.

"As we jaded queens say, 'Nobody gives a shit, honey.'" Bob stood up and went into his bedroom. From under his bed he pulled out an old typewriter protected by a clear plastic dustcover. "This beast is so heavy. I really should keep it out. Make space on the table, would you?" Sue moved away the deli leftovers and a stack of books.

Bob's typewriter was nearly as big as his grandmother's radio, a black metal antique, fitting for an apartment crammed with old, peculiar things. The typewriter was a Royal, with glass sections on the sides, like opera windows for any titmouse that might take up residence among the keys.

"Does that still work?" Sue asked.

"It's a typewriter, child. Ribbon. Oil. Paper. Happy fingers. That's all it needs. *This*, however . . ." He disdainfully picked up the record of Sue's life's work, holding it with two fingers like it was rancid melon rind. Then he grabbed a pencil and used it as a pointer. "You list only the roles you've played, not the high school you went to or the Gasbag Amateur Play School Diner. The only pro credit you have is the Arizona CLO, so you can't lie about those credits. You put it at the top in big capital letters, then list the best plays and the best roles first, not in the order you performed them. If you were in the chorus, name your part like 'Ellen Craymore' or 'Candy Beaver' toward the bottom. If anyone questions you, then say you were in the chorus. These other roles? In high school and all that?"

"Yes?"

"They go under the heading 'Regional Theater.' Embellish. Don't tell them the plays were one-acts. Don't tell them you won any trophies. Don't tell them they only ran two weekends. The play. The role. You were a working actress in the Region of Pile-of-Rocks, Arizona, and you have the credits to prove it."

"Isn't that lying?"

"They don't care." Bob took his pencil to the résumé again. "Oh, look! You've done commercials! Valley Furniture! The disease of the month! No, no, no. You put right here, 'Commercials on Request.' They will see that you have done commercials but will request not a single one."

"Really?"

"Trust Bobby Roy, Sue. The great ones all do. Now, this last bit, this sad paragraph listing your *Special Skills*. This is bullshit to anyone on the other side of the casting desk. Notice I did not say 'couch.'"

"What if they're looking for special skills?"

"They ask you. But this list? Guitar. You know three chords, right? You can juggle. Three oranges for a few seconds, right? You roller-skate. What kid doesn't? You can ski and ride a bike and skateboard. BFD! Did you actually put *Sign Language* here?"

"I learned some for Tribal Heritage Day. This means 'awkward.'"

Bob gave the one bit of sign language he knew. "This means 'bullshit.' Understand that your résumé will receive all of five nanoseconds of attention. Casting people look at your picture, then at you to see if it matches. Are you actually a girl? Do you have blond hair? You sporting a rack of any significance? If you're what they are looking for, they turn over to your résumé, scan your credits and your lies, then scribble down this magic word: *callback*."

Bob rolled paper into the old Royal, adjusted the margins and tabs, and within minutes had typed out a crisp, clear, and clean résumé that made Sue look like she was as experienced a dreamer as ever hopped a bus to the big city. She could boast of thirty roles. The one thing missing from the paper was her name at the top.

"Let's think about this for a moment," Bob said. "Over more tea." He removed the deli tray to the kitchen and lit another big match for the burner. "I'd get out more Oreos but then we'd just eat them."

"Think about what?" Sue studied her new professional call sheet. She liked herself more because of what Bobby had typed.

"Have you ever thought of changing your name?"

"My real name is Susan Noreen Gliebe. I've always been just Sue."

"Joan Crawford had always been Lucy LeSueur. Leroy Scherer was called Junior till he became Rock Hudson. You ever hear of Frannie Gumm?"

"Who?"

Bob sang the opening lines of "Over the Rainbow."

"Judy Garland?"

"*Pal of Frances* lacks the *panache* of *friend of Dorothy*, doesn't it?"

"My parents will be disappointed if I don't use my real name."

"Disappointing your parents is the first thing to do when you come to New York." When the kettle sounded off, Bob refilled the teapot sitting beside the Royal. "And say you make it big on the Great White Way—which you will. Do you really want to see *that* name in lights: Sue Gliebe?"

Sue blushed, not out of embarrassment at such praise, but because, deep inside her, she knew she had a future as an actress. She *wanted* to be big. Yes, as big as Frances Gumm.

Bobby poured more tea in both cups. "And how do you pronounce that? 'Gleeb'? 'Glee-bee'? 'Glibe'?" He pantomimed a big, fake yawn. You know what Tammy Grimes's stage name was? Tammy Grimes." He fake-yawned even wider.

"How about ... Susan Noreen?" Sue could imagine that name up in lights, no problem.

Bob flicked the paper in the Royal typewriter, snapping the new résumé with his finger. "This is a birth certificate for the new Sue. If you could go back in time and pick a brand-new name for yourself and your ma and pa, what would that name be? Elizabeth St. John? Marilyn Conner-Bradley? Holly Woodandvine?"

"I can call myself something like *that*?"

"We'll check with the union, but yes. Who do you want to be, titmouse?"

Sue held her tea. There was a name she'd once dreamed of having, in junior high school, when she sang in a folk group for her chapter of Young Life. Everyone was making up groovy names like Rainbow Spiritchaser. She came up with hers, imagining the name on the cover of her first LP.

"Joy Makepeace." She said it out loud. Bobby's face showed no reaction.

"Heap big trouble with that'um smoke signal," he said, "unless you have some Native American DNA in the Gliebe bloodline."

So it went as the afternoon wore on. Bobby came up with a constant stream of stage names, the best of which was Suzannah Woods, the worst being Cassandra O'Day. The Oreos had come back out and were now all eaten. Sue kept working the Joy angle. Joy Friendly. Joy Roarke. Joy Lovecraft.

"Joy Spilledmilk," Bobby said.

Sue used the bathroom. Even Bob's water closet was

replete with estate-sale booty. She could not imagine why anyone would want a toy bowling set with Fred Flintstone tenpins, yet there they were.

When she came out, Bobby was holding a stack of vintage picture postcards from Paris. They had considered French names like Joan (of Arc), Yvette, Babette, and Bernadette, but none of those sang out.

"Hmm." Bobby held one of the cards. He showed it to Sue. "The Rue Saint-Honoré. Pronounced 'Honor-ray.' That's the masculine. The feminine has an extra *e* on the end and is pronounced the same. *Honorée.* Isn't that lovely?"

"I'm not French."

"We could try an Anglo-Saxon surname. Something simple, one syllable. Bates. Church. Smythe. Cooke."

"None of those are good." Sue flipped through the stack of old postcards—the Eiffel Tower. Notre Dame. Charles de Gaulle.

"Honorée Goode?" Bob repeated the name and liked the sound of it. "*E*'s on the ends of both."

"They'd call me Honorée Goody Two-shoes."

"No, they wouldn't. Everyone pretends they speak French, *mon petite teet-mouse.* Honorée Goode is honestly good." He reached over and pulled a black Princess-model phone off a bookshelf and dialed a number.

"I have a friend at Equity. They have a computer so no names get duplicated. Jane Fonda. Faye Dunaway. Raquel Welch. Taken!"

"Raquel Gliebe? My parents would have no problem with that."

Bob was connected to his friend Mark. "Mark-y Mark-a-lot, Bob Roy. I know! It has? Not since she went out of town, on that cruise liner. It's good money! Can you do me a little service? Check the database for a stage name. No, for one *not* taken. Last name Goode with an *e* on the end. First name Honorée." He spelled it out. "With an accent or *schwa* or whatever on the first *e*. Sure, I'll hold."

"I don't know, Bobby." Sue was running the new name over and over again in her head.

"You can decide when you march into Equity with your first contract and a check for the dues. Then, you can be Sue Gliebe or Catwoman Zelkowitz. But I have to tell you . . ." Someone came on the phone, but it wasn't Bob's friend. "Yes, I am holding for Mark. Thank you." He turned back to Sue. "I walked into that run-through of *Brigadoon*. Up there onstage was a girl playing Fiona who was going to have a *career*."

Sue smiled and blushed. She was that Fiona. She had crushed that role, her first out of the chorus. Her Fiona had led to all the roles the ACLO had given her, had pushed her off to NYC, and had made her clean in Bob Roy's kitchen tub.

"I loved that girl," Bob said. "I loved that actress. She wasn't some bitter leading lady pissed off that New York had had enough of her. Or a painted starlet doing Civic Light Opera because the distance and makeup hid the fact she was forty-three years old. That Fiona was no mutton. No, she was a local lamb, an Arizona gal who could hold the stage like a Barrymore, sing like Julie Andrews, with a set of boobs that set the boys a-flutter. If you had introduced yourself to me as Honorée Goode, I would have said, 'Well, you certainly are!'

But no, you were Sue Gliebe. I thought, Sue Gliebe? That's just not going to fly."

Sue Gliebe felt warm inside. Bobby Roy was her biggest fan and she loved him. If he had been fifteen years younger, forty pounds lighter, and not a homosexual she would have spent the night in his bed. Maybe she would, regardless.

Mark came back on the phone. "Are you sure?" Bob asked. "That spelling, with the *e*? Okay. Thanks, Marco. I will. Thursday? Why not! Bye!" He hung up the phone, tapping it with his running fingers, and said, "Big decision time, titmouse."

Sue leaned back in her overstuffed chair. The rain had stopped outside. Her skin had been dried by the terry cloth of the robe and she smelled of delicate rosewater from the bath soap. The big radio was softly playing an orchestration of a nightclub standard, and, for the first time ever, New York City seemed like the place Sue Gliebe belonged . . .

EXACTLY ONE YEAR LATER:

WHO'S WHO IN THE CAST

HONORÉE GOODE (Miss Wentworth)—Ms. Goode trained at the Arizona Civic Light Opera. She was nominated for an Obie last year for her role as Kate Brunswick in Joe Runyan's Backwater Blues. *This marks her Broadway debut. She thanks her supportive parents and Robert Roy, Jr., for making it all possible.*

A Special Weekend

I t was the early spring of 1970 and because his tenth birthday was in a week and a half, Kenny Stahl, still thought of
as the baby of the family, did not have to go to school. He was
going to be picked up by his mother around noon to spend a
special weekend with her, so he came to the breakfast table
in his ordinary, nonschool clothes. His older brother, Kirk,
and older sister, Karen, both in their uniforms for St. Philip
Neri School, thought the deal was unfair. They wanted their
mom to come and pick them up, too—to take them away, out
of the house they had been moved into, to live again in Sacramento or anyplace else as long as they were the only kids and
the dark moodiness of their father and the constant, sunny
practicality of his second wife would not make their lives an
emotional teeter-totter.

Kenny's three stepsisters were seventeen, fifteen, and
fourteen years old. His stepbrother had two years on him.
None of them had opinions as to the fairness of the birthday

plan. They had always lived together in Iron Bend, attended the unified public schools, and never had to wear uniforms. This weekend didn't strike them as interesting, notable, or in any way special.

The small house they all lived in was far out of town on Webster Road, closer to Molinas than to Iron Bend, which was the county seat and where Kenny's father was head cook at the Blue Gum Restaurant. Eucalyptus trees—blue gums—lined both sides of Webster Road for most of the miles between the two towns, scattering their leaves and nuts all over the two lanes and both shoulders. Decades ago the messy imports from Australia were planted as windbreaks for the almond groves as well as in a misinformed attempt to farm the trees for railroad ties. This was back when big money could be made in railroad ties, as long as they were not made of eucalyptus. Fortunes were lost on the twisting, peeling, gnarly-growing trees, three of which were spaced across the front yard of Kenny's house; the constant rain of debris laid waste to every attempt to plant decent grass there. The backyard had sort of a lawn, a patch of weed-studded green, which the kids took turns mowing on occasion. Across the road were almond orchards. Almonds were a big industry then and still are now.

Kenny's father had found a new job in Iron Bend, a new home, a new school, and, it turned out, a new family. He'd moved his three kids into the small house the very same night they had left Sacramento. All the boys slept in what had been a screened-in porch. All the girls were in one bedroom with twin bunk beds.

After two school buses had come and gone, Kenny spent the morning shuffling around the house as his father slept and his stepmother quietly cleaned up the breakfast dishes. He had never been at home without the other kids and was thrilled to have the run of the place. His only instruction was that he was to keep quiet. For a while, he watched TV with the volume nearly mute, but there was just one channel, Channel 12 from Chico, and during school hours there was nothing on that interested him. He played with the model ships and planes he had made from kits, using the top of the living room coffee table as the vast sea. He went through the dresser drawers of his brother and stepbrother looking for secrets, but their treasures were hidden elsewhere. In the backyard, he punted a football, trying to clear the nearest almond trees, gambling that in failure the ball wouldn't get stuck in their branches. He tied a cut of an old bedsheet to a discarded beanpole, making a flag that he ran around with like he was leading a charge in the Civil War. He was trying to plant the flag into a hole when his stepmom called to him from the kitchen window she had cranked open.

"Kenny! Your mother is here!"

He hadn't heard the car.

In the kitchen, he was caught short by a sight he had never seen in the near decade of his life; his dad was awake and sitting at the table with his morning coffee. His mother, his real mom, was sitting at the table as well, a cup of coffee of her own. His stepmother was on her feet, leaning against the counter, sipping coffee, too. The three caretakers of his world had never been in the same room at the same time.

"There's the Kenny Bear!" Kenny's mom was beaming. She looked like a secretary in a TV show—professionally dressed, wearing heels, her trim black hair neat, her makeup showing red lips that left marks on her coffee cup. She stood and hugged him with perfumed arms, kissing the top of his head. "Go get your bag and we'll hit the road."

Kenny had no idea about any bag, but his stepmother had put some clothes into one of her daughter's small pink suitcases. He was packed. His father stood up and frazzled Kenny's hair. "I gotta shower," he said. "Go check out your mother's hot wheels."

"You got me Hot Wheels?" Kenny asked, thinking that his birthday present was going to be some miniature cars made of die-cast metal.

But no. In the driveway was an actual sports car, red, a two-seater, with wire wheels. The top was up and already littered with eucalyptus fallings. The only sports cars he'd ever seen were on television, driven by detectives and young doctors.

"Is this yours, Mom?"

"A friend let me borrow it."

Kenny was looking through the driver's side window. "Can I sit in it?"

"Go ahead."

Kenny figured out how to open the door and sat behind the wheel. The dials and switches of the car looked like they came from a jet plane. The wood paneling was like furniture. The seats smelled like leather baseball mitts. The red circle in the middle of the steering wheel said FIAT. After his mother put the pink suitcase in the car's trunk, she asked for Kenny's help putting the top down.

"We'll let the wind blow through our hair until we get to the highway, okay?" She undid the latches of the top and Kenny helped fold it back, bending the clear plastic window in on itself. His mother fired up the engine, which sounded like a dragon clearing its throat, then she backed out of the driveway—she had taken off her heels to work the pedals and put on a pair of sunglasses, the kind worn by snow skiers. Mother, son, and Fiat roared away from the house, down Webster Road, the gum tree shadows making the sunlight strobe in Kenny's eyes, the wind sounding in his ears and whipping his hair from back to front. The car was the coolest, most *boss* ride Kenny had ever seen. He was the happiest he had been since he was a little kid.

———

The attendant at the Shell station in Iron Bend was all over the car, giving it and the woman driving it his keen attention. He filled the tank, wiped the windshield, checked the oil, and marveled at the "dago motor." Kenny was offered a free soda pop from the vending machine. While he was pulling a bottle of root beer (always his choice) from the cold box, the man was helping his mother put the top back up and close the latches. The man was smiling and chatting, asking questions about if his mother was headed north or south and if she planned on coming back to Iron Bend soon. When they were back in the car and on the highway (heading south), she told her son the Shell man had "cow-eyes" and she laughed.

"Find us some music, honey," she said, pointing to the tiny radio in the wooden dashboard. "Turn that knob, then that one for a station."

Like a radio operator on a bomber, Kenny moved the red line of the dial along the numbers. The local radio station had a commercial for Stan Nathan's Shoes for the Family, a store in town. Static and voices came and went until Kenny located the beam from a station that came in loud and clear. A man was singing about raindrops on his head. Kenny's mom knew the words and sang along as she dug around in her purse at the same time she steered. She found a little leather case with a clasp on it, which she unsnapped to reveal the tips of cigarettes. They were long cigarettes, longer than those his father smoked. She had one in her lips, the red lipstick already staining the white filter, when she pushed a button on the dash. In a few seconds the button popped and she pulled the whole thing out. There was a glowing red coil on the end of the button, so hot she used it to light her long cigarette. She put the hot button back in its hole, then switched hands on the wheel to open a small, triangular window. As soon as there was a whistling crack, the smoke from her long cigarette was sucked out the window like a magic trick.

"Tell me about school, sweetie," she said. "You like school?"

Kenny told her that St. Philip Neri wasn't like St. Joseph, the only other school he had gone to, back in Sacramento. St. Philip Neri was small, not many kids went there, and some of the nuns didn't dress like nuns. As he savored his bottle of root beer with short, airy sips, he told his mom about the bus rides to school, how the uniforms were red plaid instead of blue plaid and they had some days when they didn't have to wear them, and that a kid in his class named Munson made models like he did and lived in a house with a pool, but not an inground pool like at the city park, but a circular aboveground pool. From just the one question, Kenny talked all the way from Iron Bend to the Butte City cutoff as his mother smoked. When the one radio station faded, Kenny found another, then another. His mom let him signal to the truck drivers they passed to blow their air horns. He would pump his fist up and down, and, if the drivers saw him, more often than not they would send out a toot. Once, Kenny saw a truck driver looking at them in his sideview mirror and got a blast on the horn without having to pump for it. The driver blew a kiss that was probably meant for his mom, not for Kenny.

They stopped for lunch in Maxwell at a diner called Kathy's Kountry Kafe, a place for travelers and, in season, duck hunters. The Fiat was the only sports car in the parking lot. The waitress seemed to love chatting with Kenny's mom—they talked like old friends or sisters. Kenny noticed that the waitress had very red lips, too. When she asked what to bring for the young man, he asked for a hamburger.

"Oh no, honey," his mother said. "Hamburgers are for anytime. At a restaurant we should order from the menu."

"Why not, Mom? Dad doesn't care. And Nancy lets us." Nancy was Kenny's stepmother.

"What say we make this a special rule," his mother said. "Just for you and me." This seemed like an odd rule to suddenly impose. Kenny had never been told what to order or what he could not have. "I think you'll like the hot turkey sandwich," his mother said. "We'll split it."

Kenny thought she meant a sandwich that was going to be steaming hot and was not sure he was going to like it. "Can I have a milkshake?"

"Yep." She smiled. "I'm flexible!"

Truth be told, Kenny liked the open-faced sandwich that was swimming in brown gravy and was not too hot at all. The white bread that sucked up all the gravy was just as good as the turkey meat, and mashed potatoes were his favorite food of all time. His mom had an igloo-shaped scoop of cottage cheese on tomato slices but cut up a few bites of the hot turkey for herself. His vanilla milkshake came in the freezing steel cup it was made in and twice filled up a fancy glass. He poured it himself, tapping the steel against the glass to help it along. This was so much milkshake, Kenny couldn't finish it.

When his mother went to the restroom, Kenny noticed all the men travelers following her with their eyes, turning their heads to watch her go. One of them got up to pay his check, stopping by the booth where Kenny sat alone.

"Is that your mommy, slugger?" the man asked. He wore a brown suit with a tie partly undone. His eyeglasses had flip-up sunshades that stuck out like small visors.

"Um-hmmm," Kenny said.

The man smiled. "You know, I got a boy at home just like you. But not a mommy like you got." The man laughed out loud, then paid at the register.

When his mom came back from the restroom, her lips

were freshly painted. She took a sip from what was left of Kenny's milkshake, leaving red marks on the paper straw.

———

Sacramento was more than an hour down the highway. Kenny had not been to his hometown since his father packed their stuff into the station wagon, the day they moved to Iron Bend. The buildings had a look of comforting familiarity, but when his mom turned the Fiat off the highway it was at a street he had never traveled. When he saw the sign for the Leamington Hotel he felt a smile on his face—his parents had both worked at the Leamington, but now only his mom did. He and his brother and sister had spent time there, tagging along on some weekends when their folks were still married. They played in the big conference room when it was empty and would eat at the counter of the coffee shop when the place was not busy. Dad would pay them a nickel for every tray of potatoes they would wrap in tinfoil for baking en masse. If they asked permission, they could get their own chocolate milk from the dispenser, as long as they used the small glasses. This was long ago; a big chunk of Kenny's life had passed since then.

His mother parked the Fiat in the back of the hotel and they entered through the kitchen—just as Kenny remembered doing in his dad's station wagon and his mom's Corolla. The staff all welcomed his mother and she greeted each person by name in response. A lady and one of the cooks could not believe that Kenny had grown up so much since they had last seen him, but Kenny could not remember who those people were, though he thought he recognized the lady's cat's-eye glasses with the thick lenses. The kitchen looked smaller than Kenny remembered it.

When he was little, Kenny's mother was a waitress in the Leamington Hotel coffee shop and his father one of the cooks. She wore a uniform then, but now dressed in business clothes and had an office off the hotel lobby. Her office had a desk stacked with papers and a wall covered by a bulletin board that had many index cards, all written upon in different colored inks and arranged in neat columns.

"Kenny Bear, I have a few things to do, then I'll tell you about your birthday surprise, okay?" She was sliding some papers into a leather folder. "Can you sit here for a bit?"

"Can I pretend this is my office and I work here?"

"Sure," she said, smiling. "Here're some notebooks, and look, this is an electric pencil sharpener." She showed him how to push a pencil into the opening of the machine and make the grinding noise that produced a pencil point as sharp as a sewing pin. "Don't answer the phone if it rings."

A lady named Miss Abbott came into the office and asked, "So this is your little man?" She was older than his mom and wore glasses on a chain around her neck. Miss Abbott would keep an eye on Kenny and would know where his mother was if he needed her.

"Kenny is going to do some work for us today."

"Wonderful," Miss Abbott said. "I'll give you some stamps and an ink pad to make everything official. Would you like that?"

His mother left, carrying her leather folder. Kenny sat in her chair behind her desk. Miss Abbott brought him some stamps that said the date on them and INVOICE and RECEIVED as well as a metal rectangular box with blue ink on a pad.

"You know," Miss Abbott said, "I have a nephew just your age."

———

Kenny used the stamps and ink on a few pages of a notebook, then, bored, looked through the top drawers of the desk. One drawer had dividers that separated paper clips, boxes of staples, rubber bands, pencils, and some pens that said LEAMINGTON HOTEL on the sides. Another drawer had envelopes and letter paper that said LEAMINGTON HOTEL with a little drawing of the building at the top of each sheet.

He got up from the desk, went to the door, and saw Miss Abbott at a desk of her own, typing some kind of letter.

"Miss Abbott," Kenny said. "May I use some paper that says 'Leamington Hotel' on it?"

Miss Abbott kept typing. "What's that?" she asked without looking up.

"May I use some paper that says 'Leamington Hotel' on it?"

"Go ahead," she said as she kept on typing.

Kenny used the stamps and hotel pens on the paper, drawing lines and signing his name next to the stamps. Then he had an idea.

He took the cover off the typewriter that was on its own

little desk beside his mother's. The machine was light blue, had the letters *IBM* on the front, and was really big, taking up most of its special table. He rolled a sheet of paper into the workings of the typewriter and pressed on the keys, but they were dead. Nothing happened. Kenny was about to ask Miss Abbott why the typewriter didn't work but then he saw the rocker switch that said ON/OFF and that the OFF part was depressed. He rocked it to ON and the machine hummed and vibrated. The mechanical ball with the letters on it swept back and forth once, then stopped on the left side. The carriage with the paper in it did not move, which made Kenny think the typewriter must be part computer or one of those Teletype machines.

He tried to type his name, but it came out **kkkkkkkkkkkkkkk**. That's when he discovered that if he kept the key pressed down, the letter repeated, sounding like a machine gun— **kkkk kkkkkk kkkk keeee eeeenn nnnnnnnn n n n yyyy yyy**. What confused him the most was the lack of a handle he was supposed to slap to make the page go back. There was none. There was a very big button that said RETURN on it. When he pressed that the ball moved back with a *chunk* and he could type a new line. This was now, officially, the most amazing typewriter Kenny had ever seen or heard of.

Kenny did not know how to type like a grown-up—like Miss Abbott or his mom—so he used just one finger, finding the letters he wanted but sometimes hitting ones he didn't— **kennnystdahlkl kjenny stanhl kenn sath**. By going very slowly and being very careful he finally typed his name correctly—**kenny stahl**—and rolled that page out of the

IBM. He put the date stamp next to his name along with **INVOICE**.

"How about a coffee break?" Miss Abbott was standing in the door.

"I don't drink coffee," Kenny said.

Miss Abbott nodded. "Well, let's see what else we can find, shall we?"

He followed her into the lobby, where Kenny saw his mother standing with a group of men. They were all talking business, but Kenny still called out to her.

"Mom!" he hollered, pointing toward the hotel kitchen. "I'm taking a coffee break!"

She turned to him and smiled and gave a little wave, then turned back to the businessmen.

In the kitchen, he asked Miss Abbott if he could get his own chocolate milk like he used to, but the dispenser no longer held chocolate milk. Just regular milk and something called Skim. Instead, Miss Abbott went to a silver refrigerator and pulled out a carton of chocolate milk, grabbed one of the big drinking glasses, and filled it to the top. This was more chocolate milk than Kenny had ever been allowed, which he thought was great. Miss Abbott got herself some coffee out of a round, glass pitcher that sat on a Bunn Coffee Service maker. They could not take their drinks back through the lobby, so they went into the coffee shop, which looked and smelled exactly the same as when Kenny was little. They sat in an empty booth, not at the counter.

"Do you remember me?" she asked him. "I worked here with your daddy. Before your mommy started." Miss Abbott asked Kenny more questions, mostly if he liked the same things her nephew liked—baseball, karate class, and TV shows. Kenny told her they only got Channel 12 from Chico.

———

Back in his mother's office he decided to write her a letter on the IBM typewriter. He started with a new sheet of Leamington Hotel paper and went very slowly.

Deear Mom,

How are you I am fine

    Your friends sport car is like a racecar. I like how loud the motor goes and working the radio.

    I saw you in the hotel just now and wonder what is my big surprise?????? ?

    I am going to leave this letter in a place where it will be a SURPEIZE for you. After you find it right me back on this tiperighter that is so cooooool and esy to do.

Love

Kenny Stahl RECEIVED RECEIVED INVOICE

Kenny folded the letter as best he could and put it into a hotel envelope and licked the seal, careful not to cut his tongue on the sharp edge. He wrote *TO MOM* on the front with a Leamington Hotel pen, then looked for a place to hide the letter, deciding the best place would be in a desk drawer under a few pages of Leamington Hotel stationery.

Kenny was playing with some rubber bands when his mom came back into her office. She was with a man who had dark brown skin and the straightest, blackest hair. "Kenny, this is Mr. Garcia. He let us borrow his car for the ride down today."

"Hello," Kenny said. "That's your car? The sports car?"

"It is," Mr. Garcia said. "I'm glad to meet you. But let's do it proper, shall we? Stand up."

Kenny did as he was told.

"Now," Mr. Garcia continued, "we shake hands. Grab firm now."

Kenny squeezed Mr. Garcia's hand as hard as he could.

"Don't hurt me." Mr. Garcia chuckled. Kenny's mom beamed at the two men. "Now, look me in the eye, just like I look at you. Good. Now you say, 'It's a pleasure to meet you.'"

"It's a pleasure to meet you," Kenny repeated.

"Now comes the most important part. We ask each other a question, engage each other, man to man, see? I'm going to ask you this—do you know what 'Fiat' stands for?"

Kenny shook his head, because he was confused by the question and because he had no idea what was going on. No one had ever explained to him how to shake hands.

"'Fix it again, Tony.'" Mr. Garcia laughed. "Now you ask me a question. Go ahead."

"Um." Kenny had to think of something to say. He was looking at Mr. Garcia's head of thick, jet-black hair, held stiffly in place and so shiny. That was when he remembered seeing Mr. Garcia before, when he was little, when he was playing in the hotel with his brother and sister. He remembered that Mr. Garcia did not work in the kitchen with his dad, but would come in from the lobby wearing a suit. "You work here, too, like my mom, don't you?"

Mr. Garcia and his mom shared a glance and a smile. "I used to, Kenny, but not anymore. Now I'm at the Senator."

"You're a senator?" Kenny knew what a senator was from the news on Channel 12.

"Mr. Garcia works at the Senator Hotel, Kenny," his mother said. "And he has a big surprise for you."

"You haven't told him?" Mr. Garcia asked.

"I thought it should be your treat," she said.

"Okay." Mr. Garcia looked at Kenny. "I hear you have a birthday coming up, is that right?"

Kenny nodded. "I'm going to be ten."

"Have you ever flown?"

"You mean, in an airplane?"

"Have you?"

Kenny looked at his mother. Maybe, when he was a baby, she had taken him on an airliner but he had been too little to remember. "Have I, Mom?"

"Jose is a pilot. He has a plane and wants to take you up for a ride. Won't that be fun?"

Kenny had never met a pilot before who owned his own airplane. Where was Mr. Garcia's uniform? Was he in the Air Force?

"What are you doing tomorrow?" Mr. Garcia asked. "Want to go up?"

Kenny looked at his mother. "Can I, Mom?"

"Yep," she said. "I'm flexible."

————

Kenny and his mother had their dinner at a restaurant called the Rosemount. She knew everybody who worked there. The waiter took away two place settings because his mom said that she was on "a special date with this young man," meaning Kenny. The menus were as big as newspapers. He had spaghetti and, for dessert, the waiter brought him a piece of chocolate cake as big as his shoe. He couldn't finish it all. His mother smoked her long cigarettes and drank an after-dinner coffee. One of the cooks came out, a fellow Kenny remembered from his days at the Leamington. The cook's name was Bruce. He sat at the table with the two of them and talked with his mom for a while, mostly laughing.

"Good God, Kenny," Bruce said to him. "You are growing up as fast as alfalfa." Bruce could do an amazing trick—he could throw a drinking straw into a raw potato and make it stick like an arrow. On the way out through the kitchen— Mom had parked the Fiat in the back—Bruce did the trick for Kenny. *Whap!* And the straw almost went all the way through the potato. It was amazing!

His mom lived in a two-story building with a stairway in the middle that separated the two apartments on each floor. The living room of her place had something called a Murphy bed that folded up and disappeared into the wall. When his mom pulled the bed down, it was already made. She had a small color TV on a rolling stand that she turned to face the bed, but before he could watch it she made Kenny take a bath.

The bathroom was small and the tub was tiny, so it quickly filled up with water. On one shelf there were bath soaps and other girlie things, all in colorful bottles and tubes with flowers on the labels. On another shelf was a can of Gillette shaving cream and a man's razor made by Wilkinson Sword. Kenny played in the tub until his fingers wrinkled and the water got cold. Pajamas had been packed in the pink suitcase from home, and, as he put them on, he smelled popcorn. His mom had made some, shaking it to life in a pot on her little kitchen stove.

"Find something to watch on TV, honey," she called out as she melted butter in a saucepan to pour over the popcorn.

Kenny turned on the TV and it came to life immediately, without having to warm up like the one at home. He was delighted to see all the old channels, the ones he had watched before his mom moved out of the house and his dad got married again. There were shows on Channels 3, 6, 10, and 13. And, on the other channel knob, the one that turned rather than *clicked*, there was a Channel 40. Every channel was in color, too, except the old movie on Channel 40. He settled on a show called *The Name of the Game*, which was fine with his mom.

They lay on the Murphy bed together, eating popcorn. His mom kicked off her shoes and put her arm around her son's shoulders, her fingers playing in his hair. At one point she sat up and said, "Rub Momma's neck some." Kenny rose onto his knees and tried to give her neck a massage, moving her hair out of the way and avoiding the little chain around her neck. After a few minutes she thanked him and said that she loved her little Kenny. They both lay back down. The next TV show came on—*Bracken's World*, in which grown-ups went on and on about things Kenny could not understand. He was asleep before the first commercial.

———

Music was playing on a radio when Kenny woke up in the morning. His mother was in the kitchen, having already made coffee in a glass percolator on the stove. Kenny had to hop down from the Murphy bed because it was a bit high.

"Well, hello, sleepy-bear." His mother kissed his head. "We have a big problem."

"What?" Kenny rubbed his eyes as he sat at the two-seat kitchen table.

"I didn't get milk yesterday." She did have a can of something called Evaporated Milk—there was a cartoon cow on the label—that she was using for her morning coffee. "Can you go around to Louie's Market and get a half gallon of milk? You'll need some for your cereal."

"I can."

Kenny had no idea where Louie's Market was. His mom explained that it was out the front door, one right turn, then one left turn. A three-minute walk. There were some dollar bills on her dresser in the bedroom, he could take two and buy himself a treat for later.

Kenny dressed in the same clothes he wore the day before and went into his mom's tiny bedroom. There was money on her dresser, so he took two one-dollar bills. Her closet door was open with the light on inside; Kenny could see all her shoes on the floor and her dresses and skirts on hangers. There was also a man's suit jacket and pants hanging in the closet and some ties on little hooks. A pair of man's shoes were in there with her high heels.

The streets around the apartment were lined with big trees, but not the blue gums of Webster Road. These trees had wide green leaves and branches that were thick and high. The roots of the tall, old trees had grown so large they buckled the sidewalks and made them uneven. Kenny carried the two one-dollar bills in his hand as he turned right, then left, finding Louie's Market in less than three minutes.

A Japanese man was behind the cash register, surrounded by candies and sweets on display. Kenny found the dairy case and carried a half gallon of milk over to pay for it. As the Japanese man rang up the sale he asked, "Who are you? I've never seen you before."

Kenny told him his mother lived nearby and had forgotten to buy milk.

"Who is your mother?" the man asked. When Kenny told him, he said "Oh! Your mother is a nice lady. A very pretty lady. And you are her boy? How old are you?"

"In nine days ten," Kenny said.

"I have a girl just like you," the grocer said.

For the treat he would have later, Kenny picked out a twin pack of Hostess CupCakes, chocolate with the swirl of white icing down the middle. They cost twenty-five cents, which Kenny hoped was not too much. His mother said nothing when he got back with the milk. She made him toast to eat along with his bowl of Rice Krispies and cut up sections of a seedless orange.

Kenny was watching Channel 40—a whole morning of cartoons and commercials for toys—when the phone on the wall of the kitchen rang. After saying hello, his mother said something he did not understand.

"*Que paso, mi amor?* What? Oh, no! He was looking forward to it. Are you sure?" Kenny looked at his mom, she at him as she listened. "Oh! Yes, that could work. Yes, two birds with one stone. Love it. Okay." She listened on the phone for a moment more, then giggled as she hung up.

"Kenny Bear," she sang, coming into the room. "Change of plans. Jose, Mr. Garcia, had business come up and he can't fly you in his plane today. But . . ." She cocked her head, as though a more exciting possibility was about to be floated, like there was a trip on a rocket ship available instead. "He can fly you all the way home tomorrow! We won't have to drive."

Kenny did not quite understand how a flight home on an airplane was possible. Would the plane land on Webster Road right at his house? Wouldn't they crash into the blue gum trees?

———

With the whole day now to fill, Kenny and his mom spent the late morning at Fairytale Town, a place for kids run by the Parks Department. There were little houses painted to look like they were made of straw, sticks, and stones; a long and curling version of a yellow brick road; and puppet shows every hour until 3:00 p.m. The whole family used to visit the storybook village when Kenny was little, although never with Dad, who was always sleeping at home. Since Kenny was now nearly ten years old, the fairy-tale sets were too young for him. Even the swings were for kids littler than Kenny.

The zoo was nearby. That, too, had been a favorite destination when Kenny was smaller. The monkeys still aired out their limbs by swinging on the rings in their cage, the elephants were still in a pen on the other side of the fence that was no longer as tall as it had been, and the giraffes could still be fed carrots from pails full of them, kept on hand by the zookeepers. He and his mom stayed at the zoo longer than they did Fairytale Town, lingering in the Reptile House. There was a huge python in there, wrapped around part of a tree with his head, as big as a football, right next to the window glass.

For lunch they ate at a little market that also had sidewalk tables with checkerboard cloths. Kenny had a tuna sandwich with no lettuce or tomato, just the tuna, and his mother had a small tub of pasta salad. To drink, there was golden juice that came in bottles shaped like apples—this was instead of a Coke. Kenny was disappointed at first, but the apple juice was so sweet, so thick that his whole body felt good when the drink slid down his throat and into his tummy. He imagined that must be what drinking wine was like, since grown-ups were always making such a big deal about "fine wines." He had his Hostess cupcakes for dessert.

"What shall we do now, Kenny Bear?" his mom asked. "What if we tried our hands at peewee golf?"

She drove the red Fiat onto the freeway, heading west toward the foothills. When they crossed the river, Kenny realized they were near the exit for Sunset Avenue, which was the off-ramp they used to take to get home, to his old house. He recognized the big green sign with the white arrow and SUNSET AVE, and he saw the Chevron station on one side and the Phillips 66 station on the other. But his mom didn't merge into the exit lane. She kept going. Farther down the highway a colorful little town of tiny windmills and castles appeared, the Miniature Golf & Family Fun Center. The place looked brand-new and magical.

Because it was a Saturday, there was a pretty good crowd made up of carloads of families and idle kids who had ridden their bikes or been dropped off, kids who were supplied with enough money for a day of Fun-with-a-capital-F. There was a circle of baseball batting cages with automatic pitching machines, an arcade filled with pinball and shooting games. A snack bar served corn dogs and giant pretzels and Pepsi-Cola. Kenny and his mom had to wait in line to get the balls and the right-size putters from a teenage boy who smiled at his mom with the same cow eyes as the man at the Shell station in Iron Bend. There was a choice of two courses to play and the young man behind the counter not only suggested the Magic-Land course, with the castle, but also walked them to the first hole and took pains to explain how to use the little pencil to keep score on the card. He also explained that if they got a hole in one on the eighteenth, they'd win a free game.

"I think we have the gist of it," his mom said to the kid, hoping to get rid of him. Still, he lingered until they both putted. He wished them a good round and went back to the counter to hand out more putters and colored golf balls.

They never bothered to keep score. Kenny hacked at his ball, the purple one, caring more about distance than accuracy, taking as many strokes as necessary to make the hole. His mom was a bit more careful. The most fun hole was the one where Kenny hit his ball into a polka-dotted toadstool and it disappeared for a few seconds before coming out of one of three tubes onto a lower circular green. From there, he had to hit the ball into a giant frog's mouth that moved up and down like the drawbridge on a castle. Again, the ball disappeared, coming out at an even lower green and nearly rolling right into the cup. He only had to tap the purple ball with his short putter. His mom took forever to make it through the frog's mouth.

"Peewee golf is pretty fun," he said to his mom when they were back in the Fiat. She had gotten him a corn dog, which he ate before getting into the sports car.

"You're awfully good at it," she said, shifting gears as they pulled out of the Family Fun Center parking lot and headed back into the city, back toward the Sunset Avenue off-ramp.

"Mom?" he asked. She was lighting another of her long cigarettes with the Fiat's lighter. "Can we go see the old house?"

His mother blew smoke out of her mouth, and she watched it disappear into the wind. She did not want to see the old house. She had brought Kenny home from the hospital to that house two days after he was born. His brother and sister had been born in Berkeley, but they had few memories of the apartment there. She had watched her older kids play in the backyard of that house as she carried little Kenny around in the crook of her hip. Kenny had crawled on the hooked rug— her mother's old hooked rug—in the living room until he learned to walk on it. That house carried memories of Christmases and Halloweens, of birthday parties for the kids in the neighborhood, the sweeter memories of her marriage and her life as a mother.

But unhappiness also lingered in the corners of the place, arguments sure to be echoing still, a loneliness that haunted the nights after the kids were asleep as well as the days when they were a maddening handful. To escape—the house, the kids, the boredom found in the shadows of discontent—she took a job at the Leamington Hotel. There was an opening for a waitress. She'd drive in early, before her husband came in for the lunch and dinner shift, leaving the kids with one of the Mormon teenage girls who lived down the block. The money was nice, of course, but the activity was what she looked forward to every day—having a place to go, work to do, and people to talk with. She was still Mrs. Karl Stahl, and her husband was the head of the kitchen, but everyone, including Jose Garcia, called her by her first name. She proved to be so very good with numbers that the hotel's general manager moved her from the coffee shop to a bookkeeper's desk. She had risen to the sales office after she divorced Kenny's father and was no longer Mrs. Karl Stahl.

She had walked away from that old house a lifetime ago. She did not want to see the place again.

"Sure," she said to her son. "I'm flexible."

———

She turned off the freeway, made a right at the Phillips 66 station, and continued down Sunset Avenue to Palmetto Street. She turned left on Palmetto to Derby Street, downshifted as she made the right turn, crossed Vista and Bush Streets, then pulled over and stopped in front of 4114.

Kenny had just two homes, and this was his first. He stared at it. The mailbox by the driveway was the same, the X-frame railing on the porch was as he remembered, but the tree in the front yard looked weirdly small. The lawn was mowed, he'd never seen the grass so neat, and flowers were planted in arrangements along the front of the house. They had never had flowers along the front of the house. The big window had blue curtains in it, not the white ones from when he was a kid. The garage door was closed, unlike when he lived there and it stayed open for easy access to all the bikes and toys and the back rooms of the house. Rather than his father's old station wagon or his mother's Corolla, a new Dodge Dart was parked in the driveway.

The Anhalters had lived next door. Kenny expected to see their white pickup truck, but it was not around. The house across the street had a For Sale sign in the front yard. "The Callendars are selling their house," Kenny said.

"Looks like they've already moved," his mother told him. Yes, the house looked empty. The Callendar kids, Brenda and

Steve, were not twins but looked like they'd been born on the same day. They rode Schwinn bikes, had a dog named Biscuit, had been on a swimming team, and now lived somewhere else.

Kenny and his mom sat in the Fiat for a few minutes. Kenny looked at the window of what had once been his bedroom. The shutters with the moving slats were still there, but had been painted blue, like the living room curtains. The shutters had been a natural wood when he and Kirk slept in their twin beds in that bedroom. It didn't seem right that they were now blue.

"I was born here, right, Mom?"

She was looking down the street, not at the house with the blue window shades. "You were born in the hospital."

"Oh, I know that," he said. "But I was a little baby here, right?"

His mother started the Fiat and put it into gear. "Yep," she said over the growl of the motor. On the night she left the house at 4114 Derby, her children were asleep in their beds and their father was standing in the kitchen, silent. She did not see any of them again for seven weeks. Kenny was five years old.

By the time they had driven back to the apartment, she had smoked three of her long cigarettes, the smoke sailing away in the wind of the open-top sports car.

———

She took him to dinner at the Senator Hotel, which was downtown like the Leamington, but much fancier and crowded with men in suits who all wore name tags. They ate in the coffee shop. Jose Garcia stopped by to see them as Kenny was eating his dessert, a huge slice of cherry pie with ice cream on top of it—à la mode, the waitress called it. Kenny didn't care too much for the cherries, but he finished every bite of the ice cream.

"What say we wheels up at noon?" Mr. Garcia said. "We'll see the delta for a while then head up north. Have you ever been in a plane before, Kenny?"

He had already been asked that question but politely answered again. "Never."

"You may just fall in love with the sky," Mr. Garcia said. As he left, he kissed Kenny's mom on the cheek. Kenny had never seen that happen in real life before, a man kissing a woman on the cheek. His dad never kissed Kenny's stepmom like that, just because he was leaving the room. Kissing on the cheek was something men and women did on TV.

———

Jose Garcia took them to breakfast the next morning, to a coffee shop called Pancake Parade with a décor that made the place look like a circus. The two men ordered waffles and, for Kenny's mom, another igloo of cottage cheese. As they were eating, car after car of well-dressed families came in, filling up the place. They were all in Sunday church clothes—the dads wore suits, the moms and girls were in nice dresses. Some of the boys wore neckties and were the same age as Kenny. With all those people talking and ordering breakfast the place *sounded* as loud as a circus.

When Jose and his mom finally finished their coffee—the waitress kept coming over and offering refills—Mom re-redded her lips and they went back out to the Fiat. Mr. Garcia drove, wearing a pair of gold metal-frame glasses with mirror lenses and hooks to go around his ears. His mom had on her skier's shades. Kenny sat in the little area behind the seats, where the wind was the wildest and made it difficult to hear. For the whole ride, he never knew what the grown-ups were saying.

He had fun back there, though, sitting sideways and waving his hands up in the slipstream of the open top. They drove past solid brick houses with wide lawns and a huge green park with a golf course. They came to a place called Executive Field, which turned out to be an airport, but Jose did not use the parking lot. He drove around to a gate that opened and stopped by some small airplanes that were parked side by side.

"Ready to cheat fate, Ken?" Mr. Garcia said.

"Are we flying in one of those?" Kenny pointed to the planes. They were not like the model airplanes he had at home, which were from the war—fighters and a B-17 bomber. These planes were small and had no machine guns, and they did not look like they could go very fast, even though some had two motors.

"The Comanche," Mr. Garcia said. He was walking toward a white plane with a red stripe, one of the single-engine aircraft.

The doors opened on the plane just like a car, and Mr. Garcia left them ajar to cool off the inside. Kenny got to stand on the wing and look inside, at the gauges and the dials and the steering wheel and the foot pedals. There were two of everything—plus some odd switches and controls that all looked very scientific. Mr. Garcia walked around the plane a few times, then looked at some papers he had folded into sleeves on one of the doors.

Kenny's mom came from the car with the pink suitcase. "I think you want to ride up front, don't you?" she said to him. She folded down one of the seats and climbed into the back, setting the pink case beside her.

"I get to sit *here*?" Kenny meant behind the wheel, like the copilot.

"I need a copilot," Mr. Garcia said. "Your mom's shaky on the stick." He laughed, then showed Kenny how to buckle his harness. Mr. Garcia had to pull the straps tight for him, though. Then he pulled a small pair of dark sunglasses out of his pocket and handed them to Kenny. "The sun is bright up there."

The glasses were gold metal–framed like Mr. Garcia's, but not nearly as expensive. They, too, had hooks that went around the ears. The sunglasses were oversize for Kenny's almost-ten-year-old head, but he didn't know that. He turned to show his mom how he looked. He gave her the thumbs-up and all of them laughed.

The starting of the engine was very loud, and not just because the Comanche's doors were still open. The body of the plane shook and the propeller seemed to *snap* with each turn. Mr. Garcia worked switches and knobs and made the engine roar a few times. He put on a set of earphones and did something that got the plane moving even though the doors were still open. They passed other parked planes, then wide strips of grass where little signs with letters and numbers were planted. At one end of the long runway, the plane came to a stop. Mr. Garcia reached across Kenny and latched his door closed, then did the same to the door on his own side. The motor was still very loud, but the plane was not as wobbly.

"Ready?" Mr. Garcia shouted. Kenny nodded. His mother flashed another thumbs-up. She reached forward and rubbed her son's head. If she said something, Kenny did not hear her, but he could see her large grin.

As the plane sped up and the noise got louder, a feeling came over Kenny that he had never, ever had before. They were moving faster and faster and then lifting up, making his stomach go down but the top of his head feel like it was rising. The ground quickly got smaller; soon the streets and houses and cars no longer looked real. Kenny turned to look out the side window. The wing of the plane blocked his view, so he leaned forward to see the earth and sky in front of the plane.

He saw the buildings downtown and recognized what had once been his world: the Tower Theatre and the grid of the streets, the Old Fort—Sutter's Mill, it was called, where gold was discovered in pioneer days—and there was the Leamington Hotel. He could read the sign.

Kenny's first flight in an airplane was the most amazing event of his life. His head seemed to fill up with air and his breath went short. The sun was brighter than it had ever been before, and Kenny was glad he had dark glasses. When Mr. Garcia turned the plane by dipping the wings to the left, the vast delta area of the river took up the view. There were islands down there, separated by twisted waterways and dikes. Right next to the town where Kenny was born lived farmers who needed a boat to get to town. Kenny had no idea!

"That's what the Mekong looks like!" Mr. Garcia shouted. He was pointing out the window. Kenny nodded out of habit, not sure if he was expected to say something. "That's the bargain you make with Uncle Sam! He teaches you to fly then sends you bird-dogging in Vietnam!"

Kenny knew about Vietnam because the war was on Channel 12 from Chico. What a Mekong was, he had no idea.

They flew southwest, ascending so high in the sky the cars and trucks on the highways looked like they were barely moving. The waters of the river grew wide and changed hue when they met the salt water of San Francisco Bay. Ships were down in the wide river, big ships that now looked like the toy models Kenny played with on the coffee table. When Mr. Garcia dipped the wings again, Kenny's tummy went floppy, but just for a moment.

Now they were flying north. Mr. Garcia slid half of his headset off one of his ears. "I need you to fly for a few minutes, Kenny," he said loudly.

"I don't know how to fly a plane!" Kenny looked at Mr. Garcia as if he were a crazy person.

"Can you imagine driving a car?"

"Yes."

"Take hold of the yoke," Mr. Garcia said. The yoke was

half steering wheel, half handlebars. Kenny had to sit up straight to reach the handles. "The plane will go where you point it. Pull back some and get the feel of the stick."

Kenny used more muscle than he thought he had and, sure enough, the yoke came back toward him. As it did, the sky filled the front window and the engine slowed.

"See?" Mr. Garcia said. "Now level off just as easy."

The grown man had his hand on his flight controls, but let Kenny do the work of pushing the nose of the plane back down. The earth below took up some of the window again.

"Can I turn?" Kenny yelled.

"You're the pilot," Mr. Garcia said.

Very, very carefully, Kenny turned the handlebar-yoke to the right, and the plane tipped ever so slightly. Kenny could feel the change in direction. He reversed his piloting motion and felt the plane ease back.

"If you were a little taller," Mr. Garcia said, "I'd let you work the rudder, but you can't reach the pedals. Maybe in a year. Next year."

Kenny imagined himself, at age eleven, flying the Comanche all by himself with his mom in the backseat.

"What I need you to do now is, see Mount Shasta up ahead?" Shasta, the massive volcano that loomed over the valley up north, was forever covered with snow. On clear days in Iron Bend the mountain looked like an enormous painting off in the distance. From Kenny's seat in the front of the airplane, Shasta was a triangle of white, poking up over the horizon. "Fly directly at it, okay?"

"Okay!" Kenny set his eyes on the mountain and tried to

keep the nose of the plane smack on target while Mr. Garcia pulled some papers out of the side of his seat and a ballpoint pen from his pocket. He wrote some things down, then studied a map. Kenny wasn't sure how much time went by as he flew the plane straight and true, it could have been a few minutes or most of the flight home, but he never let the plane stray. More of Mount Shasta was visible by the time Mr. Garcia folded up the map and clicked his pen closed.

"Atta boy, Kenny," he said as he took over the yoke. "You have the makings of a pilot."

"Good job, honey!" his mom called from the back of the plane. When Kenny looked over his shoulder, her smile was nearly as big as the one on his face.

Looking out the window, Kenny saw the lanes of the highway that led straight up the valley through towns like Willows and Orland leading to Iron Bend and beyond. Just two days ago he and his mom had been down below on that highway. Now, he was miles above it.

After Kenny had flown the plane he had to pop his ears, yawning widely and blowing his nose with his mouth closed. It didn't hurt. The plane was descending, the engine sounding louder as the ground grew closer and the landmarks of Iron Bend showed themselves. There was the logging yard south of town, then the two motels off the highway, the old grain silos that held no grain, and the parking lot of the Shopping Plaza with the Montgomery Ward. Kenny had never been told there was an airport in Iron Bend, but there it was, beyond the Union High football field.

The plane jiggled and shook as Mr. Garcia came in for

the landing. He did something to the engine that made it go soft and nearly silent just before the wheels *squeech*ed on the concrete runway. He drove the airplane like a car and came to a stop a few feet from where other planes were parked. When he shut the engine off, the propeller kept going around a few times until seizing up with a jerk. Without the engine, the quiet was odd, making the unclicking of the seat belts sound crisply clear, like something from a movie at the State Theater.

"Cheated death again," Mr. Garcia said without having to shout.

"Honestly," said Kenny's mom. "Do you *have* to put it that way?"

Mr. Garcia laughed, leaned back, and kissed her on the cheek.

———

The airport had a very small coffee shop. There were no customers and, it appeared, no staff. Kenny, still wearing his dark pilot glasses, sat at a table, the pink suitcase on the floor at his feet while his mom put coins into a pay phone on the wall. She dialed, waited, then hung up and put the same coins back into the phone. She dialed another number before she was able to talk to anyone.

"Well, the line was busy," she said into the phone. "Can you come get him? Because we have to get back. How long? All right." She hung up and came over to the bench. "Your dad is coming from work to pick you up. Let's see if there's some hot cocoa for you and coffee for me."

Kenny could see through the glass coffee shop door into the office of the airport. Mr. Garcia—still wearing his dark glasses, too—was talking to a man who was sitting at a desk. Kenny heard a loud *whirring* noise that turned out to be a machine that made hot chocolate. When his mom brought it to him in a Styrofoam cup, one sip told Kenny the cocoa was too watery. He didn't finish it.

His dad came, driving the station wagon. He left the motor running as he got out of the car, wearing his cook's pants and heavy shoes. He shook hands with Mr. Garcia, said a few words to Kenny's mom, then picked up the small pink suitcase and carried it out to the car.

Kenny sat in the front seat, just like he did in the airplane. As they drove out of the parking lot, his father asked him about his dark glasses.

"Mr. Garcia gave them to me," Kenny said.

Kenny told his father about aiming for Mount Shasta, then about going to the zoo and the peewee golf and seeing the old house.

"Ah," his father said. He said it again when Kenny told him the Callendars had moved away.

As they rode into town and back to the Blue Gum Restaurant, Kenny looked out the window, his eyes tinted a deep blue by his metal-framed sunglasses, scanning the sky. Mr. Garcia had probably taken off by now, and Kenny hoped to see the plane up there. His mom would be sitting in the co-pilot's seat.

But there was no sign of them. None at all.

These Are the Meditations
of My Heart

S he was not looking to buy an old typewriter. She needed nothing and wanted no more possessions—new, used, antique—not a thing. She had vowed to weather her recent personal setbacks with an era of Spartan living; a new minimalism, a life she could fit in her car.

She liked her small apartment west of the Cuyahoga River. She'd tossed away all the clothes she'd worn with him, the Knothead; she cooked for herself almost every night and listened to a lot of podcasts. She had enough money saved to see her to the New Year, allowing a lazy, agenda-free summer. January would freeze the lake and probably burst the pipes of her building, but by then she would be gone. New York or Atlanta or Austin or New Orleans. She had options galore as long as she traveled light. But the Lakewood Methodist Church on the corner of Michigan and Sycamore was having a Saturday Parking Lot Sale, raising money for community service programs like Free Day Care, twelve-step program meetings, and, she didn't know, maybe Meals on Wheels. She was neither a churchgoer nor a baptized Methodist, but she was fairly certain that sauntering through a parking lot full of card tables brimming with yard sale debris was not an act of worship.

As a hoot she almost bought a set of aluminum TV dinner trays, but three of them showed signs of rust. Boxes of costume jewelry revealed no treasures. But then she saw a set of Tupperware ice pop makers. As a kid, she had been in charge of pouring Kool-Aid or orange juice into the molds and inserting the patented plastic handles, which, when the freezer had done the physics, made for inexpensive icy treats. She could almost feel the hot wind of summer in the foothills, her hands sticky from melting, fruity ice. With no haggling, she got the set for a dollar.

On the same table was the typewriter, the color of faded Pop Art red—not an attraction. What got her eye was the adhesive label glued to the top left corner of its housing. In lowercase letters and underlined (by using the Shift and 6 key) the original owner had typed

these are the meditations of my heart

The words had been typed as many as thirty years ago, when the machine was brand new, just out of the box, perhaps a gift on a girl's thirteenth birthday. A more recent owner had typed BUY ME FOR $5 on a piece of paper and rolled it into the carriage.

The machine was a portable; the body was plastic. The ribbon was two-tone, black over red, and there was a hole in the lid where the name Smith Corona or Brother or Olivetti had once been plugged. There was also a reddish leatherette carrying case with a half-sleeve opening and push-button latch. She punched three of the keys—A, F, P—and they all *clacked* onto the paper and settled back again. So, the thing worked, sort of.

"Is this typewriter really only five dollars?" she asked of a Lady Methodist at a nearby card table.

"That?" the woman said. "I think it works but nobody uses typewriters anymore."

That was not the question she had asked, but she didn't care. "I'll take it."

"Show me the money."

And just like that the Methodists were five bucks richer.

———

At her apartment, she prepped a supply of pineapple juice ice pops for later that night. She'd have a couple when the day cooled, when she could have her windows open and watch for the first fireflies of the evening. She pulled the typewriter from its cheap case, set it out on her tiny kitchen table, and rolled in a piece of printer paper from the feed of her Laser-Writer. She tried each of the keys—many stuck. One of the four rubber feet on the bottom of the body was missing, so the machine rocked a bit. She pounded each of the keys from the top row straight across, shifting to caps as well, trying, with some degree of success, to shake loose the stickiness. Though the ribbon was old, the letters were legible. She tried the spacing of the carriage return—single and double—

which worked, although the bell did not. The margin sliders scraped and then jammed in place.

The typewriter needed a firm scrubbing and a lube job, which she expected to run, say, twenty-five dollars. But she pondered the greater conundrum, one that faces all who buy a typewriter in the third millennium: what is its purpose? Addressing envelopes. Her mom would enjoy typewritten letters from her wandering daughter. She could send poison-pen messages to her ex, like, "Hey, Knothead, you made a big fucking mistake!" with no fear of an email record. She could type out some remark, take a digital photo of it with her phone, then post that onto her blog and Facebook page. She could make to-do lists for the refrigerator door. That made for five Hipster-Retro reasons for her to own a new-old typewriter. Chuck in a few heartfelt meditations and she had six valid uses.

She typed the original owner's intent for the machine.

T hes ea re t he med it a tio n s o f m yh ea r t.

The space bar skipped, which would not do. She grabbed her phone and googled *old typewriter repair*.

Three listings gave her the choices of a shop two hours away near Ashtabula, a place downtown that did not answer its phone, or, crazily enough, Detroit Avenue Business Machines, which was just a few minutes' walk away. She knew the shop—it was next to a tire store. She had strolled past it many times on her way to a great pizzeria and, a few

THESE ARE THE MEDITATIONS OF MY HEART

doors down, to the art supply store that was soon to go out of business. She thought the small shop was for computers and printer repair so, after taking the few-minutes' walk, was amused to see, upon closer inspection of its front window, an old adding machine, a thirty-year-old telephone answering machine, something called a Dictaphone, and an ancient typewriter. The bell over the door tinkled when she entered.

One side of the shop was nothing but printers—boxes of them along with toner cartridges for any model. The other side of the shop was like a Museum for Yesteryear's Tools of Commerce. There were adding machines with eighty-one keys and pull handles, single-use ten-key calculators, a stenographer's machine, IBM Selectric typewriters, most in beige housings, and, on wall-mounted shelves, dozens of assorted typewriters gleaming black, red, green, even baby blue. They all appeared to be in perfect working order.

The service counter was in the rear of the shop. Behind it were desks and a workbench, where an old fellow was going over papers.

"How can I help the young lady?" he asked with a slight accent, most likely Polish.

"I'm hoping you can save my investment," she said. She laid the leatherette case on the counter. She unclasped the case and produced the typewriter. The old man let out a sigh at the sight of it.

"I know," she said. "This gem needs work. Half the keys are gummed up. It rocks when I type, and the space bar is kablooey. And no bell."

"No bell," he said. "Ah."

"Can you help a girl out? I have five bucks sunk into this thing."

The old man looked at her, then back at the machine. He let out another sigh. "Young lady, there is nothing I can do for you."

She was confused. From what her eyes took in, this was *the* place to get a typewriter back into working order. On the workbench behind the old man she could see disassembled machines and parts of typewriters, for crying out loud. "Because none of those parts back there match my typewriter?"

"There are no parts for this," he said, waving his hand over the dull red typewriter and leatherette case.

"You'd have to order some? I can wait."

"You don't understand." On the edge of the counter was a little case for his official business cards. He took one and handed it to her. "What do you read on this, young lady?"

She read the card. "DETROIT AVENUE BUSINESS MACHINES. *Printers. Sales. Service. Repair.* Closed Sunday, which is tomorrow," she said. "Office Hours nine a.m. to four p.m. Saturdays, ten a.m. to three p.m. My watch and your clock both show twelve nineteen." She turned the card over. Nothing on the back. "What am I getting wrong?"

"The name of this shop," the old man said. "Read the name of my shop."

"Detroit Avenue Business Machines."

"Yes," he said. "Business *Machines.*"

"Okay," she said. "Yeah."

"Young lady, I work on machines. But *this*?" Again, a wave of his hand over her five-dollar typewriter. "This is *toy*." He said the word like he was cussing: *turd*.

"Manufactured of plastic to look like a typewriter. But this is not a typewriter."

He detached the lid on the top of what he called a toy, the plastic bending until it came off with a snap to reveal the workings inside. "The typebars, the levers, the ribbon spools—plastic. The ribbon reverse. The vibrator."

She had no idea there was a vibrator in a manual typewriter.

He banged on some of the keys, flipped levers, slid the carriage back and forth, spun the platen, hit the backspace key, all in disgust. "A typewriter is a tool. In the right hands, one that can change the world. This? This is meant to take up space and make noise."

"Can you at least give it a little oil so I can take a whack at changing the world?" she asked.

"I could clean it, oil it, tighten every screw. Make the bell ring. Charge you sixty dollars and sprinkle fairy dust upon this typewriter. But I would be taking advantage of you. In a year, the space bar would still be . . ."

"Kablooey?"

"Better you take it home and put a flower in it." He slid the typewriter back into its carrying case, like he was wrapping a dead fish in newspaper.

She felt bad, as though she had disappointed one of her teachers with a lazy effort, handing in a poorly structured essay. If she had still been with the Knothead, he'd be standing next to her agreeing with the old man, saying, "I told you the thing was a hunk of junk. Five dollars? Gone!"

"Look here." The old man waved his arm at the typewriters that lined the wall-mounted shelves. "These are machines. They are made of steel. They are works of engineers. They were built in factories in America, Germany, Switzerland. Do you know why they are up on that shelf right now?"

"Because they are for sale?"

"Because they were built to last forever!" The old man actually shouted. In him, she heard her father hollering, "Who left those bikes on the front lawn? . . . Why am I the only one dressed for church? . . . The father of this house is home and needs a hug!" She realized she was smiling at the old man.

"This one," he said, moving to the shelves. He took down a black Remington 7 typewriter, a model called Noiseless. "Hand me that tablet, there." She found a pad of blank paper on the counter and gave it to him. He ripped off two pages and rolled them into the gleaming, shining machine. "Listen." He typed the words

Detroit Avenue Business Machines.

The letters whispered onto the page one by one.

"America was on the move," he said. "Work was being done in crowded offices, small apartments, on trains. Remington had sold typewriters for years and years. Someone said, 'Let's make a smaller, quieter machine. Bring down the racket.' And they did! Did they use plastic parts? No! They reengineered

the tension, the force of the keystroke. They made a typewriter so quiet it could be sold as *noiseless*. Here. Type."

He spun the machine to face her. She pecked out

Quiet down. I am typing here.

"I could hardly hear a thing," she said. "I'm impressed."
She pointed to a two-tone machine, bone white and blue with
a rounded body. "How quiet is that one?"

"Ah. A Royal." He replaced the black Remington 7 and
pulled down a gorgeous little writing machine. "A Safari portable. A decent piece of work." He rolled in two more sheets
of paper and let her go at the keys. She thought of safari-
themed words to type.

Mogambo.
Bwana Devil.
"I had a farm in Africa . . ."

The machine was louder than the Noiseless and the keys
did not fly as effortlessly. But there were features on the
Royal that postdated the engineering of the Remington. The
number 1 with an ! A button that said MAGIC COLUMN SET.
And, it was two-tone!

"Is this bit of Royalty for sale?" she asked.

The old man looked at her with a smile and a nod. "Yes.
But tell me. Why?"

"Why do I want a typewriter?"

"Why do you want *this* typewriter?"

"You trying to talk me out of it?"

"Young lady, I will sell you any typewriter you want. I will take your money and wave you goodbye. But tell me, why this Royal Safari? Because of the color? The typeface? The white keys?"

She had to think about it. Again, she felt like she was in school, about to take a test she could fail, a pop quiz when she hadn't done the reading.

"Because of my fickle taste," she said. "Because I brought that toy typewriter home and got to thinking I would like to write on a typewriter rather than in pen and pencil but the dang thing is gummed up and guess what? My local typewriter shop refuses to touch it. In my mind, I see myself at my little table in my little apartment, pecking out notes and letters. I own a laptop, a printer, an iPad, and this, too." She held up her iPhone. "I use them as much as any modern woman does, but . . ."

She stopped. She was thinking now, about what it was that had moved her to buy a five-dollar typewriter—one with an unreliable space bar and no bell—and why she was now in this shop more or less arguing with an old man, when just the day before she'd had no opinion whatsoever about old manual typewriters.

She continued. "I have loopy penmanship, like a little girl, so anything I write looks like a motivational poster in a health clinic. I'm not one who types between sips from a tumbler of booze and drags from a pack of smokes. I just want to set down what few truths I've come to know."

She went back to the service counter and grabbed the

leatherette carrying case. She yanked the plastic typewriter from inside, carried it over to the shelves, and nearly threw it beside the Royal Safari. She pointed to the sticker on the top.

"I want my yet-to-be-conceived children to someday read *the meditations of my heart*. I will have personally stamped them into the fibers of page upon page, real stream-of-consciousness stuff that I will keep in a shoe box until my kids are old enough to both read *and* ponder the human condition!" She heard herself shouting. "They will pass the pages back and forth between them and say, 'So that's what Mom was doing making all that noise with all that typing,' and I am sorry! I'm yelling!"

"Ah," he said.

"Why am I yelling?"

The old man blinked at the young lady. "You are seeking permanence."

"I guess I am!" She paused long enough to take a deep breath, letting her lungs empty in a cheek-puffing sigh. "So, how much for this Jungleland typewriter?"

The shop was quiet for a moment. The old man held a finger to his lips, thinking, wondering what to say.

"This is not the typewriter for you." He picked up the two-tone Royal and placed it back on the wall-mounted shelf. "This was made for a young girl going off to her first year of university, her head filled with nonsense, thinking she would soon find the man of her dreams. It was meant for book reports."

He pulled down a compact typewriter with a body the color of green seafoam. Its keys were just a shade lighter.

"This," he said, again rolling two sheets of paper into the carriage, "was made in Switzerland. Along with cuckoo clocks, chocolate, and fine watches, the Swiss once produced the finest typewriters in all the world. In 1959, they made this one. The Hermes 2000. The apex, the state of the art in manual typewriters, never to be bested. To call it the Mercedes-Benz of typewriters is to inflate the quality of Mercedes-Benz. Please. Type."

She felt intimidated by the green mechanical box in front of her. What in the world could she possibly say on a sixty-year-old marvel of Swiss craftsmanship? Where would she drive a vintage Benz?

In the mountains above Geneva
The snow falls white and pure
And children eat cocoa krispies
From bowls with no milk.

"The typeface is Epoca," he said. "Look how straight and even it is. Like a ruled line. That's the Swiss. See these holes in the paper guide, on either side of the vibrator?"

So, *that's* the vibrator.

"Watch." The old man took a pen from his shirt pocket and put the point into one of the holes. He released the carriage, sliding it back and forth, underlining what she had written.

In the mountains above Geneva
The snow falls white and pure

"You can use different-colored inks for different emphasis. And see this knob here on the back?" There was a thimble-size knob with a softly serrated edge. "Tighten it or loosen it to adjust the action for the keys."

She did. The keys stiffened considerably under her fingertips and she had to muscle through.

Cuckoo clocks.

"When carbon paper was needed to make three or four copies of a letter, the firm setting would strike all the way to the last page." He chuckled. "The Swiss kept a lot of records."

Turning the knob the opposite way made the keys feather light.

Clocks. Mercedes Hermes 2000000

"Nearly noiseless, as well," she said.

"Indeed, yes," he said. He showed her how easy it was to set the margins by pressing the levers on each side of the carriage. As for tabs, they were set by pressing TAB SET. "This Hermes was made the year I turned ten years old. It is indestructible."

"Like you," she said.

The old man smiled at the young lady. "Your children will learn to type on it."

She liked the idea of that. "How much is it?"

"Never mind," the old man said. "I will sell it to you with one condition. That you use it."

"Well, not to be impolite," she said, "but *duh!*"

"Make the machine a part of your life. A part of your day. Do not use it a few times, then need room on the table and close it back into its case to sit on a shelf in the back of a closet. Do that and you may never write with it again." He had opened a cupboard under the displays of old adding machines, searching through spare carrying cases. He pulled out what looked like a square green suitcase with a flap clasp. "Would you own a stereo and never listen to records? Typewriters must be used. Like a boat must sail. An airplane has to fly. What good is a piano you never play? It gathers dust and there is no music in your life."

He placed the Hermes 2000 into the green case. "Leave the typewriter out on a table where you see it. Keep a stack of paper at the ready. Use two sheets to preserve the platen. Order envelopes and your own stationery. I will give you a dustcover—free of charge—but take it off when you are at home so the machine is ready to use."

"Does that mean we are now discussing the price?"

"I suppose so."

"How much?"

"Ah," the old man said. "These typewriters are priceless. The last one I sold for three hundred dollars. But for young ladies? Fifty."

"How about something for my trade-in?" She pointed to the toy typewriter she had brought in. She was haggling.

The old man looked at her with something akin to the Evil Eye. "What did you pay for that again?"

"Five dollars."

"You were taken." He pursed his lips. "Forty-five. If my wife ever finds out I made such a deal she will divorce me."

"Let's keep it between us, then."

———

One thing about the Hermes 2000, it was a lot heavier than the toy. The green carrying case banged against her legs as she carried it home. She stopped twice, putting the machine down not because she needed to rest but because her palm had gotten sweaty.

In her apartment, she did as she had been instructed, as she had promised. The seafoam green typewriter went on her little kitchen table, a stack of printer paper next to it. She made herself two pieces of toast with avocado and sliced a pear into sections, her dinner. She pulled up her iTunes on her phone and hit PLAY, putting the phone into an empty coffee mug for amplification, letting Joni sing her old songs and Adele her new stuff as she nibbled at her meal.

She wiped her hands of crumbs and, finally, in the blush of ownership of one of the finest typewriters ever to come down from the Alps, she rolled two sheets into the carriage and began to type.

TO DO:

STATIONERY—ENVELOPES & LETTER PAPER.
WRITE MOM ONCE A WEEK?
Groceries: yogurt / honey/ 1/2 & 1/2 .
Juice variety

Nuts (variety)

olive oil (greek)

tomatos & Onions/scallions. CUKES!

Cheap record player/HiFi. Methodist Church?

Yoga mat.

Waxing.

Dental appointment

Piano lessons (why not?)

"Okay," she said aloud, to herself, alone in her apartment. "I done me some typing."

She pushed herself away from the table, from the seafoam green of the Hermes. She pulled the to-do list from the machine and put it on her refrigerator door under a magnet. She pulled the ice pop mold from the freezer and ran it under warm water in the sink, thawing free one of the pineapple pops. Knowing she would have another, she put the Tupperware into the refrigerator to remain cold until she was ready for seconds.

In her living room she opened the windows to get a bit of breeze. The sun had set, so the first fireflies of the evening would begin to flare in a bit. She sat on the windowsill and enjoyed the cold, shaped pineapple and watched as squirrels ran along the telephone wires, perfect sine waves with their bodies and tails. Sitting there, she had her second ice pop as well, until the fireflies began to float magically above the patches of grass and sidewalk.

In the kitchen, she rinsed her hands and returned the

THESE ARE THE MEDITATIONS OF MY HEART

Tupperware to the freezer. Six ice pops would be hers tomorrow. She eyed the typewriter on the table.

An idea came into her head. How is it, she thought, that the standard version of a woman, single, after a breakup, has her drinking wine alone in a sad, empty apartment until she passes out on the couch with, she didn't know, *Real Housewives* on the television? She didn't own a television, and her one remaining vice was homemade ice pops. She had never passed out from wine in her life.

She sat back down at the table and rolled two more pieces of paper into the Hermes 2000. She set the margins in close, like a newspaper column, and the spacing at 1½.

She typed

A Meditation from My Heart

then returned the carriage and started a paragraph. Her nearly noiseless typing echoed softly around her apartment and out her open window until long after midnight.

Our Town Today with Hank Fiset

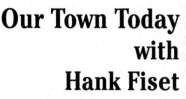

BACK FROM BACK IN TIME

OCCASIONALLY THE TYRANTS (did I say "tyrants"? I mean "Titans") who publish the *Tri-Cities Daily News/Herald* pay me for taking my wife on trips that mix business with pleasure—paid vacations to the likes of Rome (Ohio), Paris (Illinois), and the Family Compound (hers) on the shores of Lake Nixon, short trips that I then turn into a thousand words or so of A-One quality journalism, or so my staff tells me. This past week I went off on a *doozy* of a salaried adventure. I went back in time, you see! Not to the age of the dinosaurs, nor to witness the fall of the czars or to talk some sense into the captain of the *Titanic*. Rather, I time-slipped back into my own past, my hazy self-conscious, transported by a certain simple, yet magical machine . . .

* * *

INNOCENCE BREEDS ADVEN-TURE: I had set out to provide you readers with a column on the workings of the weekly swap meet at the old Empire Auto Movie Drive-In in Santa Alameda, a monster of a flea market, now in its thirty-ninth year and chockablock with sentimental debris and used hard goods. Old kitchen utensils, old clothes, old books, millions of objets d'art, both nice and rather crummy, piles of used tools and racks and racks of new ones, toys, lamps, odd chairs, and a display of hundreds of brand-new sunglasses now bring in cash where carloads of moviegoers once parked to see, say, *Krakatoa, East of Java* on a distant billboard of a screen. They heard the movie from toaster-size speakers that hooked onto the car's window. Movies in mono . . .

* * *

IMAGINE THE LARGEST yard-attic-estate sale in the Western World combined with the *Going out of Business Blowout* of every Sears store in the country and you'll have an idea of the scope of the Swap, as the regulars call it. All day, you can wander the rows of stalls, set on the hillocks between speaker posts, nibbling on chili dogs and kettle corn, wanting to buy everything the eye fancies, lim-

ited only by the cash in your pocket and the cargo space of your car. Had I wanted to, I could have paid less than two hundred dollars for a redwood burl table, a 1960s Amana refrigerator-freezer, or the front and back seats yanked out of a Mercury Montego. Luckily, I already have those things at home!

* * *

I WAS ABOUT to retire to the snack bar for a lime shave ice when I set my eyes on an old typewriter, an Underwood portable of ebony that, I kid you not, gleamed in the sun like a Springsteen hot rod. A quick inspection showed the ribbon was good once you advanced the spool a few inches, and the broken-handled case held a small supply of erasable onionskin paper. Even though a man needs a typewriter these days like he needs a timber ax, I offered the kid running the stall all of "forty dollars for this old typewriter with the broken case," and he said, "Sounds good." Should have offered a twenty. Or a fiver.

* * *

ONCE HOME, I set the machine out on the kitchen table and gave it the quickbrownfoxjumpedoverthelazydogs test. The *D* key stuck some, and the *A* key had a slight drop in it. The numbers all worked, and with some repetitive strikes the punctuation keys loosened up. I typed, I bought this typewriter today, and what do you know, the thing works ... when the bell at the end of the line sounded out clear and clean—and just like that, I was *whooshed* into the spacetime continuum for a voyage back in time which lasted either a wink of an eye or for each moment of the last forty-nine years ...

* * *

DING! First stop was the back room of my dad's old auto parts store, which is now the site of Public Parking Lot Number 9 at Webster and Alcorn. He had a big old typewriter in there though I never saw him use it. On weekends as a kid I'd poke out my name on it with my little fingers. When I grew into a teenager I avoided the store as much as I could because if I showed my face at the shop, Dad would put me to work doing inventory for the rest of the day ...

* * *

DING! I'M IN the eighth grade, the editor of the *Frick Junior High School Banner* (Go, Bobcats!), watching Mrs. Kaye, the journalism teacher, type out my "Welcome, Scrubs!" column on the ditto master that would become 350 copies of the school paper, a volume read by at least forty students. I was busting with pride at seeing my first ever byline in a published newspaper ...

* * *

DING! **I'M IN** high school now, the old campus of Logan High, on the upper floor of a building that was not earthquake safe (never felt a shudder) in a room that was meant for one subject only—Typing, levels 1, 2, and 3, for kids wanting to be professional office secretaries. Nothing but desks and indestructible typewriters overseen by a teacher so disinterested in his/her charges that I don't recall seeing our instructor. Someone put a record on a phonograph and we pecked at whatever letter was called out. One semester of Typing 1 was all I needed before volunteering for the audiovisual crew. Instead of being in a classroom, I roamed the halls of Logan, delivering movie projectors and threading up the films for teachers who didn't know how. So I never learned the many formats of business letters or what the heck a "salutation" is. I would have made a lousy secretary. Anyhow, I've been typing ever since . . .

* * *

DING! **IT IS** 2:00 a.m. in my dorm room at Wardell-Pierce College, and I'm pounding out a paper (due in eight hours) for a rhetoric class—and yes, there was such a subject. My title was "Comparative Criticism in Sports Reporting: Baseball/Track," chosen because I was a sports reporter for the *Wardell-Pierce Pioneer* and that week I had covered both a ball game and a track meet. My roommate, Don Gammelgaard, was trying to sleep, but I was on a deadline. And because it was raining there was no way I was going to tramp all the way across the quad to the Student Service Building. As I recall, I aced Rhetoric.*

* * *

DING! **I'M AT** a so-called desk in the so-called office of the *Greensheet Give-Away,* the free shoppers' guide that once provided the Tri-Cities with oodles of coupons, advertisements, and, in the back pages, local-interest stories where regular folks could see their names in print. I was crafting a piece on a dog show just held at the old Civic Auditorium—my pay was fifteen bucks!—when the most beautiful woman who ever started a conversation with me walked by and said, "You type fast." She was right, and since I was the fast type, I wooed her, wed her, and have been her main squeeze for over forty years.

* * *

THAT SAME *DISH* of American Womanhood brought me back from back in time when she came into the kitchen, telling me to move that typewriter and set the table for dinner. The grandchildren were coming over and it was going to be Make Your Own Taco Night, so a mess was due. The Underwood has powers unexplained, a vehicle for my dreams, so I locked it back into its case and carried it to a shelf in my home office, pronto. At night I think it glows in the dark . . .

* *Note: A check of transcripts shows I got a B minus in Rhetoric at W-P.*
My mistake . . .

The Past Is Important to Us

B ecause his plane was getting a new designer interior installed, J.J. Cox was hitching a ride to New York on Bert Allenberry's WhisperJet ViewLiner.

"I thought you were a smart man, Bert!" J.J. was yelling at his friend.

They'd known each other since they were twenty-year-old college kids, drivers for FedEx, full of moxie and spunk—their two heads bursting with ideas. They pooled their paychecks to rent a windowless garage on the outskirts of Salina, Kansas, which became their live-in workshop. After three and a half years of working 120-hour weeks, they'd come up with a prototype of the Shuffle-Access Digital Valve-Relay. They might as well have invented fire. Thirty years and $756 billion later, J.J. was just *now* learning that Bert had paid $6 million a pop to some outfit called Chronometric Adventures for—get this—*time travel vacations.* No, no, no!

Cindee, the fourth and youngest ever Mrs. Allenberry, was clearing the lunch china herself. She was well practiced at the chore, since she had been the flight attendant on the plane just a year ago. She had to work fast as there were but minutes before landing. Two problems with the ViewLiner: speed and vertigo. The flights from Salina to New York City took only sixty-four minutes, barely enough time to lick your fingers clean of BBQ ribs. The transparent floor and ultra-wide windows made for a nail-biter of a flight, especially if you were afraid of heights.

"I thought they had dosed us with some narcotic," Cindee called out from the plane's galley. "You wake up with a terrible headache and the room looks all different. Then you conk right back out and sleep for hours."

J.J. could not believe what he was hearing. "Let's figure out this scam. You go into a room, you fall asleep and wake up *when?*"

"Nineteen thirty-nine," Bert chirped.

"Of course you do." J.J. smirked. "But then you pass out, wake up *again* in 1939."

"Right there in the City. In a hotel on Eighth Avenue." Bert was looking down through the fuselage. Pennsylvania was becoming New Jersey. "Room 1114."

"And you spend the day sitting in a hotel room?" J.J. wanted to slap his own head, as well as some sense into that of his friend and partner.

"Everything looks real," Cindee continued as she returned to her seat to buckle up for landing. "You can touch things. You can eat and drink. And smell. The men wear stinky hair oil and the women use too much makeup and everyone smokes. And their teeth! Crooked and stained."

"Roasted coffee is in the air." Bert was smiling. "From a factory in New Jersey."

"You woke up in 1939," J.J. said. "And smelled the coffee."

"Then Cindee took me to the World's Fair," Bert said. "For my birthday. We had VIP passes."

"It was a surprise." Cindee shot her husband a smile and took his hand in hers. "The Big Six-Oh only comes once."

J.J. had a question. "Why not go back in time to see the signing of the Declaration of Independence or Jesus on the cross?"

"You can only go to 1939," Bert explained. "June 8, 1939. Chronometric Adventures has a franchise in Cleveland. You can go to 1927 and see Babe Ruth hit a home run, but I'm not a baseball fan."

"Babe Ruth. In Cleveland." J.J. nearly spit. "Jesus on the cross."

"He's gone back four times without me," Cindee said. "I'd had enough of everyone thinking we were father and daughter."

"I'm going again tomorrow." Bert smiled at the thought.

J.J. was laughing now. "Thirty-six million dollars! Bert, for half that I'll arrange for you to meet Adam and Eve in the Garden of Eden and do the naked limbo. You'll just have to trust me on how I make it happen."

"My husband would *live* in 1939," Cindee said. "But he can only stay twenty-two hours."

"Why only twenty-two hours?" J.J. asked.

Bert told him why. "Wavelength in the Time-Space Continuum is finite. You can ride the echo only so long."

"They provide this money made of paper and old-fashioned coins," Cindee said. "I bought a tiny, gold-plated space needle and globe."

"The Trylon and Perisphere," Bert corrected her.

"Right. Yeah. But when we woke up it had turned into dried-out putty."

"That's the Molecular Singularity." Bert was not buckling his seat belt for landing. He owned the plane. Screw the FAA.

"Why not go back and change history?" J.J. wanted to know. "Why don't you kill Hitler?"

"Hitler wasn't at the World's Fair that day." The Whisper-Jet began to slow, the ground rising up to meet them. The articulating engines were tilting minutely, soon to allow a vertical landing on the roof of 909 Fifth Avenue. "Besides, it wouldn't matter."

"Why the hell not?"

"Singular Dimensional Tangents," Bert said, looking down at Central Park, which hadn't really changed all that much since 1939. "There's an infinite number of tangents, but we all exist in just one."

J.J. glanced at Cindee. She shrugged her shoulders—what could she do with the old guy?

"He likes seeing what the future was going to look like. But, we're *living* in the future. You'd think that would spoil everything," she said.

———

Twelve minutes later, J.J. was zipping along the HoverLine in his Floater, headed to his private island in the sound. Bert and Cindee had taken their private elevator from the landing pad on the roof and were settling into their apartment on floors 97 to 102. Cindee immediately changed into a new outfit from one of her closets. They were going to Kick Adler-Johnson's twenty-fifth birthday party and a private hologram performance of the Rolling Stones. Bert could not stand Kick Adler-Johnson though he respected her husband, Nick, who had made a fortune buying up air and water rights around the world. Besides, the actual Stones had played the company Christmas party in 2019, when he was married to L'Audrey, wife number three. He wanted to stay home, but Cindee wouldn't allow that.

Bert wished he could go through time right then, forward to the morning, then back to 1939, to the Fair that was filled with so many promises of the world as it could have been.

———

On that first birthday visit, Cindee felt ridiculous in the old-style clothes. Bert, though, was in heaven in a double-breasted suit made to measure by the tailors of Chronometric Adventures. He marveled at every little detail, every second of the twenty-two hours they spent in 1939. How small New York City seemed! The buildings were not tall *at all*, so the sky was much more open, the sidewalks had space for everyone, and the automobiles and taxis were *huge* and *so roomy*. The cabdriver *wore a tie* and complained of the traffic out to Flushing Meadows, but if *that* were a traffic jam, Bert would take it.

The World's Fair featured the tall Trylon and the huge orb called the Perisphere, both one-of-a-kind architectural marvels that were bleach white and brilliant against the open blue sky. The Avenues of Patriots and Pioneers were meant to be taken seriously and—get this—*Courts* were dedicated to Railroads and Ships, celebrating technologies that required engines the size of his WhisperJet. There was a Giant Underwood Typewriter, an Aquacade Show, and Electro, the Mechanical Man—he walked and counted numbers on his steel fingers! Chronometric Adventures supplied a pair of VIP passes so Bert and Cindee never had to wait in line.

The fairgrounds were kept spotless. A light breeze wiggled the flags and pennants. The hot dogs cost five cents. Fairgoers were dressed to the nines, and some women even wore gloves. Hats were on most men's heads. Bert wanted to see all of the World of Tomorrow, but Cindee was uncomfortable in her ugly shoes and wouldn't eat hot dogs. They left around three in the afternoon, bound for drinks and dinner at the Hotel Astor in Times Square. Cindee was tipsy, tired, and sick of all the cigarette smoke by the time the two of them were back in room 1114 for Progression, the trip forward in time.

Two weeks later, Cindee loaded the WhisperJet with her pack of girlfriends and flew to a spa in Morocco, allowing Bert another twenty-two hours of 1939. He ordered morning coffee for just himself from Percy, the room service waiter. He had breakfast alone in the coffee shop in the Hotel Astor, the gorgeous place smack on Times Square. He had the same cabbie with the tie. Alone, he covered areas of the Fair he had missed, like the Town of Tomorrow and the Electrified Farm; he had lunch in the Heinz Dome, surveyed the Temple of Religion, and celebrated the workers' paradise that was the

Union of Soviet Socialist Republics. He listened to the conversations around him, studied the enthusiasms of the fairgoers, noting the lack of foul language and the bright colors of the clothing—not a black-on-black outfit to be seen. Fair employees seemed proud to work in their various uniforms. And it was true; a lot of people smoked.

It was on that second visit, without Cindee, when he spotted a petite, lovely woman in a green dress. She was sitting on a bench by the Lagoon of Nations, overseen by the massive sculptures of the Four Freedoms. She showed a modest amount of leg over brown shoes with straps. She carried a small purse and wore a hat with a white bud of a flower on it, more of a cap, really. She was engaged in an animated conversation with a young girl, dressed more for Sunday school than a day at the Fair.

The two of them were laughing, talking with their hands, whispering secrets to each other like they were the best of pals on the best of days in the best of places—they were the spirit of the Fair in feminine form.

Bert couldn't take his eyes off them, watching as they left the bench, heading arm in arm toward the Eastman Kodak Building. He thought to follow them, to see more of the Fair through their eyes. But his watch showed nearly 5:00 p.m., meaning there were little more than two of his twenty-two hours remaining. Reluctantly, he turned for the taxi stand that stood outside the North Entrance of the Corona Gate.

Another tie-clad taxi driver drove him back to Manhattan.

"Ain't the World Fair something?" the cabbie asked.

"It is," Bert replied.

"You see the Futurama? The trip to 1960?"

"I did not." Bert, born in 1966, chuckled to himself.

"Oh, you gotta see the Futurama," the cabbie said. "It's in the GM Building. It's a long line, but worth it."

Bert wondered if the lovely woman in the green dress had seen the Futurama. And if so, what she thought of 1960.

―――――

Although the human body takes a terrific beating by traveling back and forth in time, the Chronometric Adventures Medical Team gave Bert the go-ahead for a third trip. The World's Fair was too vast to see on just two visits, he explained to Cindee, which was true. What he didn't tell her was that, on his return to Flushing Meadows in 1939, he'd spend the day looking for the lady in the green dress.

She was not in any of the buildings dedicated to the great humanitarian works of U.S. Steel, Westinghouse, or General Electric. She was not somewhere in the Plaza of Light, the Avenue of Labor, the Court of Peace, or Continental Avenue. She was nowhere Bert had searched. So, a few minutes before 5:00 p.m., he headed to the Lagoon of Nations, and, sure enough, the woman in the green dress was there, her little friend in tow, on that bench under one of the Four Freedoms.

He sat on a bench close enough to hear them compare notes on the marvels of the Fair, their local accents turning New York into *Noo Yawk*. They simply could not decide what to do next, before the evening came and the Fountains of Light would put on a show of technical, colorful wonder.

Bert was trying to summon the courage to speak to them

when they rose up and hurried off to Eastman Kodak arm in arm, chatting and giggling. He watched them as they walked away, admiring the feminine carriage of the woman in the green dress, her hair bobbing against the back of her neck. He thought about following them, but the time was getting late and he had to return to room 1114.

For weeks, for every other minute, Bert thought of the woman in the green dress—of the way she talked with her hands and of her bobbing hair. He wanted to learn her name, to know her, if only for an extra hour or so of 1939. When Cindee announced she was joining Kick Adler-Johnson on a horseback ride through Cuba, he booked another exam with the Chronometric Adventures Medical Team.

———

He was on the bench by the Lagoon of Nations at 4:45, and yes, right on the tick of the singularity clockwork, the woman in the green dress and her young friend sat down and began their conversation. Bert guessed she was probably in her mid-thirties, though the fashions of the times made every-one look older by today's judgments. She was heavier than Cindee, than most modern-day women, as the 1939 diet was not very calorie conscious and exercise, then, was the stuff of athletes and laborers. The woman had an actual figure; the curves did her service.

He'd planned on what to say in this first conversation with a woman he had wanted to meet for over eight decades. "Excuse me," Bert said. "Do you ladies know if the Futurama is running today?"

"It is, but the line is very long," said the woman in the green dress. "We spent all afternoon in the Amusements Area. What a time we had!"

"Have you rode the Parachute, mister?" The girl could not have been more delightfully enthusiastic.

"I haven't," Bert confessed. "Should I?"

"It's not for the weakhearted," the woman said.

"You go up and up and up," the girl said, waving her hands. "You think you are going to come floating down slow and soft. But you don't. You land *ka-joink*!"

"It's true." The woman and the girl traded laughs.

"Have you seen the Futurama?" Bert asked.

"We didn't want to wait through that long line," the woman said.

"Well," Bert said, reaching into the pocket of his double-breasted suit. "I have a couple of special passes I'm not going to use."

Bert handed over the same two heavy cards Chronometric Adventures had supplied for his first trip with Cindee, the tickets embossed with the Trylon and Perisphere and the letters *VIP*. "If you show these to the attendants at the bottom of the ramp—I mean, the *Helicline*—they take you in via a secret passage."

"Oh, that's so nice of you," the woman said. "But we are definitely not VIPs."

"Believe me, neither am I," Bert said. "I have to get back to the city. Please use them."

"Can we, Aunt Carmen?" the girl asked, begged actually.

Carmen. Carmen was the name of the woman in the green dress. Carmen. The name fit her perfectly.

"I feel like a sneaky pete," Carmen said, pausing. "But let's! Thank you so much."

"Yes, thanks!" her niece said. "My name is Virginia and this is my aunt Carmen. Who are you?"

"Bert Allenberry."

"Well, thank you, Mr. Allenberry," Virginia said. "We owe our Future to you!" Arm in arm, the women headed down Constitution Mall toward the GM Building, home of the Futurama. Bert watched them go, feeling grand, happy he had returned to 1939.

For months, he daydreamed of the lovely Carmen, the sneaky pete. Though his body was in the office in Salina, the board meeting in Tokyo, on the boat off Mykonos—his mind was in Flushing Meadows, on a bench under the Four Freedoms on a day in early June of 1939. When a shareholders' meeting demanded his presence in *Noo Yawk*, he made time for another $6 million visit to room 1114.

————

The events played out as before. He offered Carmen and Virginia the VIP passes, and off they went, owing their future to him. Bert, though, wanted just a bit more time with Carmen—not long, just another half hour or so—so he stationed himself at the exit of Futurama. He waved to them as they came out.

"How was it?" he called to them.

"Mr. Allenberry!" Carmen said. "I thought you had to leave."

"Oh, I'm the boss, so I decided to change the rules."

"You're the boss?" Virginia asked. "Of what?"

"Of all the people I get to boss around."

"Since you are now in the presence of a couple of VIPs," Carmen said with a laugh, "may I treat you to some pie?"

"I happen to love pie."

"Let's go to Borden's!" Virginia piped. "We can see Elsie the Cow."

The three of them sat together with ten-cents-a-slice pie, cut into perfectly measured wedges. Carmen and Bert had nickel-a-cup coffees. Virginia had a glass of milk and talked about what marvels the year 1960 would bring, according to Futurama's predictions.

"I hope I don't still live in the Bronx in 1960," she said. Virginia's family lived in an apartment on the Parkway with her mother (Carmen's sister) and father, who was a butcher. She was in the fifth grade, belonged to the Radio Club, and wanted to be a teacher when she grew up, if she could afford college. Carmen shared a fourth-floor walk-up on East Thirty-Eighth Street with two roommates who worked as secretaries at an insurance company. She was the bookkeeper in a handbag factory downtown. All of them agreed that the World's Fair of 1939 was even better in real life than in the newsreels.

"Is your wife in New York, Mr. Allenberry?" Bert wondered how Carmen knew he was married, then realized he was wearing the wedding ring provided by Chronometric Adventures. He'd put it on by habit.

"Ah, no," he said. "Cindee is with friends. In Cuba."

"That's where Mom and Dad went on their honeymoon," Virginia said. "I came along not long after!"

"Virginia!" Carmen could not believe her niece. "Be proper!"

"It's true!" Virginia said. She had eaten all her pie filling, saving the crust for last.

"Are you married, Carmen?" Bert asked. "I'm sorry, I don't even know your last name."

"Perry," she said. "Carmen Perry. So rude of me. And, no. I'm not married."

Bert knew that already, as no ring rode her left hand.

"Mama says if you don't find a man soon, there'll be none left for you!" Virginia said. "You're almost *twenty-seven!*"

"You *hush,*" Carmen hissed, reaching over with her fork to stab the best piece of crust, then popping it into her mouth.

"You dirty rat!" Virginia laughed.

Dabbing her lips with a napkin, Carmen smiled at Bert. "It's true. I'm the last hen in the barnyard."

Carmen was only twenty-six? Bert could have sworn she was older.

After the pie, they looked at Elsie the Cow, then toured the Academy of Sports. After watching films of trick water-skiers, Bert looked at his vintage wristwatch. It was almost 6:00 p.m.

"I really do have to leave now."

"It's a shame you can't stay to see the fountains in the light show," Carmen said. "It's so lovely, they say."

"And there's fireworks every single night," Virginia piped up. "Like it's the Fourth of July all summer long."

"Virginia and I have a spot picked out to watch." Carmen's eyes were on Bert. "Are you sure you can't stay?"

"I wish I could." Bert truly wished he could. Carmen was as lovely a woman as he had ever seen. Her lips were not too thin, her smile was firm and mischievous, and her eyes were hazel, emerald green, and tinted brown.

"Thank you for a great time!" Virginia said. "We were VIPs!"

"Yes, thank you, Mr. Allenberry." Carmen offered her hand. "You've been very kind and a lot of fun."

Bert took Carmen's hand, her left hand, the hand with no wedding ring. "I've had a grand day."

In the cab on the drive back into Manhattan, Bert could almost smell Carmen's perfume—vanilla-scented lilac.

———

After one too many encores by the holographic Rolling Stones, Kick Adler-Johnson's birthday party had gone until four in the morning. Cindee was now asleep in bed, with the door closed and the blackout shades tightened down. Bert, though, was up at eight, showered and dressed, with a coffee in his hand. He had a breakfast of Mixed-Juice and an In-One protein roll, then ordered a SoloCar as he rode the elevator down to the street level.

A moment after confirming his destination as Chronometric Adventures, the car began to drive itself down Fifth Avenue at an algorithmically safe seventeen miles per hour. It crossed town on Fifty-Second, bypassing the Times Square Dome, then made three left turns before stopping on Eighth Avenue between West Forty-Fourth and West Forty-Fifth Streets.

Bert exited the car at the building that had been, in reverse order, the Milford Plaza, the Royal Manhattan Hotel, and, in 1939, the Hotel Lincoln. Most of the structure was now a service area for the Dome, which it bordered, as well as offices related to the Times Square Authority.

Chronometric Adventures was located on floors 9 through 13 of the building, not by choice or convenience, but because of historical flukes and miracles of science. Enough of the building retained the exact architectural lines of its hotel days, and one room in particular, 1114, had miraculously escaped every remodel and renovation since the place opened in 1928. With its dimensions unchanged, the room possessed the Volume Authenticity needed to echo—with pinpoint accuracy—a ripple in the Time-Space Continuum, an arc intersecting with June 8, 1939. The massive pipes, cables, and Plasma-Grids needed for Time Travel had been retrofitted to the exterior of what had been the Hotel Lincoln, above, below, and leading into room 1114; the equipment was filled with about a million of the Shuffle-Access Digital Valve-Relays invented by Bert Allenberry.

He took the lift up to the ninth floor, hearing a feminine voice announce "Chronometric Adventures" just before the door opened. The company's motto—*The Past Is Important to Us*—was inscribed on the wall, and, under it, Howard Frye was waiting.

"Mr. Allenberry. Good to see you again." Howard had

been the facilitator of every one of Bert's adventures. "I trust you are well?"

"Dandy. You?"

"Just over a cold. My son brought it home from school."

"One advantage of not having kids," Bert said. Cindee had not once said anything about wanting a child, L'Audrey before her would have made as horrible a mother as she did a mate, Mary-Lynn very much wanted to conceive but when a doctor told her that Bert's low sperm count made the biology highly unlikely, she looked to other men for satisfaction. She had remarried and quickly popped out two girls and a boy. His first marriage, to Barb, produced a baby girl. But the divorce was so filled with rancor and enmity that the only contacts Bert had with his daughter—once she turned eighteen—were occasional dinners in London, where she lived far too comfortably thanks to his support checks.

"Shall we get you to Pre-Ad?" Howard asked.

"Time's a-wasting."

"Funny, but time is actually a-plenty." Howard chuckled.

In the Pre-Adventure room, Bert was rechecked by the Medical Team. His fluids were sampled and scanned, his heart registered, and the twelve other physical properties that are affected by Progression/Reprogression were tested. He was given the five injections that would bolster his body on the molecular level and the antinausea meds to ease those initial moments of 1939. He removed his clothes as well as his rings, watch, and the thin gold chain he wore around his neck. No items from today could survive the trip to yesterday, as their molecules could irreconcilably screw up the process.

Once naked, he put on a robe with the Chronometric Adventures logo and sat through the pro-forma legal warnings.

First there was the video—slick and snappy—warning of dangers and explaining the protocols. Then came the reading material, which repeated—word for word—what had just been said. Bert already knew a person could die during Reprogression, though no one ever had; an adventurer had options for experiences—one could spend the day doing anything he or she wished—but none when it came to certain key procedures. With his thumbprint, Bert acknowledged—once again—that he understood and agreed to it all. Then Howard came into the Pre-Ad room with the large shake-like drink that would protect his digestive tract from pesky germs, circa 1939.

"Bring on the shoe leather, Howard," Bert said, toasting his glass at him.

"By now you should be able to recite this to me," said Howard, clearing his throat. As Bert sipped the blueberry-flavored liquid, Howard put into simple terms the conditions Bert had already agreed to. "You have voluntarily chosen to have Chronometric Adventures provide physical time Reprogression to this very location on June 8, 1939, for a period of no more and no less than twenty-two hours as measured by standard recognized time. From the same Volume, at 7:00 p.m. of June 8, 1939, you progress back to this place on this very day. You understand that, don't you?"

Bert nodded. "Yep."

"Chronometric Adventures in no way claims your holiday in the past is free of risk. Your adventure is governed by the same laws of physics, rules, and behavior as we know to be common."

"I fall down, I break a leg. I get punched in the nose, it's broken."

"Indeed. You will be unsupervised during those twenty-two hours. We suggest you adhere to the Agenda we have prepared with you. Another day at the World's Fair, yes?"

"You should go yourself, Howard."

Howard laughed. "Being African American, 1939 New York doesn't hold the same wonder for me."

"I get that," Bert said. On his trips back in time almost every black face he saw belonged to a porter or a janitor. Though there were black families at the Fair, taking in the same exhibits, dressed for the occasion, they were looking for promises of a future different from his.

"Should you change plans—like seeing a show or loafing in the park—there is no risk as long as you adhere to the protocols for Progression."

"I'm going back to Flushing Meadows. Maybe next time I'll loaf in the park." Bert thought of spending a day with Carmen in Central Park and wondered how he could pull that off. Virginia could ride the carousel! They could take in the zoo as it originally looked!

"Ah, yes. *Next time.*" Howard called up Bert's file on his pad. "Mr. Allenberry, I'm afraid you have reached your limit for Reprogression at this C.A. franchise."

"What?" Bert still had a third of his shake to finish.

"Your numbers from the Pre-Ad exam were a bit off from your last trip with us," Howard said. "You are showing elevated levels of Trillium in your blood and lowered measurements of cellular fluidity."

Bert didn't like the sound of that.

"Everyone's *constitution* is different, Mr. Allenberry. In fact, some of our clients have been allowed only two or three of our packages. Six is going to max you out."

"Why?"

"Molecular dynamics, Mr. Allenberry. The round trip to 1939 is a very long haul for your tissues, your body proteins, your marrow density, and your nerve endings. We can't run the risk of wearing you out. It's hypothetically possible a seventh, or even an eighth adventure to the World's Fair would be safe for you, but our insurance model disallows that. That's the bad news."

Bert was thinking of Carmen, of Virginia, of the three of them eating pie and visiting Elsie the Cow. He would do those things with them just one more time. Bad news, indeed.

"The good news," Howard chirped, "is that your Chronometric Adventures don't have to end in 1939 New York. There's Nashville in 1961. You could go to the Grand Ole Opry. We have a franchise opening in Gunnison, Colorado—a beautiful cabin in 1979. Not much goes on there, but the views are terrific."

Bert had stopped drinking. He was thinking of Carmen, of her vanilla-lilac scent and her hazel eyes.

"I am sorry, Mr. Allenberry, that's the way it is. The past is important to us, but your long life is more so."

"In that case, I'm going to need something else to take back with me," Bert said.

Bert felt the compression suit tighten as all the atoms of room 1114, including his, were jigged up by the mechanics of Chronometric Adventures. He had learned not to panic during Reprogression but still was not used to how *cold* it got, so cold that he lost all focus, all equilibrium. He knew he was lying on what would become a bed in 1939, but everything was tumbling. He fought to stay awake, alert, to see the actual process of the room reverting in time, but, as before, he passed right out.

When he felt a pounding headache, he knew he was in 1939 once again. The headaches were brutal but mercifully brief. Bert fought his way out of his compression suit—like a scuba diver's, one size too small—and sat naked on the edge of the bed, biding his time until his cranium no longer felt the crash of ball-peen hammers.

As before, the double-breasted suit was hanging in the open closet with shoes and socks on the floor. On a thin wire hanger was a button shirt and tie. Undergarments were in a basket on a chair. On the nightstand were the watch, a wedding band, a signet ring, and the wallet that contained his ID and other items that were accurate for the period and made out of pre–World War II materials. There was cash, a total of fifty dollars in the funny-looking paper currency that was once legal tender. There were heavy coins as well—a half dollar imprinted with a lady holding wheat looking toward the setting sun and ten-cent pieces, called dimes, with the head of the god Mercury. Nickels were worth five cents, and single pennies had real value in 1939.

He collected the compression suit and locked it in the vintage suitcase on the luggage stand, hiding it until he'd put it back on for Progression. Then he slipped on the vintage watch, already keeping time at three minutes after 9:00 p.m. He put the signet ring on his right hand, but remembered to leave the gold wedding band where it lay.

He saw the envelope on the desk, which would have his VIP passes for the Fair—he had ordered *three* for this, his last trip to 1939.

The window onto Eighth Avenue was open just a crack, allowing evening air to come into a room that had yet to know air-conditioning along with the sounds of traffic from Times Square. Bert wanted to get up, to get dressed and go out into the night, to walk down to East Thirty-Eighth Street, where Carmen lived in an apartment, but his body ached so. Damn the physics! He felt tired, just as before. He lay back on the bed and fell back to sleep, just as before.

He woke up when dim light was coming through the window and the city was quiet. He felt normal, like he'd taken a Green Tab and slept a healthy ten hours. His watch read ten minutes to seven. It was the morning of June 8, 1939, and he had all of twelve hours to find Carmen and Virginia. He lifted the heavy telephone receiver, pressed the only button on the phone, and was connected to the hotel operator. Once more, he asked for room service. After the same five minutes, a uniformed waiter named Percy was at his door with a tray holding a silver pot of coffee, a pitcher of real cream, cubes of sugar, a glass of water, and the morning edition of the New York *Daily Mirror*. On five previous mornings, Bert had tipped the waiter a dime, prompting a polite response of "I thank you, Mr. Allenby." This morning, Bert palmed Percy the half-dollar coin, and the man's eyed went wide. "Oh, Mr. Allenby, ain't you *flush*!"

Real cream makes coffee a thick, heavenly pleasure. Bert enjoyed the second cup as the water for his shower heated up—with the plumbing of 1939, this took a few minutes. After his scrub, he dressed. He had been taught how to knot his tie, which he thought was a silly thing to wear, but he loved the double-breasted suit that had been tailored for him nearly a century later. The fabrics were from the period, the socks did not have much elastic in them, and the shoes were like gunboats, wide and heavy, but comfortable.

Riding down in the elevator, Bert again smelled the operator's hair tonic. He didn't think it was all that stinky.

"Lobby, sir," the elevator operator said as he opened the meshed grate.

Bert was now familiar with all the smells of the Hotel Lincoln, and he liked them—the cigar smoke mixing with the wool carpets, the flowers being arranged by the black housekeepers, the florid perfume of the well-dressed ladies heading out for their day in Manhattan. Outside on Eighth Avenue, taxis idled and buses headed uptown, spewing fumes of combusted gasoline.

On foot, Bert turned right out of the lobby and right again on West Forty-Fifth Street, inhaling the scent of roasted coffee, wafting on a breeze from the Hudson River, from the Maxwell House Coffee factory in New Jersey, coffee that was good to the last drop.

This morning of June 8, 1939, he'd not take breakfast at the Hotel Astor, with its famous clock and its opulent décor. Instead Bert was going to poke his head into as many nearby coffee shops and cafes as time allowed. Carmen lived only seven blocks away. What if she was nearby, grabbing a quick breakfast before taking the subway to the Bronx to pick up Virginia? Maybe she was sitting in a Broadway diner right now, having coffee and donuts. He could meet her right then and not have to wait all day for that moment on the bench by the Four Freedoms.

He covered Times Square and the side streets, ducking in and out of cafes and peering through the windows of diners, but there was no sign of her. Reluctantly, he gave up, taking a seat at the counter of a place on Seventh, paying twenty-five cents for a breakfast of eggs, sausage, pancakes, juice, and coffee.

Bert was leaving a Mercury dime as a tip. "Ma'am," he said to the uniformed waitress with overpainted lips, "is it possible for me take the subway to the World's Fair?"

"Honey," the waitress said, "it's the best way to go." She swept the dime into her apron pocket and gave Bert directions to the IRT line.

His first ever trip on the subway cost only an Indian head nickel. The car was a jumble of people, who all smelled of *something*, if only the laundry starch of their freshly pressed clothes. No one was staring at a phone or tablet. Most of the riders read the morning papers—some oversize rectangles of newsprint and ink, others the smaller-formatted tabloids. And there were magazines with pages that held more text than pictures. Many people were smoking, even a few men with cigars and two puffing on pipes. Judging from all the guidebooks and flyers, many passengers were, like Bert, making for the World's Fair.

At each stop Bert stepped off the car just long enough to scan the stations for Carmen and Virginia because, who knows? They could be riding the IRT out to Flushing Meadows. If so, Bert could ask them for directions, they would volunteer to guide him along since they were going, too, he could confess that his *three* VIP passes were burning a hole in his pocket and why not let him treat the two ladies to a hassle-free day of no lines, no waiting? And just like that, what had in the past been less than two hours with Carmen would, in the present, become an entire day together.

But Carmen never got on the train.

"Wow! Look at that!" a rider shouted. Out the window were the Trylon and Perisphere—the Fair. Bert could see the huge globe and its attendant tower, bright and white in the morning sky. Everyone on the train gave the landmarks a glance.

The IRT discharged fairgoers at the Bowling Green Gate, where Bert paid seventy-five cents for admission and bought a guidebook for a dime.

It was only 10:30, so unless fate was to intercede there were hours before he would see Carmen again. He took a look at the Home Building Center, admired the sofa beds in Home Furnishings, and found the exhibits in the American Radiator Building just about hilarious. He kept chuckling to himself at the dazzling-in-those-days presentations by RCA,

American Telephone & Telegraph, the Communications Building, and the museum-like presentations of the Crosley Radio Corporation.

He joined the line for Democracity, the lesson in social studies that was inside the Perisphere. He was soon talking with the Gammelgards, a family of six including grandparents, who had taken the train all the way from Topeka, Kansas, to spend a week at the fair. This was their very first day, and Pop-Pop Gammelgard said to Bert, "Young man, never have I dreamed the good Lord would allow me to see such a place as this." Bert was happy to be considered a *young man*. His $756 billion afforded him every procedure in the world to look much younger than his sixty-one years.

He told the Kansans he had friends in Salina, which prompted an invitation for dinner at the Gammelgards', should Bert ever find himself in Topeka.

All morning he checked out every woman dressed in green, hoping to find Carmen. He toured every building in the Court of Power, the Plaza of Light, and along the Avenue of Labor, where uniformed ladies working for Swift & Co. demonstrated the slicing and packaging of fresh bacon. At noon, he blew two nickels on hot dogs at Childs and compared the cut of his double-breasted suit to the fashions-to-come, according to the prophets of Men's Apparel. He then walked all the way to the Amusements Area, heading for the tall iron tower that was the parachute drop. The Amusements were the Fair's most popular attractions, and the carnival crowd was thick and jumbled. Bert circled the area again and again, stopping at the parachute tower repeatedly, expecting to find Carmen and Virginia as they rose up, up, up, and came down *ka-joink*. But they were never there. So he started one last, slow walk around the area and back toward the main fairgrounds.

Then he saw her! Not Carmen at first, but Virginia! He was crossing the bridge by the Amphitheater, where the Aquacade performed, when a multicar tram passed him, Virginia sitting on the rail and, yes, Carmen beside her! They had been among the amusement rides after all, and were now en route to the Plaza of Light. Bert checked his wristwatch. If he could catch up with that tram, he'd meet Carmen nearly an hour early! He ran.

He kept sight of the tram all along the Avenue of Labor, but lost them at the Schaefer Center on Rainbow Avenue. He just couldn't keep up. The tram continued, passing the Court of States, then stopping at Constitution Mall to empty and take on new passengers. They had to be nearby! Sweating in that double-breasted suit, Bert checked Beech-Nut, Jewish Palestine, the YMCA, the Temple of Religion, and the Works Progress Administration, but no joy. Resigned to the singularity of the Time-Space Continuum, Bert was pivoting toward the lagoon benches when she appeared right in front of him.

Carmen was coming out of Brazil, holding Virginia's hand. They were laughing. Good Lord, the woman laughed so much and her smile was so adorable. He almost called out her name but remembered they had yet to meet, so instead he fell in behind them by a few yards, following them across the walkway over the man-made river that fed the Lagoon of

Nations. He didn't trail them into Great Britain but headed for the bench. A few minutes later, there she was again, with Virginia. Right on time.

"Excuse me," Bert immediately said, just as Carmen and Virginia were sitting down. "Do you ladies know if the Futurama is running today?"

"It is, but the line is very long. We spent all afternoon in the Amusements Area. What a time we had!"

"Have you rode the Parachute, mister?"

"I haven't. Should I?"

"It's not for the weakhearted."

"You go up and up and up. You think you are going to come floating down slow and soft. But you don't. You land *ka-joink*!"

"It's true."

"Have you seen the Futurama?"

"We didn't want to wait through that long line."

"I certainly don't want to miss it." Bert reached into the breast pocket of his suit. "And I have these special passes."

Bert showed them the three heavy cards embossed with the Trylon and Perisphere and the letters *VIP*. "I'm told these will get us into the Futurama via a secret passage. No waiting. I have three. And I'm alone. Would you like to join me?"

"Oh, that's so nice of you. But we are definitely not VIPs."

"Believe me, neither am I. Not sure why I even have these."

"Can we go, Aunt Carmen?"

"I feel like a sneaky pete. But let's! Thank you so much."

"Yes. Thanks! My name is Virginia and this is my aunt Carmen. Who are you?"

"Bert Allenberry."

"Well, thank you, Mr. Allenberry. We'll see the Future with you!"

The three chatted as they walked the length of Constitution Mall, below the huge statue of George Washington, and around the Trylon and Perisphere. Virginia told of all they had seen of the Fair in that day, most of it spent on the rides in the Amusement Area.

"Have you seen Electro, the Mechanical Man?" Bert asked. "He can add up numbers on his metal hands."

The General Motors Building was next to that of the Ford Motor Company. Ford showed fairgoers how their automobiles were built, then let them drive a car along a dipsy doodle of a road around the building. GM took its visitors into the future, first by ascending a long ramp, one so modern they called it a Helicline, to a cleft in the architecture so majestic it looked like a gateway into the Promised Land. The line of people waiting to see Futurama looked to number in the millions.

But, flashing their VIP cards at a pretty girl in a GM uniform, Bert, Carmen, and Virginia were taken to a door on the ground level.

"I hope you aren't tired," the girl said. "We have a few flights to climb."

The machinery of the Futurama bumped and whirred around them. They could hear music coming through the walls along with the murmur of a narration.

"You'll notice the soundtrack matches exactly what you

are seeing," the girl explained. "GM is truly proud of the engineering that went into the Futurama. It's absolutely modern."

"Are we going to be driving a *car*?" Virginia asked.

"You'll find out!" The girl opened a door revealing the starting point of the ride—sunlight and people were streaming in through the opening. "Enjoy your stay," the girl said.

There were no automobiles, but rather a long train of wheeled, sofa-like carts lined end to end, each enclosed in a shell. Passengers were climbing into the shells, which never stopped moving as the cars passed through the opening of a tunnel.

The three intrepid voyagers climbed into one, Virginia first, then Carmen, followed by Bert. Before they knew it they were in darkness. Music played and a narrator welcomed them to America, as it would be in the year 1960. The voice was so clear it was like the announcer was in the car with them.

A city appeared before them—a world in miniature that stretched to the horizon. The skyscrapers in the center stood like trophies, some connected to each other by sky bridges. The narrator explained that in just a few decades American cities would be planned and built to the specifics of perfection. Streets would be clear and ordered. Highways would flow with modern automobiles—GM cars, each of them— with traffic that never cluttered or jammed. The sky would be filled with aircraft carrying goods and passengers to terminals as conveniently placed as filling stations. The countryside would be scattered with farms, homes, and power stations, supplying 1960 with all the food, space, and electricity the American people would need.

The houses and towers and cars and trains and planes were filled with a happy, invisible populace that had tamed the wild chaos of the past; they'd figured out not only how to build the future but how to live in it side by side, in peace.

Virginia was riveted to her seat as the future rolled by. Carmen smiled at her and looked at Bert. She leaned toward him and whispered, "She'll live there and likes what she sees."

The words landed on Bert like so many soft kisses. The narration had paused, leaving only the swelling strings of violins and cellos from the musical score. He smelled Carmen's perfume, the soft whiff of lilac mixed with vanilla. Her lips stayed close to his cheek.

"Do you think it will all happen?" Carmen asked quietly. "Just like this?"

Finding her ear surrounded by the dark curl of her black hair, Bert whispered back, "If it does, it will be wonderful."

When they exited, the afternoon shadows had grown longer. As they crossed the Bridge of Wheels over the Grand Central Parkway, Virginia announced that she would be thirty years old in 1960. "I wish I could jump in a time machine right now and go there!"

Bert checked his watch—it was 5:56 p.m. In the past, he had been in a taxi by now, on his way back to room 1114. By 7:00 he had undressed, removed all the items that had been provided for his adventure, like the rings and the watch, had squeezed back into his compression suit, and was lying on the precisely placed bed for Progression out of 1939. He *should* be leaving right now; the taxi stand was just outside the gate on the other side of Chrysler Motors. Instead, he asked Carmen when the Fountains of Light show was to start.

"Not until dark," she said. "Hey, since you are now in the presence of a couple of VIPs, may I treat you to some pie?"

"I happen to love pie."

"Let's go to Borden's!" Virginia said. "We can see Elsie the Cow."

Over pie and coffee, he relearned about Carmen and her niece—of the Radio Club and the roommates on East Thirty-Eighth Street. Everything was just as it had been. Then the past took a turn.

"Do you have anyone special in your life, Mr. Allenberry?"

Bert looked into Carmen's eyes. Framed now in the décor of Borden's Food Court, they'd turned an even deeper shade of green.

"She means are you married!" Virginia teased.

"Virginia! I'm sorry, Mr. Allenberry. I don't mean to be forward, but I see you have no wedding ring and I just thought, well, a fellow like you *must* have someone special."

"I've thought so, many times," Bert said, wistfully. "I'm forever looking, I guess."

"You bachelors are so lucky. You can wait and wait for the right girl to come along and nobody says *boo.*" She rattled off the names of movie stars and athletes who had yet to marry, names Bert did not recognize. "But us ladies? If we wait too long we become old maids."

"Mama says if you don't find a man soon, there'll be none left for you!" Virginia giggled. "You're almost *twenty-seven!*"

"You *hush*," Carmen hissed, reaching over with her fork to stab the best piece of crust, then popping it into her mouth.

"You dirty rat!" Virginia laughed.

Dabbing her lips with a napkin, Carmen smiled at Bert. "It's true. I'm the last hen in the barnyard."

"How old are you, Mr. Allenberry?" Virginia asked. "I'm guessing you're like Mr. Lowenstein, my school principal. He's almost forty. Are you forty yet?"

"Young lady, I am going to throw you into the Lagoon of Nations! Mr. Allenberry, I'm sorry. My niece has yet to learn the practice of tact. Maybe by 1960."

Bert laughed. "I'm like your aunt Carmen. The last rooster in the barnyard."

They all laughed at that. Carmen reached over and took his wrist. "Aren't we a pair?" she said.

Bert should have excused himself right then. Six p.m. had passed. If a cab was available, he could be in room 1114 just in time for Progression. But this was his last day ever with Carmen. He would never see the woman in the green dress again.

Now, Bert Allenberry *was* a smart man, many say a genius. His invention of the Shuffle-Access Digital Valve-Relay had changed the world and garnered him the rapt attention of audiences at conferences full of movers and shakers—in Davos, Vienna, Abu Dhabi, and Ketchum, Idaho. He had teams of lawyers obeying his dictates, researchers and developers turning his ideas of whimsy into realities. He had more money than the GNP of most nations of the world, including those where he owned factories. He had donated to very good causes and had his name on buildings he had never even bothered to visit. He had everything a man—a very rich man—was supposed to have, need, or want.

Except for time, of course.

Chronometric Adventures said he had twenty-two hours of June 8, 1939, to do whatever he wanted. But now, what he wanted was to *stay awhile*. There must be some wiggle room, right? After all, Progression, or was it Reprogression—he was never sure—could not begin until his body, all his atoms and molecules, were in place in room 1114 of the Hotel Lincoln on Eighth Avenue. He understood why Chronometric Adventures demanded such terms—to cover their asses! Why did he *have* to be in that tight compression suit and on that bed according to the tick of the clock? Was he Cinderella at the Ball? Why couldn't he saunter into the room at, say, midnight, then slip into that rubber suit and then *whoosh* away? What was the big deal?

"Have you seen the Time Capsule?" he asked Virginia.

"I read about it in school. It's buried for the next five thousand years."

"They have what's in it on display in Westinghouse. Electro the robot, too. Do you know what television is? You just have to see television." Bert was rising from the table. "Shall we go to Westinghouse?"

"Let's!" Carmen's eyes were smiling again.

The Time Capsule was loaded with silly stuff—Mickey Mouse comics and cigarettes and whole sets of books printed on microfilm.

Though the Time Capsule and Electro were impressive, television was what had Virginia over the moon. She could see her aunt and Mr. Allenberry on a small screen, in black and white, almost like they were stars in a movie, but their images were in miniature, projecting from a screen in a cabinet no bigger than the radio at home. In fact, they were in another *room*, standing in front of a camera, one unlike any she had ever seen, and they were also in front of her. The vision was thrilling. When they switched places, Virginia waved and spoke into the microphone: "This is me, on the television saying hello from right *here* and you can see me right *there!*"

"Look at you!" Carmen said. "You look so pretty! So grown up! Oh, Bert!" She turned to him. "This should be impossible, but here it is!"

Bert was looking not at Virginia on the screen but at Carmen. He was thrilled that he was no longer Mr. Allenberry.

Checking his watch, Bert saw that it was 7:06. The deadline had passed, the twenty-two hours were up, and, lo and behold, there was wiggle room!

They visited the DuPont, Carrier, and Petroleum Industry Buildings, none of which had the socko exhibits to match television. The Glass Building, the American Tobacco exhibit, and Continental Baking were just time killers; the longer they lingered in them the sooner came darkness and the light show.

After watching films of water-skiers in the Academy of Sports, he bought cups of ice cream, which they ate with little wooden spoons.

"Here's our spot for the show!" Virginia claimed a bench for the three of them. In the growing indigo of the evening, they could see all the way from the Lagoon to giant George Washington, silhouetted against the Perisphere, surveying the great nation he had sired. As night fell, the buildings of the Fair became so many tracings of brightly lit lines on deepening black. The skyscrapers of Manhattan lit up the horizon. The illuminated fairground trees looked to be glowing from within, from their own inner light.

Bert Allenberry wanted this night to last forever, for all time. He wanted to sit beside Carmen at the Lagoon of Nations, listening to the murmur of the Fair, with her scent of lilac and vanilla stirring the warm air of 1939.

When Virginia collected their ice cream cups and took them to a trash bin, Bert and Carmen were alone for the first time ever. He reached for her hand.

"Carmen," he said. "This has been a perfect day." Carmen was looking at him. Oh, those hazel eyes. "Not because of Futurama. Or television."

"Elsie the Cow?" Carmen said, her breath catching as she smiled.

"Would you allow me to give you and Virginia a ride home when the Fair closes?"

"Oh, I couldn't do that. My sister lives too deep in the Bronx."

"We'll take a taxi. Then I can drop you off at your place. On East Thirty-Eighth Street."

"That would be very kind of you, Bert," Carmen said.

Bert wanted to hold Carmen in his arms, to kiss her,

maybe in the back of a taxi on East Thirty-Eighth Street. Or, in room 1114. Better yet, on the one hundredth floor of his building at 909 Fifth Avenue.

"I'm glad I came to the Fair today." Bert smiled. "So I could meet you."

"I'm glad, too," Carmen whispered. Her hand never left his.

Music began to play from speakers hidden around the Lagoon of Nations. Virginia ran back to the bench just as the fountains shot water into the sky, lights turning the geysers into columns of liquid color. Every patron of the Fair stopped to watch. Projections turned the Perisphere into a luminescent ball of clouds.

"Wow!" Virginia loved it.

"Beautiful," Carmen said.

The first fireworks broke into the sky, bursting into cascading comets, fading to smoke.

That's when Bert felt a ball-peen hammer strike his forehead. His eyes went painfully dry and scratched terribly. His nose and ears started to run with blood. His legs went numb, and his lower back seemed to separate from his hips. A hot, searing pain shot through his chest as the molecules that made up his lungs began to separate. He had the sensation that he was falling.

The last words he heard were Virginia yelling, "Mr. Allenberry!" The last thing he saw was the fear in Carmen's hazel eyes.

Stay with Us

MUSIC: "Mama Said Knock You Out" by LL Cool J

FADE IN

EXT: LAS VEGAS. MORNING

We know this place—the Strip. The casinos. The fountains. But wait . . . there is a new, huge, luxurious hotel on the skyline.

OLYMPUS.

Bigger than all the others. If you are a Big Roller, you frolic and gamble with the gods at OLYMPUS.

CLOSE ON: EYES OF FRANCIS XAVIER RUSTAN

A.K.A.: F.X.R. Green eyes, flecked with gold, that dance with delight at all they see.

CLOSE ON: COMPUTER SCREENS

Left screen: DETAILED ARCHITECTURAL PLANS, of a vast SOLAR ENERGY COLLECTION FIELD

Middle screen: Google Earth IMAGES of unsettled, bare parcels of land, USGS MAPS, topography CHARTS, and environmental GRAPHS

Right screen: FLOATING IMAGES. A guy catching a marlin, a guy hang gliding, a guy rock climbing, a guy white-water rafting. Steve McQueen in BULLITT. The guy is always F.X.R.

Except for Steve McQueen.

A NEWS TICKER scrolls along the bottom of this screen. Windows pop up with ALERTS and MESSAGES and NOW PLAYING, which switches from LL Cool J to . . .

MUSIC: "Mambo Italiano" by Dean Martin

A TEXT BOX pops up:

MERCURY: Boss? Breakfast as usual?

CALLER ID shows us MS. MERCURY—Jet-black hair cut short. Slashes of red lipstick.

F.X.R. replies with *clicks* of his keyboard. *F.X.R.: Called it in. Nicholas is bringing it up. MERCURY: Who? F.X.R.: New guy.*

CUT TO:

INT. SERVICE ELEVATOR—SAME

MS. MERCURY is a stunning specimen, as intimidating as a supermodel. Six feet tall, rail thin, Pilates-shaped physique. Dressed in black on black. She is a woman not to be messed with in any shape or form.

She has read the text, and screams!

MS. MERCURY

What *new guy*!?

She has been the aide-de-camp for F.X.R. over the last 12 years—a job she lives and breathes every minute of every day.

That a "new guy" is bringing her boss his breakfast is a fact that should never have escaped her!

She is tapping away on a gizmo on her wrist, a large WATCH/COMPUTER— getting MEMOS, TEXTS, SCHEDULES—and finally a series of EMPLOYEE PHOTOS. She swipes the screen until she finds . . .

NICHOLAS PAPAMAPALOS—19 years old. A look of confusion in his eyes, like a kid starting his very first job ever, which he is.

The elevator doors open and there he is—NICHOLAS PAPAMAPALOS, in the uniform of a room service waiter at Olympus, pushing a table of covered dishes.

> MS. MERCURY (CONT'D)
> *(smiling way too much)*
> Nicky my boy!
>> *Nicky is confused. Why does this tall lady know his name? He enters the elevator.*

> NICHOLAS
> I'm new here.

> MS. MERCURY
> You sure are! Look at you in your too-big uniform, with your breakfast order for F.X.R. all ready!

> NICHOLAS
> Am I in trouble?

> MS. MERCURY
> Not yet, kiddo.

> NICHOLAS
> How do you know I'm taking this to Mr. Rustan?
>> *Ms. Mercury presses the button for the 101st floor. The doors close and the elevator slowly rises.*

MS. MERCURY

Because I know everything that happens at
Olympus, Nick-chick. Do you know why?

NICHOLAS

No. I'm new here.

MS. MERCURY

Let me tell you a little about myself.
(then)
You know what I was doing until three a.m. this
morning? Seeing to it that Francis X. Rustan's
collection of one hundred and thirty-two antique
motorcycles were moved into a new climate-
controlled warehouse, where they will be kept in
perfect running order on the off chance that he
chooses to someday take one out for a spin. The last
time he did that was May of 2013. That he has yet
to inspect the new storage facilities for his collection
of antique player pianos or the vintage Burma-Shave
signs he's purchased over the years did not deter
me from having two dozen men put motorcycles in
protective wrapping and gingerly place them in a
high-tech garage the size and approximate cost of
Bruce Wayne's Batcave.
(then)
F.X.R. is a very rich man who pretends to be all-
knowing and all-seeing when it comes to his vast
empire. Accent on, line under, italicize *pretends*.
Here's something none of his millions of admirers,

acolytes, influence peddlers, and brownnosers understand about El Jefe—he couldn't make his own lunch given a kaiser roll, cold cuts, and a jar of mayonnaise. His head is in the clouds because that brain of his is so damn full of the knuckleheaded schemes that pay off so well. So, we are here—you and I—to make the life he leads possible. I to work twenty-two-hour days at his beck and call. You to prep his meals and taste-test them for poison. I'm kidding. About the poison. Or am I?

Ding! They are on the 101st floor.

INT. SERVICE HALL, 101ST FLOOR—SAME It's a long hall!

> MS. MERCURY
> *(still smiling)*
> Tell me you have his breakfast order perfect or I'll cripple you.

> NICHOLAS
> I had it all set. The seven-grain organic granola, sliced mango and pineapple, tomato juice and cinnamon cafe au lait. But then . . .

> MS. MERCURY
> *(smile? Vanished!)*
> But then?

> NICHOLAS
> Half hour ago he messaged the kitchen.

MS. MERCURY

Show me the message!

Nicholas shows her his Watch/Computer:

FXR: *Stove Team —Flag on play—Me want griddle cakes!*

MS. MERCURY (CONT'D)

Griddle cakes! GRIDDLE CAKES? No no no no!

*She lifts a cover! There, on a plate: griddle
cakes. Also known as pancakes.*

MS. MERCURY (CONT'D)

Jiminy Expletive! Those are griddle cakes!

NICHOLAS

With boysenberry syrup.

*Ms. Mercury is now beside herself with
worry.*

MS. MERCURY

Oh, Nicky—Nicky. This is not a good sign. My day
may have just been ruined, and I tell you this—if I'm
going down today I am taking you with me.

NICHOLAS

Because of griddle cakes? I didn't do anything! I'm
new here!

MS. MERCURY

The Boss only orders cakes from the griddle
when he's antsy with ideas. I'll have to arrange
an expedition to the fjords of Iceland for thirty of

F.X.R.'s closest friends so he can paddle a kayak
in open water. Or have a zip line assembled over
the gorges of the rain forest in Uganda so anyone
can look down and see chimpanzees in the wild go
by. Or make sure every employee of Olympus is
shackled to . . .

(the Watch/Computer)

. . . one of these things. And I've actually had to
make real those very orders. *Griddle cakes* mean
I'm getting a work assignment that wouldn't make
sense to hamsters. *Griddle cakes* have just ruined my
already miserable day.

NICHOLAS
Why do you do this job?

MS. MERCURY
I have no answer to that question other than my big
honker of a paycheck.

> *They are at the door of the only hotel room on*
> *the 101st floor.*

MS. MERCURY (CONT'D)
Set up by the fake waterfall. Straighten your name
tag. And smile. He likes employees who look like
they love their jobs.

> *She pauses. Takes a breath and changes her*
> *demeanor to a sunny smile. Her ability to*
> *transform this way is frightening.*
> *She knocks . . . and enters.*

INT. PENTHOUSE—DAY

A snazzy place, complete with a fake waterfall, state-of-the-art exercise equipment, wall-size video screen in front of a row of vintage movie-theater chairs. The windows look out on most of Las Vegas.

> MS. MERCURY
> *(happy as could be)*
> I have griddle cakes for the big boss man!
>> *F.X.R. rises from his computer workstation.*

> F.X.R.
> That was fast.

> MS. MERCURY
> You always say that!
>> *Nicholas sets up the room service table.*

> F.X.R.
> You Nicholas?
> *(reading the name tag)*
> Looks like it. Welcome aboard. What happened to O'Shay?

> MS. MERCURY
> O'Shay's wife had that baby, remember? And yes, I already sent over a new crib and a cold-water humidifier, along with two full-time nurses.
>> *F.X.R. sits for his griddle cakes.*

F.X.R.

Look at these beauties. If they were made in a pan,
they're pancakes. A griddle, and they are griddle
cakes. Were these made in a pan or on a griddle,
Nico?

NICHOLAS

I didn't actually see, sir. I'm new here.

F.X.R.

Sir? Around here I'm plain old F.X.
        (then)
I say they're griddle cakes.
        (he pours the berry syrup)
Ms. Mercury. I don't know what was on the docket
for today but cancel everything.

MS. MERCURY

Last time you said that you had me tramping
through Mississippi so you could buy up every kenaf
farm in the Delta.

F.X.R.

Think I nailed down the place for the Solar Pipeline
Facility.

MS. MERCURY

Wow. No kidding. Super.
        She sighs and plops herself down on the couch.
        She starts swiping around the Internet on her
        Watch/Computer.

(to herself)

Gonna be a long day . . .

> *F.X.R. picks up his plate and walks to the*
> *computers, pulls up images, and points with*
> *his fork dripping with boysenberry.*

F.X.R.

Shepperton Dry Creek ain't nothing much now.
Flat, wide. Dusty. But, a miracle of Mother Nature
that gets more sunshine than Taylor Swift gets
Facebook likes.

MS. MERCURY

(Ms. Mercury is "LIKING" a post on Taylor
Swift's Facebook page)

That's a lot.

F.X.R.

Old Route 88 cuts close to Shepperton Dry Creek.

MS. MERCURY

Does it? *I don't know anything.*

F.X.R.

Someone enterprising is going to start buying up
the land along that stretch of highway for the influx
of traffic it's gonna bring.

MS. MERCURY

(bored, examining nails)

Uh-huh.

                    F.X.R.

So, let's get goin'.

                  MS. MERCURY

Goin' where?

                    F.X.R.

Along old Route 88. It'll be fun! Just like that
trip we took in Costa Rica on the Pan-American
Highway to collect spiders.

                  MS. MERCURY

Yeah. That was a blast. I was bitten.

                    F.X.R.

You healed.

                  MS. MERCURY

Make Nick go with you today.

                    F.X.R.

I can't boss Nick around. He's in the union.
        (then)
You are in the union, right?

                  NICHOLAS

I am, sir. Er, F.X.

                  MS. MERCURY

Why can't you get married and make your wife do
this stuff?

F.X.R.

I don't need a wife. I have you, Ms. Mercury. Wives
don't put up with guys like me.

MS. MERCURY

But I have to? I've got too many things to do right
here to keep your empire afloat.

F.X.R.

A road trip will do us both good.
> *She throws up her hands.*

MS. MERCURY

You see, Nicholas! You and your griddle cakes!

NICHOLAS

What did I do?

F.X.R.

What did Nick do?

MS. MERCURY

One of these days I'm gonna quit this job and
do something dignified, like professional water
skiing . . .
> *(typing on her Watch/Computer)*

I'll get the jet ready.

F.X.R.

The big jet and the little jet. You take the little one
and scrounge up some ground transpo. I'll come in
the big jet after I've done my workout.

MS. MERCURY

Whatever you wish, O Titan of Industry. Which
fantasy automobile do you want to add to the
warehouse? A Monza? Surfer Woodie?

F.X.R.

Let's keep a low profile to blend in with the locals.
The economy bypassed that part of the nation.
    (pulls out a wad of cash)
Get me whatever car eight hundred dollars can
purchase.

MS. MERCURY

Eight hundred dollars? For a car? It'll be a hunk of
junk!
    F.X.R. pulls out a few more bills.

F.X.R.

Make it eight fifty.
    (pulls a twenty)
Nick? For you.
    Nicholas takes the money.

NICHOLAS

Thank you, Mister F.X.

CUT TO:

EXT. AIRFIELD, SOMEWHERE IN THE MIDDLE OF
NOWHERE—DAY

A single landing strip and a weathered Field Business
Office. Not many aircraft land at this place. But look here . . .

A Big Jet is taxiing up beside a parked Little Jet. Both
planes have the Olympus logo painted on the sides.

Ms. Mercury—still in her black on black—sits behind the
wheel of a 1970s-era Buick convertible with the top down.

The stairs of the Big Jet pop open, and there is F.X.R. in
clothes he thinks the common people wear—a fruity-
looking western shirt with too much piping tucked into
an old pair of Jordache designer jeans, a belt with a huge
Marlboro cigarettes belt buckle, and flame-red cowboy
boots.

He wears a too-perfectly-broken-in John Deere cap and has
a straw cowboy hat in his hand.

> MS. MERCURY
> Hey, Duke, or Bo, or whoever you are. Is my boss in
> that plane?

> F.X.R.
> *(re: his costume)*
> Pretty good, huh? Authenticity is the key.

> MS. MERCURY
> Glad some of the casino showgirls let you raid their
> dressing room.

F.X.R.

(re: the car)

How's she running?

MS. MERCURY

I've burned half a tank of gas and a pint of oil just driving from the lot. Good news is, I bargained down to seven hundred bucks.

F.X.R.

Put the change in petty cash. Here.

(the cowboy hat)

Blend in!

He plops the hat on her head.

F.X.R. (CONT'D)

(laughing)

Don't we look great?

MS. MERCURY

All that fortune and your idea of fun is dressing up like a poor mortal with no fashion sense. I can arrange this to be permanent. Just give me all your money and you'll live happily ever after.

F.X.R. runs around to the passenger seat, trying to hop in over the door. He lands in a heap on the front seat, one foot hooked on the door.

MS. MERCURY (CONT'D)

Gangway for adventure!

> *She hits the gas and the car spins out and*
> *away, spewing dust and gravel.*

MUSIC: "I've Been Everywhere" by Hank Snow

EXT. HIGHWAY 88—LATER

> *The Buick chugs along down the highway.*
> *F.X.R. smiles into the wind.*

F.X.R.

I should get out of that penthouse more often!

MS. MERCURY

Two weeks ago you were boogie boarding on the
Great Barrier Reef!

F.X.R.

To see America. Don't see enough of my native land.
Open road. Big sky. Asphalt ribbon with nothing but
a dotted line and the horizon. I love this country!
God help me, but I do love it so!

> *(then)*

It's good for the soul to come down from the
mountaintop sometimes, Ms. Mercury. Otherwise,
all you see are the tops of mountains. I should put
that in a memo to all the employees.

MS. MERCURY

Do that. It would inspire us all.

> *(then)*

So, where are we going, cochise?

Sending a message from his Watch to hers . . .

F.X.R.

Here. A little town called Phrygia.

(he tries three different pronunciations)

Population 102.

WATCH: *Photos, facts, information about Phrygia . . .*

F.X.R. (CONT'D)

Formerly a major stop on Route 88 that once billed itself as America's Hospitality Capital. Let's see how hospitable they are to the likes of us.

MS. MERCURY

Before you buy up every square inch and acre.

(studying her Watch)

Oh, hell. This drive will take us hours! I'm gonna fry!

EXT. A HUGE SIGN—Faded, ancient, with broken neon tubes and peeling paint that says MOTEL OLYMPUS . . .

Still barely visible are the large figures of a man and woman, both waving to nonexistent traffic, calling out in sun-bleached letters *"Stay with us!"*

MUSIC: *"Que Te Vaya Bonito"* on an accordion

SUBTITLES IN ENGLISH OF THE SPANISH LYRICS

"I don't know if your absence will kill me

even if my chest is made of steel . . ."

CUT TO:

EXT. MOTEL OLYMPUS, PHRYGIA—DAY—SAME

Nothing at all like its namesake in Las Vegas . . . Nothing at all.

Like the sign, the Motel Olympus has seen better days. The best that can be said of it? It's clean.

The MUSIC is coming from JESUS HILDALGO, who plays the final bars of a song so beautiful it even sounds great on an accordion.

SUBTITLES: "But no one will call me a coward

Without knowing how much I love her . . ."

An old couple—PHIL and BEA (yes, that's them on the sign)—applaud as Jesus packs away his instrument and loads it into his old pickup truck.

PHIL

Talent like I never seen!

BEA

Every time you play I find myself all *misty*. You have a gift, Jesus.

JESUS

You make me feel so good, Mr. Phil and Mrs. Bea. You have always made me feel I was at home.

BEA

That's because you have been, Jesus. You've been at our home.

PHIL

Good luck there in Chesterton. I hear they get benefits galore at that windshield factory.

JESUS

Thank you. I will come back to see you many times. I promise I will.

BEA

Bring us a windshield you made yourself.
> *Jesus climbs in, and the pickup truck pulls out of the motel lot, honking. Phil and Bea watch the truck disappear down the road. They are quiet for a moment.*

PHIL

There goes our only guest. One less bed to make.

BEA

Lord, am I going to miss him playing that 'cordine.

PHIL

Sixty-two less dollars a week. Why would anyone
want to leave this little spot of paradise to live in a
podunk burg like Chesterton . . .

BEA

Oh, stop serving crab apples. Do some weeding.
        Phil sizes up the woman he married. The
        woman he still finds so very beautiful . . .

PHIL

Don't treat me like some hired hand.

        (then)
Unless you wearing that pretty dress means you
want to play Seduce the Hired Hand.

BEA

You go out there with the weedwacker and flex your
rippling muscles, maybe I'll get all heated up.

PHIL

Tell you what, woman. Give me twenty minutes to
clear the south forty, then meet me in room 10. I
just might be naked in the shower.

BEA

It's a date.
        A Buick convertible is coming down the road,
        its turn signal blinking.

BEA (CONT'D)

Hold on. Looks like we have guests.

PHIL

Rats.

(shouting)

Come back in an hour, folks!

> *The car pulls in to the motel. Hey, it's none
> other than F.X.R. and Ms. Mercury! The top
> is still down.*
>
> *He is smiling. She looks like hell after
> driving three hours in a convertible with
> the top down. They pull right up to Phil
> and Bea.*

F.X.R.

Howdy!

PHIL

Howdy-do?

BEA

Howdy-do to you.

MS. MERCURY

How-diddly-dee-dooty-do.

F.X.R.

(all "folksy")

As you can see, we happen to be weary travelers
who have been on the road too long.

MS. MERCURY

With no sunblock.

F.X.R.

We seek a respite from our journey. You know—
some real hospitality.

BEA

How about trying a motel of some kind?

F.X.R.

Know any good motels around?

BEA

Well, let's think here. Motels. You need a motel . . .

PHIL

Best motel in the world is right here on the
outskirts of Phrygia. Called the Olympic or the
Olympian or something.

F.X.R. looks at the faded sign.

F.X.R.

Motel Olympus!

PHIL

That's the one.

F.X.R.

Ms. Mercury! Motel Olympus! This is fate!

*Ms. Mercury wants out of the car and into a
shower ASAP.*

MS. MERCURY

It must be. This parking lot screams *destiny*.

BEA

Welcome. I'm Bea. He's Phil. Stay with us!

> *These two adorable old folks immediately*
> *freeze in the positions of the sign behind them,*
> *complete with waving arms.*
>
> *F.X.R. and Ms. Mercury share a look.*
> *Phil and Bea have not moved. They are still*
> *frozen in their "sign" position. They remain*
> *so. For a beat. Then another.*
> *And another.*

MS. MERCURY

So, do you have a vacancy?

BEA

(breaking her pose)

Nothing but.

CUT TO:

INT. MOTEL OFFICE—SAME

CLOSE ON:

A faded photo from fifty years before—young Phil and Bea, in that same pose. Obviously the model for the sign back when it was constructed.

The office is clean and cozy. F.X.R. inspects the photo as Bea prepares the paperwork.

F.X.R.

Too firm and I can't move my neck in the morning.

(he tries a pillow, grabs his neck)

Ouch! No way!

BEA

We sleep with some good down models. We'll put fresh cases on them and let you have them for the night.

F.X.R.

And, finally, this picture here over the bed.

The one of a babbling brook and a farmhouse.

F.X.R. (CONT'D)

It reminds me of a foster home I once spent an eternity in. Do you have some other painting we could hang?

Ms. Mercury mouths the words "foster home"?

PHIL

Room twelve has one with some ducks.

F.X.R.

I have a fear of waterfowl.

PHIL

There's one with some wagon wheels on it in Eight.

MS. MERCURY

Wagon wheels? Why paint wagon wheels? I don't understand.

PHIL

There's a clown face in Room Thirteen.

No way. The thought makes F.X.R. shudder.

BEA

How about we just remove all the artwork?

F.X.R.

Problem solved.

CUT TO:

INT. MOTEL ROOM—DAY

Later. Phil is moving in a new mattress. Ms. Mercury is marveling at the softness of the bath towels, and Bea is putting pillowcases on the borrowed pillows.

MS. MERCURY

(completely amazed)

What do you use to make this towel so soft? It's like mink!

BEA

I just wash 'em, honey. Then I hang them out to dry.

MS. MERCURY

I can't wait to take a shower!

BEA

When you do, let the hot water run. It takes a while.

F.X.R.

Okay. Last item. How does a soul get nourishment around here?

PHIL

Used to be a cafe right across the road. Truman's, it was called. Great pie. Even better pot roast. Closed in 1991.

BEA

Fast-food places over in Chesterton. Thirty-six miles as the crow flies.

PHIL

I'd rather eat crow than fast food in Chesterton.

MS. MERCURY

Just as well. We're stuck here. The car blew its oxyspoiler.

PHIL

(remembering, and bolting)
I gotta call Tommy Boyer!
As he leaves . . .

MS. MERCURY

Any chance of room service?

BEA

If you don't mind getting your hands a little dirty.

CUT TO:

EXT. BACK OF MOTEL—LATER

A mini-farm. Complete with henhouse and garden.
Beautifully kept. Bea is expertly inspecting vegetables while
Ms. Mercury tries to get tomatoes off a vine.

> MS. MERCURY
> *(tossing into a basket)*
> Okay. Tomatoes. Radishes. Those long green things.
> And half of my fingernails.

> BEA
> Wouldn't avocados be perfect? I've got to plant some
> avocado trees.

> MS. MERCURY
> They grow on trees?

> BEA
> Yes. But you need two. One male tree and one female
> tree. Otherwise no avocados.

> MS. MERCURY
> The trees . . . have sex?

> BEA
> Once a week. Just like that old man and me.
> > *Bea LAUGHS. Even the chickens SQUAWK*
> > *in jest.*

MS. MERCURY

That is way too much information . . .

CUT TO:

EXT. POOL AREA—DUSK

> *Phil has been preparing an old barbecue,*
> *where a scrawny chicken rotates on a spit. The*
> *pool, empty of water . . .*

F.X.R.

So you never had kids?

PHIL

(shakes his head)

Couldn't. Didn't mind though. Back in the
old days this place was swarming with kids all
the time. That's 'cause of this swim pool. A dozen
motels along Eighty-eight before the interstate
cut us off. Only three had swim pools. I put up
signs every twenty miles, saying, 'Mount
Olympus—Swim Pool.' Guess where the kids
demanded to stay?

F.X.R.

With Phil and Bea.

PHIL

You ever work in the hospitality business?

F.X.R.

Not legitimately.

Phil gives him a look.

> PHIL
>
> It's a line of work you can't learn. Has to come natural. You have to like people and trust 'em. And lie a little when those with crazy eyes ask if there's a vacancy. No shame in that. Wisdom.

> F.X.R.
>
> You must like the motel business.

> PHIL
>
> I like this motel. Could use a bit more business.

MUSIC: "Last Date" by Floyd Cramer

CUT TO:

EXT. LANDSCAPE—SUNSET

At the very moment the sun blinks out, gone, beyond the horizon.

CUT TO:

EXT. MOTEL OLYMPUS—THE WHOLE PLACE—NIGHT

The sign is not lit up itself, but has only a cheap garden light shining up on it.

Down by the pool we see that a picnic dinner has been
enjoyed by the two innkeepers and their guests.

PHIL

Tell me something. How long you kids been
together?

MS. MERCURY

What?

PHIL

You two. You an item?

BEA

Phil, whose business is that?

MS. MERCURY

(her eyes go wide!)
Are we an item? An item? *Item?*

PHIL

A man and a woman drive up. In a car together.
Check in together. Have a room together. It's only
happened about a million times . . .

*Ms. Mercury rolls her eyes. Then she shakes
her head. Then she laughs to herself.*

MS. MERCURY

(pointing to F.X.R.)
This man could no sooner be my half of an "item"
than I could fart toast.

BEA

Oh, I'm gonna steal that.

F.X.R.

As Ms. Mercury says, we have an employer-
employee relationship that is proper in every way.

MS. MERCURY

If he isn't sleeping on the couch, and he isn't because
he's never slept on a couch, I sure as hell am!

PHIL

Okay.
> *(then)*

You a gay lesbian, Ms. Mercury?

MS. MERCURY

No, I'm not that fashionable. I'm just single.

BEA

No man in your life?

MS. MERCURY

Look . . . Let me explain this aspect of my life to two
relative strangers, as nice as you are.
> *(then)*

A man would complicate my life in the extreme. I
need a man right now like your chicken coop needs a
satellite dish. I am unattached, connected to no one.
The day will come when I chuck it all and bid my
boss adieu, and go for the mate, the kids, the hand-

made Halloween costumes, all of it. Until then, I'm happily solo, working for this guy . . .

(F.X.R.—who nods)

Who drives me nuts but can take a joke. I'm making good bank and I see the world, from Tasmania to this lovely inn. I. Have no room. For a boyfriend.

Things are silent for a beat.

BEA

Then there's my answer.

And another beat. The quiet is all-encompassing, beautiful.

F.X.R.

Listen to that.

MS. MERCURY

To what? I don't hear anything.

F.X.R.

You're not listening.

MS. MERCURY

I sure as hell am.

BEA

The quiet. He means listen to the quiet.

MS. MERCURY

Oh.

(she does)

I am really trying here . . . but I don't hear anything.

F.X.R.

The only time I feel like this quiet makes me feel
is . . .

(whenever it is he keeps it to himself)
And it never lasts.

PHIL

It does around here.

BEA

I've come to marvel in its totality. No matter the
problems or worries, there's solace in the quiet of
the night.

*Phil looks at his wife. F.X.R. also looks at
Bea. Ms. Mercury looks out into the night.*

MS. MERCURY

Oh. I hear it now. Nothing. You mean the sound of
nothing.

(she listens)
Ooh. Aah.

*A distant CAR HORN honks. Headlights
appear, and a panel truck pulls into the motel
lot.*

F.X.R.

So much for that.

BEA

That's Tommy Boyer.

PHIL

With that part for Bachelorette Number One's car.

(to Ms. Mercury)

Since you're not fashionable, you might like Tommy.

MS. MERCURY

(more eye rolling)

Gosh, let me fix my hair . . .

PHIL

(calling)

Tommy!

> *From out of a truck comes TOMMY BOYER.*
> *He is the most gorgeous male creature on the*
> *planet Earth.*

MS. MERCURY

That's Tommy Boyer?

(she is transfixed)

My lord . . .

> *She* immediately *starts primping her hair.*

MS. MERCURY (CONT'D)

Oh my. My my my . . .

BEA

He loves to cook.

MS. MERCURY

(licking her hair into place)

Are. You. Shitting. Me?

*The great Tommy Boyer approaches. He
carries an engine part.*

TOMMY BOYER

Evening, Bea. Folks.

BEA

You eat, Tommy?

TOMMY BOYER

I did, thanks. You call for an old GM fuel pump,
Phil?

PHIL

Yep. For this little lady right here.
*Everyone can see that Ms. Mercury is smitten
with Tommy.*

TOMMY BOYER

Hi.

MS. MERCURY

(giddy)

Howdy-oo-doody-doo!

TOMMY BOYER

Car problems, huh?

MS. MERCURY

Yes indeedy. Terrible that pesky little car problems
with of mine.

TOMMY BOYER

That it over there? The Buick.

MS. MERCURY

Is it a Buick? Yes. Our sad, bad broken Buick . . .

TOMMY BOYER

Let's see if we can't get 'er running.

MS. MERCURY

Okeydokey. I'll come pop the hood . . .
(whispers to Bea)
I keep talking like a six-year-old. Help me.

BEA

Tommy divorced three years ago. Has a little girl.
Gave up smoking last summer. Reads a lot.

MS. MERCURY

Got it. Thanks.
Off she goes with Tommy Boyer.

PHIL

Once again, the Motel Olympus works its magic
spell.

BEA

(rising)
I'm going to clean up. You men waste time like you
always do when women start cleaning up.

PHIL

Okay.
(then to F.X.R.)
Care to patrol the perimeter?

CUT TO:

EXT. MOTEL OLYMPUS—EDGE OF PROPERTY—NIGHT
Out on the perimeter of the motel property,
Phil and F.X.R. walk.

                    PHIL
          (pointing)
I was hoping to do something with those ten acres
over there, but nothing ever came of it. I once
almost put in a snake hut.

                    F.X.R.
A snake hut?

                    PHIL
Yeah. We'd have signs out on Eighty-eight—"Visit
the Snake Hut: 140 miles." "Snake Hut: 62 miles.
Air-Conditioned!" But then Bea pointed out that I
knew very little about raising snakes. So, we just
made do with the motel.

                    F.X.R.
It's a lovely motel. An hospitable little place. I love
the name.

                    PHIL
Can't stay here 24/7 without going nuts. One day
a week, each of us gets a solo trip to Chesterton to
go to the bank, do some shopping. Use the wi-fi at

Theo's Coffee Hutch. Connect to the outside world a couple of hours a week.

F.X.R.

(wistful)

That's the way to do it.

(recovers his "folksy" personality)

If I ever get one of those laptop computer pads, I'll try that.

Phil eyes F.X.R. as they walk.

PHIL

What middle name starts with *X*? Other than Xavier?

(then)

Francis Xavier Rustan.

F.X.R. stops. Knows he's been busted.

Bea fingered you, when you signed the register.

F.X.R. You ever heard the phrase 'nom-dee-plume'?

F.X.R.

(no longer "folksy")

I'm sorry I was dishonest with you.

PHIL

You weren't. Other than being a rich and famous man in a poor man's car.

(then)

You on some incognito vacation lark?

F.X.R.

Well, no.

PHIL

You going to sue us over the name, like Olympus is a trademark you own?

F.X.R.

I don't operate that way.

PHIL

You're one of the few.

F.X.R.

I'm looking for land and sunshine.

PHIL

Lotta both around here. The land will cost you. The sun is free.
(then, pointing)
We own from over there to over there. We ain't going to be around much longer, according to both the doctors and common sense. We would like to close out our days someplace as nice as what we've had here.

F.X.R.

So, should I make you an offer?

PHIL

(stopping him with a hand)
You talk business with Bea. She's my boss.

(then)

I'm going to head back for a cup of Ovaltine.

F.X.R. watches the old man go.

CUT TO:

EXT. MOTEL OLYMPUS, PARKING LOT—NIGHT

The hood is up on the Buick. Ms. Mercury is holding the light for Tommy Boyer, passing him tools.

MS. MERCURY

So, the metric tools are *different* from standard tools?

TOMMY BOYER

Them's the facts.

(then)

Okay. Try to start 'er up.

She hops behind the wheel.

MS. MERCURY

Okay! Startin' me up!

She turns the key. The Buick roars into life!

MS. MERCURY (CONT'D)

Hot damn! You must have read a lot of books on car fixing!

F.X.R. walks up.

Boss! Tommy Boyer and me are going to take the car out . . . for a test drive.

TOMMY BOYER

We are?

MS. MERCURY

Gotta see how it handles a long stretch of Eighty-
eight! We'll be gone for a while. So don't wait up.
Not that you would. Wait up. For me to come back.
From test driving the car . . .

(finally, to Tommy)

Wanna take shotgun?

> *Tommy gets in the car and buckles his seat*
> *belt. Ms. Mercury hits the RADIO on and then*
> *gears into REVERSE. She and Tommy peel*
> *out into the night.*

MUSIC: "We've Only Just Begun" by the Carpenters

INT. MOTEL OFFICE—NIGHT

TYPING is heard. F.X.R. enters to find Bea at a desk pecking
on a typewriter. An Olympia.

F.X.R.

It true you have Ovaltine?

BEA

The hot plate.

> *F.X.R. finds a pan of milk, a cup, a jar, and*
> *makes himself a hot malty beverage.*

BEA (CONT'D)

I'm gouging you a little on the facilities, knowing you'll tear everything down anyway.

You planning on getting all the land around here?

F.X.R.

If I can.

BEA

Then we'll be your first purchase. Kind of an honor for us.

He looks at the photograph of Bea and Phil, the original source for the dead sign out front.

F.X.R.

How old were you when this was taken?

She sees him looking at that photo.

BEA

I was nineteen. Phil was twenty-three. Our honeymoon. In Greece. An island so warm, so quiet we didn't want to leave. Had to, of course. He went into the Air Force. I finished school. Came driving up old Eighty-eight and saw a place to sink all our savings into. Worked out pretty well.

She pulls the paper from the machine and hands it to him.

Your lawyers will put their fingerprints all over this, but it's the basics—take it or leave it.

He doesn't even look at it.

F.X.R.

Ever go back to Greece? On vacation?

BEA

We're moteliers. Every day is a vacation.

CUT TO:

EXT. MOTEL OLYMPUS, PHRYGIA—PARKING LOT—
LATER

F.X.R. folds a typed piece of paper, tucks it into his breast
pocket as he walks back to his room. Behind him, the lights
go off in the office, and the dim spotlight goes out on the
old sign.

He pauses in the quiet night . . .

FADE OUT.

MUSIC: *"Mi Reina y Mi Tesoro"*

SUBTITLES: "Now I know

That I truly love her . . ."

FADE IN

EXT. MOTEL OLYMPUS, PHRYGIA—EARLY EVENING

The sun is well down as the light of day fades to blue.

SUBTITLES: "I will work hard

To conquer her heart . . ."

A PARTY is going on. LIGHTS strung across the parking lot bring a magic to the growing night.

Jesus Hildalgo is there with his BAND playing to COUPLES dancing. As he sings about his queen and loving her with all his heart, his extended family is there, with KIDS splashing in the newly filled swimming pool.

Tommy Boyer is there with his little DAUGHTER and her PALS playing JUMP ROPE with a very different looking Ms. Mercury, who now sports jeans and a halter top.

WORKMEN swarm around trucks, storing away tools, finally quitting work for the day.

Nicholas, the room service waiter, puts the finishing touches on a superb dinner that looks like something served on the lido deck of the Love Boat.

LOCALS from as far away as Chesterton have come around for the big party, having brought their own lawn chairs.

F.X.R. is dressed in a fine, yet casual suit. He is talking over plans on a blueprint with a HALF DOZEN ARCHITECTS.

In two chairs, dual places of honor, sit Phil and Bea, who both have *To Tell the Truth*–style blindfolds over their eyes.

                    BEA

Oh, I've missed that man and his 'cordine!

                    PHIL

From the way things sound, we're gonna see a circus when we take these things off.

> *As Bea sways to the Mexican melody, a*
> *Foreman, COLLINS, comes over and whispers*
> *something to F.X.R., who then smartly*
> *dismisses the architects.*

                    F.X.R.

Ms. Mercury! We're ready.

                MS. MERCURY
            (turning that jump rope)

Who is Ms. Mercury?

                    F.X.R.

Oh. Sorry. Old habit.
            (tries again)

Diane! We're ready!

                MS. MERCURY

Okay, F.X.! Be right there!
            (to Tommy's daughter)

Come on, Lizzie. Let's go see the show!

> *Jesus concludes his music with a flourish.*
> *There is applause for the band.*
> *F.X.R. goes to Phil and Bea.*

F.X.R.

You guys peek? Tell the truth.

PHIL

No!

BEA

You aren't lining up a firing squad, are you?

F.X.R.

Diane, is it dark enough?

MS. MERCURY

I say yes.

F.X.R.

Okay. Collins!

Collins is at the main power switch.

COLLINS

Shutting down!

*Collins shuts OFF all the lights in the motel
lot. The place is dark now.*

F.X.R.

Okay. You may remove your blindfolds.

They do. All is dark.

PHIL

Hell, I can't see a thing.

BEA

Where am I supposed to look?

PHIL

Where's the bloody circus?

F.X.R.

(a shout)

Let there be light!

> *Collins throws another switch. The parking*
> *lot, and all the people in it, are suddenly*
> *bathed in . . . shades of red, blue, and golden*
> *neon light.*
>
> *Ms. Mercury's face sees something so very*
> *beautiful. Tommy Boyer is with her, holding*
> *his daughter.*

TOMMY BOYER

Wow . . .

> *The guests, every one of them glowing, look*
> *up in awe into the sky.*

MS. MERCURY

Oh, lord! What a heavenly light!

CLOSE ON: Phil and Bea, the lights playing across their faces like a magic show in the heavens, are silent . . .

THE SIGN

Big Phil and Big Bea, illuminated in colors brilliant and bold, greet the world like twin giants in the nighttime sky.

"Stay with us!" they say, arms raised, bright, hospitable, young.

The sign is beautiful. Truly beautiful.

> *Bea reaches out and takes her husband's hand.*
> *They look into each other's eyes.*

BEA

It's like we'll live here forever . . .

> *F.X.R. hears this. He looks up at the sign. The*
> *colors play on his face, too.*

CUT TO:

EXT. MOTEL OLYMPUS—THE WHOLE PLACE—SAME

The sign dominates the vision of the Motel Olympus.

And then . . .

The landscape slowly TRANSFORMS into that of a . . .

BUSTLING CROSSROADS.

The empty desert becomes filled with neatly ordered buildings, each an architectural gem.

The OLYMPUS SOLAR ENERGY COLLECTION FIELD has been built, stretching far into the distance.

Phrygia has grown into a lovely small city . . .

Around that landmark of a sign . . .

Around Bea and Phil, who will, for generations, bid all who pass by to *Stay with us.*

FADE TO BLACK.

Go See Costas

———

I brahim had been true to his word. For the price of one bot-tle of Johnnie Walker Red Label, he had provided Assan with two, most certainly stolen but that didn't matter to either of them. In those days, American liquor was more valuable than gold, even more valuable than American cigarettes.

With both bottles clanking in his knapsack, Assan, dressed in his nearly new blue pin-striped suit, searched the many tavernas of the port city of Piraeus, looking for the chief of the *Berengaria*. It was known that the chief savored the taste and effects of Johnnie Walker Red Label. It was also known that the *Berengaria* was taking cargo to America.

Assan found the chief at the Taverna Antholis, trying to enjoy his morning coffee. "I don't need another fireman," he told Assan.

"But I know ships. I speak many languages. I am good with my hands. And I never brag." Assan smiled at his little joke. The chief did not. "Ask anyone on the *Despotiko*."

The chief waved to the waiter boy for another coffee.

"You are not Greek," he said to Assan.

"Bulgarian," Assan told him.

"What is this accent of yours?" During the war, the chief had done a lot of business with Bulgarians, but this one talked in an odd cadence.

"I'm from the mountains."

"A Pomak?"

"Is that a bad thing?"

The chief shook his head. "No. Pomaks are quiet and tough. The war was hard on the Pomaks."

"The war was hard on everyone," Assan said.

The boy brought the chief his other coffee. "How long have you been on the *Despotiko*?" the chief asked.

"Six months, now."

"You want me to hire you so you can jump ship in America." The chief was no idiot.

"I want you to hire me because you have the oil fuel. A fireman checks the bubble in the tube is all. He doesn't shovel the coal. Too long with a shovel and it becomes all a man knows."

The chief lit a cigarette without offering one to Assan. "I don't need another fireman."

Assan reached into the knapsack between his feet, pulled out a bottle of Johnnie Walker Red Label in each fist, and set them on the table beside the chief's morning coffee. "Here. I am tired of carrying these around."

———

Three days out, some of the crew began giving the chief troubles. The Cypriot steward had a bad leg and didn't clean up after meals fast enough. The seaman Sorianos was a liar, saying he had checked the scuppers when he had not checked the scuppers. Iasson Kalimeris's wife had left him—again—so his hot head was even faster to flare. Every conversation with him turned into an argument, even over dominoes. Assan, though, caused no worries. He was never idle with a smoke in his lips, but was always wiping down valves or taking a wire brush to the rust. He played cards and dominoes quietly. And perhaps best of all he stayed away from the eyes of the captain. The captain noticed everything, the chief knew. But he did not notice Assan.

Past Gibraltar the ship met the heavy seas of the Atlantic. At sea, the chief rose early every morning, to wander the *Berengaria*, looking for possible headaches. This day, as usual, he climbed up to the bridge for the coffee that was always there, then worked his way down. He found all was well until he came to the fuel station and heard Bulgarian being spoken.

Assan was on his knees, rubbing the legs of a man leaning on the bulkhead, a man black with oily grime, his damp clothes sticking to his skin.

"I can walk now, let me stretch," said the filthy man, taking wobbly steps back and forth on the steel deck. He, too, spoke Bulgarian. "Ah. Feels good." The man drank deep from a bottle of water, then wolfed down a thick slice of bread from a wrapped bandanna.

"We are in the ocean now," Assan said.

"I could feel it. The ship, rocking." The man finished the bread and drank more water. "How much longer?'

"Ten days, maybe."

"I hope it's less."

"You better go back in," said Assan. "Here, your can."

Assan handed him an empty tin that once held biscuits, taking from the filthy man a can that was once for coffee but was now, the chief could smell, filled with sewage. Assan covered the tin with the bandanna and then handed over a corked bottle of water, and the filthy man crawled back into a hole, a narrow gap in the decking from where a plate had been lifted. With some struggle the filthy man squeezed through and was gone. Assan used a bar to lift and slide the steel plate back into place, like a puzzle piece.

———

The chief did not report what he saw to the captain. Instead he went back to his cabin and looked at the Johnnie Walker Red Label, two bottles, one for Assan, the other for his friend hiding in the half meter of space between the steel decking. On ships heading to America stowaways were not uncommon, and life was easier if eyes saw nothing and questions were not asked. Of course, sometimes a full coffin was offloaded as a result.

Ah, the world was a mess. But it seemed a little less messy after a drink from the first open bottle. If someone else discovered the filthy man crawling around in the black space between decks, there would be hell to pay, plus all the paperwork for the captain. It was up to Assan. If the captain never found out, well, he would never find out.

———

Two storms at sea slowed down the *Berengaria*, then the ship had to wait two days at anchor until a harbor pilot finally came out in the little boat, climbed up the pilot ladder, and made his way to the bridge to guide the ship into the port. It was night by the time she was tied up at the dock, one ship of so many. The chief saw Assan at the rail, looking at the skyline of a city in the distance.

"That is Philadelphia, Pennsylvania. America."

"Where is Chee-ca-go?" asked the Bulgarian.

"Farther from Philadelphia than Cairo is from Athens."

"So far? Son of a gun."

"Philadelphia looks like paradise, eh? But when we dock in New York, New York, you will see a real American city."

Assan lit a smoke, offering one to the chief.

"Better cigarettes in America." The chief smoked, eyeing the Bulgarian, who had caused no problems for him. Not a single one. "Tomorrow they search the ship."

"Who?"

"American big shots. They search the ship, high and low, looking for stowaways. Communists."

At the mention of Communists, Assan spit over the rail.

"They count heads," the chief continued. "If the numbers don't match up, it's trouble. If they find nothing, we off-load and then go to New York, New York. I will take you for a shave there. Better than the Turks can shave."

Assan said nothing for a moment. "If there are Communists on this ship I hope they find them," he said, spitting over the rail again.

———

Assan lay in his rack faking sleep as other crewmen came and went. At 4:00 a.m. he dressed quietly and slipped into the passageway, checking around each corner to make sure he was not seen. He made his way to the fuel station and used the iron bar to lift one plate of the steel decking and slide it open.

"It's now," Assan said.

Ibrahim crawled up from below, his elbows and knees rubbed raw and bleeding from living in the low, dark space between the deck and the ship's inner hull. How long had he been down there? Eighteen days? Twenty? Did it matter? "Let me get my can," Ibrahim whispered in a croak.

"Leave it. We go. Now."

"A second, please, Assan. My legs."

Assan massaged Ibrahim's legs for as long as he dared, then helped his friend to stand. Ibrahim had been on his feet only a few minutes each day. His back ached horribly and his knees were actually shaking.

"We have to go," Assan said. "Follow me by two meters. We wait at every corner. If you hear me speak to someone, hide where you can."

Ibrahim nodded, taking small steps, following.

A ladder led to a hatch that led to a room that led to another hatch and another passageway and another ladder. At the top of it, another passageway and one more ladder, though this was more like a stairway. Assan pulled on a heavy steel door that opened inward and halted. Ibrahim smelled fresh air for the first time in twenty-one days, that's how long it had been since the *Berengaria* had left Piraeus with Ibrahim hiding under the steel decking.

"It's okay," Assan whispered.

Ibrahim stepped through the doorway and was finally outside, the night a blessing, as his eyes tried to adjust. The air was warm, the air of summertime. They were at the portside rail, facing away from the dock, the water twelve meters below. Hours earlier, the ship's Pomak fireman had tied a rope, anonymous as any on deck, to the lowest rung of the rail. "Climb down this. Swim around to the dock and find a way up."

"I hope I can still swim," Ibrahim said. He was laughing like it was a funny joke.

"There are bushes nearby. Hide in them until I come tomorrow."

"What if there are dogs?"

"Make friends with them." That made Ibrahim laugh again as he swung over the rail, the rope in his hands.

———

The chief was with the captain on the starboard wing of the pilothouse taking their morning coffee. The longshoremen had off-loaded most of the cargo, and the docks were busy with trucks and cranes and workers.

"We'll go to the Waldorf Hotel," the captain said just as the chief saw Assan walking down the gangway and off the ship, with his knapsack that once held bottles of Johnnie Walker Red Label. He was carrying, too, a parcel under his arm. Crewmen returned to the ship with parcels, filled with goods they could buy only in America, under their arms. But here Assan was leaving with one.

"Big steaks, like this." The captain held up his fingers showing the thickness of what his steak would be. "The Waldorf Astoria Hotel. They have the steaks."

"That's a good place," the chief said as Assan disappeared into some bushes.

———

Assan found no sign of Ibrahim and was worried that American big shots had searched the bushes for Communists and uncounted heads with no papers. Not wanting to call out, he howled like a dog. He heard a dog howl back, but it was Ibrahim, who came out of the bushes, stripped to the waist and carrying his grease-caked shoes.

"Who's a big dog?" he asked, smiling.

"Were you all right through the night?"

"I made a bed of reeds," Ibrahim said. "Soft. And the night never got a chill."

Assan opened the parcel, showing some clothes and soap and food and a shaving kit. There was also a folded newspaper bound in twine. Inside was Ibrahim's share of the drachmas the two had saved from all the odd jobs they had worked in Greece. Ibrahim pocketed the bills without counting. "How much will a train cost to get to Chee-ca-go, Assan?"

"How much from Athens to Cairo? Find a money changer at the train station."

After Ibrahim had eaten and washed, Assan sat him down

on a rock and took the razor to his face, shaving his friend, as there was no mirror for him to do it himself.

———

From the bridge wing, the chief searched the bushes through a pair of glasses. In a gap between waving branches, he saw Assan shaving the face of a man he could not recognize. A problem had left the ship without bothering the captain. No need for a coffin, either. Assan was one smart Pomak.

As Ibrahim ran a comb through his wet hair, Assan tried to clean his friend's shoes. "The best I can do," he said, handing them over.

Ibrahim reached into his pocket and pulled out a single drachma and slapped it into Assan's hand. "Here. A perfect shine on perfect shoes." Assan took a bow and both men laughed.

They walked together to the end of the dockyards, able to mingle with others coming and going. They saw huge cars, trucks the size of houses grinding gears and pulling big loads, and more ships, some much larger and newer than the *Berengaria*, others rusted buckets. They saw men eating rolls with sausages in them at a kiosk with a sign Assan could spell out—he had been learning the American letters— H O T D O G S. Both Bulgarians were hungry but neither had American money. At the end of the dockyards there was a gate with a guard in an office, but every American walked past without so much as a pause.

"Assan. I will see you in Chee-ca-go one day," Ibrahim said. Then in English he said, "Tenk choo berry mich."

"All I did was carry your shit away," Assan said, taking one cigarette, then giving the pack to Ibrahim. He smoked it while watching his friend walk to the gate, pass the guard with only a nod, and disappear down the road toward the skyline of Philadelphia.

———

Returning to the ship, Assan kept busy all morning, not getting to the galley until the first meal was nearly over and only a few of the crew were around. He collected what bread, vegetables, and soup was still available and sat at a table. The Cypriot with the limp brought him a coffee from the galley.

"America for the first time?" he asked Assan.

"Yeah."

"America is the top, I tell you. New York, New York, has anything you want. Wait until you see."

"The big shots. When do they come on board?" Assan asked.

"What big shots?"

"The Americans who search the ship. Looking for Reds. Making big trouble."

"The fuck you talking about?"

"They make sure our heads match. The chief told me. Big shots come and search the whole ship."

"Search for what?" The Cypriot went back to the galley for a coffee for himself.

"They check our papers, right? Line us up and check our papers?" Assan had lined up so many times to have his papers checked, it made sense that he'd do the same in America.

"The captain takes care of that shit." The Cypriot downed half of his coffee. "Hey, I know a whorehouse in New York City. Bring money tomorrow and I'll get us laid."

———

Back in his village, Assan had seen black-and-white movies flickering on a white wall. Sometimes the movies were American, with cowboys on horses shooting pistols that threw out long plumes of smoke. He liked best a newsreel that showed factories and construction sites and a new building rising to the sky in a city called Chicago; Chicago had many tall buildings and streets jammed with black sedans.

But New York, New York, looked like a city with no end, a city that threw a haze into the night sky, making the low clouds golden and the water shimmer like colored smoke. A hot wind blew as the ship moved slowly up the wide river, the city passing like a brilliant jeweled curtain; a solid mass of a million lighted windows, bright towers shining like castles, and twin lights of cars, so many cars, buzzing every which way like insects. Assan stood at the rail, the wind rippling his clothes, his mouth open, and his eyes wide.

"Son of a gun," he said to New York, New York.

———

In the morning, the chief found him at the fuel station. "Assan, put on that striped suit of yours. I want a shave."

"I have duties, here."

"I say you don't, and I'm the chief. Let's go. And leave your money here so you don't get pickpocketed on your first day."

Cars flew down the streets, many of them colored yellow with words printed on their sides, screeching to stops at corners as people got out and different people got in. Lights in boxes mounted on poles flashed red then green then orange again and again. Signs were everywhere, attached to poles, walls, and in windows; so many that Assan stopped trying to make out the letters. Rich-looking Americans walked fast. Americans who didn't look rich hurried, too. Three black men, with muscles ripping at their sweat-stained shirts, were moving a large wooden crate up a stairway into a building. There was shouting and music and engines and radio voices coming from everywhere.

A young man rode a two-wheeled motor bicycle, roaring by so fast, almost hitting Assan and the chief as they crossed a broad street. Assan had seen a newsreel with policemen on big motored bicycles, but that young man was not a cop. Could anyone ride such a thing in America?

They passed a kiosk selling papers, candy, drinks, cigarettes, magazines, combs, pens, and lighters. Two minutes later they passed another, selling the same goods. It turned out the kiosks were everywhere. A river of moving cars, people, crowded buses, trucks, and even horses pulling wagons flowed along streets that stretched to the edge of sight.

The chief walked fast. "In New York, New York, you have to walk like you are late for an important meeting or thieves mark you." They crossed street after street and rounded many corners. Assan had draped his blue pin-striped jacket over his arm. He was sweating and dizzy, his head too full of America.

The chief stopped at a corner. "Let me see. Where are we?"

"You don't know?"

"I'm just thinking of the best way to go from here." The chief looked around and saw something that made him laugh. "Will you look at that?"

Assan tilted his head and looked, too, up at a window on an upper floor of a building. He saw a flag in the window, posted like a sign—the blue and white flag of Greece with the cross for the church and the stripes for the sea and sky. A man in shirtsleeves and a loosened tie stood in the window, shouting into a telephone and waving a cigar.

"We Greeks are everywhere, no?" The chief laughed again, then held up the palm of his hand. "Look. New York, New York, is a simple city to learn. It is shaped like your hand. The numbered avenues are long and run from your fingertips to your wrist. The numbered streets run across the palm. Broadway is the lifeline and curves the length around. The two middle fingers are the Central Park."

Assan studied his own palm.

"Now those signs"—the chief pointed to two signs forming an X on a post—"tell us we are at Twenty-Sixth Street and Seventh Avenue. That puts us about right here, see?" The chief pointed to the map of his hand. "Twenty-Sixth and Seventh. Understand?"

"Like my hand. Son of a gun." Assan felt as though he understood. They continued walking up the shaded side of Seventh Avenue, then turned a corner. The chief stopped at steps that led into a basement barbershop.

"Here's the place," he said and stepped down to the door.

The place was for men only, not unlike barbershops in the old country. Everyone looked over at the chief and Assan when they came in. A radio was playing, not music, but a man talking and talking over the sounds of a crowd in the background. Sometimes the crowd would roar or applaud. The shelves were lined with bottles of different-colored liquids. Cigarettes were smoked, so many that two standing ashtrays were overflowing with butts.

The chief spoke English to the older barber—there was another, younger barber, the son perhaps—then took a seat off to the side. Assan sat next to him, listening to the English and looking at the magazines with pictures of crooks with guns and women in tight skirts. Three Americans waited as well, until one of them took a place with the other barber, sitting in a big, comfortable chair made of leather and steel. After a customer paid and said something that made the men all laugh, he walked out the door and up the steps to the street. When another customer was done, he said something funny, too, gave the barber some coins, and was gone.

The chief took a seat in the big leather barber chair and spoke, pointing to Assan like he was explaining something. The barber looked at Assan and said "Yoo bet-cha." He draped a white cloth over the chief, pinned it tight behind his neck, then gave the chief a shave. Three times with the hot towel, the lather, and the razor, as close a shave as the Turks give a man in Constantinople. Then he trimmed the chief's hair, shaving around his ears and the back of his neck with the lather and razor. The men laughed and told stories, the chief using so much English he must be fluent, thought

Assan. The Americans laughed and looked at Assan, as if he were in on the jokes.

When the chief was clean and smelled of spicy cologne, he paid the barber with paper money, said something in English, and pointed at Assan. The barber said "Yoo bet-cha" again and waved Assan into his chair.

As the barber draped his cloth around Assan, the chief spoke in Greek.

"A free shave. I paid already. And this is for you." The chief handed Assan a wad of folded paper money. American money. "A smart man like you will do well in America. Good luck." The last Assan saw of the chief was his shoes, climbing the steps back up to the street.

———

Assan walked, feeling his smooth face and smelling the cologne, as the late summer night fell on New York, New York, and the lights took on new warmth. He saw so many amazing things: a window filled with dozens of roasting chickens rotating on mechanical spits, a man selling windup toy cars on a box with a wooden rail nailed to the top to keep the toys from rolling off, and a restaurant with one wall all glass, where inside Americans sat at tables and on stools at a long counter. Waitresses swung around, carrying platters of complete meals and small dishes of cakes and pastries. Assan passed a long stairway that led down below the street, fenced in with decorated iron and crowded with people going up and others going down, all in a hurry and none of them easy marks for pocket pickers.

The buildings stopped and the sky opened up, and on the other side of a busy street there were thick trees. Assan figured he must be at his middle fingers, at the Central Park. He did not know how to cross the broad street but followed with others when they walked. By a low rounded wall a man with a cart was selling H O T D O G S, and Assan was suddenly very, very hungry. He pulled out the paper money the chief had given him, finding a bill with the number 1 on it. He handed the money to the man, who kept asking him questions that Assan had no answer for. The only word he could make out was Coca-Cola, the sum total of his English, really.

The man handed over a sausage sandwich that was dripping with sauces of red and yellow and stringy, wet onions and a bottle of the Coca-Cola. Then the man gave Assan a fistful of coins of three different sizes, which he pocketed with his free hand. Assan sat on a bench and ate a most delicious meal. With half the Coca-Cola left, he went back to the man. He held out the coins, the man took one of the thinnest, and made another richly burdened sausage sandwich.

The sun had gone down and the sky was dark and the lampposts were shining as Assan walked along the paths of the beautiful park, finishing the Coca-Cola. Assan saw fountains and statues. He saw men and women as couples, holding hands and laughing. A rich lady walked a tiny dog, the funniest dog Assan had ever seen. He almost howled at it as a joke, but Assan thought maybe the rich lady would complain to a cop, and the last thing he wanted was a cop asking for his papers.

At a side entrance to the park, a gate in a wall, Assan came to where the city began again. It was late now, and people were crossing the street, heading into the park with blankets and pillows. Assan could see these people were not like the rich lady with her dog, but families of white and black and brown people with giggling kids and men and women who looked tired from a day's work. Assan suddenly felt so very tired, too. He followed a family back into the park, coming to a big field of grass, where others were laying out blankets and bedding to sleep outdoors in the hot, humid night. Some were already asleep. Others hushed their kids and made sleeping spots near the trees on the border of the field.

Assan found a spot with soft grass. He removed his shoes and used his jacket as a pillow. He fell asleep to the sounds of distant traffic and quiet conversations between husbands and wives.

———

Assan washed his face in a public restroom in a stone building. Flicking his fingers, he brushed his pants and suit jacket and shook out his nice shirt, then put his clothes back on, wondering where he would walk today.

That was when he thought of the man who had been shouting into a telephone, the man who made the chief laugh, the man in the window with the Greek flag. Where was that again? He looked at the palm of his hand, at the map there, and remembered the chief saying Twenty-Sixth Street and Seventh Avenue, and Assan knew he could find it again.

No one was in the window at Twenty-Sixth and Seventh when Assan looked up, but the Greek flag was there. Assan found an entryway nearby that had a small sign with another small Greek flag on it and words in Greek: THE HELLENIC INTERNATIONAL SOCIETY. Assan went through the door and up the stairs.

The day was already hot and the office was sweltering, even with the door ajar and the windows cracked open. Assan heard music playing—a slow tune with a voice repeating words. *Ay . . . ay . . . ay . . . space . . . es . . . es . . . es . . . space.* A *clacking* typewriter noise came with each word. *Dee . . . clack . . . dee . . . clack . . . dee . . . clack.* At the office door, Assan saw only a messy desk and some easy chairs.

Eff . . . clack . . . eff . . . clack . . . eff . . . clack . . . space . . . thunk. Assan stepped inside. A girl was in the small inner office, sitting in front of a small green typewriter on a tiny table. She was concentrating on the fingers of her left hand, pressing the keys that matched the instructions on the record. Assan stayed quiet, not wanting to disturb the typing lesson.

"Tikanis."

Assan turned. The man who had been yelling into the telephone yesterday was walking in, carrying a small paper bag. "Who are you?" the man asked in Greek.

"Assan Chepik."

"Not Greek?"

"No, Bulgarian. But I come from Greece. I saw the flag."

The man pulled a cardboard cup filled with what smelled like coffee from the paper bag, along with a round cake with a hole in the middle. "You did not tell me you were coming today, Assan, or I would have brought you breakfast!" The man laughed out loud. "Dorothy! We need another coffee for Assan, here."

Ell . . . ell . . . ell . . . space. "I just started a lesson!"

"Pick up the needle. When Bulgarians are hungry they get nutsy." The man turned to Assan. "Dorothy will get you a coffee. At least it's what they say is coffee here."

———

Assan sipped a hot drink, mostly milk and sugar with something of a coffee taste. Dorothy was back at her typewriter, *clacking* along with the record. *You . . . you . . . you . . . space . . . eye . . . eye . . . eye . . . space.* Demetri Bakas, which was the man's name, asked questions of Assan. Assan told of his job on the *Berengaria* and that just yesterday he had left the ship, but said nothing of Ibrahim hiding between the decking or getting off in the city called Philadelphia.

Assan also said nothing of the four years since the war ended, nothing about all his attempts at crossing the border between Bulgaria and Greece. He did not tell of the early morning when his brother made the mistake of starting a fire to heat some water. They were in the mountains, had slept between two rocks, and were planning to move along quickly, but Assan had some coffee in his pocket. His brother wanted just one cup, for energy he said, but he really wanted the taste of hot coffee on a cold morning. The Communist bounty hunters had been trailing after them and saw the smoke from the fire. Assan had been taking a shit on the other side of a copse of trees. Unseen, he watched his brother put up a fight and a Communist shoot him in the head. He didn't tell Demetri about the man he'd had to kill, either. Assan was drinking from a stream that ran alongside a path when a local man almost stumbled upon him. The man wore a Party pin on his threadbare jacket, and the look in his eyes said all Assan needed to know. The man was running back to whatever village was nearby to report seeing a traitor making for the border, but Assan chased him down, hit him with a rock, then threw his body down into a gully. And Assan was silent about the time he finally arrived in Athens and made a friend who told him to go to a certain house where refugees like him lived together. When Assan went to the house, he was beaten up, thrown into an unmarked truck, and taken back across the border into Bulgaria, handcuffed to others who had fallen for the traitor's trick. Assan said nothing of the Communist captain who chained him to a chair, then yelled questions at him and, not liking the answers, used his fists and then special tools as he yelled the questions again and again. Assan said nothing of the camp, of the prisoners he saw shot in the camp, of the prisoners he saw hanged in the camp.

He said nothing of the girl he met after his release, of their short romance, or of how hungry they always were. He didn't say her name was Nadezhda or tell of her becoming pregnant, or of their marriage just months before a boy was born, his son, named Petar. He said nothing about his young wife struggling during the birth and the midwife not knowing how to stop the bleeding. Without his mother's milk, the boy lived only a month. Demetri did not hear of Assan's son, Petar.

Assan said nothing of his arrest for stealing empty bottles, even though he had not stolen any empty bottles. His name was on a list, so he was again sent to prison. Assan said nothing of his fourth attempt at escape, his arrest, his year in the work camp, of meeting Ibrahim there and the night the train came by and separated them from the guards on the other side of the track and how they threw down their shovels and jumped into the river. He said nothing of the farmer who found them miles away, wet and freezing, who could have turned them in to the Party official in the village, but instead gave them hot food as their uniforms dried. He gave them some money, too—twenty levs each.

Assan and Ibrahim bought tickets for the bus to the mountains near the border with Greece. When the police came on board to check papers, they had none. But their prison uniforms happened to be the same as the ones for privates in the army, just with no patches or insignia. When Assan told the cop that they were reporting to the Army Hospital because they were carriers of typhus, the cop's eyes went huge at the word *typhus* and he nearly ran off the bus.

They crossed the border high in the mountains. In Athens they earned drachmas with picks and shovels, with their hands and their backs for most of that year until Assan got the fireman job on the *Despotiko*, shoveling coal into the boiler as the ferry made its way between Piraeus and the many Hellenic islands.

Assan said nothing of all that, but only of being a fireman on the *Berengaria* with the oil bubble in the tube, and now here he was in America having jumped ship.

Demetri knew there was much more to Assan's story but didn't care. "Do you know what I can do for you, out of this office?"

"Teach me to type?" Dorothy was now pecking out *Cap* . . . *thunk* . . . *Cue* . . . *clack* . . . *space* . . . *thunk* . . . *Cap* . . . *thunk* . . . *Double-You* . . . *clack* . . . *space* . . . *thunk*.

Demetri laughed loudly. "We have good people who will help us help you. It will take time. But let me tell you right now, if you get into any problem with the law—any problem with the police—everything becomes trouble. Understand?"

"Sure. Of course."

"Okay. Now. You are going to learn to speak English. Here is an address of a free school. It meets nights. Just walk in, sign up, and pay attention."

Assan took the address.

"You have anything of value you can sell? Anything gold or fancy from the old country?"

"Nothing. I left everything on the ship."

"My old man did the same thing. In 1910." Demetri pulled a cigar from his jacket pocket. "Come back in a few days and we'll have some spare clothes for you. Dorothy! Size up Assan for a couple pairs of pants. Some shirts, too!"

"When I'm done!" Dorothy never looked away from her keyboard. *Cap. Tee. Space. Cap. Gee. Space. Thunk-clack-thunk-clack* . . .

"You have any lines on a job, Assan?" Demetri lit his cigar in a ball of fire that came from a huge match.

Assan had no lines on a job.

"Go here. It's downtown." Demetri wrote something

on another piece of paper and handed it to Assan. "Ask for Costas."

"Costas. Okay." Assan was leaving the office just as the typing record stopped and Dorothy turned it over for lesson two.

———

The address was very low on Assan's palm, down where streets had no numbers and went every which way. He spent most of the day tramping the odd-shaped blocks, going round and round and passing the same points more than once. He finally found the place, a little restaurant, with a sign that said OLYMPIC GRILL surrounded by a Greek key border. There were all of four little tables connected to the wall with leather benches and eight of the pole stools at a counter. Every seat was taken and the cafe was hot. A woman was behind the counter, too busy to look at Assan until he stood in one place a bit too long. She barked at him in Greek: "Wait outside for a seat, fool!"

"I am here to see Costas," Assan said.

"What?" the woman shouted.

"I am here to see Costas!" Assan shouted back.

"Honey!" the woman hollered, turning her back on Assan. "Some fool is asking for you!"

Costas was a short man with a brush for a mustache. He had no time to speak to Assan but did anyway.

"What do you want?"

"Are you Costas?" Assan asked.

"What do you want?"

"A job," Assan said with a laugh.

"Oh, Jesus," Costas said, turning away.

"Demetri Bakas sent me to see you."

"Who?" Costas was clearing dishes and taking money from a customer.

"Demetri Bakas. He told me you would have a job for me."

Costa stopped what he was doing and looked Assan in the eye; he was so short he had to lean back to glare at the Bulgarian.

"Get the fuck out of here!" The customers who spoke Greek looked up from their meals. The ones who only spoke American kept on eating. "And don't come back!"

Assan turned and got the fuck out of there.

———

The walk back to the two middle fingers of the Central Park took a very long time. The air was so hot and thick—Assan's shirt became wet against his back and didn't dry. He walked and walked along one avenue, until bright flashing lights shone down on a place where nine streets seemed to collide in a storm of people, buses, yellow cars, and even soldiers on horses, or maybe they were cops. Assan had never been in the middle of so many people, with everyone going everywhere.

In a huge cafeteria, he spent coins on another sausage H O T D O G and a paper cup filled with sweet juice, ice cold, and as delicious as any drink he'd ever had—even Coca-Cola. He stood as he ate, like most of the people in the place, though he wanted to take off his shoes more than anything in the world. Across the triangle of streets and humanity, he recognized what was a cinema, with a chain of lights chasing each other around and around. Assan saw the price—forty-five cents. That was four of the smallest coins in his pocket and a larger, thicker coin that had a humpbacked cow printed on one side. Assan suddenly wanted to sit in a nice seat, take off his shoes, and see a movie. He hoped it would be about Chicago.

The cinema was like a cathedral, with uniformed men and women directing a stream of people to seats, chattering couples, and young men in groups, everyone talking loud and barking in laughter. The columns were like those in the Parthenon in Athens, modern angels were etched in gold on the wall, and a deep red curtain stood thirty meters tall.

Assan took off his shoes just as the curtain opened and a short movie appeared on a screen as big as the hull of the *Berengaria*. Music played as fancy words flipped and spun on the screen, appearing and disappearing so fast Assan couldn't sound out a single letter. The movie showed ladies dancing and men arguing. Then another short movie played, with more music and flying words. This movie had boxers in it and skies full of airplanes. A third short movie showed a very serious woman saying very serious things, then weeping, then running down a street calling out a name, then that movie was over. A moment later the screen burst into vivid colors as a funny-looking man dressed like a cowboy, but not a real cowboy, and a gorgeous woman with black hair and the reddest of lips sang songs and said things that made the cathedral echo with laughter. Despite that, Assan soon fell asleep hard and deep.

The next day there was no one at the Hellenic Society. The whole city seemed quiet, with fewer people coming up out of the stairways that led to tunnels and many of the buildings empty. Assan found the address for the English lessons, a building on Forty-Third Street, but there was no one around the place to speak English with.

When Assan returned to the park, though, it seemed like all the buildings surrounding the two middle fingers had emptied into the trees, the paths, the playgrounds, and the broad green fields. Kids and families were everywhere—in a zoo, in rowboats, sliding around on shoes with wheels attached, at a concert of music, with dogs playing, and kids throwing, catching, and kicking all kinds of balls. Assan liked the dogs the most and watched them for the longest time.

When clouds darkened the sky late in the afternoon, the families packed up, the games of ball stopped, and the park emptied. Rain came soon after, so Assan found a covered archway and ended up spending the night there, sharing the spot with a few other men who slept on boxes and covered themselves with only their jackets. None of them spoke any of the languages Assan knew. None of the others seemed happy at all, but Assan had been stuck in the rain before and was not at all miserable. He had hidden under bridges, been in wet clothes, walked for days, even run from men in the old country who had the same faces of misery as these guys. This? This was nothing.

In the morning, Assan woke with a cough in his throat.

———

"These pants should fit you." Dorothy was speaking Greek. "The boots, too. Try them on in the lavatory in the hall."

"What is the lavatory?" Assan had never heard that word.

"The toilet. The men's room."

The pants fit well enough. The used boots not only fit his small feet but were already broken in. Dorothy gave him stockings, a few different shirts, two pairs of heavy pants— all felt good after so many days in his blue pin-striped suit, which Dorothy took from him for cleaning.

"What happened to that Bulgarian guy who was here Friday?" Demetri walked in with a bag of round cakes with holes in the middle and more sweet American coffee. "Assan? You look like you live in Jersey!"

Dorothy sat down at her typewriter again and put on another record. Music played in a faster tempo—*Cap tee aitch eee space cue you eye see kay space*—as Dorothy clattered at the keys.

"Did you see Costas?" Demetri asked.

Assan sipped his coffee and bit into a round cake, which hurt his throat but tasted good. "Yeah. He told me to get the fuck out." Assan glanced through the door to Dorothy, who luckily did not hear his foul language.

"Hah! Costas must not have liked the way you looked. But now, you look like a guy from Hoboken, like Sinatra on a weekend." Assan had no idea what that meant. "Costas owes me, so you go back and tell him I sent you. You did tell him I sent you, right?"

"He didn't care who sent me."

"Tell him I sent you."

———

Assan again walked all the way downtown, arriving at the Olympic Grill when only half its seats were occupied. Costas sat on the stool farthest away from the door, reading a newspaper with a cup of coffee in front of him, so short he swung his legs back and forth, like a little boy. Assan approached, waiting for Costas to look up from his paper. But he didn't.

"Demetri says you will give me a job."

Costas kept reading. "Huh?" he said, writing a word on an open tablet with a pencil. There were many words on the page.

"Demetri Bakas. He sent me to see you."

Costas didn't move, but managed to change his focus from the newspaper and the list of words to Assan.

"What the hell? What is this?"

"Demetri Bakas. Said to see you for a job. Because you owe him."

Costas turned back to his reading and writing. "I owe Demetri Bakas shit. Order something or get out of here."

"He said to see you for a job."

Costas was off the stool with fire in his dark eyes. "Where are you from?" he shouted.

"Bulgaria, but I come from Athens."

"Go back to Athens! I can do nothing for you! You know where I was when you were jerking off in your shit-filled barn in Bulgaria? I was here! I was in America. And you know what I was doing? Getting my ass kicked for even thinking about this restaurant!"

"But Demetri said to go see Costas. So, I came."

"He can kiss my ass and you can go piss in a hat! I feed cops here! They'll crack your head open if I ask. Come back again and it's the cops for you!"

Assan hurried out of the diner. What else could he do? He didn't want trouble with any cops.

———

The day was as hot as ever. The roar of cars and buses was as loud as a storm wind. The chatter of so many people who all had jobs and money in their pockets and few worries clogged Assan's ears. His throat was burning and his legs felt like bags of sand.

He was heading to Forty-Third Street and the English lessons, but stopped in a tiny, triangular patch of grass and trees as a wave of ache came over him. A new pain in his head knocked and knocked, right above his eyes. At a drinking fountain he cupped his hand to collect enough water to slurp but the fire in his throat would not go out. He saw two men sharing a bench in the shade, a bench large enough for four, and he wanted to sit down very quickly. Then a violent, invisible punch to his stomach bent him in two and sickness came out of his insides.

A man was asking him questions he could not understand as another led him by the shoulder to the shade of the bench and someone, a lady maybe, gave him a kerchief to wipe his mouth. Someone handed him a bottle of warm soda water, which Assan used to rinse and spit out. Someone yelled at him for doing that, but Assan said nothing. He leaned his head back on the bench and closed his eyes.

———

He thought he slept for a few minutes, but when he opened his eyes the shadows were longer and different people were in the tiny park. Americans who ignored a napping man on a bench.

Assan reached into his pocket. His American paper money was gone. Some coins remained, that was all. Just as the Chief had warned, he had stopped moving and a thief had pocket-picked him. His head ached as he sat for a very long time.

As the afternoon became early evening, he didn't want to walk all the way up to the Central Park, but a cop came around and eyed him. So, he got moving. An hour or so later he was asleep under a park tree, his head on his rolled-up pair of extra pants.

———

There were other people in Demetri's office, all wearing suits and carrying leather cases filled with papers. None of them were Greeks. Demetri was standing in the window, yelling into the telephone, in English, as he had the first day Assan saw this place. Two of the men in suits laughed at something Demetri said, others lit cigarettes. One man blew smoke rings. Assan could hear Dorothy typing, *clack clack clack* without the aid of the record playing music.

"Hold on," Demetri said, seeing Assan, cupping his hand around the telephone. "Dorothy has your suit. Dorothy!"

Every eye in the office looked at Assan, his rumpled clothes, the growth of his beard, seeing another of the poor, ignorant bastards that were forever showing up in Demetri's office. Dorothy came out with the suit on a wire hanger; the jacket and pants were crisp and fresh, his shirt folded into a square like a tablecloth. Assan took his clothes and backed out of the office, nodding his thanks. The eyes and faces of the men in the office had him feeling small, like in the old country when soldiers searched him, roughed him up, and checked his papers longer than necessary, like when the guards made him stand and answer questions over and over, or like when he and the other prisoners in the camps were lined up for the roll calls that took hours.

As he descended the steps to the street, he heard a burst of laughter from the men and Dorothy taking back up her typing: *clack-clack clack. Clack.*

———

As Costas was counting out his supply of change in the cash register, a man in a clean blue-striped suit took a stool at the counter. The lunch rush would be picking up soon, the regulars would come and go until after 3:00 p.m., and Costas would need to make change for paper money. After that, Costas would have time to read the paper and find his list of new words. English was not a hard language to learn as long as you studied the newspaper every day and had a lot of American customers to listen to talk and talk and talk.

His wife was wiping down the tables, so it was Costas who asked the man in the clean and pressed blue pin-striped suit, "What can I bring ya, pal?"

Assan laid his few coins on the counter, the last of the money in his pocket. "A coffee, please. American coffee, sweet, with milk."

Costas recognized Assan and flushed with anger. "You some kind of joker?"

"I make no jokes."

"Demetri send you back here? Again?"

"No. I just came for a coffee."

"Bullshit you came for just a coffee!" Costas was so angry he slammed a mug down so hard in front of the coffee urn he cracked it. "Nico!" he yelled.

A boy, as short as Costas, popped out from the kitchen. "Huh?"

"More coffee mugs!"

Nico carried out a tray of heavy mugs for the American coffee. There was no way the boy was not Costas's son. The only differences between them were twenty years and ten kilos.

Costas almost tossed the hot coffee into Assan's lap. "That's a nickel!" he said, taking one of the thick coins off the counter, the one with the humpbacked cow. Assan poured milk and sugar into the mug and stirred slowly.

"You walk into my place and think that because you made it to America a job is waiting for you." Costas was leaning on the counter, so short his eyes were equal with Assan's. "You go cry to that Corfu bastard and he says, 'Go see Costas,' and I'm supposed to pay you to work for me?"

Assan sipped his coffee.

"What the hell is your name?"

"Assan."

"Assan? Not even Greek and here for a job!"

"Today I'm here for coffee."

Costas was rocking on his heels, like a man so angry he could leap across the counter and start a fight. "I'm supposed to be so rich I must have jobs for anyone, eh? 'Costas is a big shot! He has his own restaurant! He does so much business he has jobs coming out of his ass! You can come to America and work for him!' Bullshit!"

Assan's mug was almost emptied. "Can I have another, please?"

"No! No more coffee for you!" Costas stared Assan in his eyes for a long moment. "Bulgarian, huh?"

"That's right." Assan had finished the coffee, setting the mug on the counter.

"Okay then," Costas said. "Now take off that nice jacket and hang it on a hook in the back. Nico will teach you how to scrub the pots."

Our Town Today with Hank Fiset

YOUR EVANGELISTA, *ESPERANZA*

CUPPA JOE, PAL? Addicted to the stuff! Coffee, that is. I'm a newsman, you see, and the newsroom that doesn't run on coffee puts out a lousy paper, I'll bet. The pots here at the *Tri-Cities Daily News/Herald* are filled to the brim, even as most of the staff head out for the ubiquitous high-end spots, the ones with baristas and flavor shots for six bucks a throw. A tour of the caffeine parlors in our three conjoined metropolises will prove that good wake-'em-up is roasted, brewed, pressure-steamed, and poured in damn fine style. Try Amy's Drive-Thru, a converted taco stand on the Miracle Mile. She'll pop your eyes wide with a triple-bang espresso with a hot-pepper stirrer. ... The Corker & Smythe Coffee Shop in the old Kahle Mercantile Building on Triumph Square just recently offered takeout, and reluctantly at that. Better to sit at the counter and sip that *nectar d'noir* out of those deep porcelain mugs. ... Kaffee Boss has three stores—one at Wadsworth and Sequoia—serving the locals in leather-sleeved mason jars. Whatever you do, don't ask for milk or creamer. They are coffee purists and make a point of telling you why. Java-Va-Voom on

Second Boulevard at North Payne in East Corning has something no other coffee place can match—a unique sound. There is the *whissh* of the frother, the chitter-chatter of the staff and customers, and music, soft, in the background, like the musical score of a movie playing next door. Occasionally, there is also the *click-clack* made by a typist, but in no ordinary sense of the word.

* * *

ESPERANZA CRUZ-BUSTERMENTE, born and raised in nearby Orangeville, is an Account Adviser for a local bank, though, to many people, that is her *second* job. Many folks know her as an *evangelista*, a typist who uses her words-per-minute skills for other people. In Old Mexico, educated nuns served their flocks by typing important documents— applications, receipts, official papers, tax records, sometimes even love letters for the illiterate and those who lacked access to the once-technological marvel that is a typewriter. Esperanza's parents, like many others, learned touch typing from the *evangelistas,* then made a living by typing the messages, missives, and memoranda needed by the public. No one got rich, but sentences got stamped into paper.

* * *

ESPERANZA HAS A table at a Java-Va-Voom, where, with her large drip-with-soy, she works from a stack of blank, naked pages at the ready beside her typewriter. She's been using the place for a while now. For those unfamiliar with the sound and rhythm of a typewriter in use, Esperanza's *clacking* took some getting used to. "There were complaints at first," Esperanza told me. "I'd be typing away and get asked why I wasn't working on a laptop, which is quieter and easier. Once, two policemen walked in and I thought, Have they called the cops on me? Turns out, they were just coming in for lattes."

* * *

WHY GO ANALOG? "My email was hacked," Esperanza told me. By who? "The Russians? The NSC? Fake Nigerian princes? Who knows? My data was stolen. My life was such a mess for months." These days she uses the Internet sparingly and has an old-style flip phone, with which she can text but which she prefers to use the old-style way—by getting and receiving actual telephone calls. She never has to ask for the wi-fi password. And as for Facebook, Snapchat, Instagram, et al.? "Gave them up," she says, almost bragging. "When the hack happened and I went off social media, my day gained, like, six hours! I spent so long checking my phone every few minutes. Never mind how much time I wasted playing SnoKon, catching colored balls of ice in a little

triangle cup for points." The only negative? "My friends had to be taught how to get ahold of me." What is written, exactly, on that typewriter of hers? "Lots! I have a big family. Birthdays, the nieces and nephews get a letter and a five- or ten-dollar bill. I write memos for work that I either copy or rewrite and email at the office. And here . . ." She held up a page filled with the neatest, most perfectly formatted document you could ask for. "This is my grocery list."

* * *

OTHER CUSTOMERS SEEK Esperanza for her Little Nun services. "The kids are fascinated by my typewriter. I let them peck out their name as Mom waits for her order. Older ones type out raps and poems." Grown-ups seek her services, too. "No one has typewriters anymore, none that work. But typewritten letters are special. Some folks come with letters they've composed on a computer they want me to type out for them and make one of a kind. Before Valentine's or Mother's Day, I could sit here for hours and type notes for folks lined up around the block. If I charged, I'd be as rich as a good florist." For such personal service Esperanza may accept a free coffee. Regular in the mornings. Decaf in the afternoon.

* * *

"THIS ONE FELLOW was waiting for his coffee and started telling me about an old typewriter he had thrown out. He wished he still had it. He was going to ask his girlfriend to marry him. If he did so in a typed letter, it and the moment would last forever. What could I do but roll in a new sheet and let him dictate? I was his Steno-of-Love. We did six different drafts." What did he say to pop the question? I asked. "None of your business." Did the girlfriend say yes? "I have no idea. He read over the letter a dozen times to make sure the words fit the occasion. Then he left with it and a vanilla-shot cappuccino and has not been seen since."

* * *

HER PORTABLE TYPEWRITER allows Esperanza to take her keyboard services anywhere, but Java-Va-Voom is her faux Plaza Centrale. "This place puts up with me and gets my mind churning. I like having people around," she said. "And, some of them have come to need me." Oh, more than you may know, *Evangelista* Esperanza!

Steve Wong Is Perfect

B ecause videos go around the world in nanoseconds, little pigs are celebrated for saving little lambs from drowning. No, wait. That video was an Internet hoax. What Steve Wong did was real, it happened, in front of witnesses, even, so he went viral.

We went bowling one night, you see, and Steve truly was the alley-ooper who threw or rolled—who *bowled*—an impossible number of strikes, so he deserves the reverence of all who bowl for fun and profit. Still, if you had not been there to eyeball Steve's run, you might think Anna, MDash, and I had faked it all.

Steve's accomplishments were not falsified, nor were they a fluke. He'd been the captain of the Freshman Bowling Team at St. Anthony Country Day High School, winning trophies at Young Bowler Tournaments at the Surfside Lanes. He even had a perfect game—twelve consecutive strikes for a score of 300—when he was only thirteen years old. His name was in the paper and he was given a lot of free swag from the Surfside.

When MDash hit the Year-One anniversary of his becoming a U.S. citizen, we celebrated by taking him bowling. We convinced him that it was a great American Tradition, that immigrants from Vietnam, Chile, et al. went bowling after a year of citizenship and that he should, too. He bought it. Steve Wong brought his professional-quality glove for his rolling hand as well as his custom-made bowling shoes! We wore crummy rentals with mismatched laces that were kept in dank cubbies behind the front desk while he wore one-of-a-kind yellow and brown bowling slippers, STEVE and WONG written across the toes, with three Xs on each heel—xxx—representing the final frame of that perfect game of years before. The shoes came in a matching bag in the same hideous two-tone brown-yellow. We kept rubbing them, hoping to summon a genie as if they were magic lamps. When our beers arrived, I hollered, "My wish came true!"

MDash had never bowled in his native sub-Saharan village, so we got him his own lane and had the staff pull up the kiddie rails, the things that help little kids keep their balls out of the gutter. With his ball ricocheting from bumper to bumper, he always hit some pins for a high score of 58. My top game was 138—respectable as hell, what with all the Rolling Rocks I'd chugged. Anna, bless her, focused so much on her mechanics that she beat my high by six pins—a 144. Flushed with the thrill of victory over me, she was giddy, wrapping up MDash in her taut-as-coiled-rope arms and calling him "our American friend."

But the surprise of the night was Steve Wong and his alley prowess. His three games—236, 243, and a final high of 269—made moot our competitive loop. He was so good we grew fatigued marveling at the splits he turned into spares. At one point he rolled eleven straight strikes over two games. I threatened to steal that glove of his and burn it.

"Next time I'll bring my own ball," he told us. "I couldn't find it."

"But you keep those ugly shoes where you can grab them in a jiffy?"

We bowled again the next week, the four of us. Steve found his ball with my help. I picked him up from his too-big house in Oxnard and went through the garage and three closets. His bowling ball bag—that lovely yellow and brown leather— was behind an old, beat-up plaid typewriter case on the highest shelf in what had been his sister's closet, next to a box that held about a hundred old Barbie dolls with vacant smiles and impossibly trim waists. The ball was also that odd color combination, like a sphere of fake puke from a novelty store. The Chinese character for lightning was stamped within the trinity of finger holes. When we got to the Ventura Bowling Complex, he put the ball in a machine that turned out to be a bowling ball polisher. And he fitted Anna with her own glove, one with a lot of wrist support.

MDash was still on the bumpered lane beside our alley— his four games topped out with a high of 87. My first game was a 126, then I stopped caring because, well, we had bowled the week before and to my sensibility four games of bowling in one year is a fine total. Anna? Possessed! Again! She changed balls three times in the first game before going back to the rack for her original choice. With that special glove of hers, her concentration on her stride and on her release point, and constantly drying her palm with the little fan above the ball return, the woman flirted with 200 all night, finally topping out at 201. She was in such a good mood she took swigs from my beer.

And Steve Wong? With those three fingers of his slotted into the precision-fitted holes in that shiny orb, he put on a show of shows. His years of experience appeared in the grace of his footwork, the arc of his swing, the release of his ball hand sweeping upward to the projected computer scoreboard. He had the balance of a dancer, his cantilevered foot splayed behind his left shoe, his right toe tapping the hardwood in a triple-X kiss of brown and yellow. He never bowled less that 270 that night, finishing with a score of . . . 300.

That's right. The computer flashed PERFECT GAME PERFECT GAME PERFECT GAME as the manager rang an old ship's bell behind his desk. Other patrons—who take bowling seriously—came around and shook Steve's hand and slapped his back and paid for every Rolling Rock I ordered, proving that yes indeed, his were magic shoes.

We played again a couple of days later—at MDash's demand. He'd been dreaming about the game. "Sleeping, I can see the black ball, curving to the 1 pin, to knock down all of them, but they don't smash like I want. I want to smash them all down!" Breaking 100 was now a Vision Quest for him. On what would be only his third trip to the lanes, he eschewed the kiddie bumpers and promptly rolled five gutter balls in a row.

"Welcome to the varsity squad," I told him before missing the 9 and 10 pins by a foot. Score me an open-frame 8. Anna picked up a spare by nicking the 7 pin so was already beating me. Last up, Steve Wong rolled a strike.

A flash flood begins with a drop of rain on stone. A forest fire tells with just a whiff of distant smoke. A perfect game of bowling is a possibility only when an *X* is recorded in the little box in the corner of frame number 1, the first of twelve in a row. Steve Wong racked up nine straight strikes, so in the tenth and final frame of our first game that night—MDash posted a 33, and I had a 118, Anna a 147—a gang had gathered around our lane, about thirty people (by frame 6 the other games had quit to watch what might be Steve Wong's second perfect game in a row—an oddity and marvel as rare as twin rainbows).

He opened the tenth with a strike. The crowd crowed and Anna screamed out, "Atta baby!" A hush fell, Steve strolled and swiped, and all ten pins fell again, his eleventh strike of the game with one more needed for perfection redux. It would be a bad joke to say, "You could hear a pin drop," but you could. Dead silence met Steve's final roll. When PERFECT GAME PERFECT GAME PERFECT GAME honked on the computer scoreboard, you'd have thought it was New Year's Eve on the same night the Brooklyn Bridge opened, Neil Armstrong walked on the moon, and Saddam Hussein was dragged from his spider hole. Wong-mania was in full force, and we didn't get out of the place until exactly three in the morning—3:00. Get it?

Had we bothered with a second game that night, you might not be reading this. Steve could have bowled a 220 and then played pinball. But Fate is a kooky dame. Four nights later, bowling for free as a prize for his twenty-four consecutive "tens-at-one-blow," we returned for a goofy night of watching MDash try for something other than an open-gutter 33. But Steve Wong altered the tenor of the evening by rolling Chinese *Lightning* for a strike. He then rolled another. And, well, holy cow, as they say at bowling alleys on the subcontinent of India.

Steve rolled strike after strike, talked less and less, and entered a Concentration Zone that blocked out the rest of existence. He said nothing, never sat down, and never looked at what was happening behind him. People were texting their bowl mates to get down to the lanes on the PDQ. Free pizza was delivered. Smart-phone cameras came out in force, and a family of six showed up, the little kids in their pajamas, pulled out of bed because a sitter could not be found and Mom and Dad did not want to miss another perfect game. Steve Wong had yet to bowl anything other than a big black *X* for his third game in a row. In an atmosphere of utter wonder and magic, he kept right on smacking down thirty-point frames for his fourth, fifth, and—wait for it—sixth game. In a row.

We were openmouthed and hoarse from screaming, the three of us, huddled around the little desk between lanes 7 and 8, surrounded by a crowd of 140 and then some. I had stopped bowling. Anna began pacing instead of playing in the fifth frame of game 2, not wanting to somehow mar the alley and screw up Steve's run. Only MDash kept rolling, two gutter balls to every one that found the stack.

Huzzahs rose and fell from lofty levels to silences thick with stilled lungs. Anna's "Atta baby" became the common cheer not just for each of Steve's strikes but, charitably, for MDash's knockdowns as well. When the seventy-second consecutive strike for S. Wong was computed as his sixth perfect game in a row, the man-in-full stood at the foul line rubbing his eyes, his back to the berserk crowd, which screamed and stamped and pounded bottles of beer and cups of soda. None of us had ever been present for that kind of achievement—trivial to some, as what is bowling but a game? But come on! Six perfect *anythings* are a permanent memory.

Check out the Internet for videos of the evening and you'll see Steve stone-faced as strangers and pals celebrate him like a congressman-elect. Look at the comments: about 90 percent of the Anonymous Horde call it a hoax, but never mind them. The next day Steve was fielding calls from media outlets that wanted comments, photos, and appearances on camera. He went on the local news, the four channels shooting him individually on lane 7 as he stood stiffly, the embodiment of on-camera discomfort. You actually roll all those perfect games? How's that feel, rolling all those perfect games? What were you thinking? You ever think you'd roll so many strikes? Yes. Good. Trying to get another. Nope.

Each camera crew asked him to finish the interview with a roll down the alley. He obliged with four strikes, on camera, on cue. The string continued. The capper was a call from ESPN for an appearance on a show called *Alley Nation*. They'd pay him seventeen hundred bucks for just showing up, and if he rolled *another* perfect game, he'd get one of those six-foot-tall checks for $100,000.

You'd think such a heady few days would be fun, with an invite to be on TV and all. But Steve comes from a long line of quiet, humble Wongs. He clammed up. MDash saw him at work at Home Depot, standing stock-still in Power Tools, supposedly racking saber saw blades, but all he was doing was staring at two different blades in their clamshell packaging like the labels were written in a foreign language. He woke up at night with the dry heaves. When we picked him up in my VW Bus to drive to the ESPN gig, he almost forgot the bags with his monogrammed shoes and Chinese *Lightning*.

The show was going to be at Crowne Lanes in Fountain Valley—a long drive, so we stopped at an In-N-Out burger before hitting the freeway. In the drive-thru lane, Steve finally confessed what had been bothering him. He did not want to bowl on TV.

"You against the idea of getting free money?" I asked him. "The closest I've ever been to a hundred K was a Powerball ticket with two numbers right."

"Bowling should be fun," Steve said. "Laughs in an informal social contract. We roll when our turn comes up and no one cares about the score."

MDash wanted him to take his winnings in silver dollars.

Steve continued as we crawled through the line. In-N-Out is always busy. "I stopped competitive bowling at St. Anthony

Country Day when it became a letter sport. You had to file an application and sign score sheets. Keep up an average. It wasn't fun anymore. It was stressful then. It's stressful now."

"Look at me, Stevie baby," Anna said, reaching around the seat and grabbing his face in her hands. "Relax! There is nothing you can't do on a day like today!"

"On what waiting room poster did you read that?"

"I'm just saying, turn this day into fun with a capital *F*. Today, Steve Wong, you are going to go on TV and you are going to have fun. Fun fun fun fun."

"I don't think so," Steve said. "Nope, nope, nope, nope."

Crowne Lanes had been a site for PBA tournaments. There were grandstand-style seats and ESPN banners, lights for the TV, and multiple cameras. When Steve saw the seats filled with avid bowling fans, he let out a cussword, rare for Steve Wong.

An exhausted woman with a headset and a clipboard found us.

"Which one of you is Steve Wong?" MDash and I raised our hands. "Okay. You'll be on lane 4 after the game between Shaker Al Hassan and Kim Terrell-Kearny. The winner of that plays the winner of the Kyung Shin Park–Jason Belmonte game for the final. Nothing's expected of you until then."

Steve went out to the parking lot to pace with Anna on his heels, talking about how *fun* it must be to work at ESPN. MDash and I grabbed sodas and sat in a VIP section to see Kyung Shin Park beat Jason Belmonte by 12 in what was a damn fine exhibition of the hardwood game of tenpin. In the second game, MDash rooted hard for Shaker Al Hassan—he knew a lot of Al Hassans before coming to the USA—but Kim Terrell-Kearny (who was a woman pro, by the way) nipped him 272–269. While the cameras were being rolled over to lane 4 and the crew started tweaking the lights, the crowd milled about and Anna came looking for us.

"Steve is throwing up in the parking lot," she told us. "Between the TV trucks."

"Nerves?" I wondered.

"Are you an idiot?" she asked.

MDash left us to get a selfie with Shaker Al Hassan.

I found Steve sitting outside on a low wall by the entrance, his head in his hands like he was fighting a fever and might *chook* again.

"Wong-o," I said, squeezing his shoulder. "Here's what you are going to do today. You roll Chinese *Lightning* a couple of times. You go home seventeen hundred bucks to the better. Easy. Breezy."

"Can't do that, man." Steve raised up his head, eyes to the horizon across the parking lot. "Everyone expects god damn perfection. Drive me home right now."

I sat with him on the low wall. "Let me ask you a question. Is this bowling alley not like every bowling alley on the planet, with the foul line and the arrows in the wood? Are there ten pins down at the other end of the lane? Will your ball come back to you magically via an underground slot?"

"Oh, I see. You are giving me a pep talk."

"Answer my insightful questions."

"Yes. True. Golly, jeepers, I see that you are right. Everything will be hunky-dory now that you have talked some sense into me." Steve was speaking in a monotone. "I'm special and I can do anything I set my mind to and dreams do come true if I just carpe diem."

"Atta baby," I said. We did not move for a couple of minutes. The exhausted woman in the headset came yelling for us that it was *post time* for Steve Wong.

He ran his fingers through his jet-black hair, and then rose up, letting loose with a string of very un-Wong expletives. Good thing his parents weren't around.

When Steve put on those ugly bowling shoes, a ripple of "hey . . . that's that *guy . . .*" went through the crowd. His Internet legend had preceded him. When the tape was rolling and he was introduced by the host of *Alley Nation*, the place echoed with applause. Even the pro bowlers looked over at lane 4.

"Steve Wong," the host intoned. "Six perfect games in succession. Seventy-two strikes in a row. But questions linger as to whether your incredible streak has been the creation of clever editing and computer special effects. What is your reaction to such allegations?" The host stuck the microphone up to Steve's lips.

"Makes sense, what with the Web being the Web." Steve's eyes darted from the host to the crowd to us to the floor and back to the host—all so fast it looked like he was having an attention-induced seizure.

"Have you ever thought you'd reach such a level of technique and form that so many closed frames would be in your game?"

"I just bowl for fun."

"The official record for straight strikes is held by Tommy Gollick at forty-seven, but here you claim to have rolled twenty-four consecutive Turkeys. Many in the bowling world wonder if such a string is even possible."

I turned to a fellow next to me who, with his bowling shirt emblazoned with a Crowne Lanes logo, must have been a citizen of Alley Nation. "What does he mean by *Turkeys?*" I asked him.

"Three strikes in a row, dipshit. And no way in hell did that punk roll twenty-plus of 'em." He then yelled *"Hoax!"* at the top of his lungs.

"As you may hear, Steve Wong, there are some who doubt not just your claim but also the word of the manager of your home alley, the Ventura Party, Billiards, and Bowling Complex."

Steve looked the crowd over, probably seeing only the glaring eyes of unbelievers. "Like I said. I bowl for fun."

"Well, as I always say, the proof of any bowler is in the crash of pins, so, Steve Wong, step up to the line and show us what game you brought with you today. And remember, folks, a great time is waiting for you and your family at your nearby Bowling Alley and Fun Center. Take up bowling and get on a roll."

Steve walked to the ball return, strapping on his glove as the three of us hooted and hollered "Atta baby." Some in the crowd catcalled. Steve heaved a sigh so deep and soulful we could see his shoulders sag, and we were perched far away in the upper row. He turned his back to us all and sighed again. By the time he took Chinese *Lightning* into his hands and placed his fingers into the ball's custom-drilled holes, we who knew Steve Wong could tell this about him—he was not having fun.

And yet, his movements were still a vision of grace, his release of the ball smooth and effortless, the flick of his hand applying the same spin we had seen so many times, his fingers reaching for the ceiling in one hand waving free, the toes on his right foot tap-tapping on the hardwood akimbo to his left shoe, xxx flashing from his heels.

Rumble. Smash. Strike. Cries of "Lucky!" echoed throughout Crowne Lanes. Steve, his back to the world, cooled his hand waiting for Chinese *Lightning* to appear from below. With ball in hand, he assumed the pose and did it again. Rumble. Smash. Strike number 2.

Then came strikes number 3 through 6, netting a score of 120 in the fourth frame. Steve had turned the crowd decidedly in his favor, but I doubt he noticed. He didn't so much as glance our way.

Shaker Al Hassan was asked what he thought of Steve's form. "Unworldly magnificent!" he said on camera to all citizens of Alley Nation.

Strikes 7, 8, and 9 had all four professionals weighing in on Steve's balance, his mechanics, his cool-under-pressure command, in what Kyung Shin Park called "the Tunnel" and

Jason Belmonte knew as the "Line of Fate." Kim Terrell-Kearny said the PBA had a place for a competitor as poised as Steve Wong.

When ten *X*-ed frames were superimposed on the TV monitors, the host became flabbergasted—actually saying, "I am flabbergasted by the performance of this fine young example to bowlers everywhere!" The crowd was on its feet shouting encouragements equal to those for the gladiators of Ancient Rome. Steve's eleventh roll was a surreal moment in time, a dream ballet, a free fall out of the sky that hit the perfect pocket between the 1 and 3 pins and *kablooey* went all eight of the rest of them.

With one last strike needed for a perfect game, $100,000, and ESPN immortality, Steve soft-shoed to the ball return without any tell of emotion—no expectation, no anxiety, no fear. No fun, either. As far as I could tell from the back of his head, his face must have looked like an open-eyed death mask.

As he held his ball before his heart in preparation for his windup, something more encompassing than silence fell on Crowne Lanes—a void of sound, like the room had been vacuum-pumped of atmosphere, robbing sound waves of their purchase. Anna's fingers were digging into MDash's and my arms, the words *atta baby* forming mutely on her lips.

The exact moment of the beginning of Steve's twelfth and final roll was imperceptible, like the slow liftoff of a rocket to the moon, so heavy a thing that nothing moves despite the ignition of boosters and all the flames and fury. The nanosecond Chinese *Lightning* hit the hardwood a roar exploded so loud you'd have thought every member of Alley Nation was on the cusp of simultaneous orgasm with the love of his or her life. A SABRE jet engine is not as loud as the roof-busting blare that grew and grew as that brown and yellow orb spun along its arc. Just inches from the impact of ball on pin, Crowne Lanes was engulfed in a wall of sound.

The smash of ball in the pocket just between pins 1 and 3 happened in some other place, a clap of thunder a hundred miles away. We all saw the flash of white, like the smile of a giant with perfect teeth suddenly busted, all ten pins scattering and clattering until what was left was empty space and dead soldiers—ten of them.

Steve stood at the foul line surveying the emptiness at the other end of the alley as upright pins appeared on automatic reset. As the host was yelling into his headset, "Steve Wong is perfect!" our friend knelt on one knee, appearing to thank God-as-he-knew-God for such a triumph.

Instead, he was unlacing his left shoe—STEVE. He took it off and set its toe on the foul line. He did the same to WONG on the right, neatly setting his custom-made bowling footware so that xxx showed on TV.

In stocking feet, he padded to the ball return and took up that which had already been delivered. Carrying Chinese *Lightning* in two hands like it was nothing more than a paving stone, he set it on top of his shoes in a gesture that Anna, MDash, and I knew to mean, "I will bowl no more. Forever."

As he tossed his bowling glove into the crowd—setting off a melee for the memorabilia hounds—Kim Terrell-Kearny ran up and kissed his cheek in an embrace, while the other pros offered handshakes and head rubs.

By the time we made our way through the adoring bowlers—all of them now fans—Anna was weeping. She threw her arms around Steve Wong and sobbed so deeply I was worried she would pass out. MDash kept saying something in his native language, a superlative, I am sure. I toasted Steve with a beer I had found in a cooler by one of TV cameras, then grabbed his stack of bowling gear and stuffed it all in his bowling bag.

Only the three of us heard him say, "I'm glad that's over."

———

None of us went bowling again for the next few months, though not by plan. I had a dime-size growth on my leg that went all raised up and spooky on me, so I scheduled outpatient surgery to have it removed, sliced away, potato-peeled off. Nothing serious. MDash got a new job, walking away from his career possibilities at Home Depot for a position at Target, his new workplace separated from his former job by a vast, shared parking lot. He walked to the other store, changed his polo shirt, and never looked back. Anna took fly-fishing lessons at a place run by the Parks Department—at the Stanley P. Swett Municipal Casting Ponds, a place no one had ever heard of or could find without Google Maps. She tried to get me to sign up along with her, but I look on fly-fishing as a companion sport to luge racing—never will I do either one.

Steve Wong's life settled down. He figured out how many ESPN dollars would go to taxes and planned accordingly. He went back to work, had to take selfies with customers for a while, and told MDash that leaving Home Depot for Target was like emigrating from his sub-Saharan home country to North Korea (such is the competitive rhetoric of Home Depot management). One thing Steve never did talk about was bowling.

But one night, there we were, bowling for free, the regulars at the lanes sidling up to Steve for bumps with the fist that had rolled those perfect games. Steve and I arrived first. I had picked him up, but he came out of his house empty-handed!

"You dope!" I said as he climbed into the shotgun seat of the VW Bus.

"What?"

"Go back inside and get your stuff. Your shoes and your bag and Chinese *Lightning*."

"Okay," he said, after a long pause.

By the time Anna arrived, then MDash, I had finished a Rolling Rock and Steve was pumping quarters into a video motocross game. We carried his equipment down to our assigned lane, changed into our rental shoes, and picked out our bowling balls, Anna considering every single one, I think. When we called to Steve that we were ready to begin, he was still racing on the machine and just waved blindly for us to start without him. We ended up playing two games, just the three of us. Anna won both, I lost them, and MDash was crowing about being a Silver Medalist over me.

Steve came down to our lane and watched the last frames of that second game. We were debating whether or not to go again, since it was getting late and it was a Thursday night.

I wanted to go home, MDash wanted to beat Anna for the Gold, and she wanted to crush all our dreams for the third straight time in one evening. Steve didn't care what we did, saying he would sit out the next line and maybe have a beer or two.

"You aren't going to bowl with us?" Anna was incredulous. "When did you get so stuck-up?"

"C'mon, Steve," MDash pleaded. "You and bowling mean America to me."

"Put your shoes on," I told him. "Or you are walking home."

Steve sat there for a moment, then called us a bunch of jerks and took off his street shoes to change into his ugly bowling footwear.

I rolled first, hitting a paltry four on my first ball, then missing the remaining pins by millimeters. MDash nearly died laughing. His first ball left three standing, which he then clobbered to pick up the spare.

"Tonight," he hissed at Anna, "you are going to die!"

"Bit heavy with the taunts," she told him. "No one dies bowling unless a tornado is involved." She then knocked down nine of the pins and expertly closed the frame on her second ball—she and MDash were tied.

Then came Steve Wong, sighing as he took his custom ball out of its custom bag, the spherical tool of his legendary alley work. I may exaggerate by saying the bowlers in the place stopped what they were doing to watch a master at work, that the whole joint suddenly went silent, wondering if, somehow, _Lightning_ would strike again and start another chain reaction of perfect games, proving that Steve Wong was the true God of Turkeys. I think it was mostly in my head.

He stood still on the lane, holding the ball once again to his heart, his eyes locked on the faraway wedge of ten white pins. Then he began his swing and step-step-stepped to the lip of the foul line and released *Lightning*, lifting his bowling hand up to the sky. His right toe tapped the floor behind his left heel, the total of six Xs displayed for all to see. His ball curved and spun down the long lines of the shiny hardwood, headed for that pocket between the 1 and 3 pins, looking to be a strike for sure.

Acknowledgments

Many thanks to Anne Stringfield, Steve Martin, Esther Newberg, and Peter Gethers—the four in-laws of these married words.

Special credit to E. A. Hanks for her blue pencil and sharp, honest eyes.

Plus, a tip of the cap and a buck apiece to Gail Collins and Deborah Triesman.

And thanks to all those at Penguin Random House who examined, admired, improved, and made presentable these stories.

A NOTE ABOUT THE AUTHOR

Tom Hanks has been an actor, screenwriter, director, and, through Playtone, a producer. His writing has appeared in *The New York Times*, *Vanity Fair*, and *The New Yorker*. This is his first collection of fiction.

THE
SCHOOL STORY

Also by Andrew Clements

Frindle
The Landry News
The Janitor's Boy
The Jacket
A Week in the Woods

THE
SCHOOL STORY

Andrew Clements

Illustrated by Brian Selznick

ALADDIN PAPERBACKS

New York London Toronto Sydney Singapore

First Aladdin Paperbacks edition September 2002

Text copyright © 2001 by Andrew Clements
Illustrations copyright © 2001 by Brian Selznick

ALADDIN PAPERBACKS
An imprint of Simon & Schuster Children's Publishing Division
1230 Avenue of the Americas, New York, NY 10020
All rights reserved, including the right of
reproduction in whole or in part in any form.

Also available in a Simon & Schuster Books for Young Readers hardcover edition.
Book design by Paula Winicur
The text of this book is set in Revival.
The illustrations are rendered in pencil.

Manufactured in the United States of America
14 16 18 20 19 17 15
The Library of Congress has cataloged the hardcover edition as follows:
Clements, Andrew, 1949-
The School Story / by Andrew Clements; illustrated by Brian Selznick.
p.cm.
Summary: After twelve-year-old Natalie writes a wonderful novel, her friend Zoe helps her devise a scheme to get it accepted at the publishing house where Natalie's mother works as an editor.
ISBN 0-689-82594-3 (hc)
[1. Authorship—Fiction. 2. Publishers and publishing—Fiction.]
I. Selznick, Brian, ill. II. Title
PZ7.C59118 Pu 2001
[Fic]—dc 21
00-049683
ISBN-13: 978-0-689-85186-5 (ISBN-10: 0-689-85186-3) (Aladdin pbk.)

For Stephanie Owens-Lurie and
Rick Richter—without whom, less
—A. C.

THE
SCHOOL STORY

CHAPTER 1

Fan Number One

Natalie couldn't take it. She peeked in the doorway of the school library, then turned, took six steps down the hall, turned, paced back, and stopped to look in at Zoe again. The suspense was torture.

Zoe was still reading. The first two chapters only added up to twelve pages. Natalie leaned against the door frame and chewed on her thumbnail. She thought, *What's taking her so long?*

Zoe could see Natalie out of the corner of her eye. She could feel all that nervous energy nudging at her, but Zoe wasn't about to be rushed. She always read slowly, and she liked it

1

that way, especially when it was a good story. And this one was good.

The Cheater by Natalie Nelson
page 12

I catch up with Sean between Eighty-second and Eighty-first Streets. His legs are longer than mine, so I'm panting. I grab his arm and he stops in front of a bodega.

He says, "Why are you following me?"

"I've got to talk to you."

"Yeah, well, too bad. You had your chance to talk during the Penalty Board hearing. And you didn't."

"But if I told the truth, then the whole school would know I cheated. I'd get expelled."

He just looks at me. "But you really did cheat, right? . . . And I really didn't steal that answer key, right? . . . And you know I didn't steal it because *you* did, right?"

I nod yes to all the questions.

Sean is almost shouting now, his eyes wild. "So first you steal, then you cheat, and now you've lied. And me? You've left me to take the punishment."

The shopkeeper is worried. He moves from the counter to the doorway of the bodega, looking at us.

Sean ignores him and gets right into my face, screaming. "Well, guess what, Angela. We're not friends now—and I don't know if we ever were!"

He storms away, hands jammed in his pockets, shoulders hunched, stabbing the sidewalk with every step.

Me, I cry.

Zoe let page twelve slip onto the table and then stared at it, deep in thought.

"So, what do you think?"

Natalie was right behind her, and Zoe jumped six inches. "Jeez, Natalie! Scare me to death! And you ruined a nice moment too."

"But what do you think? Is it any good?"

Zoe nodded. "I think it's very good."

"Really?" Natalie pulled out a chair and sat down, leaning forward. "I mean, you're not just saying that because we're best friends?"

Zoe shook her head. "No, I mean it. It's good. Like I can't wait to read the whole thing. Can you bring the rest tomorrow?"

Natalie smiled and reached into her backpack. She pulled out a blue folder with a rubber band around it. "Here. I've still got to write about five more chapters. I just needed to know if the beginning was any good, but you can read what I've got done if you want."

Zoe took the folder carefully and said, "This is great. But you *are* going to finish it, right? Do you know the whole story already—like all the way to the end?"

Natalie said, "Not *all* the way to the end . . . but almost. I know how the end *feels*, but not exactly what happens—at least, not yet."

Natalie's book had begun by accident on the bus with her mom late one afternoon back in

September. Sixth grade was already three weeks old, and both she and her mom had settled into the routine of commuting together. It was a Friday afternoon, and they were going home on the 5:55 coach, thundering through the Lincoln Tunnel from New York City to Hoboken, New Jersey.

Her mom looked exhausted. Natalie studied the face tilted toward her on the headrest. It was a pretty face—*Prettier than mine*, she thought. But there were little lines at the corners of her mother's eyes and mouth. Care lines, worry lines.

Natalie said, "Hard day, Mom?"

Eyes still closed, her mom smiled and nodded. "The editorial department met all day with the marketing department—all day."

Natalie asked, "How come?" When her dad died, Natalie had decided she needed to talk to her mom more. Sometimes she pretended to be interested in her mom's work at the publishing company even when she wasn't. Like now.

Her mom said, "Well, the marketing people keep track of what kinds of books kids and parents and teachers are buying. Then they tell us, and we're supposed to make more books like the ones they think people will buy."

Natalie said, "Makes sense. So, what kinds of books do they want you to make?"

Hannah Nelson lifted her head off the seat back and turned toward Natalie. "Here's the summary of a six-hour meeting. Ready?"

Natalie nodded.

Her mom used a deep voice that sounded bossy. "People, we need to publish more adventure books, more series books, and more school stories." In her regular voice she said, "That was it. A six-hour meeting for something that could have gone into a one-page memo—or a three-line E-mail."

Then Natalie asked, "What's a school story?"

"A school story is just what it sounds like—it's a short novel about kids and stuff that happens mostly at school."

Natalie thought for a second and then said, "You mean like *Dear Mr. Henshaw*?"

And her mom said, "Exactly."

Then Natalie said to herself, *Hey, who knows more about school than someone who's right there, five days a week, nine months a year? I bet I could write a school story.*

6

And that was all it took. Natalie Nelson the novelist was born.

Or almost born. Her career as an author didn't officially spring to life until about four months later—on that afternoon in the school library after Zoe read the first two chapters.

Because it's the same for every new author, for every new book. Somebody has to be the first to read it. Somebody has to be the first to say she likes it. Somebody has to be that first fan.

And of course, that was Zoe.

CHAPTER 2

A Portrait of the Author as a Young Girl

Some
people are writers, and some people
are talkers. Natalie had always been a writer.

Like all writers, first she was a reader. As a baby
and then a toddler, Natalie loved it when her mom

or dad read to her. She loved how the same story would change, depending on who was reading it.

Mom read calmly, evenly, thoughtfully. Even if the story was exciting or scary or sad, Natalie always felt warm and safe when Mom was reading.

But not with Dad. He was loud and reckless. He made funny voices for all the firemen and ducks and princesses. He made sound effects for the trains and the caterpillars, and if the words weren't exciting or silly or scary enough, he threw in some new ones. When Dad was reading, anything could happen.

And so Natalie got her first taste of reading in the very best way, from people who loved good books almost as much as they loved her.

By the time she was four, Natalie couldn't wait any longer. She wanted more stories than her parents had time to read to her. She already knew her ABCs, and she made her mom and dad point at every word as they read to her. Then Natalie would sit and turn the pages of her picture books again and again. She started being able to see the words and hear the sounds they made, and once she began to crack the code, there was no stopping her. Natalie became a reader.

Even after Natalie could read by herself, her mom and dad read stories to her at bedtime—Dad one night, and Mom the next. Natalie always got to choose the story from her shelf of favorites.

The car crash changed all that. Natalie was in second grade, and after the accident there was only Mom to read at bedtime. And that was when Natalie hid some of her favorite books in the back of her closet. She didn't want her mom to read them anymore. Those were Daddy's books. Sometimes late at night, or on a quiet Sunday afternoon, Natalie would open up *The Sailor Dog* or *The Grouchy Ladybug*, and she could hear her father's voice reading to her.

The writing part came gradually, naturally. At first it was imitation. If Natalie read a good poem, she tried to make up one like it. If a character grabbed her imagination, Natalie would talk to her stuffed animals and pretend she was the Sailor Dog or the Steadfast Tin Soldier or Raggedy Ann. She would act out parts of a story and make up words for everyone to say. Sometimes she pretended to be Gretel, helping Hansel push the wicked witch into the oven. Other times she pretended to be the wicked witch.

And always, always, Natalie thought about the authors. She thought about Hans Christian Andersen or Margaret Wise Brown or Beatrix Potter, and she imagined these people sitting in a garden or a cabin or an attic, making up new stories. And she knew that one day she would sit down in a garden or a cabin or an attic and try it out for herself.

When Natalie got to fourth grade, she began to spend more time writing. She made herself a little writing place in the back corner of the loft that she and her mom had moved to. Her desk was a door laid flat across two small filing cabinets. She sat in her dad's old red desk chair and used his old Macintosh computer. Not quite a cabin or an attic, but close enough—and it was as close as Natalie could get to her dad.

CHAPTER 3

Mystery Man

"So, what are you going to do with the book," asked Zoe, "you know, when it's all finished?"

"Don't know yet." Natalie gathered up the first twelve pages from the library table in front of Zoe. "Maybe print out a copy for you, and maybe one for Lill and Sparky . . . maybe let some other kids read it. I might even show it to Ms. Clayton—maybe get some extra credit in English." Natalie handed the pages to Zoe, and she tucked them into the blue folder with the rest of the manuscript.

Zoe shook her head, and her curly brown hair bounced from side to side. "It's way too good for that. I think you should get it all done and then give it to your mom. She should get it published—you know, for real."

Natalie snorted. "Yeah, like my mom is going to take it to her boss and say, 'Guess what? My daughter wrote this wonderful little book,' and then her boss goes, 'Gee, that's great—let's pay her a bunch of money and start printing her book right away!' Get real, Zoe. You don't know anything about publishing."

"Do too," said Zoe. "My dad gets this magazine called *Publishers Weekly* at his office, and when I go there, I read all about what the bestsellers are and who's making the big deals." Zoe's dad was a lawyer, and she always bragged to Natalie about big deals and famous clients.

Natalie shook her head. "Well, I've seen that magazine too, *and* I've also been to my mom's office at her publishing company, and I've seen stacks and stacks of envelopes filled with new books from new authors, and most of them don't get published. So there!"

"Shhh!" Mr. Levy glared at the girls from his perch at the front desk. Even though it was after three on a Thursday afternoon and they were the only kids in the room, it was still his library, and he liked it quiet.

Natalie whispered, "Let's go."

Zoe never admitted that there was something she did not know or could not do. They gathered up their coats and backpacks, and by the time they had walked halfway down the stairs toward the front door of the school, Zoe had a good idea—no, a *great* idea. But she wasn't going to just blurt it out. What's the fun of that? Zoe wanted to make Natalie work for it.

So she said, "I know how to get your book published."

Natalie shifted her backpack to the other shoulder and glanced sideways at Zoe. She said, "Oh, really?" There was just a trace of sarcasm, but Zoe heard it loud and clear.

Zoe said, "Yes, really."

Natalie and Zoe had been best friends since their first day of kindergarten at the Deary School. From the start it had been a push-and-pull friendship, the kind that can happen when two very different people like each other a lot.

They stepped out onto the sidewalk. It was sunny, but a cold wind whipped across the

Hudson River and skittered off the buildings on Riverside Drive. January in New York wasn't picnic weather. Pulling up the hood of her parka, Natalie said, "So, what's your big idea?"

Zoe said, "Ever hear of Ted Geisel?"

Natalie shook her head and said, "No . . . does he go to school here?"

Zoe looked amazed, shocked. She put her hands on her hips and said, "You mean you've never heard of Ted Geisel? Really? Well. Then *that's* your homework assignment."

Natalie laughed. "You don't have an idea at all—you're just trying to send me on some wild goose chase."

Zoe shook her head and put on an air of superiority. "No, I really *do* have a plan, and it's a very good plan. But until you know who Ted Geisel is, it won't make any sense to you. So go learn what you have to learn, and we'll talk about it tomorrow, maybe."

Natalie lifted her nose into the air and said, "Fine!" She turned on her heel and headed south. She had to walk down to Seventy-second Street and then east to Broadway to catch a bus to her mom's office in midtown. Most of the schoolkids in the city used the subway. It was a lot faster, but Natalie always felt too closed in down there. Besides, the buses smelled better. Natalie was never in a rush anyway. Today, like almost every school day, it would be about another three hours before she got home.

Zoe would be home in twenty minutes, and all she had to do was put up her hand. When she did, a yellow cab pulled out of the traffic on Riverside Drive. It veered over and lurched to a stop at the curb. Zoe lived on East Sixty-fifth Street, and she always went home in a taxi. As Zoe opened the rear door of the cab she yelled to Natalie, "Remember—Ted Geisel!"

Natalie was almost to the first cross street. She looked back over her shoulder, made a face, and stuck out her tongue. Then she turned and kept walking, smiling to herself.

Zoe could be a pain, but once in a while she really did come up with a great idea. Natalie couldn't wait to find out something about this Ted Geisel.

CHAPTER 4

City Kid

Natalie's mom was nervous when her twelve-year-old daughter had to get around New York City on her own—so she was nervous almost every afternoon. She didn't like it, but she didn't have any choice. Every weekday morning she put Natalie into a taxi at the bus station. The cab drove straight uptown to the Deary School at a time of day when most of the traffic was going the other direction. Even so, that ride still cost about nine dollars. But an afternoon cab ride to her office building near Rockefeller Center took much longer, and the fare was almost twice as much. Hannah Nelson just couldn't afford to pay that much for transportation every single school day.

She worried, but she knew Natalie was a good city kid—always had been. Back when Natalie was only three and they still lived in Manhattan, her dad had taught her to look for a police officer if she ever got lost. If she couldn't see a police officer, Natalie learned she should talk only to a lady with children, because a mother or a nanny would always help a lost child. She also learned how to dial collect from a pay phone and how to use 911. Her dad had taught her well.

Natalie knew she had to be careful in the city, but she also knew that she didn't have to walk around feeling afraid all the time. She felt fine about her daily trip to her mom's office. She was tall for a girl of twelve and looked as if she might be fourteen or fifteen. She had plenty of street smarts, but she was also well equipped. Natalie had a whistle on the lanyard around her neck and a twenty-dollar bill under the liner in her left shoe. Hannah Nelson also made her daughter carry an emergency cell phone. Natalie could push one button that sent a message to the police, to her mom at the office, and to her uncle Fred. Fred Nelson was her dad's younger brother, and he'd made a point of spending time with Natalie ever since the accident. He lived a few blocks from the Deary School, and his office was on Madison Avenue. If there was ever a problem, Natalie would have plenty of help.

Still, at least once a week her mom would remind Natalie of the basic rules: If a person begins bothering you, yell and start running. Never get into a car or a van, and if someone asks you to come closer, run the other way. Always stay on the main streets, where there are plenty of people. If someone ever grabs hold of you, bite, scratch, kick, scream—do whatever it takes to get away, and then run, keep calling for help, and hit 911 on the cell phone. Don't get into an empty bus or an overcrowded one. Sit or stand at the front, near the driver. Never go into a strange building.

Like most city kids, Natalie had developed a kind of radar. Scanning the sidewalk ahead of her, if she saw a person who looked shady or someone asking for money or acting pushy or weird, she'd find a way to avoid a face-to-face meeting. If she had to, she could always cross the street, but usually it was just a matter of watching for the right moment to pass by. At age twelve, and after years of walking in New York, avoiding trouble had become almost automatic for Natalie.

Still, it's impossible to plan for everything. There was the time a woman on the bus started yelling at Natalie's backpack like it was a dog that was trying to bite her. Natalie was scared, but she stayed calm. When the driver shouted, "Hey, lady—shut up or get off!" the lady got off and started screaming at a trash can on the corner. And then there was the time Natalie thought this tall boy wearing sunglasses was following her. He walked behind her all the way from Seventy-ninth Street to the bus stop at Seventy-second Street and Broadway. When he took the same bus she did, Natalie got really scared. She thought he was looking at her from behind his dark glasses. Just when she was about to ask the bus driver for help, the boy stood up and got off at the next stop, and Natalie saw him walk into a big bookstore on Fifty-seventh Street. False alarm.

Today's trip was uneventful, and when Natalie got to the lobby of her mom's building, she signed in at the desk, got in the elevator, and pushed the button for the fourteenth floor. The elevator hummed up to the third floor, and three more people got on. They pushed the buttons for floors five, seven, and eight. People got on and off the elevator at almost every floor, and soon Natalie was squeezed against the back wall.

The first time she had come to visit her mom at work was about four years earlier. Back then Natalie was sure that making children's books had to be the most exciting job in the world. Natalie had expected to see mountains of books and a huge, noisy workshop. Some people would be painting book covers, others would be printing and folding the pages, and over in a corner someone would be gluing everything together.

What she actually saw on that first visit was a large, quiet room filled with a maze of little offices. Here and there small groups talked quietly at large tables, and everywhere people sat at computer screens, tapping away. True, there were plenty of books around—stacks and boxes and bookcases of them—but they were all finished. Natalie was disappointed. A publishing company was a pretty boring place.

The elevator door opened on fourteen, and Natalie stepped out onto the thick green carpet of the reception area. The receptionist was talking into his headset, but he gave her a smile and a wave, and then pushed the security button. The door to the right began to buzz. Natalie pushed it open and walked into the editorial department of Shipley Junior Books.

The sign beside the opening of her mom's small, windowless office said HANNAH NELSON, EDITOR. The room had a door and a ceiling, but in all other respects it was a basic cubicle. The office contained a desktop that made a U, and bookcases lined the walls. Every inch of space was loaded with piles of paper and books. There was a

computer, two small filing cabinets, one swivel chair, a plastic trash basket, and one straight-backed chair just inside the doorway. All the furniture was gray or green.

Balanced above the computer screen was a single photograph in a clear plastic holder—Dad and Mom and Natalie in a sailboat. Every time she came to the office, that picture was the first thing Natalie saw. All three of them looked like they were having such a good time, but Natalie couldn't remember being there. She always wished she could.

"Hi, Mom."

Hannah Nelson spun around in her chair and pulled Natalie into a hug. She held both of her daughter's hands a moment and then reached up to push a wisp of brownish blond hair out of Natalie's eyes. "Have you had a good day, sweetheart?"

Natalie nodded. "Except everyone gave a ton of homework. Can I go get a snack?"

"Uh-huh . . . here." Her mom swung her chair around, pulled open a drawer, and swiveled back. She handed Natalie a small stack of quarters. "Could you get me a Sprite, or maybe some apple juice? You can start your homework in Ella's office. She's away all week."

It was fifteen minutes later—soda drained and cookies gone—before Natalie remembered Zoe's assignment. She jumped up out of Ella's chair, grabbed a dictionary from the shelf near the doorway, and flipped to the Gs. *Game, gargoyle, geisha*—no *Geisel*.

Turning around, Natalie sat down at the desk and moved the mouse next to the keyboard, and the darkened computer screen jumped to life. She'd used Ella's computer before, so she knew what to look for. She clicked on a folder labeled REFERENCE and then clicked again on ENCARTA.

The encyclopedia opened up, and a few clicks later she had it in search mode. Natalie typed *Geisel*, and then hit the return key.

And there he was: *Geisel, Theodor.* End of mystery.

CHAPTER 5

The Plot Thickens

"Dr. Seuss."

Those were Natalie's first words to Zoe on Friday, whispered during the morning meeting.

When Natalie had discovered that Theodor Geisel was the real name of Dr. Seuss, at first she didn't see Zoe's point. She thought about it on the bus ride home Thursday, and then off and on all night. By Friday morning Natalie had a pretty good idea why Zoe had made her learn about Ted Geisel.

But as the morning meeting ended and they headed toward the science rooms, Natalie pre-

26

tended she didn't have a clue. That way, Zoe could explain everything. Natalie knew that was what Zoe always preferred.

"So, do you get it?" asked Zoe.

Natalie looked at her blankly. "Get what?"

"The idea—you know—Ted Geisel, Dr. Seuss?" prompted Zoe. "You can get your book published by using a different name. That way your mom won't know it's you! She reads, she likes, she publishes! Great idea, right? You get to pick a pseudonym, a phony name!"

Natalie paused a few seconds, then said, "You mean I get to lie to my mom, right?"

Zoe made a face. "Oh, come on."

Zoe and Natalie had different ideas about what was and was not a lie. Natalie always got the best results with the whole truth. Zoe wasn't a liar, but as long as the truth was not entirely absent, Zoe felt just fine. They'd had this discussion before, and Natalie usually held out for complete honesty.

But today Zoe was prepared. She said, "Okay, tell me this: Was Dr. Seuss lying to forty gazillion kids just because they didn't know his real name? Was that a lie?"

Natalie started to reply, but Zoe kept on building her case. "Was Samuel Clemens lying when everybody thought some guy named Mark Twain wrote *Huckleberry Finn*? It's not lying, Natalie. Authors use made-up names all the time. And you're an author, so it's okay."

Natalie said, "Well . . . but do you think Ted Geisel lied to his *mother*? Don't you think *she* knew he was also Dr. Seuss?"

Zoe had to think about that, but only for a few seconds. She said, "Yeah, but . . . but I bet his mother wasn't an editor. If she was, and if he sent her a bunch of his wacky pictures and stories, she'd probably have said, 'Oh, Ted—this is cute, but it's not really a book. Now, you run along outside and play baseball.' And then millions of kids would never have gotten to read *The Cat in the Hat* or *Green Eggs and Ham* or anything. All because he forgot to use a pseudonym. I bet if his mom had been an editor, he'd have kept his real name a secret—at least for a while. Remember, Natalie, she's not just your mom. She's your *editor*."

Zoe reached behind her chair and pulled the blue folder out of her backpack. She handed it to Natalie and said, "Here. I stayed up until eleven last night to read it. It's great, even better than I thought it would be. And I can't wait until it's finished. It's going to make a great book."

Natalie was quiet as she sat down at their worktable in science class. Zoe could feel victory, but she didn't want to rush things. Zoe knew better. Natalie always had to think things through for herself. So Zoe pretended to be busy with her lab notebook and then started assembling the string and weights they would need for their experiment about simple machines.

Natalie put the manuscript away. As she slowly pulled her science book from her backpack she said, "Cassandra . . . Cassandra Day. I've always wished my name could be Cassandra. Do you think Cassandra Day is a good name?"

Zoe grinned. "It's a *great* name!" She stuck out her hand, and when Natalie took it, Zoe pumped it up and down and said, "Cassandra Day, I'm so glad to get to meet such a wonderful author!"

CHAPTER 6

Reality Attack

Zoe's excitement was like a river. All day Friday it swept Natalie along. But after school, alone, riding the bus to her mom's office, Natalie started to face facts.

First of all, her book wasn't finished. And even when it was, would it be something a real editor would want to look at? Just because Zoe liked it, that didn't mean her mom would. And what if other people thought the book was really bad?

By the time Natalie arrived at Shipley Junior Books, she had talked herself out of the whole crazy idea. Standing in the opening of Ella's cubicle, Natalie sipped on a strawberry-kiwi drink and looked at the mounds of mail from writers all over the country. Brown envelopes, white envelopes, red-and-gold envelopes with fancy lettering. Manuscripts from writers in California and Illinois and Texas and Florida. Hundreds of them. Some of them had been mailed more than six months ago. Some of the envelopes hadn't even been opened. It was like a morgue for dead books.

Natalie finished her drink and slumped down into Ella's chair. She picked up the phone, punched "9," then dialed Zoe's number, the one for her private line in her bedroom. Zoe actually had two private phone numbers, because she also had her own cell phone. Zoe picked up during the first ring.

"Zoe Reisman's room at the Reisman residence, Zoe Reisman speaking."

"Zoe? It's me. It's a stupid idea."

"What?"

"Trying to get my story published—it's a stupid idea, Zoe. Even if I get the book done, and even if it's halfway decent, no one will ever read it, and even if they read it, there are probably a million books that are better. So what's the point?"

It was silent on the other end of the line.

Natalie said, "Zoe? Are you there?"

Zoe's voice was hard. "Let me talk to Cassandra Day."

"Give it up, Zoe. Cassandra Day is dead."

Zoe was fierce now. "If you don't put Cassandra Day on the phone this instant, then I'm going to call the police and tell them that a girl who looks

just like you is hiding there in that building on the fourteenth floor and has kidnapped an amazingly talented person named Cassandra Day. Now you just put Cassandra on the line, or the next thing you'll hear is sirens."

Natalie smiled. She knew Zoe wasn't going to let up, so she paused a moment. Then in a quiet voice a little deeper than her own she said, "Yes? This is Cassandra Day."

Zoe said, "Thank God you're all right! Now listen, Cassie—"

Natalie broke in, enjoying her new voice. "Oh, my . . . no, no, no, dear. No one *ever* calls me *Cassie*. It's Cassandra, always Cassandra."

Zoe never liked being interrupted, but she held on to her focus. "Fine. Okay, Cassandra. Listen, Cassandra. Don't you believe one thing

that that deadbeat Natalie tells you. You are a great writer. One day your grandchildren are going to read all the books you've written. And we are going to get this first one published, okay? You've got to trust me on this. Are you with me?"

Natalie sighed, but still speaking as Cassandra she said, "Yes, I am with you. . . . But I must say that you are an extremely annoying and cantankerous person."

"Miss Day, let me worry about me. You just make sure you keep your head clear. Now, you go home and do some writing this weekend, okay?"

Natalie didn't answer. Five seconds. Ten seconds.

Zoe said, "Cassandra? . . . You *are* going to go home and finish another chapter this weekend—right?"

"I guess so. Sure. I'll keep writing."

"And Cassandra?"

"What?" said Natalie.

"I'm proud to know you, Cassandra. Goodbye."

"Thanks, Zoe. Bye."

CHAPTER 7

Business Lesson

Cassandra Day was still alive, but she wasn't exactly in tip-top shape. After saying good-bye to Zoe, Natalie sat in Ella's chair, staring at the stacks of unread manuscripts, imagining what it would be like to have her own story there among them. It was too depressing, so she went to her mom's office and sat on the chair just inside the doorway. Her mom was absorbed in a manuscript, leaning over the stack of paper, red pencil in one hand, gum eraser in the other. Natalie didn't want to interrupt her, but she had to. She cleared her throat and said, "Mom, what's with that big stack of envelopes? Are they all manuscripts?"

Hannah looked up from her work and said, "The ones in Ella's office, or the ones over in Tim's space?"

Natalie's mouth dropped open. "You mean there are more?"

Her mom smiled. "Lots more. You put them all together and it's called the slush pile. When someone sends us something without asking us first if we want to see it, it goes into the slush pile. Those are called unsolicited submissions. Someone writes a story, thinks it should be published, sticks it in an envelope, finds our address in a reference book or somewhere, and sends it off to New York City. The people in the mail room bring us nine or ten new ones every single day, and twice as many on Mondays."

Natalie asked, "Does anyone ever read them?"

Her mom nodded. "Eventually. Everyone will at least get a letter that says thanks, but no thanks. Digging through the slush pile is one of the jobs you get when you're brand-new in the editorial department. Whenever Ella and Tim have some time, they chip away at it. When it gets too huge, we get a couple of interns from NYU or Brooklyn College and have them power through the whole stack. Most of those people get sent a rejection letter."

Natalie frowned. "It doesn't seem fair. How can someone just take a quick look and right away say no?"

Her mom was about to answer, when Letha appeared in the doorway. Ignoring Natalie, she said, "Hannah, I need that Trevor manuscript on my desk before you leave today. Are you nearly done?" Letha Springfield was Hannah's boss, the editor in chief at Shipley Junior Books. She stood there, one eyebrow arched, arms folded. Natalie's eyes were drawn to Letha's long fingernails, bloodred against the pale yellow silk of her blouse.

Hannah said, "I'll be done with it in about an hour . . . will that be all right?"

Letha smiled, but there was no warmth. She said, "I really needed it yesterday. . . ." Then glancing at Natalie, she continued, "But I know you're very busy. Just be sure I have it today, all right?" And then she was gone. Natalie stared at the dents that the woman's high heels had left in the carpet.

Hannah said, "Gotta get back to work, sweetheart. Try to stay out of sight, okay?"

• • • • •

Settled next to her mom on the bus an hour and a half later, Natalie said, "I still want to know how a person in your office can take one quick look at someone's story and decide it's a reject. That's not fair."

"I used to think that too," said her mom, "but then I spent a week or so working on the slush pile myself. With ninety-nine percent of them you can tell it's not good enough after reading one page, or even less. Bad writing, weak characters, old idea, dull plot. It's pretty discouraging. Then once in a great while you open up an envelope and you find a story that has some originality, some real style. The good ones stand out like roses in a snowbank. And if you find only one like that, then you know why we keep reading the slush pile."

Natalie shook her head. "But if so few of them are any good, where do you get all the books you publish every year?"

"Well, first of all, there are writers we know, good ones we've worked with. Or authors who have written for other publishers. When an established writer sends us something, it doesn't go into the slush pile. We look at it right away.

We don't always publish it, because it still has to be right for us. But it always gets looked at seriously. And then there are new stories that agents send us."

"Agents?" asked Natalie. "Like FBI agents?"

Her mom laughed. "No, like literary agents. Agents work for writers—illustrators, too. An agent brings us something he or she thinks is good, and if we buy it, then the writer or the artist pays the agent part of the money. Most of the new books we publish come from agents."

Natalie nodded and turned to look out the window of the bus. There wasn't much to see. They were crawling along in heavy traffic, midway through the Lincoln Tunnel. The orange glow of the tunnel lights bounced off the tiles on the ceiling and walls. Natalie always imagined the boats and barges steaming along on the Hudson River above them, and she thought about the enormous weight of all that water pressing down on the tunnel. It made her feel trapped.

So did the business lesson from her mom. It was more fun back when she didn't know anything, back when a bookstore was like a wonderland and new books just kept showing up like magic.

At home that night, when dinner and dishes were done, Natalie went to the video store with her mom and they rented two movies. Natalie Nelson didn't feel like writing at all, and by Saturday morning Cassandra Day was nowhere to be found.

CHAPTER 8

A Portrait of the Bulldog as a Young Girl

Some people are talkers, and some people are writers. Zoe had always been a talker.

Like all talkers, first she was a listener. She listened to her mom. She listened to her two sisters. She listened to her nanny. She listened to her dad. And even before she knew any real

Deary School

IDENTIFICATION

Reisman
Zoe

GRADE SIX

words, she joined every conversation, waving her hands and gurgling.

Zoe's first word was "da"—and everyone assumed it meant "Dad." But really it was an all-purpose word. For a while everything was "da." Or "Da-da?" Or "Da! Da-da-da!" As Zoe's vocabulary grew she learned that talking had a purpose. It was how to give orders, how to let people know what she wanted. Zoe's first sentence was "Have dat!" And by the time Zoe was three, her two older sisters knew better than to get in an argument with her. Zoe always won. Always.

Like Natalie, Zoe loved books too. Her mom and her nanny read to her all the time when she was little. But Zoe never tried to imagine herself as an author. She had no interest in that. Instead she imagined what it would be like to talk to the authors. She wished she could pick up the phone and ask Roald Dahl how come James didn't find a giant pickle instead of a giant peach. *James and the Giant Pickle.* Now *that* would have been a *really* funny book.

When Zoe's parents went to their first conference with her preschool teacher, there wasn't much good news. Zoe was not very good at sharing. Zoe had trouble listening to others. Zoe would not put her hand up and wait to be called on. She just talked. When the teacher began to read a book to the class, if Zoe had already heard it, she would say, "I know this story," and then blurt out how it ended.

And Zoe always argued. She argued about the snacks. She argued about nap time. She argued about which puppet was the best puppet. Endlessly arguing. The teacher said, "For example, she's learned the names of the primary colors all right, but she argues with us about the names of the secondary colors. Zoe insists that purple should be called grapy, and orange should be called juicy. We're just trying to get her ready for school, you know, and I have to say that the staff and I have some concerns."

In the cab going home Zoe's mom was concerned too. Amy Reisman shook her head. "I knew it. We've been spoiling her. I should have spent more time with Zoe. I should have taught her how to get along better."

But Zoe's dad said, "Relax. There's nothing wrong with Zoe. She's plenty smart, and once she figures out that she needs to work with other people in this world, she'll do fine."

It turned out that both her parents were right. Zoe was a little spoiled and a little headstrong, but when she met Natalie Nelson in kindergarten, she learned very quickly that if she wanted to have a friend, she couldn't have her own way all of the time—just *most* of the time.

On Saturday morning Zoe woke up at seven. First she remembered it was Saturday. She turned over and started to go back to sleep. Then she remembered about Natalie's book. Zoe sat straight up, instantly awake. Cassandra Day was still in danger, so it would have to be Zoe to the rescue.

Zoe got up, got dressed, and then did a quick cleanup of about half the mess in her room, just in case her mom decided to make an inspection tour. She was pretty sure her dad would be going to his office, and she wanted to go with him. Her dad worked late almost every night, and Sunday was usually spent with the whole family. Zoe adored her dad, and if she wanted to get some time alone with him, it had to be on Saturday. And besides, today she really needed to go to his office.

Zoe's bedroom was the smallest one on the third floor of her family's brownstone. She closed her door silently, tiptoed past her sisters' rooms, and headed down the stairs. At the second-floor landing she smelled coffee.

When Zoe opened the first-floor door to the kitchen, her dad looked up from his newspaper, mug in one hand, and smiled at her. "Hello there, Miss Early Bird. Are you my assistant this morning?"

Zoe beamed at him and said, "I thought I was your partner, not just your assistant."

"Oops—my mistake." He gave Zoe a one-armed hug and a coffee-flavored kiss on the cheek. "You hurry up and grab some breakfast, partner. Then we'll leave a note for your mom and hit the street."

It was about eight o'clock when Zoe and her dad left the house, so the city was still pretty quiet. They walked west to Lexington Avenue, hailed a cab, and rode down to Forty-sixth and Third. Zoe didn't talk much on the cab ride or on the elevator ride up to the forty-seventh floor. She was too busy thinking, and her dad seemed to know it. Most of the time Zoe thought her dad was easy to be with. If she felt like talking, so did he. If she was quiet, he was too. That's what made it easy.

Robert Reisman was the senior managing partner at his law firm. The offices of Crouch, Pruitt, and Reisman were modest but well appointed. To Zoe, the place seemed huge. There was a comfortable reception area with a leather couch and a pair of deep armchairs. There was a library with tall bookcases and a ladder that rolled along on a track. There was a big conference room with a long wooden table. There were smaller conference rooms and lots of offices for the associates and junior members, and there was even a spiral staircase that went from the forty-seventh floor down to the rest of the offices and the filing area on the forty-sixth.

Zoe thought her dad's office was the best. From his windows she could look down the East River all the way to the Brooklyn Bridge. Sometimes Zoe would sit on the broad windowsill for an hour watching the boats and the helicopters and listening to her dad talk on the phone. He was a talker too, and like Zoe, he was good at winning arguments.

Today her dad had a lot of E-mail to answer, so Zoe made herself scarce. She went to the reception area and poked through the magazines until she found what she was looking for: a recent issue of *Publishers Weekly*. She hadn't been lying when she told Natalie that she'd read the magazine at her dad's office. But she hadn't ever looked at it carefully. She took the issue into the main conference room, closed both doors, and sat in the big armchair at the head of the table. Spreading the magazine out before her, she turned past sixteen pages of ads before she found the table of contents.

Flipping from section to section, Zoe read part of an article about horror books. Then she read about a deal to make a movie out of a children's book. There were pages and pages of ads everywhere and a whole lot of reviews of new books—fiction books, nonfiction books, travel books, mystery books, children's books, history books, and on and on and on.

After almost an hour of reading, Zoe felt like her head was spinning. Looking in the magazine reminded her of when she had looked under a big, flat rock at their farm in Connecticut last summer. She had seen thousands of little ants and bugs running every which way. There were paths and tunnels, tiny rooms and bigger rooms, with workers scurrying all over the place carrying twigs and leaves and eggs—a whole little world. And now she was peeking into the world of books and the people who make them. Zoe had to admit it. Publishing wasn't so simple after all.

Zoe had won the argument with Natalie about trying to get her book published, and then she had won the argument about not giving up. Shaking her head, Zoe thought, *But what now? Natalie's book is really good, and I want to help her, but how?*

Zoe walked out of the conference room, put the magazine back, and went into her dad's office. He was looking at the notebook computer on his desk, tapping away, his reading glasses perched on the end of his nose. Zoe flopped down on the sofa beside the tall windows.

When her father paused and looked up at

her, Zoe said, "Dad, if you wrote a book, how would you get it published?"

He looked at her. "Me? A book? Why would I want to write a book? I'm never going to write a book."

"Okay, okay, but let's say that you *did* write a book. How would you get it published?"

Her dad pushed back from his desk and slowly swiveled his chair back and forth. He narrowed his eyes and scratched his chin. Zoe loved watching her dad think. He pursed his lips and said, "What kind of a book?"

Zoe shrugged. "How should I know—any kind of a book."

Her dad smiled. "All right, then. First of all, what do I always tell you? I tell you that up to a certain point, it's not *what* you know, but *who* you know. So first I'd get a great agent, a real bulldog. The kind of agent who won't take no for an answer. Then we'd map out a strategy, we'd target the best people at the best publishers. Then I just point my bulldog at the red meat, and I say, 'Go get 'em!' That's the 'who you know' part. That's why you hire an agent. It's the agent's job to get the book to the right person so the book gets a fair shot. After that the book has to stand on its own, right?"

Zoe nodded and said, "Right."

"So if the book's any good, and it gets into the right hands, then *Boom!*—it gets published. Any questions?"

Zoe shook her head.

Then her dad said, "So what got you going on this?"

"Oh . . . just curious. I found a copy of *Publishers Weekly* out in the reception room, and it got me thinking." Zoe knew this wasn't the whole truth, but it was enough for now.

Her dad scooched his chair back toward his desk. "Well, I'll be done here in another five minutes or so. You ready to go?"

Zoe nodded. "Whenever you are."

Zoe was quiet on the cab ride home. She was busy thinking, and for Zoe, that meant she was arguing with herself: *First of all, Natalie's book is good. How come you're so sure about that? Because I am. Can you think of any books you've read that are better? No? So, like I said, the book is good. So that means if the book gets to the right editor, the editor will like it, right? Right. So all we have to do is find an agent to make sure that Cassandra Day's first novel gets looked at, right? Right.*

The rest of the weekend Zoe was busy. She spent some time searching for information on the Internet, and she spent some time using the computer and the printer in her mom and dad's little office in the study on the second floor of her house. And she spent a lot of time thinking.

Zoe wanted to get this book published. Sure, she loved the challenge of it. But there was more. She didn't want to do it just to prove she could get it done. It was something she wanted to do for Natalie, something for Natalie and her mom.

Because Zoe saw things. When you stay friends for a long time, you see things. Zoe remembered Natalie's dad. He was not someone you could forget. Bill Nelson hadn't really been a handsome man, but he was so kind, so funny, that you thought he was handsome, too. He owned an ad agency called Nelson Creative that he had started with his brother, Fred. Fred was the businessman, and Bill supplied the imagination.

Natalie's dad had loved writing ads, especially funny ones. His first big campaign was some TV ads for the Brennan Furniture Company. The first ad showed a couch lying in a huge bed, and the couch was having a dream. And the couch dreamed it had wings. And the couch flew up into the sky with a dozen other couches, flying in a V like geese. And then a jet flew by. And the camera followed the jet, and inside the jet, instead of airplane seats, there were rows of Brennan couches with people looking very comfortable. And the punch line was "Stop dreaming. Fly Brennan." The ads were a big hit, and Brennan couches flew out of furniture stores all around the country. And from then on, companies lined up to have Bill Nelson at Nelson Creative make people feel good about their products.

Of course, Zoe hadn't known all that. All she knew was how much Natalie loved her dad, and how hard it was for her to lose him. That was when they were in second grade. About four months after the accident Natalie came for a sleepover at her house. And at bedtime, Zoe's dad came into her room to tuck them in. He bent over and gave Zoe a kiss good night, and at that moment Zoe looked over at Natalie. Zoe never forgot the look on Natalie's face—angry and soft and hurt and strong all at the same time. Zoe had been careful ever since not to talk about the good times she had with her dad. She didn't want to hurt her friend.

And now, four years later, when she read Natalie's book, Zoe saw things. Not about the girl in the book, because Angela wasn't much like Natalie at all. It wasn't that part. It was when the girl's father got involved in the story. Because it was the girl's father who stood by Angela all the way through. Even when the girl got caught cheating, her dad didn't give up on her. He saw she was alone, and he stepped in. The father knew the cheating had to be about something else. And when the school came down hard on Angela in the story, it was the dad who took on the headmaster and the administration. And the way he did it—by showing how the school had been cheating everyone, all the kids and the teachers, too—made Angela's dad the hero.

When Natalie talked about her book, she said the story was about Angela and her friends. But

Zoe knew there was more to it. It was about a girl and her dad. The book was like a good-bye poem from Natalie to her father.

That's why Zoe spent the weekend thinking and planning. Getting the book published would be good for Natalie, and good for her mom, too.

And by Monday morning Zoe had her ducks all in a row.

CHAPTER 9

The Agent

Zoe was waiting at the curb in front of the school when Natalie got out of her taxi on Monday morning. Her first look into Natalie's face told Zoe everything: Cassandra Day was dead again.

With a little too much forced cheerfulness in her voice Zoe said, "Hi, Nat. Get some good writing done over the weekend?"

Natalie pressed her lips together, shook her head, and frowned. She stepped around Zoe and went up the front steps.

Zoe was right behind her. "Come on, Natalie. Don't give up. I've got a whole new idea, a really good one."

Just inside the glass doors Natalie turned around. "Listen, can we just stop talking about this? I'm sorry I ever showed you my stupid story. So let's just forget about it, okay?" But Natalie knew better, even as she was saying the words. Asking Zoe to stop something halfway was like asking a chimp to lay off the bananas.

Zoe was all business. "Are you done pouting now? Because I've got something important to say. I talked with my dad, and I did some thinking, and all Cassandra Day needs is a good agent. You know what an agent is?"

Natalie heaved a sigh and shrugged off her backpack, letting it thump onto the floor behind her. "Yes, I know what an agent is. And I talked with my mom, so I also know that it's almost as hard to get an agent for a book as it is to get a book published."

"Well, what would you say if I told you that I've already got you an agent?"

"You're kidding, right?" said Natalie.

"Not kidding," said Zoe.

"So . . . who is it?" Natalie was cautious but interested, even a little flattered.

Zoe smiled. "Okay, her name is Sherry Clutch,

and she's known my dad for more than ten years, and thanks to me, she knows all about your story, and she's really interested . . . even if the book's not completely finished yet."

Natalie narrowed her eyes and looked sideways at Zoe. "So, what's the catch? There's got to be a catch."

"No, really. There's no catch . . . except—"

"Aha!" Natalie cut in. "Except what? Sounds like a catch to me. C'mon, out with it."

Zoe went on, "Well . . . you know how you're Cassandra Day? Well, Sherry Clutch . . . she's me! Get it? I'm your agent!"

Natalie's face was a dictionary of emotions. Horror. Disbelief. Disappointment. Then anger. She grabbed her backpack, wheeled around, and started up the stairs. "That's not funny, Zoe. It's not funny at all."

Again Zoe was at her heels. "But listen, Nat. I can do this, I really can. An agent is just someone who works for a writer. It's just a person who really believes a writer is great. I know your book is good. I know I can get your mom to take it seriously. It's gonna get a fair shot, I know it!"

Natalie didn't stop and she didn't turn

around. She turned left at the first corridor and headed for her locker, taking long purposeful strides. Zoe sprinted ahead, turned, and planted herself in Natalie's path. Natalie was a whole head taller, and Zoe half expected to be knocked over.

But Natalie stopped. Jaw clenched and eyes hard, she looked down into Zoe's face.

Zoe said, "Please, Natalie. Just let me give it a try. It'll be fun, and I know I can do this . . . I *know* I can. And don't you think Sherry Clutch is just *the* most perfect name for an agent?"

Part of Natalie just wanted to push right past this girl and never talk to her again. But her training as a writer stopped her. In a fraction of a second, in that way that writers do, she took a mental step back and considered the scene before her. There was Zoe. Ridiculous? Yes, but also completely loyal, completely enthusiastic, completely confident. Here they stood in the hall, face-to-face. Dozens of kids streamed by in both directions, lockers slammed, laughter and shouts and noise rose all around them. And in that instant Natalie saw what mattered. It wasn't whether the book got published or not.

It wasn't whether Zoe was absolutely crazy—which she was. The important thing was Zoe herself, her friend.

So Natalie had to roll her eyes and smile. She had to. And then she put out her hand and shook Zoe's. Then in her author's voice Natalie said, "Ms. Clutch, I'm Cassandra Day. My friend Zoe says you're a terrific agent. Can you tell me a little about yourself?"

In bits and pieces during their morning classes Zoe told Natalie about her plans. Natalie had to admit they were impressive—crazy, but still impressive. Except that, as usual, Zoe wanted to do everything herself.

But during lunch Natalie said, "It all sounds good, Zoe, but I want to have Ms. Clayton read my book too. She might have some ideas about how to get it published."

Zoe looked hurt. "Ms. Clayton? What does she know?"

Natalie shrugged. "I don't know. That's what I want to find out."

"But I've already thought of everything."

Natalie narrowed her eyes. "Everything? I

don't think so. I mean, like, look at this." Natalie pointed at the piece of stationery that Zoe had designed and printed up on her computer at home over the weekend. "Zoe, I hate to tell you, but this stationery doesn't look real."

"I know," said Zoe. "It's just the prototype. I'll take it to a Kwik Kopy and have fifty sheets printed up on nice paper."

Natalie said, "That's not what I mean." She pointed at the top of the page, below where it said SHERRY CLUTCH LITERARY AGENCY. "Look. There's no office address, there's no phone number, no E-mail address, no fax number. No one's going to believe this."

Zoe gave Natalie one of her Do-you-really-think-I'm-that-dumb? kinds of looks. She patted Natalie's arm and said, "Trust me. I've got it all figured out, I really do. That's my job, remember? But if it'll make you feel better to have Ms. Clayton get involved, then fine. That'll be fine. I'll figure that out too. All *you* have to do is finish the book and leave the rest to me."

Natalie wished it could actually be that simple, but she knew better. With Zoe in charge, nothing was simple.

CHAPTER 10

The Chosen Grown-Up

LAURA CLAYTON

Laura Clayton sorted the remains of her lunch into the recycling bins in the teachers' room—glass, paper, plastic. As she rinsed her salad container she caught a glimpse of herself in the mirror above the sink. She looked exhausted. It was her second year of teaching, and it was January, and Laura Clayton had to keep reminding herself that she loved her job.

Ms. Clayton glanced up at the clock, then opened the hallway door and walked briskly toward her classroom. She didn't feel prepared for sixth period. She never felt prepared for sixth period. It was her most challenging group of kids, and the hour between twelve thirty and one thirty was when her daily energy level hit rock bottom.

Nothing—not her own years in New York's best private schools, not her bachelor's degree from Barnard College, not her master's degree from Bank Street College, not even her student teaching—nothing had prepared her for the daily grind of classroom teaching, and especially teaching her sixth-grade class on a Monday afternoon.

The Deary School emphasized writing, and Laura Clayton agreed wholeheartedly. The curriculum required at least three writing assignments per week. Again, Ms. Clayton agreed. Writing was a vital skill. But she taught five English classes a day to grades five through eight. Even though Ms. Clayton's average class size was only thirteen students, if she gave a simple, one-paragraph writing assignment to each kid, that meant at least four hours of reading and commenting and evaluating for her.

A group of Laura's friends from Barnard College still lived in the city, and they couldn't understand why she wouldn't go out to clubs and shows with them on weeknights anymore. They had jobs at places like banks and ad agencies, department stores and publishing companies— one of her friends even worked at the United Nations. They had jobs where a person could slide by on four hours of sleep once in a while. Ms. Clayton had tried teaching five English classes on four hours of sleep once or twice. Now she knew better.

The sound of chirping robins came from the speaker below the clock in Ms. Clayton's room. That was the class-passing sound for February. Four years back the new headmaster had replaced the bell timers with a programmable sound system. So far this year the passing sounds had been a humpback whale song, the honking of migrating geese, a bouncing basketball, the sound of bamboo wind chimes, and a Mozart flute solo.

The old alarm bell was gone, but chirping birds had the same effect. Kids burst from their walled containers all over the school, and for seven minutes a cheerful chaos shook both buildings of the Deary School. Then the sound of chirping robins—played much louder for the start-of-class signal—magically guided each student to the doorway of another walled container. For fourteen of the sixth graders at the Deary School that meant English class in the Linden Room. Ms. Clayton braced herself, and sixth period began.

Fifty-three minutes later robins chirped again in the Linden Room. Ms. Clayton handed out an assignment sheet explaining how to write a short persuasive essay, and then she dismissed the class. The kids left the room heading for their exercise period, and Ms. Clayton picked up an eraser and began clearing the chalkboard. As she methodically swept the board clean she took stock. Overall it had been a pretty decent class. They had read editorials on the same subject from three different news magazines. They had identified the persuasive words and techniques of each writer. The discussion had been lively but not too unruly, and the students did most of the talking. All in all, it had been a very good session. And now she had a full hour before her last class of the day. Another Monday was almost over.

When Ms. Clayton finished erasing the board and turned around, Zoe and Natalie were standing beside her desk.

Ms. Clayton said, "Yes, girls? What is it?"

As arranged, Natalie spoke first. "Ms. Clayton, Zoe and I want to start a writing club, and we were wondering if you could be our adviser."

Ms. Clayton smiled at them and sat down in her chair. "A writing club? You mean like creative writing?"

Natalie nodded. "Yeah, that's right. Creative writing."

Ms. Clayton was pleased. Natalie was a talented writer, easily better than any of her other students, even the kids in grades seven and eight. No matter what writing assignment she gave, Natalie Nelson's work always stood out.

She turned to Zoe. Zoe's writing was all right, but it was nothing like Natalie's. Ms. Clayton said, "And you, Zoe? You want to be in the writing club too?"

Zoe said, "Oh, yes, I do."

"And do you want to invite students from the upper grades to join," asked Ms. Clayton, "or were you just thinking of having it be a sixth-grade club?"

Zoe said, "Well . . . really we were hoping that it could be just me and Natalie in the club. 'Cause . . . well, we want it to be more like a . . . like a publishing club."

Ms. Clayton's eyebrows went up. "A publishing club?"

"Yeah," said Zoe, "because, you see, well, I mean, you know how Natalie's a great writer? Well, you see, she's almost done with her first novel, and it's a really great novel—it's really, really good—and, and . . . Natalie's book has got to get published. It's . . . it's *got* to. So, really we want to start a publishing club. Like I said."

"A . . . publishing . . . club." Ms. Clayton was having trouble getting her mind around the idea.

Zoe nodded. "Uh-huh. Natalie's the writer, I'm her agent, and you . . . you're our adviser. You help us. You help us get Natalie's book published. So it's a publishing club."

Both girls stood waiting. Natalie was blushing, looking down at her feet, embarrassed. Not Zoe.

Zoe leaned forward, both her hands on the teacher's desk, looking at Ms. Clayton's face.

Ms. Clayton didn't know what to say. It made sense, in a sixth-grade sort of way. But somehow—she wasn't quite sure why—it felt like trouble. She was just about to start shaking her head, just about to start making excuses, just about to say, "No thanks," when Zoe reached into her backpack, pulled out Natalie's manuscript, and laid it on the desk.

Zoe said, "Well, we've got to run to gym now, so we'll come and talk to you tomorrow before school. And here's the manuscript. You should read it—it's really good. See you tomorrow."

As the robins began chirping from the speaker below the clock, Zoe took Natalie's hand and pulled her toward the doorway.

And Ms. Clayton gave them a wave and a half-dazed little smile and said, "Yes . . . fine. See you tomorrow."

CHAPTER 11

welcome to
the club

Laura Clayton sat at her desk. The school had slowly become silent in the late afternoon, but she had not noticed. She had been reading. And now she was done.

Zoe had told the truth. "The Cheater," by Natalie Nelson, was a remarkable novel. Ms. Clayton had read part of the manuscript during her free period, right after Zoe put it on her desk. After school she sat down at her desk again and didn't move until she'd finished the last page. Like Zoe, Ms. Clayton couldn't wait to read the rest of the book.

The novel was intense, but it was also funny. Ms. Clayton had been pulled into the lives of four friends at a private school in New York. The plot was clever, and the book also explored some big ideas, like loyalty and friendship, and learning the difference between right and wrong.

There was one passage that really got her, close to the end. It was when the girl watched her dad. He was inside the headmaster's office, and she was outside, watching him through a glass wall.

My father sits and listens politely to Dr. Sipes. Dr. Sipes is doing his best to send me to a special school, a school for problem kids. I don't need to hear his words. I can read his face. He wants to make an example of me. It's not about me. It's about his rules. It's about keeping his school under control. I can see all this in his face.

Dr. Sipes stands up and paces now, but he stays behind his desk, always behind his desk. The desk is a barrier. It is a drawbridge. It is the moat of his castle. He hides there. When he stays behind his desk, he feels safe.

Suddenly my father stands too. I am seeing the side of his face. He shakes his head no. He will not hear these bad things. Not about me. He knows better. He knows me better. My father leans forward. He leans over the desk. Dr. Sipes steps back, as if pushed by a finger on his chest.

My father has asked a question. I can see the question in the tilt of his chin. I can see the question hang there in the air above the wide desk. And I can see that it is a challenge. It is a glove tossed onto the draw-bridge.

And Dr. Sipes does not move. He cannot answer the challenge. He does not pick up the glove. It lies there smoldering on his desk. And I can see my father has won. He has done battle. For me. And he has won.

I stand up as he comes out of the headmaster's office. My father smiles at me, and it is like the sun coming from behind a cloud. "Come on, Angela. We're going home now."

My father walks out and does not look back.

Neither do I.

There was a power and a depth to Natalie's writing that surprised Ms. Clayton. If the ending was anywhere near as good as the first fifteen chapters, "The Cheater" was a book Ms. Clayton would buy for herself and her classroom, and she'd also recommend it to all her friends. If she hadn't been Natalie's writing teacher for the past five months, she never would have believed a twelve-year-old had written it.

Ms. Clayton walked toward her room on Tuesday morning, bulging briefcase in one hand, coffee cup in the other. When she turned the corner on the second floor, there beside her locked door stood Natalie and Zoe.

"Good morning, Ms. Clayton," said Natalie, and Zoe waved and said, "Hi."

Ms. Clayton smiled and said, "Good morning, girls." She set her briefcase down, took a key ring from her coat pocket, and unlocked the door. Zoe pulled it open for her and then followed her into the Linden Room. Natalie hung back in the doorway, but Zoe motioned her to come in, so she did.

Ms. Clayton put her coffee on the desk, set her briefcase on her chair, and then walked over to the large wardrobe to hang up her coat and scarf. With her back to the girls, she said, "I've read the manuscript. I read it here at school yesterday, and again at home last night." Turning to look at Natalie, she smiled. "Zoe's right, Natalie. It's an excellent novel, and once you finish it, I'm almost sure someone will want to publish it."

Natalie blushed and gulped. She said, "Do you really think so?"

Ms. Clayton nodded and said, "Well, I'm no publisher, but I've read a lot of books, and I think I know a good one when I see it." Coming over to her desk, Ms. Clayton pulled the manuscript folder from her briefcase and set it on the green blotter. Then she moved her briefcase to the floor and sat down. "Pull a couple of chairs over here, and let's talk about this idea for a club."

The girls took off their coats and sat, Zoe on the left and Natalie on the right. Ms. Clayton said, "Now, since this is New York City and we know a lot of publishers are located here, we could just open up the Yellow Pages and find the addresses of three or four publishers. Then when Natalie finishes her book, we can send the manuscript to one of them . . . or maybe even to three or four at once. I'll be happy to help you figure out how to do that, and then we can wait and see what happens. Is that what you have in mind?"

Zoe shifted in her chair and said, "Well, not exactly."

Natalie said, "You see, my mom works at a publishing company, and I've been there and I've seen what happens when writers just send stuff. If we do what you said, my manuscript will just get dumped into a big pile with all the other mail."

Zoe added, "And my dad said that unless you have an agent, no one will ever read your manuscript. That's why I'm Natalie's agent."

"You're her agent?" Ms. Clayton sipped her coffee and then said, "Oh, yes—I think you said that yesterday. What else?"

Zoe sat up on the front edge of her chair, her eyes bright. "And, well, we want Natalie's mom to be the first editor to read the book, but we don't want her to know Natalie wrote it because—"

"Because you want her mom to be objective— not be influenced one way or the other, right?" said Ms. Clayton.

And Zoe said, "Right."

Then Zoe sketched out her plan. While Zoe explained, Natalie watched Ms. Clayton's face. The signs were not good.

"And that's all there is to it!" said Zoe. "So, what do you think?"

Ms. Clayton pushed her chair back from the desk a little and sat up straight. "I don't know. The pseudonym . . . and then you pretending to be Natalie's agent—that doesn't seem quite honest . . . and I'm not even sure it's legal."

Natalie kicked Zoe's chair. "See?" she said, and then turning to Ms. Clayton she added, "That's what I told Zoe. I told her that making up all these names was just like lying, and I told her I didn't want to do it."

Ms. Clayton said, "Changing *your* name isn't the part I'm concerned about, Natalie. Zoe's right. Using a pen name is perfectly acceptable, and many writers through the years have done it. The man who wrote *Alice's Adventures in Wonderland* used a pseudonym, and there was a French woman who used the name George Sand, and lots more—that part is just fine. It's Zoe pretending to be an agent—that's what worries me."

Zoe shook her head. "But I'm not pretending to be her agent. I *am* her agent. I know I'm just a kid, but does it say somewhere that an agent has to be old?"

Ms. Clayton squinted and took another sip of coffee. Then she said, "Well, most agents *are* grown-ups, but if Natalie has asked you to try to get her novel published, then . . . I guess that makes you her agent. Still, there's no such agency as this Sherry Clutch company."

Zoe said, "But don't people just make up names for their companies sometimes? You know, just make up a new name? That's okay, isn't it?"

Ms. Clayton said, "Well, yes . . . I guess so."

"So I'm making up the name of a new company—the Sherry Clutch Literary Agency," said Zoe.

Natalie said, "But you said *your* name was going to be Sherry Clutch."

Zoe gave Natalie a withering look and said, "Not if our *adviser* says it shouldn't be. If that's a problem . . . then . . . then I'll use my own name, so it'll be me contacting your mom from the Sherry Clutch Agency."

Natalie snorted. "Yeah, like my mom won't know right away that it's you."

Zoe wheeled to face Ms. Clayton. "People are allowed to have nicknames, right?"

Ms. Clayton nodded her agreement but looked puzzled.

Zoe continued, "So I'm going to use the name my grandma calls me. It's my nickname—Zee Zee. I'm going to be Zee Zee from the Sherry Clutch Agency—Zee Zee . . . *Reisman.*" And when Zoe said her last name, it sounded like "raceman."

Natalie said, "Your name doesn't sound like that. It sounds like 'rice,' not like 'race.' And besides, when you sign a letter, the spelling will still be the same, and my mom will know."

Zoe snapped back, "I'm not the only Reisman in New York City, Natalie. Open up the phone book. Go ahead, take a look. Tons of people spell their name like mine. And who says I have to say my name to sound like 'riceman'? Who says? I can pronounce my name any way I want to—isn't that right, Ms. Clayton?" And Ms. Clayton, now a referee, nodded again in favor of Zoe.

Zoe was in full argument mode now. "So, here's how it works. It's okay for Natalie to become Cassandra Day, because she's an author; and it's okay to name a new company and call it the Sherry Clutch Agency; and it's okay for me to call myself Zee Zee 'Raceman,' because it's still my real name and I'm just changing it a little to protect the identity of my author. So I guess everything's okay, right?"

Zoe looked from Natalie to Ms. Clayton. Ms. Clayton looked from Zoe to Natalie. And then Natalie and Ms. Clayton both looked at Zoe. Ms. Clayton sighed and said, "I should probably get my head examined, but I have to agree with you, Zoe. I think everything you described is perfectly legal. And the novel is certainly real, so it's not like we're trying to commit a fraud on anyone. So . . ." Ms. Clayton reached across her desk and shook Natalie's hand and then Zoe's. She smiled and said, "Ladies, I think we have a publishing club. So, what's next? Any ideas?"

Natalie said, "Ideas? That's Zoe's department—and you're going to be sorry that you ever asked."

As is turned out, Natalie was right.

CHAPTER 12

In or Out?

Now that a grown-up was involved, Natalie felt better about everything. Zoe didn't seem quite as insane, and it was exciting that Ms. Clayton liked her book. Natalie felt like she could write again. So for the rest of the week she wrote for two hours every night, and then she worked all afternoon on both Saturday and Sunday. It turned out that all the story needed was three more chapters, and by Sunday night her book was done.

Riding into the city on Monday morning, her mom said, "We didn't get to spend much time together this weekend, Nat. And you look so tired. Is it my imagination, or do you have a lot more homework lately?"

Natalie smiled and said, "Yeah, there's more homework, but I'm also doing some creative writing. That's why I've been so busy."

"Creative writing for your English class?"

Natalie paused and then said, "Well, sort of."

"Sometimes I think your English teacher goes overboard with the work. I mean, she's good, and her comments on your assignments are excellent. But still, kids shouldn't have to slave every second. I'm sorry I didn't get to your open house so I could have met her. I have half a mind to call her and tell her to lay off every once in a while."

Natalie shook her head. "No, it's not like that, Mom. This writing, it's mostly something I've been working on—on my own."

Her mom smiled. "Well, I'm glad you enjoy writing, but you really need to get enough rest. And if you have enough time to go shopping with me or go to the movies now and then, that'd be nice too."

Natalie smiled back. "Sorry, Mom. Next weekend will be different, I promise."

When the Publishing Club met in the Linden Room on Monday afternoon, Natalie gave a finished manuscript to Zoe and another one to Ms. Clayton. Blushing a little, she said, "I finished the book. You'll have to read it and see if the ending's any good."

Zoe hugged the stack of paper and said, "I can't wait!"

Ms. Clayton beamed and said, "Neither can I. I'm sure it's going to be great, Natalie."

And when they met again early Tuesday morning, everyone agreed that the ending was perfect. The book was done. It was time to send it to a publisher.

Now that the manuscript was ready, Zoe put her plan into high gear. At the end of English class on Tuesday afternoon Zoe handed Ms. Clayton a big brown envelope. During her free period Ms. Clayton opened it. There was a neatly typed letter from Zoe, and when she opened a separate, smaller envelope, she let out a gasp. The envelope contained five hundred dollars in cash.

Ms. Clayton began reading Zoe's letter:

Dear Ms. Clayton:

First of all, don't get scared about the other envelope. I know it's a lot of money, but it's all mine from birthdays and holidays, and I can spend it any way I want to. It's really mine. So don't worry about that. Here's what we need to do.

As Ms. Clayton read Zoe's detailed instructions her eyes got wider and wider.

Mr. Archer, the headmaster, happened to walk past the open doorway of the Linden Room as Ms. Clayton was reading the second page of Zoe's letter. He stopped and took a step into the room.

"Laura?" he said.

Ms. Clayton jerked her head up, saw Mr. Archer, and then slapped Zoe's letter facedown onto the envelope of money.

Mr. Archer looked concerned. He said, "Is everything all right?"

"All . . . all right?" stammered Ms. Clayton. "Oh, oh yes, everything's fine. I'm just . . . I . . . I'm just getting ready for my last class."

Mr. Archer smiled. "Sorry to startle you, but you looked as if you'd seen a ghost."

Ms. Clayton's laugh was forced and a little too shrill. "A ghost? Oh, no, I'm just a little tired, that's all. I'm fine . . . really. Just fine."

"Well, good. I'm glad you're fine." Mr. Archer started to turn, and then stopped and said, "Oh, I've been meaning to remind you— we need to talk sometime this week to set up another classroom observation. I'll put a note in your mailbox, all right?"

Ms. Clayton nodded. "That'll be fine. Thanks, Arthur."

Mr. Archer left, and Ms. Clayton turned the letter over and finished reading it. Then she went to the intercom by the door and called the office.

"Yes, what is it?" The tinny speaker made the secretary's voice sound even more nasal and harsh than it did in person. Mrs. Fratchi had been at the Deary School since the days when all the letters were typed on a manual typewriter and all the grade reports were written by hand. Of all the staff at the school, Mrs. Fratchi was the only one that Ms. Clayton hadn't learned to call by her first name, which was Edna.

"Mrs. Fratchi? This is Laura Clayton."

"I already know that. What is it, Miss Clayton?" Mrs. Fratchi didn't believe in calling anyone "Ms." To her, a woman was either a "Miss" or a "Mrs."

"Mrs. Fratchi, will you please ask Zoe Reisman to stop in and see me after school today?"

"Do you have her schedule?"

"N-no, but I know she's in the gym this period."

"Very well. I'll try to get the message to her."

"Thank you, Mrs. Fratchi."

There was no response. Mrs. Fratchi didn't believe in saying "You're welcome," either.

When Zoe showed up at the Linden Room after school, Ms. Clayton didn't mince words. She held up Zoe's letter and the envelope of money and said, "Listen, Zoe. I just don't feel right about this. You're asking me to go and spend a lot of money. You want me to rent an office and hire a receptionist and everything else, and I . . . I . . . I just don't know. Where will all of this end up?"

Zoe was unmoved. "Where will it end up? With Natalie's book getting published, that's where. And we're not really renting an office. Did you read my whole letter? We're just going to one of those instant office places. We pay three hundred fifty dollars, and for that we get to use their mailing address, and we get our own phone number and a fax number and an answering machine, and if someone calls during business hours, the reception lady answers the phone and says, 'Sherry Clutch Literary Agency, may I help you?' We only have to pay for a month at a time, and none of this is wrong. People do this all the time when they want to go into business. If I was old enough, I could do it myself—but I'm not, so that's the part that you have to do."

Ms. Clayton felt trapped. She imagined herself having to explain all this to Mr. Archer. She saw herself sitting in a heavy chair in the oak-paneled boardroom on the fifth floor, facing all the sober, frowning trustees of the Deary School. She imagined being charged with unprofessional behavior and never being able to teach again.

She gave a little smile and said, "I know what you're asking me to do, Zoe, but I'd feel so much better if I could talk to your parents about it. In fact, don't you think you should ask *them* to help you do all this? Why not get them involved?"

Zoe pressed her lips together. "I'm *not* getting my parents involved, because when you get parents involved, they take over—at least that's what mine would do. This is something that Natalie and I want to do on our own. If we got my dad or my mom into it, then it wouldn't be like doing it ourselves, that's all. It just wouldn't be. And we came to you because, well . . . because you're nice. And smart."

Zoe paused for about five seconds, and then she said, "But if you don't want to be our adviser, that's okay. I mean, Natalie thought you would be the best one, and so did I. But if you don't think you can help us, then I guess we'll have to ask someone else." Zoe paused again and then said, "I think Mr. Karswell might help us, don't you?"

Ms. Clayton saw what Zoe was doing. Zoe was calling her a coward, and she was saying that Mr. Karswell wouldn't be. And Zoe was probably right. Mr. Karswell taught social studies. He had been at the school for about five years, and he had a reputation for being sort of a rebel. He was the editor of the school newspaper, and he coached the varsity soccer team. He was always bursting with energy, and he ran in the New York Marathon every fall, and last summer he had paddled his kayak up the Hudson River all the way to the Adirondack Mountains. And on top of all that, he was good looking. Sooner or later almost every girl at the Deary School got a crush on Mr. Karswell. Even Ms. Clayton.

Ms. Clayton blushed. Zoe had cut off every possible escape. If she backed out now, she would brand herself a coward. And she was not a coward. Even if she had never run a marathon.

Ms. Clayton was learning the same lesson that Zoe's older sisters had learned years ago: to argue is to lose.

Forty-five minutes later Laura Clayton was sitting at a small desk in the reception area of

Offices Unlimited, filling out paperwork.

Name of Business: _Sherry Clutch Literary Agency_

Nature of Business: _author representation_

Renter's Name: _Laura S. Clayton_

Term of Rental: _x_ monthly ____ yearly

That part of the form was simple. It was all
simple, just like Zoe had said it would be. Zoe
had done her research well.

Then Ms. Clayton checked off the services
Zoe had asked for:

REQUIRED SERVICES:

_X_ phone answering   _X_ voice-mail service   _X_ beeper   _X_ fax receiving

___ E-mail _X_ postal service ___ stenographic service ___ messenger service

___ Federal Express service   ___ desktop computer   ___ laptop computer

___ Internet access ___ office space, furnished ___ office space, unfurnished

There was a lot of fine print at the bottom of
the form, and then a line for a signature. Laura
paused, then took a deep breath, signed the
sheet, and stood up to hand it across the counter
to the office manager. The young woman calcu-
lated the first month's rent, then looked up and

said, "That'll be three hundred forty-seven dollars and seventy-five cents. How will you be paying today?"

Laura opened her purse and started to reach for Zoe's cash, then had a flash of inspiration. Instead of Zoe's money she grabbed her own billfold, opened it, and pulled out her MasterCard. She handed it to the lady. "I'll be using this, thanks."

Instantly Ms. Clayton felt so much better. Maybe helping the girls was a crazy idea, and maybe she shouldn't be doing it at all, but at least she could keep every bit of Zoe's cash safe and sound. No one would be able to accuse her of wasting the money of a poor, defenseless child. Thinking of Zoe as "a poor, defenseless child" almost made Ms. Clayton burst out laughing.

Three minutes later the office manager handed Ms. Clayton four things: a small black beeper; a sheet that listed the new phone number, the new fax number, and the mailing address; a separate sheet that told "How to Record Your Company's Outgoing Voice-Mail Message," "How to Call and Retrieve Your Voice-Mail," and "How to Use Your Beeper." The fourth thing she gave Ms. Clayton was a receipt for the payment.

Offices Unlimited was on upper Broadway, only about five blocks from Ms. Clayton's apartment. So on her way home she stopped at her bank and opened a new savings account. She deposited $347.75 of Zoe's cash. Ms. Clayton tucked the new passbook into the bottom of her purse. Then she put the receipt for the office in the envelope with the leftover money. That way, when she gave Zoe the envelope, it would look like she had used the cash to pay for the office.

Walking up Broadway with a spring in her step, Ms. Clayton felt alive, energized. The smell of pizza mixed with the exhaust from the 104 bus, and the streetlights seemed bright and cheery in the gathering dusk. As she turned right onto Ninety-eighth Street, Ms. Clayton thought about what she'd just done—the office, the money, the beeper, the new savings account. And she smiled. She was glad she hadn't sent Zoe and Natalie looking for another adviser. She thought, *I did it! The Sherry Clutch Literary Agency is ready for action. I am Ms. Clayton the Fearless, Ms. Clayton the Bold!*

Then after another ten steps she thought, *Yeah, right. Who am I kidding? I'm the slightly wacky Ms. Clayton, that's who I am. But whatever happens, I'm going to be right in the middle of it—and it's going to be an adventure!*

CHAPTER 13

Open for Business

By Friday afternoon everything was set.

Zoe had put all the right numbers on the Sherry Clutch stationery, and she had had fifty sheets printed up on good-quality paper at a Kwik Kopy shop on Lexington Avenue. She'd also had twenty-five large self-stick address labels printed.

Natalie made some last-minute changes to her novel and then printed two double-spaced copies of the manuscript, one for the publisher and one to keep for herself. The manuscript was ninety-seven pages, and the title page said:

The Cheater

by Cassandra Day

Looking at it gave Natalie goose bumps.

The first phone call to Hannah Nelson would be important, and Zoe was worried.

Zoe and Natalie were in gym class on Friday afternoon. Zoe said, "So, when I call your mom today, she's got to say it's okay for me to send her the manuscript, and then when she gets it, she's got to want to read it." Zoe was quiet for a minute. Then she said, "My dad told me that when you want a person to agree with you, never ask a question they can answer by saying no. But I don't get how to do that, do you?"

Natalie shook her head and shrugged. They were both quiet, sitting on a rolled-up tumbling mat, waiting for their turn on the balance beam.

Then Natalie had an idea. She said, "How about if you don't talk to her at all?"

Zoe said, "What do you mean?"

And when Natalie told her, Zoe nodded and said, "Of course! That's it! Why didn't I think of that?"

Natalie grinned and said, "Because sometimes brilliant writers have to help their stupid agents, that's why."

· · · · ·

By 3:10 the Deary School had gotten pretty quiet. At exactly 3:15 Natalie called her mom from the pay phone on the wall outside the office.

"Hannah Nelson."

"Hi, Mom, it's me. I'm still at school, so I'm going to be a little late. How's your day going?"

As soon as her mom answered, Natalie turned and gave a thumbs-up to Ms. Clayton, who was watching from down the hall. Ms. Clayton walked briskly to the Linden Room, stuck her head inside the door, and said, "Okay, Zoe. Natalie's talking to her mom."

Zoe sat down at Ms. Clayton's desk and quickly dialed seven numbers on her cell phone, then pushed the Send button. Ten seconds later she heard Natalie's mom's voice: "You've reached Hannah Nelson at Shipley Junior Books. I'm on another call or away from my desk right now. Please leave your name and number after the tone and I'll call you back."

Zoe had practiced her agent voice for the past two days, driving Natalie nuts with it. Zoe always talked fast anyway, but Zee Zee talked even faster. Zee Zee's voice was also deeper, but most of all it was louder. Zoe had decided that Zee Zee should be loud.

So after the beep on the voice mail Zee Zee jumped right into her prepared message. Ms. Clayton stood guard in the hallway outside the Linden Room, and she could hear Zoe's performance right through the door: "Hannah—this is Zee Zee Reisman from the Sherry Clutch Agency? Listen, I've got this terrific manuscript by an author named Cassandra Day. You've got to read this. I've got a messenger bringing it to your

office this afternoon. You really have to read this. Even though this is her first novel, I know a lot of editors will be interested, but Cassandra wanted Shipley to see it first because she likes a lot of the other books

you've done there. I'm in and out a lot, but you can phone me at 212-555-8878. If I'm not in, the office will beep me. Let me know what you think as soon as you can, 'cause like I said, this is a hot one. Thanks a lot—bye."

Zoe's heart was racing as she hung up the phone.

Ms. Clayton walked back to the corner of the hallway and waved to Natalie. Natalie ended her talk with her mom by saying, "Well, I'll be leaving in a few minutes, so I'll be there in about half an hour or so."

Her mom said, "No need to hurry. I'd like to get out of here early this afternoon, but I don't think it's going to happen. Letha's on the warpath, and my phone's been ringing all day long. So bring your homework, honey. See you soon."

．．．．．

Natalie got off the elevator at Shipley Junior Books at 4:25. She walked to the desk and handed a thick brown envelope to the receptionist. Natalie smiled and said, "A messenger brought this—it's for my mom. Do you need to check it in, or can I take it right back to her?"

He looked at the address label and said, "All it needs is a date stamp and my initials." The stamp made a mechanical *ca-chonk* sound as he pressed it onto the front of the envelope, and then he scribbled his initials below the date. Now the package looked official. "Here you go." He handed the envelope back to Natalie, then pushed the security button to open the door for her.

Natalie wound her way through the maze to her mom's office. Her mouth was dry. Even though she'd been here a hundred times, she felt like a spy sneaking into a strange building.

"Hi, Mom."

As her mom swung her chair around and smiled, Natalie glanced at the phone console on the desk beside the computer screen. The Message Waiting light was dark. That meant her mom had already listened to Zee Zee's message.

"Here," Natalie said, and she handed the envelope to her mom. "This is for you."

Hannah Nelson looked at the envelope. The large address label was printed in bright green ink. She read the return address aloud. "'The Sherry Clutch Literary Agency'? I just had a message from this agent, but I don't think I know her. . . . Oh, well." And she dropped the envelope onto the papers beside her computer. "Could you get me a juice or something, Natalie? I didn't even stop for lunch today."

Natalie returned with two bottles of apple juice and some shortbread cookies. Her mom held up her bottle for a toast, and when Natalie clinked it, her mom said, "Here's to our weekend!"

And at that moment Letha walked in. She stepped across the space carefully and leaned over to look at Hannah's computer screen. Natalie caught the sharp scent of Letha's perfume and took a step backward.

With a strained smile Letha said, "I love the weekend too, but I don't think it's quite here yet. Have you double-checked all those revisions, Hannah? The production manager is calling me for that text every half hour, and we

Shipley Junior Books

Letha
Springfield

EDITOR IN CHIEF

can't get out of here until it's released."

Glancing around Hannah's workspace, she snatched up the new envelope and said, "What's this?"

Hannah said, "That? It's just a manuscript. Must be a new agency—Sherry something."

Letha read the label. "Sherry Clutch . . . oh, yes, I believe I've heard of her. She's supposed to be very bright. Listen—buzz me the second you're sure all those revisions check out, okay? And I want you to give this a look over the weekend." Letha dropped the envelope on Hannah's lap and swept out of the office.

Hannah shook her head and gave Natalie a wry smile. "So much for the weekend, eh?

Listen, I've got to get back to work. Tim is probably gone by now, so you can hang out over there, okay?"

Natalie said, "Sure, Mom."

As she walked over to Tim's cubicle, Natalie tried not to smile. The editorial director of Shipley Junior Books had just pretended that she knew all about the Sherry Clutch Literary Agency. And then she had ordered her best editor to read a novel written by a twelve-year-old.

Alone in Tim's office, Natalie grinned. For the first time ever she was glad that her mom's boss was a fire-breathing, stuck-up know-it-all.

CHAPTER 14

Judgment Day

After Letha told her mom to read the manuscript, Cassandra Day couldn't wait to tell her agent about this unexpected development.

Natalie actually picked up the phone in Tim's office and dialed half of Zoe's number. Then she stopped and said to herself, *Do I really want Zoe calling me every five minutes all weekend long asking me, "Has she read it? Has she read it yet?"* Natalie hung up the phone.

Then she picked it up and dialed the number again. Zoe deserved some kind of a progress report. *But she doesn't need to know everything—bad enough that one of us has to worry the whole weekend.*

"Zoe Reisman's room at the Reisman residence, Zoe Reisman speaking."

Natalie kept her voice low because her mom's office was only about ten feet away. "Zoe? It's me. The manuscript is here. It's in my mom's office."

Zoe was excited. "Great! Is she going to read it? Did she listen to my message? Do you think she suspects anything?"

"I know she got your message, and she doesn't suspect a thing. And I'm pretty sure she's going to read it. So we'll just have to see what happens next."

"You know," said Zoe slowly, "you could maybe help things along. You know, like pick up the envelope and say, 'I wonder if this one's any good'—something like that."

Natalie smiled, but she talked in a serious voice. She wanted Zoe to calm down. "No, I think we better just let things move ahead on their own. If there's no action in a week or so, then maybe you can call her again."

Zoe did not like that idea. "A week? Are you crazy? A week is forever! If I don't hear from her in three days, then I'm going to turn the heat up—way up!"

"Look, Zee Zee, relax. I've got to get off the phone now, but I'll let you know if anything else happens, okay?"

Zoe said, "Hey! Maybe you could offer to read it for her—you know, help out around the office?"

"Zoe?" said Natalie. "No. No, no, no. Just be patient."

"Yeah," said Zoe, "easy for you to say."

"No, it isn't easy for me to say, Zoe. I want to know what she thinks about it as much as you do. But we're just going to have to let it move along one step at a time, okay?"

There was a pause, and then Zoe said, "Okay. You're right . . . I guess."

"I'll call you if there's any news, I promise."

"Okay," said Zoe. "Bye."

When they finally left the office at seven-fifteen on Friday night, Natalie could see the envelope from the Sherry Clutch Literary Agency sticking up from the outside pocket of her mom's briefcase.

Natalie tried to think. She tried to decide what she was feeling. She couldn't figure out if she was happy or scared or numb or what. Because what Zoe had said at the very beginning was true now. All of a sudden her mom wasn't just her mom. She was her editor. Hannah Nelson would be the first person to read "The Cheater" in a professional way. Her own mom would be comparing Natalie's story to all the other manuscripts she had read during the past five years at Shipley Junior Books—manuscripts written by successful, established, professional authors. Part of Natalie wanted to snatch that envelope out of her mom's briefcase and toss it into a trash barrel. But it was too late for that. The day of judgment had arrived.

But that day wasn't Friday. Friday night when they got home, Natalie and her mom went right out again and ate at a Chinese restaurant and then caught a late movie at the local theater—one of those British movies where half the actors wear fancy clothes and the other half look like beggars. It was a lively story with plenty of action and a little bit of romance, but Natalie couldn't stay focused on it. Her mind kept wandering back to that envelope, still in the briefcase, sitting on a chair in the entryway of their loft.

And Saturday wasn't judgment day either. In the morning they went grocery shopping, and then there was the laundry, and then they both spent two hours cleaning the loft from one end to the other. And then it was dinnertime.

Natalie went to her room to read after dinner, hoping that if she left her mom alone, she'd remember the manuscript. At about nine o'clock Natalie opened her bedroom door and walked softly toward the living-room area. Peeking from behind the big, leafy plants that framed the living room, she saw her mom. She was asleep on the couch, feet propped up on the coffee table, open magazine on her lap, bathed in flickering light from the muted TV.

Lying in bed later, Natalie tossed and turned. She thought about the heap of envelopes stacked up in Ella's darkened office. For every envelope there was a person somewhere, and Natalie knew how each of them felt. Those people were out there tonight, sleeping in hundreds of different beds in hundreds of different towns in dozens of different states. Every day each person woke up and thought, "Maybe the editor will read my story today," or "Maybe the editor will call me today." Every day each writer wondered if the mail would bring a letter, maybe good news from New York City.

And Natalie felt guilty. *Her* envelope wasn't in a heap somewhere in a dark office. Her story was in the editor's briefcase. The editor's boss had assigned *her* story as homework.

Natalie sat up in bed and looked at the clock. It was almost midnight. She groped for the phone on her bed stand and punched the glowing buttons.

Zoe answered on the third ring, groggy and grumpy. "Hello?"

"It's me, Zoe. I've got to tell you what happened."

It took Natalie about two minutes to tell Zoe how her story found its way home with the editor for the weekend.

Zoe was wide awake now. "So she read it? Did she like it? What did she say when she finished it? C'mon, tell me, tell me!"

"Well . . . she hasn't read it . . . not yet."

"She hasn't read it? So why did you call me in the middle of the night?"

Natalie hesitated. "Because . . . because I feel

bad. I feel like the girl in my book. I feel like I'm a cheater too. All those other stories at my mom's office, stories that she'll never even look at? And here's my story, and it's all the way up at the head of the line. It just doesn't feel fair. That's all."

"Not fair? Who said things are fair? It's never fair, Natalie. You're a great writer, and someone like me isn't—is that fair? Is it?

"Well . . . no. I guess not," said Natalie. "But you're great at things I stink at."

"Exactly," said Zoe. "It all evens out. It seems unfair, but it's not. Your mom is a good editor at a good publishing company, and someone else's mom isn't. Is that fair?"

"No . . . not really."

"Of course it's not fair. It's just the way it is. Didn't you have to work hard to write your book—just as hard as those other writers did?"

Natalie nodded as she answered. "Yeah, I did. I worked hard."

"So do you know why your book is going to get looked at and some of those other ones aren't? It's because you are who you are, and your mom is who she is, and you worked hard to write a great book."

Zoe paused to let that sink in. Then she said, "And there's another reason your book will get published and most of those others won't."

Natalie asked, "Why's that?"

In her best agent voice Zoe said, "Because you have a great agent, and those other schnooks don't! Now listen, Cassandra. I'm giving you good advice, you hear me? You hang up now and get a good night's sleep. And just stop thinking so much. You artists are all alike—thinking, thinking, thinking! Not to worry, darling. Zee Zee is going to take good care of you."

After hanging up, Natalie felt better, but it still took her another hour to get to sleep.

And even after her lecture to Cassandra, Zee Zee lay awake doing some thinking of her own.

Then on Sunday it happened. It was late in the afternoon, and after finishing her math and English, Natalie settled into her beanbag chair to read about ancient Egypt in her social studies book. The chair was so comfortable, and she had stayed up too late the night before. The next thing Natalie knew, her mom was shaking her awake.

"Natalie, you won't believe this! You know this manuscript Letha made me bring home? Well, I opened it up, you know, just so I could tell her I looked at it? And I started reading it, and it's just . . . well, I couldn't stop reading! It's one of the best things I've read in a long time—and besides that, it's even a school story! Isn't that great?"

Natalie wanted to throw her arms around her mom's neck and burst into tears. She wanted to say, "It's mine, Mom! I wrote that! I wrote it for you, and I wrote it for Dad, and I'm so happy that you like it!"

But she couldn't, so she didn't. Instead Natalie gulped, and she smiled and said, "That's great, Mom. So, it's really good?"

Her mom nodded excitedly. "It's got such a wonderful feeling all through it . . . I mean, it needs some work here and there, but this Cassandra Day—that's the author—it's her first novel, and for a first novel it's terrific. I can't wait for you to read it."

And Natalie nodded and said, "I'd love to."

But as she walked back to her workroom Hannah wished she hadn't said anything to

Natalie about the book. Because the strongest section of the book was the part about this girl and her dad.

Hannah worried about Natalie. Ever since she lost her dad, Natalie had kept much more to herself. She seemed happy enough, and she didn't seem to need to talk about not having a dad, but maybe that was a problem. Hannah was glad that Fred made the effort to be part of the family, and she knew that Natalie loved him. But having an uncle who loved you wasn't the same. Nothing could ever be the same.

Hannah shook off the fear. *After all*, she thought, *isn't that why I love my work? That's the whole idea of a good book, right? It's supposed to hit you where you live. That's the point.*

Which was easy for her to see as an editor.

But seeing it as a mom was a different story.

CHAPTER 15

A New Island

Natalie and Zoe burst into Ms. Clayton's room right before first bell on Monday morning. Breathless, Zoe said, "Guess what? Natalie's mom got the manuscript, and her boss made her read it over the weekend, and her mom read it, and—she *loves* it! Isn't that terrific? We did it!"

Natalie nodded. "It's true, just like Zoe said! My mom raved about it last night, and she even mentioned it again this morning—I think she really wants to publish it!"

Ms. Clayton smiled and reached out to take both girls' hands, swept up in the excitement. "This is wonderful! And she doesn't have any idea that her own daughter wrote it—this is just too *cool*!" Then Ms. Clayton caught herself, and in her teacher voice she said, "Well, I think you both should be very proud. Neither one of you could have done it without the other."

"Or without you," said Natalie.

Ms. Clayton blushed and said, "Well, anyway, things are jumping now, aren't they? Keep me posted, and let me know if I can help, okay?" Robins started chirping, so Zoe and Natalie rushed out of the Linden Room to go to their lockers and get ready for morning meeting.

Alone, Ms. Clayton shook her head and smiled, half amused, half worried. She wished she could be twelve again. Back then all she would have seen was the fun of a moment like this. But she was twenty-six, and she was supposed to be the mature, grown-up teacher. And there were probably dangers ahead. There were still plenty of things that could go wrong with this little publishing adventure. If things started to turn sour, Ms. Clayton the Bold could easily be renamed. And her new name just might be Ms. Clayton the Idiot.

In science class Zoe was trying to pour exactly thirty cubic centimeters of distilled water into a graduated cylinder. Natalie was watching her, and all of a sudden Zoe started spilling water all over the lab table. It splashed onto Natalie's notebook, and she said, "Hey! Watch out!"

Behind her safety goggles Zoe's eyes were as big as golf balls. She slammed the water bottle down on the table and grabbed at the belt of her skirt. She pushed something into Natalie's hand, and it lay there jiggling. Zoe hissed, "It's the beeper! It's ringing! That's the silent ring—when it vibrates!"

Natalie turned the beeper and looked at the display. "Look!" she whispered, pointing it at Zoe. "Look! It's my mom's number! My editor is calling my agent!"

When lunchtime finally arrived, Zoe and Natalie ate in about six minutes and then hurried to the library. Mr. Levy was at lunch, and two eighth graders, a boy and a girl, were in charge. They were flirting with each other at the front desk, and they didn't even look up as two sixth-grade girls hurried to the back of the room and went into the foreign language booth and shut the door. Natalie sat down at one of the stations and put on a set of headphones. She opened her Spanish book, but she didn't start a tape. Zoe sat down at the workstation opposite Natalie, away from the glass wall and completely hidden by a study carrel. She quickly dug her cell phone out of her backpack. She had already entered the voice-mail number at Offices Unlimited into her speed dialer, so in ten seconds she was listening to the message.

Natalie said, "What'd she say?"

"Shhh!" hissed Zoe. "I'm still listening!"

The fifteen seconds that followed seemed like years to Natalie.

Then Zoe passed her the phone over the top of the carrel. "Here—push the star button quick, and the message will replay!"

Natalie glanced over her shoulder to be sure the eighth graders weren't looking, then pushed the star button and slipped the slim cell phone under the headphone cup covering her right ear. It was her mom's voice.

"Zee Zee? This is Hannah Nelson at Shipley Junior Books. I read the manuscript you sent me this weekend, and I think we may be interested in it. I can't say for sure just yet, but I'd appreciate it if you'd let me respond before you start sending it to any other publishers. It's certainly not perfect, but I think the flaws are manageable, and it might just fit in with our program. So, if you'd give me a call at 555-9091, we can talk about it. Again, that's 555-9091. Good-bye."

Zoe took the phone back and turned it off. Her eyes sparkled, and she said, "Great, eh? She wants to talk."

Natalie frowned and pulled off the headphones. "But it sounds like she doesn't like it as much anymore. Do you think she's changing her mind about it?"

Zoe made a face. "Of course not, silly. It's just business. She's not going to tell me that she loves it, because then I'd make her pay more money for it. She's just playing it cool. And she's afraid I'm going to show it to other publishers, because then she'd have some competition for it."

Natalie said, "But we don't want some other publisher."

Zoe smiled. "*I* know that, and *you* know that, but *she* doesn't know that—and that's good. That way, we'll get a better deal."

Natalie narrowed her eyes and said, "Zoe, I don't want you messing this up, trying to make some big deal. Let's just get the book published."

Zoe waved her hand and said, "Relax. I've got it all under control. Put your headphones back on and listen to your agent go to work."

Natalie pulled on the headphones, and Zoe sat down, turned on her phone, and dialed Hannah Nelson's number. She answered right away, and Natalie thought, *Poor woman, she's working through her lunchtime again.*

Natalie could hear only Zoe's half of the conversation.

"Hannah? This is Zee Zee Reisman from the Sherry Clutch Agency, and I'm returning your call. I am so glad you like Cassandra's book. I think you're very smart to pick up on it right away. . . . Yes, yes, I can understand that . . . but still, if you're asking me to stop sending the book to other publishers, then you must have a very strong interest. . . . Uh-huh, yes—of course. . . . I understand. So, Hannah, what is the next step here? . . . Yes, that sounds good. . . . Sure, but Wednesday would be better. I don't want to let this cool off. . . . Fine. . . . Yes, I understand. . . . This is good, and I'll talk to you on

Wednesday. . . . And thank you. Good-bye, now."

Natalie yanked off the headphones and stood up to look over the top of the partition. "Well?" she said. "Does she want to publish it?"

Zoe nodded. "I can tell she does, but she says she has to talk to the rest of the editorial committee. She's trying to sound like she's not excited about it, but when I asked her to call me Wednesday instead of Thursday, she said yes right away. I think she really wants this book!"

Five minutes after her first conversation with Zee Zee Reisman, Hannah Nelson knocked lightly on Letha Springfield's open door and stuck her head inside the office. Letha was on the phone, but she motioned for Hannah to come in and sit down. Letha's office was four times the size of Hannah's, complete with a couch and a little round conference table next to windows that looked down into a plaza with trees and a fountain. Hannah sat at the table and tried to look like she wasn't listening.

When Letha hung up the phone, she said, "So, did you talk to the agent?"

Hannah said, "Yes, and she said she'd like to hear back from us on Wednesday. So could you look this over and see if you agree with me? I really think this is a good one, and if we can come to terms quickly, this book could even make it into the summer catalog."

Letha's eyebrows went up and she pursed her lips. "So you really think this book is worth the rush?"

Hannah paused. Talking with Letha was dangerous. She enjoyed making her people take a strong position on everything. That way, if there were problems later on, it was never her fault. But Hannah felt sure about this book, so she said, "Definitely—and I'll put in the extra hours to get it done right."

Letha stood up, and so did Hannah. Letha said, "Fine. I'll read it tonight, and we'll talk about it tomorrow. And I'm glad I had you read it over the weekend."

Hannah handed her the envelope with the manuscript. "Thanks, Letha."

On the bus Monday afternoon Natalie didn't want to talk about the book. She was afraid she might jinx it or say something stupid and give away her secret. But just before they got to the terminal in Hoboken, her mom brought it up.

"You know that new book I told you about last night?" she said.

Natalie gulped and nodded. "Yeah?"

"Well, I talked to the agent today, and Letha's reading it tonight. I'm really excited about it."

Natalie couldn't resist. She said, "So, what do you know about the author?"

Her mom shrugged. "Nothing, really. Except that she's a good writer. And she has a good ear for the way kids talk, and she knows how to keep a story moving forward." Her mom paused and looked out the window. Then she said, "I think finding a new writer is even more fun than working with someone who's already great. It's like . . . it's like finding a new island out in the middle of the ocean. And once you find it, from then on that island goes on every new map. Then every time you look at a map, you see the island, and you say to yourself, 'That's the one I found!'"

"That's neat, Mom." It was quiet for a minute or so, and then Natalie said, "You really like being an editor, don't you?"

"Yes, I do." Hannah turned to smile at Natalie. "There's only one thing I like better—and that's being your mom."

Natalie smiled back, and the bus pulled into the station.

CHAPTER 16

Poker, Anyone?

Right in the middle of Wednesday's morning meeting Zoe's beeper started jiggling. She nudged Natalie, pulled her sweater up, and pointed at it. Natalie craned her neck to read the number and then frowned.

In the hall on the way to science Natalie said, "I don't get it. I can tell the call is from Shipley, because all the numbers there start with 555. But it's not my mom's number."

"Maybe she called from a meeting in a different room," suggested Zoe. "But anyway, we know her number, so I'll just call her at lunchtime like we did Monday."

When Zee Zee called Hannah Nelson from

her soundproof office in the Deary School library, Natalie listened. Right away she could tell there was something wrong.

"Hannah? This is Zee Zee from the Sherry Clutch Agency. What's the news? . . . Oh. . . . I see. Well, I'm sorry about that. . . . All right. Good-bye."

Natalie tore off the headphones and stood up. "They're saying no? But she liked it so much! I don't get it."

Zoe shook her head. "No, that's not it. The good news is that they like the book, and they definitely want it . . . but your mom said someone else is going to be the editor. She didn't sound very happy about it. It's someone named Letha Springfield."

The color drained from Natalie's face, and she sat down with a *thump*. Zoe stood up and looked at her. "Are you all right?"

Natalie said, "Letha—she's my mom's boss, the one I'm always telling you about. She *can't* be the editor. She's awful! And she doesn't even like kids. Whenever she sees me, it's like she wants to push me into a closet or something. I really want my mom to be the editor.

Can't we do something?"

Zoe said, "I'm not sure."

After school Ms. Clayton listened while the girls told her the good news and then the bad news.

Natalie said, "I'm not kidding. I do *not* want that lady to be the editor. There must be *something* we can do."

Ms. Clayton looked out the window a few moments and then said, "Well . . . there is something you could try . . . but it might upset the whole deal. It all depends on how much they want your book."

Natalie frowned, "I don't care. I'll try anything."

Ms. Clayton turned to Zoe and said, "You're going to have to be a pretty tough agent if this is going to work. Do you think you're ready to play some poker?"

"Poker?" said Zoe. "I *love* poker. I beat my dad and my sisters at it all the time."

Ms. Clayton smiled wryly, looking from Zoe to Natalie, and said, "Why am I not surprised?"

Natalie frowned. "But this time you're not

playing for matchsticks, Zoe."

"No problem," Zoe said.

And Natalie thought, *Yeah, that's what the captain of the* Titanic *said.*

Even after Ms. Clayton had explained her idea, Natalie still felt like she was on a sinking ship.

Hannah Nelson hurried to Letha's office at three o'clock on Wednesday afternoon. Letha was pacing behind her desk, her high heels clicking as she crossed and recrossed the hard plastic chair mat.

Hannah said, "What's up?"

Letha stopped, face toward the windows, her back to Hannah. Turning around, she grabbed the high back of her gray leather desk chair, her fingernails digging into the padding. "The *nerve* of that woman! Talking to me that way . . . giving me an *ultimatum*! Unbelievable! Tell me—did you make some sort of promise to her? Think very, *very* carefully before you answer me."

Hannah was confused. "Promise? To whom?"

"To that *woman*!" stormed Letha. "Zee Zee, the agent from the loony bin, that's who! What did you tell her about that manuscript?"

Hannah gulped. Letha was never a picnic to work for, but when she was like this, things got broken, things like vases and computers—and careers. "I . . . I didn't say anything out of the ordinary. I told her the manuscript had promise, and that we wanted to think about it—and I asked her not to send it anywhere else until we got back to her today."

"And that's all?" There was a threat in Letha's voice, lurking below the shrill surface.

Hannah met Letha's glare without blinking. "Yes," she said evenly. "I'm certain I said nothing more."

Momentarily satisfied, Letha wheeled away, setting her chair spinning. "Then what we're dealing with is crazy people, both her and her writer! Because Zee Zee says that Cassandra Day has fixed on the idea that no one but *you* can edit her book!"

Hannah hid her feelings and asked, "And what did you tell her?"

"Tell her?" raged Letha. "Tell her? I told her things don't work that way in the real world, and that she'd better go and shake her author by the shoulders and get her to wake up. I told her that *I'm* the editor in chief at Shipley Junior Books, and that I like this manuscript enough to take it on and edit it myself, and that if her little Miss Day doesn't care for that, then she could take her manuscript and throw it off the Empire State Building! *That's* what I told her!"

Hannah wished she could leave, but she nodded slowly and said, "Oh . . . I see. . . ."

Letha wasn't done. "And do you know what she said to me? She said, 'Well, Ms. Springfield, I *always* try to do all I can for my writers, so perhaps we both had better think about this—as if *I'm* suddenly going to change my mind! The *nerve* of that woman!"

There was a moment of quiet, and Hannah asked, "So, what are you going to do?"

Letha planted both feet and crossed her arms. "Unless I get an apology, we will not publish that book." Then, pointing with one long index finger, Letha added, "And if you have *any* contact with that agent, I want to hear about it, is that clear?"

Hannah nodded. "Certainly."

Letha sat in her chair and spun away to look out the window. The meeting was over.

Hannah got out quickly, glad that she still had her job. Letha's door had been open, and everyone on the floor must have heard her shouting. She was glad Natalie wasn't around. Natalie had called right after school to say she'd be waiting for her in the lobby at five.

Hannah was suddenly desperate for a candy bar, so she walked to the elevator and headed toward the employee snack room on the fifteenth floor. Four minutes and one Hershey bar later Hannah sat alone at a small, round table feeling sorry for herself. She would have loved to edit that book. And she felt sorry for the author. It was a bad break. This could delay the publication of the book for at least six months, maybe more—maybe forever. And it was such a good book. It would be a gain for some other publishing house, and a loss for Shipley.

But most of all Hannah felt sorry for Zee Zee. Hannah was puzzled. Zee Zee had seemed so smart, so capable—but now it appeared very likely that Zee Zee was about to get run over by a steamroller. Hannah had thought that everybody in the New York publishing world knew about Letha Springfield. Letha was the wrong person to have for an enemy. And by the time someone figured that out, it was usually too late.

Natalie knew why her mom was so silent and tense on the cab ride to the Port Authority Bus Terminal Wednesday evening. Once they'd boarded and the bus was heading down the ramp toward the Lincoln Tunnel, Hannah Nelson settled back in her seat and let out a deep sigh.

Natalie said, "Another one of those long meetings today, Mom?"

With a grim smile her mom said, "No, actually it was two short ones, both with Letha."

"Oh?"

"Yup—one first thing in the morning, and then another one in the afternoon. They were both about that manuscript, 'The Cheater.'"

"What—didn't she like it?"

Her mom let out a bitter little laugh. "That's not the problem. She liked it a lot—you'd have to be a moron not to. But first thing in the morning she calls me in and says, 'This is a terrific book. This writer really knows kids, don't you think? You can just feel the zits popping out on their faces. Thanks for spotting it. I'm going to handle it myself.'" Hannah turned to look out the window.

Natalie said, "Can she do that, like, just take it away?"

Turning back to Natalie, her mom said, "Letha? Letha can do pretty much whatever she wants to. What's so upsetting is she does this all the time. I find a good property, and then she takes it over and steals all the glory, if you can call it that. It's not the glory I want. It's just that I'm trying to build a career here, and Letha's already got a great one. And this book, well, it has real promise, especially since it's a first novel. This is what an editor like me hopes for— a new writer with a strong first book who has the promise of developing into something more. That's how an editor gets noticed in this business. I just happen to be cursed with a selfish boss, and there's not much I can do about it."

"What about the second meeting?" asked Natalie.

"At about three she yells for me to come to her office, and then she rants and raves about this agent—her name is Zee Zee—because she called Letha and said that the author wants *me* to be the editor for her book. So Letha practically accuses me of going behind her back and making promises to the agent—which I would never do. So now Letha's got her high heels dug in, and she's saying if it doesn't happen her way, then it doesn't happen. So the book is probably not going to get published, at least not at our company." Hannah paused and then said, "What I don't get is, why would the author be so determined to have me be her editor, anyway?"

Natalie said, "It's because you're a great editor, that's why. And the author probably heard about you, and the agent could probably tell just from talking with you that you're nice, too—not like that witch Letha. Don't you just *hate* her?"

"No, I don't hate her. . . . I just don't understand her, that's all. It seems like it would be so easy for her to ease up a little. She's got all this talent, she looks great, she makes good money, and she really is an amazing editor. I guess she just has some other issues that make her feel like she has to keep grabbing more and more for herself. In a way I feel sorry for her." She almost added "And I feel even sorrier for myself," but she didn't.

Hannah fell silent and turned to look out the window again.

Natalie was quiet too. She wished she could comfort her mom. She'd say, "Don't worry, Mom. Because if Ms. Clayton and Zoe know how to play poker half as well as they think they do, then help is on the way."

CHAPTER 17

High Stakes, Aces wild

When a package arrived by messenger at nine fifteen on Thursday morning, Kelley Collins double-checked the address label.

Kelley had been Tom Morton's secretary for the past six years as he worked his way up through the ranks at Shipley Publishing Company. Whenever he had jumped a rung on the ladder, Kelley had jumped with him. And now Tom was the president and publisher of Shipley Junior Books, and Kelley was his Executive Assistant.

Mr. Morton didn't usually get packages from agents, but this one was clearly addressed to him, so Kelley opened it. He wouldn't be in the office until one o'clock today, so she had plenty of time to get his correspondence and his afternoon appointments organized.

She started to read the cover letter from the agent, and when she got to the name Letha Springfield, she stiffened. Her eyes narrowed and her mouth formed an involuntary frown. Kelley had been watching Letha Springfield carefully for the past two years. Every time Letha and the other editors in chief came to a meeting on the sixteenth floor, Kelley had the feeling that Letha was measuring the windows in Tom Morton's office for curtains—*her* curtains.

Kelley finished reading the letter and then looked at the manuscript. *Good title*, she thought. Kelley flipped the title page over and began reading. After three pages she was hooked. She read the story off and on all morning and then finished it over the noon hour. And when she got back from lunch, Kelley put the letter and the manuscript at the top of the stack in Mr. Morton's in box.

At one fifteen on Thursday afternoon Tom Morton called to Kelley through his open door.

"Kelley, would you take this down to fourteen and give it to Letha? She really ought to handle this herself." When Kelley walked in, he was holding out the manuscript and the letter from the agent.

Kelley took the manuscript from him, and Tom looked down at the next item on his desk. But Kelley didn't leave, and when he noticed, Tom looked up again and said, "Something else?"

Kelley shifted her weight from one foot to the other, then plunged in. Holding up the letter, she said, "Mr. Morton, I know this situation is sort of a can of worms, but did you look at the story? It's a great book—I read the whole thing . . . over my lunch hour. I think it might be worth taking a look at . . . if you don't mind my saying so."

Tom Morton never minded Kelley saying what was on her mind. She had kept him from making at least a dozen mistakes over the years—several mistakes that could have delayed his promotions, and one or two that could have cost him his job. She had the instincts of a mother lion, and Tom was glad to have her looking out for him.

With a smile he pushed the papers on his desk to one side, took the manuscript back from her, and began reading. Kelley turned and left his office, pulling the door shut behind her.

Ten minutes later Tom Morton buzzed Kelley on the speakerphone.

"Yes, Mr. Morton?"

"Kelley, hold my phone calls for an hour or so, would you? I'd like to finish reading this manuscript."

Kelley Collins smiled at her phone and said, "Will do."

At precisely 3:46 on Thursday afternoon Letha Springfield and Hannah Nelson each received an E-mail message, and the little mail-delivery chime bonged on both of their computers. Letha ignored the chime because she was on the phone, but Hannah clicked on her E-mail icon and read the message right away.

---

tmorton@shipleybooks.com/ed/smpt//inhouse/

3:45 PM ***2.19.00

From: Tom Morton

To: Letha Springfield

Cc:

Bcc: Hannah Nelson

Re: The Cheater manuscript

Letha—

It's odd for an agent to send anything directly to me these days, so I took note when someone named Zee Zee Reisman messengered me a manuscript this morning. It's called The Cheater, and from the cover letter, I gather you've seen it too.

I started reading it—couldn't stop. Made me remember all those years I spent as an editor. I hate to step in, but it's clear that unless we put Hannah on this project, we'll lose the book, and frankly we can't afford to. I smell a hit here, and if we have to let a headstrong author have her own way in order to keep the book, then I say we let her.

I've called Susan Yau in marketing and asked her to save a half page for this in the summer catalog. I know a June pub date is pushing it, but this one could build nicely and be strong right into the fall.

Have Hannah handle the deal and the editing, and I'd like her to keep me in the loop on this. Susan will call her in a day or so for catalog information.

Thanks,

Tom

As Hannah read the E-mail, her throat tightened up. Her heart raced and she felt as if she couldn't breathe. Hannah knew this feeling. It was fear.

Looking at the heading of the E-mail again, she saw that her copy was a "bcc"—a blind copy. That meant Tom Morton had sent Hannah a copy of his message to Letha, but Letha didn't know about the copy.

Hannah took several deep breaths to try to clear her head. She thought, *Doesn't Tom know what an impossible situation this puts me in? Doesn't he know it's already hard enough to work for Letha?*

Nervously Hannah jumped up from her chair. Standing on her tiptoes in her doorway, she peeked over the top of the cubicle dividers to look across at Letha's office. Letha was there, talking on the phone, smiling and nodding. Hannah thought, *She must not have read it yet.*

Hannah sat down again and looked at the E-mail still open on her computer screen. She tried to think calmly, but she couldn't. The message was like a time bomb in Letha's computer, ticking away. Any minute now Letha would click it open and—*boom!*

Hannah shook her head. She had to admire this Zee Zee Reisman. Sending the manuscript directly to Tom Morton was a gutsy thing to do. She thought, *This woman is incredibly brave— or else she's incredibly stupid.*

"Hi."

Hannah almost jumped out of her shoes. She wheeled around. "Oh! . . . It's you, Natalie! Ooohhph—you surprised me." Instantly Hannah turned around and grabbed her purse from the bottom drawer of her desk. She pulled out two dollars and said, "I think you'd better go up to the lunchroom and study this afternoon, honey. Here's some snack money."

Natalie looked at her mom. She said, "Are you okay, Mom? You look . . . you look kind of . . . funny."

Hannah laughed nervously. "Just a lot going on today, that's all. Now, you run along—and stay put. I'll come up there and get you on my way out, okay?"

"Sure, Mom. See you later."

· · · · ·

Letha Springfield stomped off the elevator onto the sixteenth floor. It was six minutes after four o'clock. Five minutes earlier Letha had read her E-mail from Tom Morton.

Grim, unsmiling, Letha didn't slow down. She glared at the receptionist, who scrambled to push the security button just as Letha reached the door to the executive offices.

Striding on, Letha approached Tom Morton's office. She had a piece of paper in her hand. As she went marching right past Kelley Collins into Tom Morton's office, she waved it and said, "Mr. Morton is *expecting* me!" The office door slammed shut behind her.

Kelley kept tapping away at her keyboard. A nearly invisible smile tickled the corners of her mouth. She wished she could be a fly on the wall in her boss's office.

At four forty-five Hannah was working on a letter to one of her authors. She heard a rustle of papers behind her. The hairs on the back of her neck stood up. Hannah tensed and then turned her chair to face the doorway. It was Letha.

"Here." Letha's voice sounded like a shovel plunging into a pile of gravel. She handed Hannah a manuscript. Hannah didn't have to look to know what it was, but she did. Then she did her best to look surprised. Letha said, "I've decided you should handle this one. After all, we don't want our sensitive little Miss Author to get her tummy all tied up in knots, now do we? So I want you to take it from here."

Hannah tried to keep the right mixture of surprise, confusion, and obedient acceptance in her voice and gestures. She said, "But . . . well . . . I'll be glad to. Are you sure you want me to?"

Coldly, evenly, Letha said, "Very sure." And with that, she turned and walked briskly back toward her office.

Hannah took three or four deep breaths. She thought, *If I ever get fired from here, I'll go train tigers for Ringling Brothers—it'll feel like a vacation!*

When her mom came to get her in the snack room, Natalie thought her mom's face looked strange. She seemed to be in a big hurry, too. She was silent in the elevator, and once on the ground floor, she took Natalie's hand and practically dragged her across the lobby and then squeezed into the same compartment of the revolving door with her. Once they were out of the building and down the block near where they caught their cab, her mom started to laugh and swing Natalie's arm back and forth, almost giddy.

Natalie said, "What's all this about?"

Hannah stopped to catch her breath and at the same time held up her hand to flag a vacant cab. Then she giggled and said, "You'll never *believe* what happened at work today!"

But her mom was wrong. Natalie believed every word of it.

CHAPTER 18

The Long Arm of the Law

Ms. Clayton sat at a small, round table in the Linden Room with Natalie and Zoe on a Thursday afternoon. It had been just a week since they sent Tom Morton a copy of Natalie's manuscript, but with Hannah Nelson handling the project, there had been rapid progress.

Hannah had found Zee Zee Reisman to be a very cooperative agent. When Hannah offered a royalty advance of six thousand dollars, Zee Zee accepted right away—not a single counteroffer. Hannah could have paid as much as ten thousand dollars for the book—she had authorization from Tom Morton himself. Zee Zee, on the other hand, had been told by

Natalie to take the first offer with absolutely no negotiating. Accepting that offer without arguing was one of the hardest things Zoe had ever done.

Thanks to Hannah's efficiency and Zee Zee's cooperation, the entire membership of the Deary School Publishing Club was now staring at a stack of paper on the little, round table. It was the contract, all fourteen pages of it, in triplicate. By signing the contract, Cassandra Day ("hereinafter referred to as THE AUTHOR") would grant permission to Shipley Junior Books ("hereinafter referred to as THE PUBLISHER") to publish *The Cheater* ("hereinafter referred to as THE WORK") for "the full duration of copyright"—which meant all of Cassandra's life plus another fifty years after she died.

At the end of the fourteen pages there was a place for Zee Zee Reisman ("hereinafter referred to as THE AGENT") to sign, and there was a place for Cassandra Day to sign. Cassandra Day also had to write her Social Security number on the contract. All three copies had to be signed and dated and returned to Shipley Junior Books as soon as possible.

Patting the stack of paper, Ms. Clayton spoke first. "I know I'm supposed to be your adviser, but I really don't know what to tell you. This contract is a legally binding document. I'm pretty sure you have to be at least eighteen years old to sign a contract yourself, maybe even twenty-one—and I know you should completely understand all the words before you ever sign anything."

Zoe had been enjoying her role as the big-shot agent, the queen of the problem solvers. With a little toss of her head she said, "I know all about contracts. You write down the deal, then you sign it, and then you do what you said you would. My dad says that's all there is to it."

Natalie gave Zoe a sideways look. "If that's all there is to it, Zoe, then every cab driver in New York City would become a lawyer."

Zoe made a face at Natalie and then said, "So, what do you think we should do, Ms. Clayton?"

Looking from Zoe to Natalie, she said, "I don't think we have any choice, girls. We need to talk to a lawyer."

Natalie nodded, and glancing at Zoe, she said, "I agree—a *real* lawyer. I think we should talk to Zoe's dad."

"No way," said Zoe. "No parents, remember?"

"But remember what you said to me about my mom? It's the same kind of thing. He's not just your dad, Zoe. He's your *lawyer*."

"But what if he says he has to tell your mom about everything?" said Zoe. "He might feel like he really has to."

"Not if I tell him he can't," said Natalie. "If you tell something to a lawyer, he's not allowed to tell anyone else, right, Ms. Clayton?"

Ms. Clayton nodded. "That's true. So what do you think, Zoe?"

Zoe shrugged and said, "Well, I guess it'll be all right. I know my dad can figure out what we should do . . . and he probably won't charge us anything either."

At noon on Friday, Natalie called her mom. She asked if she could ride home with Zoe after school. Her mom said, "That'll be fine. How about I pick you up at her house at six o'clock. We'll get some food in the city—and maybe I'll

147

call your uncle and see if he wants to see a movie with us."

So it was all settled. Except Natalie and Zoe weren't going to Zoe's house after school—at least not right away. First they had to have a talk with their lawyer.

Zoe and Natalie walked into the reception area of Crouch, Pruitt, and Reisman at three fifteen. Zoe had been to her dad's office only once or twice on a weekday, and that was a long time ago. The receptionist didn't recognize her.

The tall young woman put her hand over the mouthpiece of the telephone headset looped over her right ear. She smiled and said, "May I help you?"

Zoe said, "We're here to see Robert Reisman."

The receptionist's smile dimmed, and she said, "I see. Do you have an appointment?"

Zoe said, "No, but I know he's here." Zoe had called her dad's secretary from school at noon to make sure about that.

The receptionist frowned slightly and raised one eyebrow. "And who may I say is here to see him?"

Zoe smiled sweetly and said, "Tell him it's his favorite daughter, Zoe."

Three minutes later a surprised Robert Reisman was sitting in a chair across from Zoe and Natalie. Zoe had settled back into the cushions of the couch, but Natalie sat on the front edge.

Looking from face to face, he said, "So, what's going on here? I mean, I'm happy to see you, Zoe, and you, too, Natalie . . . but let's hear what's on your mind—unless this is a purely social visit."

As planned, Natalie spoke first. Opening her backpack, she took out the contract and handed it across the coffee table to Zoe's dad. "No, this is a business visit, Mr. Reisman. I need to have a lawyer look at this contract."

Zoe's dad was already doing that, peering down through his reading glasses, flipping from page to page. Nodding his head, he said, "This is a publishing contract—looks pretty standard. What's this got to do with—" He stopped in midsentence, his eyes fixed on the last page. Looking up quickly at Zoe, he said, "'Zee Zee Reisman, agent for THE AUTHOR'? Is this a coincidence? This is a project for a class, and you want me to look at it, right? Is that it?"

Zoe smiled a knowing little smile at her dad and nodded toward Natalie, as if to say, "Ask her." On cue, Natalie said, "No, it's a real contract. I wrote a book, and my pen name is Cassandra Day. And Zoe—that is, Zee Zee—she's been my agent."

Robert Reisman sat back in his chair and looked at his daughter. "No kidding?"

Zoe said, "No kidding. We wanted to get Natalie's book published, and we're *this* close, but our adviser at school said we needed to talk to a lawyer to see if we could even sign this contract."

Leaning forward again, Mr. Reisman said, "Your *adviser*? At school?"

Natalie nodded. "Ms. Clayton. She's our English teacher. She helped us rent the office where we get mail and phone calls."

"You have . . . you have an *office*?" Robert Reisman looked from girl to girl as they both nodded yes.

Natalie ignored the lawyer's amazement and quickly described the steps that had led to the

contract. Then she said, "So what we need to know is, can we sign this contract and have it be . . . you know, legal?"

"Legal?" Mr. Reisman was at a loss for words, something that did not happen to him very often. Making a visible effort to think like a lawyer, he said, "Well, you are both underage—but you have in fact already delivered the manuscript to the publisher, correct?"

Natalie nodded.

The lawyer went on, "And it could be argued that concealment of the author's age was not an effort to commit fraud but was merely part of the same principle leading her to use a pseudonym in order to have her work taken seriously—is that a fair statement of the facts?"

Natalie nodded again, expecting that any moment he would ask her to put her hand on the Bible and swear to tell the truth, the whole truth, and nothing but the truth.

"And at any time did any person at the publishing company indicate that the age of either the agent or the author might affect whether or not the work was acceptable or this contract could be issued?"

Each girl shook her head no to that.

"And did anyone ever ask you your age, or did either of you ever volunteer false information about your age to anyone at the publishing company?"

Again, each girl shook her head no.

"Then I think that each of you should be able to sign this contract and have it be legally binding—provided, of course, that you each have a parent sign an affidavit that says you are entering into the agreement with their full knowledge and consent." He winked at Zoe and said, "I think I can find someone to vouch for Zee Zee."

Natalie looked at Zoe and then back to Mr. Reisman. Natalie said, "But that's a problem for me. You see, my mom? . . . Well, she works at Shipley Junior Books. She's an editor . . . and she's the editor for this book. So I can't really have her sign that . . . whatever you called it, saying it's okay. I mean, I'm sure it would be fine with her, but I don't want to let her know it's me until the book is all edited. And my dad, well, you know about my dad."

Robert Reisman sat back in his chair again

and rubbed his chin. "Hmm. Yes, I can see the problem. You don't feel free to get your mom's prior consent because if she knew, she could be accused of giving you special treatment—it's called a conflict-of-interest situation. Hmm . . ." And the lawyer paused again. Then he asked, "How about a grandparent, or some near relative we could inform of the situation? That way, if this matter ever came before a judge, we could show that we wanted to make sure you had guidance from an adult who had your best interest in mind. Anyone who fits that description?"

Instantly Natalie said, "Uncle Fred! He's my dad's brother. He lives here in the city, and he's the one who helped us with everything after my dad died, and sometimes we go on trips with him in the summer, and he comes to our house all the time, and we go to his—he's a close relative, right?"

Zoe's dad asked, "Do you know his phone number?"

Natalie said, "No, but I know his address, and I know he runs an advertising company called Nelson Creative."

Mr. Reisman handed Natalie a pad of yellow paper and a pen, and she wrote down Frederick T. Nelson's address.

Three minutes later Natalie was talking to her uncle at his office through the speakerphone on Mr. Reisman's desk. "Uncle Fred? It's me, Natalie."

"Natalie? This is a surprise! Is everything all right? Your voice sounds funny."

"That's because I'm using a speakerphone. Everything's fine, but I need to ask you something. I'm calling you from the office of my friend Zoe's dad. He's a lawyer, and he's helping me with . . . a problem."

Natalie took about five minutes to tell her uncle what was happening, and Zoe chimed in whenever she thought Natalie left something out. Then Natalie introduced Mr. Reisman, and he and Uncle Fred talked about the details. When he'd explained the legal situation, Mr. Reisman said, "I've looked over the contract, and it's a fairly standard publishing agreement—which means it heavily favors the publisher. Still, if you can sign an affidavit that states you and Natalie understand what's going on, and that until her mom can be informed, you are acting as next-of-kin adviser, then I see no reason why my daughter and your niece can't sign the contract and move ahead with this."

Fred Nelson said, "Well, if you think it's all right for your daughter, then I guess it should be fine for Natalie. If you send me the affidavit, I'll sign it and get it notarized and get it back to you right away." Then Uncle Fred said, "Natalie?"

"Yes?"

"Way to go, kid. Sounds like a great book, and I can't wait to talk to your mom after she finds out it's yours. And another thing—tell your agent there that whenever she's ready, I've got a job waiting for her here at Nelson Creative."

Zoe had been slumped on the couch, feeling a little neglected. She perked up and said, "Thanks, Mr. Nelson."

Grinning across his desk at Zoe, Mr. Reisman said, "Sorry, Fred, but Zoe's already an honorary partner right here at Crouch, Pruitt, and Reisman."

Then Natalie said, "Hey! I want everyone to remember that first of all she's *my* agent!"

Uncle Fred said, "Well, hang on to her, Natalie—she's pure gold."

Natalie beamed at Zoe and said, "I know, Uncle Fred . . . I know."

The buzz of the intercom startled Ms. Clayton as she sat at her desk marking some eighth-grade essays.

It was Mrs. Fratchi. The school secretary didn't like teachers getting phone calls at school, and when Mrs. Fratchi disapproved of something, she never tried to hide it. "Miss Clayton? There's a *personal* telephone call for you on line two in the teachers' room."

Ms. Clayton said, "Thank you," but Mrs. Fratchi had already clicked off the intercom.

Thinking it must be Natalie, Ms. Clayton hurried down the hall and into the empty lounge. She picked up the handset and punched the blinking button. "Hello?"

A woman's voice said, "Ms. Clayton?"

"Yes . . ."

"Please hold a moment."

Then a clear, strong voice said, "Ms. Clayton, this is Robert Reisman. I'm Zoe's father."

"H-hello, Mr. Reisman." She gulped, and her heart started pounding. "Did . . . did the girls come and . . . and talk to you?"

"Yup—just left. Tell me about this office, Ms. Clayton."

Laura Clayton couldn't tell much from his voice. He didn't sound mad, but it wasn't really a friendly tone either. She gulped again and said, "Well, it's one of those instant office places on upper Broadway. It's near where I live, so I stop in to pick up the mail. And they have a beeper service so that we . . . I mean, so that Zoe can return phone calls."

"Zoe talked on the phone with these people?"

"Well, yes," said Ms. Clayton, "but . . . but not a lot. Just when she had to."

"How about the rent on this office, Ms. Clayton?"

"I . . . I was going to explain that to you. When Zoe got the idea to rent the office—"

Mr. Reisman broke in, "Renting the office was Zoe's idea?"

"Oh, yes. I . . . I was just her . . . well, her helper."

"Okay," he said, "go on."

"Well, Zoe brought me an envelope of money."

"How much money?"

Ms. Clayton winced and said, "Well . . . it was five hundred dollars."

"Did you say five *hundred*?"

"Yes, five hundred dollars."

"In cash?"

"Yes, all in cash." Laura Clayton did not feel this conversation was going well.

Robert Reisman was silent, so Ms. Clayton continued. "Zoe said it was her money, and I didn't doubt it, but . . . but I didn't want to spend that money without . . . well, without permission. So I paid for the office with my own credit card."

"And what about the cash?"

"I . . . I opened a new savings account at my bank. It's all there."

The lawyer was quiet for a few moments. Then

he said, "Ms. Clayton, I'm going to say something, and I hope you are listening very carefully."

Ms. Clayton was having a hard time hearing anything except the thumping of her runaway heartbeat. Weakly she said, "Yes?"

Robert Reisman continued, "Ms. Clayton, I don't know if helping the girls to do all this was wise on your part. However, I do know this. You have been very courageous, and I can't thank you enough. I wish you could have been here to listen to these two kids tell me about this deal. This is real learning here, you know what I mean? Real stuff in the real world? I can tell you one thing—I will never again groan when I pay Zoe's tuition bill. If it helps to pay your salary, Ms. Clayton, then it is money well spent."

Ms. Clayton was stunned, and a silly grin crept over her face. She managed to say, "Thank you, sir."

"And Ms. Clayton, send me a bill for that rent right away, here at my office. Zoe'll give you the address, all right?"

"Yes . . . yes, of course, Mr. Reisman."

"Don't take this the wrong way, Ms.

Clayton, but I hope you stay a teacher for a long, long time. Kids need teachers who aren't afraid of life, don't you think?"

"Yes . . . yes, and thank you."

"No, Ms. Clayton," said the lawyer, "thank *you*!"

Cassandra Day
c/o The Sherry Clotch Literary Agency
723 West 93rd St.
NYC 10023

CHAPTER 19

The Red Pencil Blues

Six days after the contract had been signed and returned to Shipley Junior Books, Ms. Clayton stopped at Offices Unlimited on her way home. Today the office manager handed her a large brown envelope addressed to Cassandra Day, care of the Sherry Clutch Literary Agency.

In English class the next afternoon Ms. Clayton passed a note to Natalie and Zoe asking them to come to a meeting.

When they were sitting at the small, round table after school, Natalie opened the envelope. It was a five-page letter from her editor, along with a copy of her story. The manuscript was littered with dozens of Post-it notes—the yellow ones were editorial suggestions, and the pink ones flagged grammar questions. It looked like Hannah Nelson had worn out at least three red pencils.

The letter began, "Dear Cassandra: Thank you for this wonderful first draft. Now that your contract is all squared away, we can get down to work."

Natalie's heart sank. She thumbed through the manuscript, flipping from note to note. "Look at all these—this is going take forever! I thought the book was done, and I thought it was good, too. And . . . look."

Ms. Clayton took the letter from Natalie. As she read through the first two pages the teacher began to nod and smile. She was impressed. She said, "So now we know what real editors do. This is a wonderful letter, Natalie. She's telling you how to make a good book into a great book, that's all. Your mom really knows what she's doing."

Natalie said, "Yeah, she knows what *she's* doing, but what about me?"

Zoe wasn't sympathetic. "Quit whining, Natalie. You wanted to be an author, and now you are one. So your editor gives you a bunch of good ideas to make the book better—so what? You're an author now, so you have to do the work."

"Well, you're a big help, Miss Know-it-all!" snapped Natalie.

"Girls!" said Ms. Clayton. "We don't need any sarcasm—and we don't need criticism, either." Then in a gentler tone she said, "Natalie, just take this home this weekend and see how it goes—maybe spend only half an hour on it. It doesn't all have to be done at once. If you get stuck, well, that's why you have an editor. It's her job to help you do your best work."

Natalie and Zoe went down the front steps of the school. Ms. Clayton had sent them on their way together, but neither had said a word on the walk through the halls.

Natalie got to the bottom of the steps and turned left as if she was just going to walk to her bus, but Zoe took her by the arm.

"Wait, Natalie." Natalie stopped and turned to face her. Zoe said, "Listen . . . I'm sorry I called you a whiner. It's just that . . . well, I feel like my part in all this is over, and I . . . and I don't know what to do."

"So how do you think *I* feel?" snapped Natalie. "I wish we hadn't started this. I mean, my mom almost got fired, and she still could, for all I know. And now I've got all this extra work to do, and I'm still not sure the book is going to turn out right. And then it gets published, and then what if the book reviewers hate it and no one buys it—then what?"

Zoe looked into Natalie's eyes. The fear and the worry was so intense it made Natalie look feverish. Instantly Zoe was furious with herself for being so stupid . . . so . . . so selfish.

"Then what?" asked Zoe. "If some reviewer doesn't like it? So what? It just means he's an idiot. How could anyone *not* like this book, Natalie? This book is so good that even Lethal Letha the Grumphead liked it, remember? And all those little changes your mom—I mean, your *editor* wants you to make? I know you can figure them out. You're good at this. And your book? It's only gonna get better and better, honest."

Natalie smiled a little and said, "Do you think so?"

Zoe nodded and said, "I *know* so!"

Already Zoe could see Natalie's eyes chang-

166

ing. She could see her smart, talented, confident friend coming back to life. And with a surge of fierce joy Zoe could see that her part in all this *wasn't* over, not by a long shot.

Natalie discovered that the editing process wasn't glamorous, and it wasn't a lot of fun, but at least it was creative. It was work—slow, steady work. It was a careful look at every word, every sentence, paragraph, and chapter. It was a methodical tracing of each character, each story-line, each rise and fall of the action, each of the points along the path that led to the end of the book. And always, everything had to be judged to see if it supported the overall theme and the deeper ideas that made her book more than just a story.

During four weeks of revisions the book got steadily better. Every day, and especially during their bus rides home, Natalie was tempted to ask her mom about the book she was editing. But she didn't. Natalie felt like that would have been unfair . . . like cheating.

She also learned that the editing process was when an author and an editor got to know each other. When one said, "Let's cut this out of the book," and the other said, "No, I really think it should stay," each learned something new about the other. It was like a very long conversation about . . . about life. Natalie felt she was getting to know her mom in a way she never had before. When a note from her mom asked Cassandra Day, "Does Sean really have to seem so mean at this part of the story?"—Natalie could hear her mom and dad telling her how important it was to be kind.

And when Cassandra Day wrote back and said, "Sean's not really being mean here, it's just that his feelings are hurt, and the narrator hasn't figured it out yet," Hannah read the note and smiled, and suggested a way to make that clearer to the reader without giving too much away too soon.

And during the editing process the author and the editor came to respect each other's ideas and insights more and more.

Near the end of the manuscript there was a note from the editor about Angela's father. Of all the notes, it was the one that meant the most to Natalie.

Cassandra—
There are only a few small
changes I'd suggest here. This
part of the story is so strong,
so tender. I think you've
caught the essence of the way
daughters feel about their
dads, and the way dads will do
anything for their daughters.
Every time I read this, I
think about my own life, and
my father, and my own
daughter's life too. And each
time I read it, I weep — it's
that good.

Several times during the editing Hannah
Nelson invited Cassandra Day to drop by the
office if she was in the area, or just pick up the
phone anytime something wasn't clear. Each
invitation to visit was politely refused, and the
author continued to communicate only by mail.

Hannah also found Cassandra's handwriting
hard to read. Cassandra's notes were written
with a thin pencil in tiny letters, and the writing

had an unusual slant. They looked like that because Zoe was a lefty. After Natalie wrote each note and comment, Zoe copied it out again in her cramped little scrawl. Natalie was sure it was driving her mom nuts, but she didn't want to risk having her handwriting recognized.

Finally, on the fourth pass, the manuscript came back in a new form. The words had all been set into type and laid out in pages. It was called a galley proof, and now each page looked like two side-by-side pages from a book—a real book! Best of all, there were only two Post-it notes on the whole thing, two small errors that were a snap to fix. The book was done.

Two weeks later Ms. Clayton brought Natalie a puffy mailing envelope. It was heavy, and when Natalie pulled the strip to open it, out tumbled two paperback books. Natalie gasped. "The book! It's done!"

But it wasn't the book. It was a paperback printed on flimsy paper, and the cover looked like it had been made from a cheap color Xerox of the jacket. On a black rectangle at the bottom of the cover white letters spelled out this announcement:

Ms. Clayton picked up a handwritten note that had slid onto the table with the books. She glanced at it and then began reading aloud.

Dear Cassandra:

Our marketing department is excited about your book, so we've printed up five hundred of these advance reader's copies. So far, our salespeople have been using our catalog to tell booksellers about your book, and now they will send these ARCs to all their key bookstore accounts. The subsidiary rights department will be sending them to the book clubs, the specialty markets, and our overseas agents. Also, the publicity department will be sending out more than two hundred

ARCs to the trade, institutional, and consumer review media. I'll let you know when we start getting reviews. The hardcover is already in production, and we'll be shipping the advance orders by mid-May. The advance orders aren't great, but a few good reviews should give the sales a boost. I know we rushed a little on the revisions to meet the deadlines, but the book turned out great. You should be very proud.

Yours truly, Hannah.

Natalie held one of the paperbacks with both hands. She *was* proud. It wasn't the real book yet, but it was so close.

Zoe held the other reading copy. She was proud too, but she was also indignant. "What does she mean, the orders aren't so great?

What's the matter with these people? They should be selling these books like crazy. Their publicity people must stink, that's all I can say."

Natalie said, "Remember how my mom said that every year there are more than five thousand new children's books published in the United States? They can't all be bestsellers, Zoe. It's amazing to get one published at all."

Zoe made a face and shrugged. Actually, Zoe had heard only about half of what Natalie had said. Natalie and Ms. Clayton kept talking, but Zoe was busy. She was having a brainstorm. It took only about thirty seconds for the whole idea to take shape, and when it had, Zoe held up the reading copy and said, "Can I have this one, Natalie?"

Natalie smiled and said, "Of course you can." Then Natalie handed her copy to Ms. Clayton and said, "And I want you to have this one. I'll ask my editor to send another one for me."

Ms. Clayton felt choked up, but she swallowed hard and said, "Thank you, Natalie. I'm going to treasure this my whole life."

Absentmindedly Zoe said, "Yeah . . . me too, Natalie." But Zoe's thoughts were elsewhere.

She had just decided it was time for Zee Zee Reisman to develop some new skills. Zoe thought, *I mean, being an agent was fun, but now my client needs something else. What she really needs is . . . publicity!*

CHAPTER 20

Family and Friends

Most books are published quietly. They don't get big ads in the newspaper, they don't get written about in *Time* magazine, and they don't get a publication party. If it's a book by a famous author, or by an author that the publisher wants to impress, then the publisher might send out some invitations and throw a little party. Publishers do this to create some news and, hopefully, sell some books.

So when Zee Zee Reisman called Hannah in mid-April to suggest that Shipley Junior Books might want to throw a little publication party to launch *The Cheater*, Hannah's first reaction was, "It's a nice idea, but I don't think it makes sense."

But then her curiosity took over. All through the negotiations and the editing Cassandra Day and Hannah Nelson had never sat at a worktable together, never gone out to lunch, never even talked on the phone. She felt close to Cassandra Day and had loved their little exchanges about the manuscript. So she thought, *Zee Zee's right. A little party might be nice—and then I'll finally get to meet this lady.*

But Hannah had so much to do that she never focused on the idea. Letha had been piling extra work on her ever since the day she'd been appointed as Cassandra Day's editor.

Then, three days after Zee Zee's call, the first review arrived. It was from *Kirkus Reviews*, and the reviewer gave *The Cheater* special notice with a "star," which is like giving a book an A++. Hannah liked the last three sentences best: "*The Cheater* grabs hold of your heart and never lets go. This writer speaks with a fresh and honest voice, something always welcome in middle-grade fiction. If this first novel is an indication of things to come, then Cassandra Day could emerge as a major new talent."

With the review in her hand Hannah went

upstairs to talk to Tom Morton. Hannah read him the review, and then she proposed a simple publication party on a Friday afternoon in June. Tom Morton agreed instantly, and that was that.

Getting back on the elevator, Hannah had second thoughts. Letha would not be happy about this party, and she'd be furious that Hannah had asked Tom instead of coming to her first.

Hannah almost stepped out of the elevator to go back and call it off. But then she stopped and let the doors glide shut. On the short ride from the sixteenth down to the fourteenth floor, she realized something: Letha was not as scary as she used to be. And then Hannah said to herself, *No, that's not it. Letha is actually scarier than ever. It's just that* I'm *not afraid of her anymore.*

Back in her office Hannah called and left a message for Zee Zee. She said there would be a small "pub party" in honor of Cassandra Day's first novel. It would be on the sixteenth floor of the Shipley Publishing Company building on the second Friday in June. Zee Zee was free to invite anyone she'd like to be there. And everyone was very excited about actually getting to meet the author.

When Zoe got the phone message, she was excited, too. But she kept it to herself.

Natalie had finally gotten Zoe to shut up. For a solid week Zoe had bugged her and begged her and driven her batty. She wanted Natalie to ask her mom if she could bring Zoe and Ms. Clayton to see Shipley Junior Books—just to have a look around.

Natalie thought it wasn't such a good idea, but Zoe wouldn't let up. "It'll be like a field trip for the Publishing Club—and besides, school's almost over. Ms. Clayton probably won't even be our teacher next year."

Finally Natalie agreed to ask her mom if she could bring Zoe and her English teacher to see the publishing office—it wouldn't be a long visit, just in and out.

And her mom said, "Of course you may, sweetie. Just bring them with you after school one day. If I'm too busy to show you around, Ella can do the honors."

So it was all settled. They had an open invitation, and Zoe stopped pestering Natalie. And the day that looked the best for everyone was a Friday afternoon—the second Friday in June.

• • • • •

At three thirty on Friday, June 12, the editorial staff of Shipley Junior Books started straggling up to the sixteenth floor for the publication party. The manuscript had floated around a little, and there was a definite buzz about this book—and early in the day the third starred review had arrived. Everyone was excited about meeting Cassandra Day.

Hannah had already been up to the large conference room twice, once to check on the caterers, and once to be sure that the big banner had been hung up. When Hannah got off the elevator the third time, she could hear that the party had begun. As she walked into the room the first thing she noticed was the camera crew. A woman with a large video camera was taking a shot of the banner while a skinny young man behind her held up a bright light. The young man wore a jacket labeled ABC NEWS. A man with perfect hair, perfect teeth, and a pinstriped suit was talking with Tom Morton. Glancing across the room, Hannah caught the eye of Jody Cross, the publicity director. Jody nodded toward the camera crew, smiled, and gave

Hannah a thumbs-up. Hannah smiled and nodded back. She was impressed that Jody had managed to get some news coverage of such a small event.

When Zoe and Natalie and Ms. Clayton arrived at the fourteenth-floor reception area, Phil buzzed them right in. Her mom wasn't in her office, so Natalie just started walking her guests around the floor. Natalie had been dreading Zoe's little field trip, but now that they'd arrived, she began to enjoy herself.

They started in the art department and slowly worked their way clockwise from area to area. It struck Natalie as odd that there were so few people around, but she just figured that people had left early on a Friday afternoon. It was nice because they didn't have to be as quiet.

Natalie was showing them the stages of a book's cover art, but Zoe interrupted her. "Let's go find your mom, Natalie. You know, so we can ask her some questions too."

Natalie shook her head. "If she's not in her office, it means she's busy. We'll find her later."

Natalie really understood the publishing

process now, and Ms. Clayton had a lot of questions. It was fun to teach her teacher, and it would have been perfect, except that Zoe was so impatient.

They were almost back to her mom's office, and Natalie was standing in Ella's cubicle pointing at the huge pile of envelopes on her worktable. "And that's the slush pile. I've seen it when it was even bigger." Turning around, Natalie said, "And over there in Tim's office—" She stopped midsentence. Letha stood in the corridor outside her office, ten feet away.

Crossing her arms, Letha walked toward them. She smiled faintly and said, "Well, this is a cheery little group . . . and I see you have a tour guide."

Natalie gulped and said, "This is my friend Zoe and my English teacher, Ms. Clayton—and this is my mom's boss, Letha Springfield."

Ms. Clayton stepped around Natalie and held out her hand. "Pleased to meet you, Ms. Springfield."

Letha looked at Ms. Clayton's hand and then shook it briefly. "Yes. Well. We're happy to have you visit us."

Natalie said, "We . . . I was going to wait for my mom, but I don't think she's back yet. If she's not back in a few minutes, then we'll just go. We don't want to bother anyone."

Letha said, "Actually, your mother is . . . just upstairs." Then with an amused smile she added, "But I know she'd want to see you . . . and your friends, too. Just take the elevator up to the sixteenth floor. And be sure to tell her that I sent you to see her."

Natalie nodded and said, "Sure . . . okay. Thanks."

And Letha said, "Oh, you're quite welcome."

As the elevator door opened onto the six-teenth floor an alarm went off in Natalie's head. It didn't sound right. It sounded like . . . like a convention or something. Her first instinct was to push another button—any but-ton—and get away fast. Before she could act, Zoe grabbed her hand and pulled her out of the elevator. Ms. Clayton followed, and Zoe headed right toward the open double doors of a large room where fifty or sixty people were standing around in small groups, talking loud enough to be heard over the talking of everyone else.

Natalie said, "Zoe! I don't think we'd better—"

But Zoe said, "Look, there's your mom," and she tightened her grip on Natalie's hand and headed straight toward Hannah Nelson like a locomotive. Ms. Clayton stopped in the doorway, just barely overcoming her urge to flee.

Halfway across the floor Natalie saw the banner:

THE CHEATER
BY CASSANDRA DAY

CONGRATULATIONS
TO OUR NEWEST AUTHOR!

The camera operator swung to face Zoe and Natalie, and her assistant turned on the lights. All but a few of the people at the edges of the room stopped talking. Everyone craned their necks to see what the camera was targeting. Natalie tried to make sense of the scene around her, but it was happening too fast. In another three seconds Zoe was standing in front of Hannah Nelson.

Hannah had been talking to Tom Morton, trying to act completely at ease. So what if the guest of honor was already thirty minutes late? The lights from the camera suddenly blinded her, and when she looked again, Zoe and Natalie were standing right in front of her.

Zoe looked up into her face and said, "Mrs. Nelson, I know this is going to be a shock, but I want to introduce you to Cassandra Day."

Hannah looked from Zoe to Natalie and then over their heads. Standing in the doorway of the room was a shy-looking young woman wearing a black skirt and a green cardigan sweater. Hannah's face broke into a relieved smile, and she said, "Well, this is . . . great. Come on, Tom, let's go welcome her."

Zoe looked over her shoulder and then turned back and said, "Mrs. Nelson, that's not her." Putting her arm gently around Natalie's waist, Zoe said, "*This* is Cassandra Day. That's her pen name. Cassandra Day is Natalie Nelson."

The camera operator saw it all. As the tape rolled she thought, *It doesn't get better than this.* And she was right.

The camera saw everything so clearly. It saw

the woman look at the girl, completely baffled. It saw the mother's eyes widen, her eyebrows furrow into a question mark and then smooth to understanding. It recorded the ballet of emotions that danced across both faces.

The microphone heard the woman's sharp intake of air, almost a gasp, and then the long breathing out, almost a sigh. And it heard the girl whisper, "It's true, Mom."

Mother and daughter looked at each other for a long moment, and when they hugged, the people and the room and the building and the city around them disappeared.

Pulling away, Natalie looked around and then reached out to take Zoe's hand. "And Mom, this is Zee Zee Reisman." The woman's face did another dance, and then the hug held three.

And standing over in the doorway, tears streaming down her cheeks, Ms. Clayton felt as if she'd just won the New York Marathon.

The publicity director dabbed a tear from her eye and whispered to Tom Morton, "I don't know how Hannah got ABC News to show up, but I'm sure glad she did."

Tom whispered back, "She didn't set this up,

Jody—she said *you* got them here."

The camera was there because Zoe had sent her advance reading copy to a producer at ABC, along with a full explanation of the story behind the book. And she guaranteed the producer that the author would be revealing her identity at a publication party on the sixteenth floor of the Shipley Publishing Company building at four o'clock in the afternoon on the second Friday in June.

The Party was pretty much over by 4:30, and Tom Morton invited all the Shipley employees to get an early start on the weekend. After Zoe and Ms. Clayton said good-bye, Natalie and her mom walked the eight blocks to the Port Authority Bus Terminal.

It was a beautiful June afternoon, but neither of them noticed the blue sky or the springtime bustle along Eighth Avenue. They were too busy. The walk was one long question-and-answer session, punctuated by bursts of laughter, half a dozen hugs, and outrageous impersonations of Zee Zee the agent and Letha the fire-spitting boss.

When their bus rolled down the ramp toward the Lincoln Tunnel, mother and daughter sat side by side, exhausted but glowing.

Hannah cleared her throat. "You know, I almost didn't want you to read this book by Cassandra Day—because of the parts about Angela and her father. I thought those sections might be too hard on you."

Natalie nodded. "Those parts were hard to write. But I wanted to remember Daddy. I wanted to feel what it would be like if he was still here. I don't want to forget about him, not ever."

"Of course not. You won't. He'd be so proud of you right now."

Natalie looked up into her mom's eyes. "Do you think so, Mom?"

Her mom nodded. "I know so."

Two weeks later ABC ran a half-hour story on one of its weekly news shows. The segment was called, "The Publishing Club." The man with the perfect hair and the perfect teeth sat in the studio talking with Zoe, Ms. Clayton, Natalie, and Hannah Nelson. As the story unfolded, the viewers saw location shots of the Deary School, the Linden Room, Shipley Publishing Company, Offices Unlimited, and the law firm of Crouch, Pruitt, and Reisman. At the right places in the story there were short interviews with Arthur Archer, Tom Morton, Robert Reisman, and Fred Nelson. Letha Springfield even got a little airtime, just enough to smile into the camera and say, "I guess it's just the result of experience, sort of a sixth sense I have, but somehow I just *knew* that Hannah Nelson was the right editor for this book."

The program was perfectly timed with the publication of *The Cheater*. It offered the kind of opportunity that a good publicity director dreams about. Jody Cross went right to work, and during the next two weeks Natalie and Zoe spent a lot of time on TV talk shows. They were on *Nickelodeon News for Kids*, plus their picture was on the cover of *People* magazine.

The production manager at Shipley Junior Books almost went crazy trying to keep up with the demand. By the end of August the hardcover book had been reprinted six times, and it was number five on the *New York Times* Children's Bestseller List.

Zoe Reisman received six offers to purchase the rights to use the name of her company, the Sherry Clutch Literary Agency. After consultation with her lawyer, each offer was refused.

Three weeks after the program aired on ABC, the president of one of the largest publishing companies in New York called Letha Springfield. He asked her to become the vice president and editorial director of his Children's Division, and he promised that she would have complete editorial control. His offer was accepted.

By mid-August applications for new student enrollment at the Deary School had reached an all-time high. Arthur Archer and the board of trustees sent a letter of commendation to Ms. Clayton for "embodying so well the ideals of the Deary School." And Mr. Karswell asked her if she'd like to go kayaking some Saturday morning.

The fall alumni newsletter of the Bank Street Graduate School of Education featured an interview with Ms. Laura Clayton. The last question was the hardest for her to answer.

BANK STREET COLLEGE: If you had to give one piece of advice to the men and women who are preparing to become teachers, what would that be?

LAURA CLAYTON: I've been a teacher for only two years now, so I can't pretend to be some great expert. But I think it's important not to be afraid. Don't be afraid to really listen to your students. Remember what it was like to be a kid, and how brave you had to be to try something new. As a teacher, I want to try to be as brave as my students have to be.

One week after the departure of Letha Springfield, Hannah Nelson was promoted. She became the editor in chief of Shipley Junior Books. It was a big jump for her, but Tom Morton felt sure she could handle it.

Sitting in her new office, Hannah Nelson looked out at the Manhattan skyline. She picked up a copy of *The Cheater* off her desk. Opening it, she stared at the title page. She smiled, closed the book, set it back on her desk, and turned to look out the window again.

Then she remembered something. Months ago she had asked Cassandra Day for the last few bits of text needed to complete the book. She recalled handing the note with those final words to her editorial assistant, with instructions to be sure they got added in the right place. Spinning around, she grabbed the book and flipped it open.

There. Just past the title page.

It was the dedication.

Of course, thought Hannah. *How could it be anything else?*

for Dad and Mom,
for Zoe and Ms. Clayton
—N. N.

On the Saturday afternoon before Labor Day the girls sat on the front steps of Zoe's house eating Italian ices, strawberry for Natalie and lemon for Zoe. It was the first time they'd been together in a month.

Natalie and her mom had taken a trip to the Grand Canyon with Uncle Fred. They stayed at the campground in the forest on the North Rim. It was her mom's first two-week vacation in four years. They did a lot of hiking, and a lot of just sitting around, talking, and reading. The peace and quiet was just what Natalie needed.

Zoe and her mom and sisters had spent August at their farm in Connecticut, and Mr. Reisman had driven up on weekends. Zoe loved being at the farm, but the peace was a little too peaceful and the quiet was way too quiet. By the middle of the second week Zoe couldn't wait to get back to the city.

But summer was over now, and school was in the air. Zoe pulled the little wooden spoon out of her mouth and said, "Too bad we don't have Ms. Clayton for English this year."

"Yeah," said Natalie. "And I heard that Mr. Allston is a lot harder, too."

They fell silent again, spooning out chunks of the sweet flavored ice and trying to imagine what seventh grade would be like.

Zoe said, "So, what are you going to do with your first royalty check?"

Natalie shrugged. "College fund, mostly. I might get to spend some, but not much. And there won't be any money coming until next March, you know."

"I know," said Zoe. "I know *exactly* when the royalties get paid, because agents don't get paid until authors do. The checks come every six months. And I know about how much I'm going to get from that first check too. My dad helped me figure it out—it's fifteen percent of whatever they pay you."

Natalie blushed. "I know that's what the contract says . . . but really, Zoe, you should get a lot more than that. I mean, without you that story would just be sitting in a pile at my house."

Zoe wiped a drip off her chin and shook her head. "Maybe so . . . but without your book there'd have been nothing. I helped get it to the right person, but after that, it was all you. My share's just right."

They were quiet, eating again.

Then Zoe said, "You know, when you write another book, Natalie? It won't hurt my feelings if you want to hire a real agent."

Natalie stopped, a last bit of strawberry ice halfway to her mouth. "What, are you crazy? Who could be more real than you?"

The friends looked at each other and smiled. And Natalie thought, *The way this feels right now? I want to put this feeling into a book someday.*